# A GENTLEMAN OF FRANCE

# STANLEY WEYMAN

# A Gentleman of France

### BEING THE MEMOIRS OF GASTON DE BONNE SIEUR DE MARSAC

*Introduced by* Hugh Greene

## THE BODLEY HEAD

LONDON   SYDNEY

TORONTO

# INTRODUCTION

The three writers who gave me most pleasure when I was a boy were Rider Haggard, Anthony Hope and Stanley Weyman. I should judge that the least remembered of these, the one with fewest readers, is Stanley Weyman.

To return, as I have done recently, to the favourites of one's youth can be hazardous. Some writers whom one loved seem now to be entirely without merit. But the three I have mentioned, alike in being great story-tellers, pass the test, not least Stanley Weyman. One finds on re-reading him that there is something very firm and durable about his writing: it is not, apart from the occasional 'Zounds, Sir', mere Wardour Street fustian.

As a historical novelist he based his books on very close study and he was fond of the sort of detail which places them firmly in their period and fixes the attention of the reader. The opening sentences of *A Gentleman of France*, Weyman's second novel, may seem plain, but they have the cunning of the Ancient Mariner and tell one a lot very concisely: 'The death of the Prince of Condé, which occurred in the spring of 1588, by depriving me of my only patron, reduced me to such straits that the winter of that year, which saw the King of Navarre come to spend his Christmas at Saint-Jean d'Angely, saw also the nadir of my fortunes. I did not know at this time—I may confess it today without shame— whither to turn for a gold crown or a new scabbard, and neither had nor discerned any hope of employment.'

Although Weyman's books have many settings he is at his best with France and the French sixteenth and seventeenth

5

centuries. His later books with a nineteenth-century English setting, although they are praised by T. E. Welby in the Dictionary of National Biography at the expense of the historical novels, seem to me to be Trollope and water.

*A Gentleman of France* is the story of a down-at-heels, stolid, middle-aged soldier who is given a mysterious and dangerous mission by Henry of Navarre. The opening chapter, 'The Sport of Fools', is a painful picture of thoughtless cruelty which in one's schooldays seemed only too close to everyday reality and still rings true. The adventurous rides along the roads of France, the skirmishes in the narrow, filthy streets of ancient towns, the encounters in wayside inns, the last chase through a misty and plague-ridden countryside retain all the sense of danger and excitement one felt as a boy. Whatever happens the attention to detail is unfailing. When at a moment of danger the hero leaps to his saddle he is careful to explain that it had always been his habit to teach his horse to stand for him and that he did not know of any accomplishment more serviceable at a pinch.

The story gains enormously through being told by a cautious, awkward and, in his own eyes, elderly man rather than by a romantic and reckless youth. There is no romance in the hero's heart when the dangerous mission begins: 'I could think of nothing but the three long days before us, with twenty-four hours to every day, and each hour fraught with a hundred chances of disorder and ruin.'

Until he turned to writing Stanley Weyman, who lived from 1855 to 1928, was a struggling barrister whose earnings were sometimes as low as £50 a year and never more than £300. He joined the Oxford Circuit, which he used to describe as 'the most gentlemanly Circuit'. As he later admitted he was too shy and nervous to be a success at the Bar, and once he was so badly bullied by a judge that he drank a pint of champagne to stop himself from being sick. After a few years he went home to Ludlow, apparently a complete failure.

He had tried his hand at writing while still at the Bar with no success at all. Then when he was thirty-one years old, he had an adventure which seems to have stirred his imagination. He was travelling in the French Pyrenees with a friend when they were arrested by the gendarmes. 'They took us for Belgian spies', he said in an interview with *The Idler* magazine in 1895, 'connected with the Carlist rising over the frontier. They marched us, under bayonets and revolvers, many miles along the high roads: and if I refused to walk they dangled handcuffs in my eyes. We passed one night in a cell—and that was an adventure.

'There was', he added wistfully, thinking, perhaps, of the gallant exploits he was afterwards to describe, 'no chance to escape.'

The first of his long series of historical novels, *The House of the Wolf*, about the massacre of Saint Bartholomew, appeared in 1890. It was a success, though all he earned at the time from serial and book rights was £200, and it has been more often reprinted than any of his other books. 'Only a few weeks ago', he told *The Idler* interviewer five years later, 'the publishers of this book sent me a complimentary cheque of £100. Why I do not know: it was not needed now.'

So the quiet little man with a big walrus moustache settled down happily in his mother's house in Broad Street, Ludlow, where he had been born, working steadily for five hours a day, during which he would produce a thousand words. Now he could afford his pleasures and he hunted regularly on his favourite mare Emerald.

It is pleasant to learn that among Stanley Weyman's admirers was Oscar Wilde, who wished to procure his books as suitable reading for the other inmates of Reading gaol.

For this edition a map has been provided of the Sieur de Marsac's journeys.

Hugh Greene

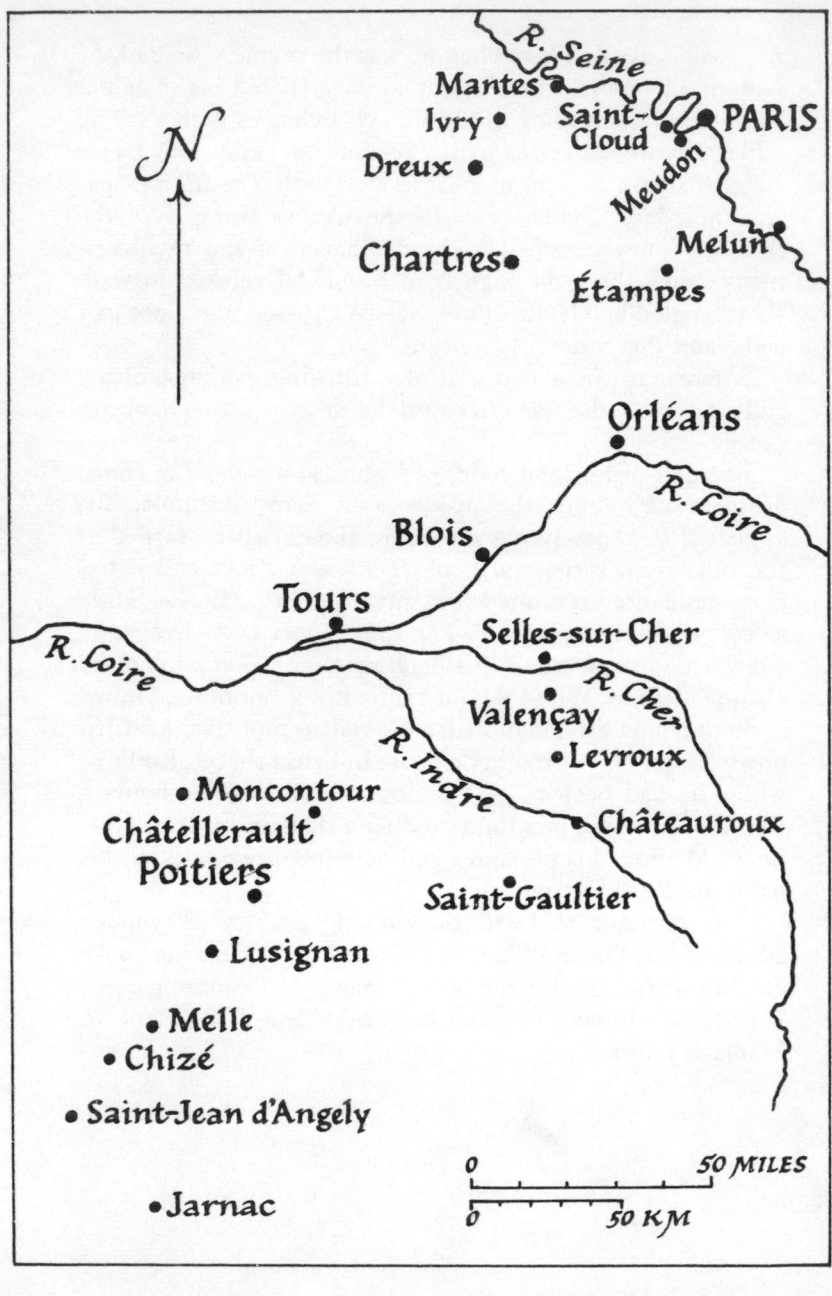

# CONTENTS

# I

# The Sport of Fools

The death of the Prince of Condé, which occurred in the spring of 1588, by depriving me of my only patron, reduced me to such straits that the winter of that year, which saw the King of Navarre come to spend his Christmas at Saint-Jean d'Angely, saw also the nadir of my fortunes. I did not know at this time—I may confess it today without shame—whither to turn for a gold crown or a new scabbard, and neither had nor discerned any hope of employment. The peace lately patched up at Blois between the King of France and the League persuaded many of the Huguenots that their final ruin was at hand; but it could not fill their exhausted treasury or enable them to put fresh troops into the field.

The death of the Prince had left the King of Navarre without a rival in the affections of the Huguenots; the Vicomte de Turenne, whose turbulent ambition already began to make itself felt, and M. de Chatillon, ranking next to him. It was my ill-fortune, however, to be equally unknown to all three leaders, and as the month of December which saw me thus miserably straitened saw me reach the age of forty, which I regard, differing in that from many, as the grand climacteric of a man's life, it will be believed that I had need of all the courage which religion and a campaigner's life could supply.

I had been compelled some time before to sell all my horses except the black Sardinian with the white spot on its forehead; and I now found myself obliged to part also with my valet de chambre and groom, whom I dismissed on the same day, paying them their wages with the last links of gold chain left to me. It was not without grief and dismay that I saw myself thus stripped of the appurtenances of a man of birth, and driven to groom my own horse under cover of night. But this was not the worst. My dress, which suffered inevitably from this menial employment, began in no long time to bear witness to the change in my circumstances; so that on the day of the King of Navarre's entrance into Saint-Jean I dared not face the crowd, always quick to remark the poverty of those above them, but was fain to keep within doors and wear out my patience in the garret of the cutler's house in the Rue de la Coutellerie, which was all the lodging I could now afford.

Pardieu, 'tis a strange world! Strange that time seems to me; more strange compared with this. My reflections on that day, I remember, were of the most melancholy. Look at it how I would, I could not but see that my life's spring was over. The crows'-feet were gathering about my eyes, and my moustachios, which seemed with each day of ill-fortune to stand out more fiercely in proportion as my face grew leaner, were already grey. I was out at elbows, with empty pockets, and a sword which peered through the sheath. The meanest ruffler who, with broken feather and tarnished lace, swaggered at the heels of Turenne, was scarcely to be distinguished from me. I had still, it is true, a rock and a few barren acres in Brittany, the last remains of the family property; but the small sums which the peasants could afford to pay were sent annually to Paris, to my mother, who had no other dower. And this I would not touch, being minded to die a gentleman, even if I could not live in that estate.

Small as were my expectations of success, since I had no one at the king's side to push my business, nor any friend at Court, I nevertheless did all I could, in the only way that occurred to me. I drew up a petition, and lying in wait one day for M. Forget, the King of Navarre's secretary, placed it in his hand, begging him to lay it before that prince. He took it, and promised to do so, smoothly, and with as much lip-civility as I had a right to expect. But the careless manner in which he doubled up and thrust away the paper on which

I had spent so much labour, no less than the covert sneer of his valet, who ran after me to get the customary present—and ran, as I still blush to remember, in vain—warned me to refrain from hope.

In this, however, having little save hope left, I failed so signally as to spend the next day and the day after in a fever of alternate confidence and despair, the cold fit following the hot with perfect regularity. At length, on the morning of the third day—I remember it lacked but three of Christmas—I heard a step on the stairs. My landlord living in his shop, and the two intervening floors being empty, I had no doubt the message was for me, and went outside the door to receive it, my first glance at the messenger confirming me in my highest hopes, as well as in all I had ever heard of the generosity of the King of Navarre. For by chance I knew the youth to be one of the royal pages; a saucy fellow who had a day or two before cried 'Old Clothes' after me in the street. I was very far from resenting this now, however, nor did he appear to recall it; so that I drew the happiest augury as to the contents of the note he bore from the politeness with which he presented it to me.

I would not, however, run the risk of a mistake, and before holding out my hand, I asked him directly and with formality if it was for me.

He answered, with the utmost respect, that it was for the Sieur de Marsac, and for me if I were he.

'There is an answer, perhaps?' I said, seeing that he lingered.

'The King of Navarre, sir,' he replied, with a low bow, 'will receive your answer in person, I believe.' And with that, replacing the hat which he had doffed out of respect to me, he turned and went down the stairs.

Returning to my room, and locking the door, I hastily opened the missive, which was sealed with a large seal, and wore every appearance of importance. I found its contents to exceed all my expectations. The King of Navarre desired me to wait on him at noon on the following day, and the letter concluded with such expressions of kindness and good-will as left me in no doubt of the Prince's intentions. I read it, I confess, with emotions of joy and gratitude which would better have become a younger man, and then cheerfully sat down to spend the rest of the day in making such improvements in my dress as seemed possible. With a thankful heart I concluded that I had now escaped from poverty, at any rate from such poverty as is disgraceful to a gentleman; and consoled myself for the meanness of the appearance I must make at Court with the reflection that a day or two would mend both habit and fortune.

Accordingly, it was with a stout heart that I left my lodgings a few minutes before noon next morning, and walked towards the castle. It was some time since I had made so public an appearance in the streets, which the visit of the King of Navarre's Court had filled with an unusual crowd, and I could not help fancying as I passed that some of the loiterers eyed me with a covert smile; and, indeed, I was shabby enough. But finding that a frown more than sufficed to restore the gravity of these gentry, I set down the appearance to my own self-consciousness, and, stroking my moustachios, strode along boldly until I saw before me, and coming to meet me, the same page who had delivered the note.

He stopped in front of me and with an air of consequence, and making me a low bow—whereat I saw the bystanders stare, for he was as gay a young spark as maid-of-honour could desire—he begged me to hasten, as the king awaited me in his closet.

'He has asked for you twice, sir,' he continued importantly, the feather of his cap almost sweeping the ground.

'I think,' I answered, quickening my steps, 'that the king's letter says noon, young sir. If I am late on such an occasion, he has indeed cause to complain of me.'

'Tut, tut!' he rejoined, waving his hand with a dandified air. 'It is no matter. One man may steal a horse when another may not look over the wall, you know.'

A man may be grey-haired, he may be sad-complexioned,

and yet he may retain some of the freshness of youth. On receiving this indication of a favour exceeding all expectation, I remember I felt the blood rise to my face, and experienced the most lively gratitude. I wondered who had spoken in my behalf, who had befriended me; and concluding at last that my part in the affair at Brouage had come to the king's ears, though I could not conceive through whom, I passed through the castle gates with an air of confidence and elation which was not unnatural, I think, under the circumstances. Thence, following my guide, I mounted the ramp and entered the courtyard.

A number of grooms and valets were lounging here, some leading horses to and fro, others exchanging jokes with the wenches who leaned from the windows, while their fellows again stamped up and down to keep their feet warm, or played ball against the wall in imitation of their masters. Such knaves are ever more insolent than their betters; but I remarked that they made way for me with respect, and with rising spirits, yet a little irony, I reminded myself as I mounted the stairs of the words, 'whom the king delighteth to honour!'

Reaching the head of the flight, where was a soldier on guard, the page opened the door of the antechamber, and standing aside bade me enter. I did so, and heard the door close behind me.

For a moment I stood still, bashful and confused. It seemed to me that there were a hundred people in the room, and that half the eyes which met mine were women's. Though I was not altogether a stranger to such state as the Prince of Condé had maintained, this crowded anteroom filled me with surprise, and even with a degree of awe, of which I was the next moment ashamed. True, the flutter of silk and gleam of jewels surpassed anything I had then seen, for my fortunes had never led me to the king's Court; but an instant's reflection reminded me that my fathers had held their own in such scenes, and with a bow regulated rather by this thought than by the shabbiness of my dress, I advanced amid a sudden silence.

'M. de Marsac!' the page announced, in a tone which sounded a little odd in my ears; so much so, that I turned quickly to look at him. He was gone, however, and when I turned again the eyes which met mine were full of smiles. A young girl who stood near me tittered. Put out of countenance by this, I looked round in embarrassment to find someone to whom I might apply.

The room was long and narrow, panelled in chestnut, with a row of windows on the one hand, and two fireplaces, now heaped with glowing logs, on the other. Between the fireplaces stood a rack of arms. Round the nearer hearth lounged a group of pages, the exact counterparts of the young blade who had brought me hither; and talking with these were as many young gentlewomen. Two great hounds lay basking in the heat, and coiled between them, with her head on the back of the larger, was a figure so strange that at another time I should have doubted my eyes. It wore the fool's motley and cap and bells, but a second glance showed me the features were a woman's. A torrent of black hair flowed loose about her neck, her eyes shone with wild merriment, and her face, keen, thin, and hectic, glared at me from the dog's back. Beyond her, round the farther fireplace, clustered more than a score of gallants and ladies, of whom one presently advanced to me.

'Sir,' he said politely—and I wished I could match his bow—'you wished to see——?'

'The King of Navarre,' I answered, doing my best.

He turned to the group behind him, and said, in a peculiarly even, placid tone, 'He wishes to see the King of Navarre.' Then in solemn silence he bowed to me again and went back to his fellows.

Upon the instant, and before I could make up my mind how to take this, a second tripped forward, and saluting me, said, 'M. de Marsac, I think?'

'At your service, sir,' I rejoined. In my eagerness to escape the gaze of all those eyes, and the tittering which was audible behind me, I took a step forward to be in readiness to follow him. But he gave no sign. 'M. de Marsac to see the King of Navarre' was all he said, speaking as the other had done to those behind. And with that he too wheeled round and went back to the fire.

I stared, a first faint suspicion of the truth aroused in my mind. Before I could act upon it, however—in such a situation it was no easy task to decide how to act—a third advanced with the same measured steps. 'By appointment I think, sir?' he said, bowing lower than the others.

'Yes,' I replied sharply, beginning to grow warm, 'by appointment at noon.'

'M. de Marsac,' he announced in a sing-song tone to those behind him, 'to see the King of Navarre by appointment at noon.' And with a second bow—while I grew scarlet with mortification—he too wheeled gravely round and returned to the fireplace.

I saw another preparing to advance, but he came too late. Whether my face of anger and bewilderment was too much for them, or some among them lacked patience to see the end, a sudden uncontrollable shout of laughter, in which all the room joined, cut short the farce. God knows it hurt me: I winced, I looked this way and that, hoping here or there to find sympathy and help. But it seemed to me that the place rang with gibes, that every panel framed, however I turned myself, a cruel, sneering face. One behind me cried 'Old Clothes,' and when I turned the other hearth whispered the taunt. It added a thousandfold to my embarrassment that there was in all a certain orderliness, so that while no one moved, and none, while I looked at them, raised their voices, I seemed the more singled out, and placed as a butt in the midst.

One face amid the pyramid of countenances which hid the farther fireplace so burned itself into my recollection in that miserable moment, that I never thereafter forgot it; a small, delicate woman's face, belonging to a young girl who stood boldly in front of her companions. It was a face full of pride, and, as I saw it then, of scorn—scorn that scarcely deigned to laugh; while the girl's graceful figure, slight and maidenly, yet perfectly proportioned, seemed instinct with the same feeling of contemptuous amusement.

The play, which seemed long enough to me, might have lasted longer, seeing that no one there had pity on me, had I not, in my desperation, espied a door at the farther end of the room, and concluded, seeing no other, that it was the door of the king's bedchamber. The mortification I was suffering was so great that I did not hesitate, but advanced with boldness towards it. On the instant there was a lull in the laughter round me, and half a dozen voices called on me to stop.

'I have come to see the king,' I answered, turning on them fiercely, for I was by this time in no mood for brow-beating, 'and I will see him!'

'He is out hunting,' cried all with one accord; and they signed imperiously to me to go back the way I had come.

But having the king's appointment safe in my pouch, I thought I had good reason to disbelieve them; and taking advantage of their surprise—for they had not expected so bold a step on my part—I was at the door before they could prevent me. I heard Mathurine, the fool, who had sprung to her feet, cry 'Pardieu! he will take the Kingdom of Heaven by force!' And those were the last words I heard; for, as I lifted the latch—there was no one on guard there—a sudden swift silence fell upon the room behind me.

I pushed the door gently open and went in. There were two men sitting in one of the windows, who turned and looked angrily towards me. For the rest the room was empty. The king's walking-shoes lay by his chair, and beside them boot-hooks and jack. A dog before the fire got up slowly and growled, and one of the men, rising from the trunk on which he had been sitting, came towards me and asked me, with every sign of irritation, what I wanted there, and who had given me leave to enter.

I was beginning to explain, with some diffidence—the stillness of the room sobering me—that I wished to see the king, when he who had advanced took me up sharply with, 'The king? the king? He is not here, man. He is hunting at Saint-Valery. Did they not tell you so outside?'

I thought I recognised the speaker, than whom I have seldom seen a man more grave and thoughtful for his years, which were something less than mine, more striking in presence, or more soberly dressed. And being desirous to evade his question, I asked him if I had not the honour to address M. du Plessis Mornay; for that wise and courtly statesman, now a pillar of Henry's counsels, it was.

'The same, sir,' he replied abruptly, and without taking his eyes from me. 'I am Mornay. What of that?'

'I am M. de Marsac,' I explained. And there I stopped, supposing that, as he was in the king's confidence, this would make my errand clear to him.

But I was disappointed. 'Well, sir?' he said, and waited impatiently.

So cold a reception, following such treatment as I had suffered outside, would have sufficed to have dashed my spirits utterly had I not felt the king's letter in my pocket. Being pretty confident, however, that a single glance at this would alter M. du Mornay's bearing for the better, I hastened, looking on it as a kind of talisman, to draw it out and presented it to him.

He took it, and looked at it, and opened it, but with so cold and immovable an aspect as made my heart sink more than all that had gone before. 'What is amiss?' I cried, unable to keep silence. "Tis from the king, sir.'

'A king in motley!' he answered, his lip curling.

The sense of his words did not at once strike home to me, and I murmured, in great disorder, that the king had sent for me.

'The king knows nothing of it,' was his blunt answer, bluntly given. And he thrust the paper back into my hands. 'It is a trick,' he continued, speaking with the same abruptness, 'for which you have doubtless to thank some of those idle young rascals without. You had sent an application to the king, I suppose? Just so. No doubt they got hold of it, and this is the result. They ought to be whipped.'

It was not possible for me to doubt any longer that what he said was true. I saw in a moment all my hopes vanish, all my plans flung to the winds; and in the first shock of the discovery I could neither find voice to answer him nor strength to withdraw. In a kind of vision I seemed to see my own lean, haggard face looking at me as in a glass, and, reading despair in my eyes, could have pitied myself.

My disorder was so great that M. du Mornay observed it. Looking more closely at me, he two or three times muttered my name, and at last said, 'M. de Marsac? Ha! I remember. You were in the affair of Brouage, were you not?'

I nodded my head in token of assent, being unable at the moment to speak, and so shaken that perforce I leaned against the wall, my head sunk on my breast. The memory of my age, my forty years, and my poverty, pressed hard upon me, filling me with despair and bitterness. I could have wept, but no tears came.

M. du Mornay, averting his eyes from me, took two or three short, impatient turns up and down the chamber. When he addressed me again his tone was full of respect, mingled with such petulance as one brave man might feel, seeing another so hard pressed. 'M. de Marsac,' he said, 'you have my sympathy. It is a shame that men who have served the cause should be reduced to such straits. Were it possible for me to increase my own train at present, I should consider it an honour to have you with me. But I am hard put to it myself, and so are we all, and the King of Navarre not least among us. He has lived for a month upon a wood which M. de Rosny has cut down. I will mention your name to him, but I should be cruel rather than kind were I not to warn you that nothing can come of it.'

With that he offered me his hand, and, cheered as much by this mark of consideration as by the kindness of his expressions, I rallied my spirits. True, I wanted comfort more substantial, but it was not to be had. I thanked him therefore as becomingly as I could, and seeing there was no help for it, took my leave of him, and slowly and sorrowfully withdrew from the room.

Alas! to escape I had to face the outside world, for which his kind words were an ill preparation. I had to run the gauntlet of the antechamber. The moment I appeared, or rather the moment the door closed behind me, I was hailed with a shout of derision. While one cried, 'Way! way for the gentleman who has seen the king!' another hailed me uproariously as Governor of Guyenne, and a third requested a commission in my regiment.

I heard these taunts with a heart full almost to bursting. It seemed to me an unworthy thing that, merely by reason of my poverty, I should be derided by youths who had still all their battles before them; but to stop or reproach them would only, as I well knew, make matters worse, and, moreover, I was so sore stricken that I had little spirit left even to speak. Accordingly, I made my way through them with what speed I might, my head bent, and my countenance heavy with shame and depression. In this way—I wonder there were not among them some generous enough to pity me—I had nearly gained the door, and was beginning to breathe, when I found my path stopped by that particular young lady of the Court whom I have described above. Something had for the moment diverted her attention from me, and it required a word from her companions to apprise her of my near neighbourhood. She turned then, as one taken by surprise, and finding me so close to her that my feet all but touched her gown, she stepped quickly aside, and with a glance as cruel as her act, drew her skirts away from contact with me.

The insult stung me, I know not why, more than all the gibes which were being flung at me from every side, and moved by a sudden impulse I stopped, and in the bitterness of my heart spoke to her. 'Mademoiselle,' I said, bowing low—for, as I have stated, she was small, and more like a fairy than a woman, though her face expressed both pride and self-will—'Mademoiselle,' I said sternly, 'such as I am,

21

I have fought for France! Some day you may learn that there are viler things in the world—and have to bear them—than a poor gentleman!'

The words were scarcely out of my mouth before I repented of them, for Mathurine, the fool, who was at my elbow, was quick to turn them into ridicule. Raising her hands above our heads, as in act to bless us, she cried out that Monsieur, having gained so rich an office, desired a bride to grace it; and this bringing down upon us a coarse shout of laughter and some coarser gibes, I saw the young girl's face flush hotly.

The next moment a voice in the crowd cried roughly, 'Out upon his wedding suit!' and with that a sweetmeat struck me in the face. Another and another followed, covering me with flour and comfits. This was the last straw. For a moment, forgetting where I was, I turned upon them, red and furious, every hair in my moustachios bristling. The next, the full sense of my impotence and of the folly of resentment prevailed with me, and, dropping my head upon my breast, I rushed from the room.

I believe that the younger among them followed me, and that the cry of 'Old Clothes!' pursued me even to the door of my lodgings in the Rue de la Coutellerie. But in the misery of the moment, and my strong desire to be within doors and alone, I barely noticed this, and am not certain whether it was so or not.

2

# The King of Navarre

I have already referred to the danger with which the alliance between Henry the Third and the League menaced us, an alliance whereof the news, it was said, had blanched the King of Navarre's moustache in a single night. Notwithstanding this, the Court had never shown itself more frolicsome or more free from care than at the time of which I am speaking; even the lack of money seemed for the moment forgotten. One amusement followed another, and though, without doubt, something was doing under the surface—for the wiser of his foes held our prince in particular dread when he seemed most deeply sunk in pleasure—to the outward eye Saint-Jean d'Angely appeared to be given over to enjoyment from one end to the other.

The stir and bustle of the Court reached me even in my garret, and contributed to make that Christmas, which fell on a Sunday, a trial almost beyond sufferance. All day long the rattle of hoofs on the pavement, and the laughter of riders bent on diversion, came up to me, making the hard stool seem harder, the bare walls more bare, and increasing a hundredfold the solitary gloom in which I sat. For as sunshine deepens the shadows which fall athwart it, and no silence is like that which follows the explosion of a mine, so sadness and poverty are never more intolerable than when hope and wealth rub elbows with them.

True, the great sermon which M. d'Amours preached in the market-house on the morning of Christmas-day cheered me, as it cheered all the more sober spirits. I was present myself, sitting in an obscure corner of the building, and heard the famous prediction, which was so soon to be fulfilled. 'Sire,' said the preacher, turning to the King of Navarre, and referring, with the boldness that ever characterised that great man and noble Christian, to the attempt then being made to exclude the prince from the succession—'Sire, what God at your birth gave you man cannot take away. A little while, a little patience, and you shall cause us to preach beyond the Loire! With you for our Joshua we shall cross the Jordan, and in the Promised Land the Church shall be set up.'

Words so brave, and so well adapted to encourage the Huguenots in the crisis through which their affairs were then passing, charmed all hearers; save indeed, those—and they were few—who, being devoted to the Vicomte de

23

Turenne, disliked, though they could not controvert, this public acknowledgment of the King of Navarre as the Huguenot leader. The pleasure of those present was evinced in a hundred ways, and to such an extent that even I returned to my chamber soothed and exalted, and found, in dreaming of the speedy triumph of the cause, some compensation for my own ill-fortune.

As the day wore on, however, and the evening brought no change, but presented to me the same dreary prospect with which morning had made me familiar, I confess without shame that my heart sank once more, particularly as I saw that I should be forced in a day or two to sell either my remaining horse or some part of my equipment as essential; a step which I could not contemplate without feelings of the utmost despair. In this state of mind I was adding up by the light of a solitary candle the few coins I had left, when I heard footsteps ascending the stairs. I made them out to be the steps of two persons, and was still lost in conjectures who they might be, when a hand knocked gently at my door.

Fearing another trick, I did not at once open, the more as there was something stealthy and insinuating in the knock. Thereupon my visitors held a whispered consultation; then they knocked again. I asked loudly who was there, but to this they did not choose to give any answer, while I, on my part, determined not to open until they did. The door was strong, and I smiled grimly at the thought that this time they would have their trouble for their pains.

To my surprise, however, they did not desist, and go away, as I expected, but continued to knock at intervals and whisper much between times. More than once they called me softly by name and bade me open, but as they steadily refrained from saying who they were, I sat still. Occasionally I heard them laugh, but under their breath as it were; and persuaded by this that they were bent on a frolic, I might have persisted in my silence until midnight, which was not more than two hours off, had not a slight sound, as of a rat gnawing behind the wainscot, drawn my attention to the door. Raising my candle and shading my eyes I espied something small and bright protruding beneath it, and sprang up, thinking they were about to prise it In. To my surprise, however, I could discover, on taking the candle to the threshold, nothing more threatening than a couple of gold livres, which had been thrust through the crevice between the door and the floor.

My astonishment may be conceived. I stood for full a minute staring at the coins, the candle in my hand. Then, reflecting that the young sparks at the Court would be very unlikely to spend such a sum on a jest, I hesitated no longer, but putting down the candle, drew the bolt of the door, purposing to confer with my visitors outside. In this, however, I was disappointed, for the moment the door was open they pushed forcibly past me and, entering the room pell-mell, bade me by signs to close the door again.

I did so suspiciously, and without averting my eyes from my visitors. Great were my embarrassment and confusion, therefore, when, the door being shut, they dropped their cloaks one after the other, and I saw before me M. du Mornay and the well-known figure of the King of Navarre.

They seemed so much diverted, looking at one another and laughing, that for a moment I thought some chance resemblance deceived me, and that here were my jokers again. Hence while a man might count ten I stood staring; and the king was the first to speak. 'We have made no mistake, Du Mornay, have we?' he said, casting a laughing glance at me.

'No, sire,' Du Mornay answered. 'This is the Sieur de Marsac, the gentleman whom I mentioned to you.'

I hastened, confused, wondering, and with a hundred apologies, to pay my respects to the king. He speedily cut me short, however, saying, with an air of much kindness, 'Of Marsac, in Brittany, I think, sir?'

'The same, sire.'

'Then you are of the family of Bonne?'

'I am the last survivor of that family, sire,' I answered respectfully.

'It has played its part,' he rejoined. And therewith he took his seat on my stool with an easy grace which charmed me. 'Your motto is "*Bonne foi*," is it not? And Marsac, if I remember rightly, is not far from Rennes, on the Vilane?'

I answered that it was, adding, with a full heart, that it grieved me to be compelled to receive so great a prince in so poor a lodging.

'Well, I confess,' Du Mornay struck in, looking carelessly round him, 'you have a queer taste, M. de Marsac, in the arrangement of your furniture. You—'

'Mornay!' the king cried sharply.

'Sire?'

'Chut! your elbow is in the candle. Beware of it!'

But I well understood him. If my heart had been full before it overflowed now. Poverty is not so shameful as the shifts to which it drives men. I had been compelled some days before, in order to make as good a show as possible—since it is the undoubted duty of a gentleman to hide his nakedness from impertinent eyes, and especially from the eyes of the *canaille*, who are wont to judge from externals—to remove such of my furniture and equipage as remained to that side of the room, which was visible from without when the door was open. This left the farther side of the room vacant and bare. To anyone within doors the artifice was, of course, apparent, and I am bound to say that M. du Mornay's words brought the blood to my brow.

I rejoiced, however. a moment later that he had uttered them; for without them I might never have known, or known so early, the kindness of heart and singular quickness of apprehension which ever distinguished the king, my master. So, in my heart, I began to call him from that hour.

The King of Navarre was at this time thirty-five years old, his hair brown, his complexion ruddy, his moustache, on one side at least, beginning to turn grey. His features, which

Nature had cast in a harsh and imperious mould, were relieved by a constant sparkle and animation such as I have never seen in any other man, but in him became ever more conspicuous in gloomy and perilous times. Inured to danger from his earliest youth, he had come to enjoy it as others a festival, hailing its advent with a reckless gaiety which astonished even brave men, and led others to think him the least prudent of mankind. Yet such he was not: nay, he was the opposite of this. Never did Marshal of France make more careful dispositions for a battle—albeit once in it he bore himself like any captain of horse—nor ever did Du Mornay himself sit down to a conference with a more accurate knowledge of affairs. His prodigious wit and the affability of his manners, while they endeared him to his servants, again and again blinded his adversaries; who, thinking that so much brilliance could arise only from a shallow nature, found when it was too late that they had been outwitted by him whom they contemptuously styled the Prince of Béarn, a man a hundredfold more astute than themselves, and master alike of pen and sword.

Much of this, which all the world now knows, I learned afterwards. At the moment I could think of little save the king's kindness; to which he added by insisting that I should sit on the bed while we talked. 'You wonder, M. de Marsac,' he said, 'what brings me here, and why I have come to you instead of sending for you? Still more, perhaps, why I have come to you at night and with such precautions? I will tell you. But first, that my coming may not fill you with false hopes, let me say frankly, that though I may relieve your present necessities, whether you fall into the plan I am going to mention, or not, I cannot take you into my service; wherein, indeed, every post is doubly filled. Du Mornay mentioned your name to me, but in fairness to others I had to answer that I could do nothing.'

I am bound to confess that this strange exordium dashed hopes which had already risen to a high pitch. Recovering myself as quickly as possible, however, I murmured that the honour of a visit from the King of Navarre was sufficient happiness for me.

'Nay, but that honour I must take from you,' he replied, smiling; 'though I see that you would make an excellent courtier—far better than Du Mornay here, who never in his life made so pretty a speech. For I must lay my commands on you to keep this visit a secret, M. de Marsac. Should but the slightest whisper of it get abroad, your usefulness, as far as I am concerned, would be gone, and gone for good!'

So remarkable a statement filled me with wonder I could scarcely disguise. It was with difficulty I found words to assure the king that his commands should be faithfully obeyed.

'Of that I am sure,' he answered with the utmost kindness. 'Were I not, and sure, too, from what I am told of your gallantry when my cousin took Brouage, that you are a man of deeds rather than words, I should not be here with the proposition I am going to lay before you. It is this. I can give you no hope of public employment, M. de Marsac, but I can offer you an adventure—if adventures be to your taste—as dangerous and as thankless as any Amadis ever undertook.'

'As thankless, sire?' I stammered, doubting if I had heard aright, the expression was so strange.

'As thankless,' he answered, his keen eyes seeming to read my soul. 'I am frank with you, you see, sir,' he continued, carelessly. 'I can suggest this adventure—it is for the good of the State—I can do no more. The King of Navarre cannot appear in it, nor can he protect you. Succeed or fail in it, you stand alone. The only promise I make is, that if it ever be safe for me to acknowledge the act, I will reward the doer.'

He paused, and for a few moments I stared at him in sheer amazement. What did he mean? Were he and the other real figures, or was I dreaming?

'Do you understand?' he asked at length, with a touch of impatience.

'Yes, sire, I think I do,' I murmured, very certain in truth and reality that I did not.

'What do you say, then—yes or no?' he rejoined. 'Will you

undertake the adventure, or would you hear more before you make up your mind?'

I hesitated. Had I been a younger man by ten years I should doubtless have cried assent there and then, having been all my life ready enough to embark on such enterprises as offered a chance of distinction. But something in the strangeness of the king's preface, although I had it in my heart to die for him, gave me check, and I answered, with an air of great humility, 'You will think me but a poor courtier now, sire, yet he is a fool who jumps into a ditch without measuring the depth. I would fain, if I may say it without disrespect, hear all that you can tell me.'

'Then I fear,' he answered quickly, 'if you would have more light on the matter, my friend, you must get another candle.'

I started, he spoke so abruptly; but perceiving that the candle had indeed burned down to the socket, I rose, with many apologies, and fetched another from the cupboard. It did not occur to me at the moment, though it did later, that the king had purposely sought this opportunity of consulting with his companion. I merely remarked, when I returned to my place on the bed, that they were sitting a little nearer one another, and that the king eyed me before he spoke— though he still swung one foot carelessly in the air—with close attention.

'I speak to you, of course, sir,' he presently went on, 'in confidence, believing you to be an honourable as well as a brave man. That which I wish you to do is briefly, and in a word, to carry off a lady. Nay,' he added quickly, with a laughing grimace, 'have no fear! She is no sweetheart of mine, nor should I go to my grave friend here did I need assistance of that kind. Henry of Bourbon, I pray God, will always be able to free his own lady-love. This is a State affair, and a matter of quite another character, though we cannot at present entrust you with the meaning of it.'

I bowed in silence, feeling somewhat chilled and perplexed, as who would not, having such an invitation before him? I had anticipated an affair with men only—a secret assault or a petard expedition. But seeing the bareness of my room, and the honour the king was doing me, I felt I had no choice, and I answered, 'That being the case, sire, I am wholly at your service.'

'That is well,' he answered briskly, though methought he looked at Du Mornay reproachfully, as doubting his commendation of me. 'But will you say the same,' he continued, removing his eyes to me, and speaking slowly, as though he would try me, 'when I tell you that the lady to be carried off is the ward of the Vicomte de Turenne, whose arm is well-nigh as long as my own, and who would fain make it longer; who never travels, as he told me yesterday, with less than fifty gentlemen, and has a thousand arquebusiers in his pay? Is the adventure still to your liking, M. de Marsac, now that you know that?'

'It is more to my liking, sire,' I answered stoutly.

'Understand this too,' he rejoined. 'It is essential that this lady, who is at present confined in the Vicomte's house at Chizé, should be released; but it is equally essential that there should be no breach between the Vicomte and myself. Therefore the affair must be the work of an independent man, who has never been in my service, nor in any way connected with me. If captured, you pay the penalty without recourse to me.'

'I fully understand, sire,' I answered.

*'Ventre Saint Gris!'* he cried, breaking into a low laugh. 'I swear the man is more afraid of the lady than he is of the Vicomte! That is not the way of most of our Court.'

Du Mornay, who had been sitting nursing his knee in silence, pursed up his lips, though it was easy to see that he was well content with the king's approbation. He now intervened. 'With your permission, sire,' he said, 'I will let this gentleman know the details.'

'Do, my friend,' the king answered. 'And be short, for if we are here much longer I shall be missed, and in a twinkling the Court will have found me a new mistress.'

He spoke in jest and with a laugh, but I saw Du Mornay

start at the words, as though they were little to his liking; and I learned afterwards that the Court was really much exercised at this time with the question who would be the next favourite, the king's passion for the Countess de la Guiche being evidently on the wane, and that which he presently evinced for Madame de Guercheville being as yet a matter of conjecture.

Du Mornay took no overt notice of the king's words, however, but proceeded to give me my directions. 'Chizé, which you know by name,' he said, 'is six leagues from here. Mademoiselle de la Vire is confined in the north-west room, on the first floor, overlooking the park. More I cannot tell you, except that her woman's name is Fanchette, and that she is to be trusted. The house is well guarded, and you will need four or five men. There are plenty of cut-throats to be hired, only see, M. de Marsac, that they are such as you can manage, and that Mademoiselle takes no hurt among them. Have horses in waiting, and the moment you have released the lady ride north with her as fast as her strength will permit. Indeed, you must not spare her, if Turenne be on your heels. You should be across the Loire in sixty hours after leaving Chizé.'

'Across the Loire?' I exclaimed in astonishment.

'Yes, sir, across the Loire,' he replied, with some sternness. 'Your task, be good enough to understand, is to convoy Mademoiselle de la Vire with all speed to Blois. There, attracting as little notice as may be, you will inquire for the Baron de Rosny at the Bleeding Heart, in the Rue Saint-Denys. He will take charge of the lady, or direct you how to dispose of her, and your task will then be accomplished. You follow me?'

'Perfectly,' I answered, speaking in my turn with some dryness. 'But Mademoiselle I understand is young. What if she will not accompany me, a stranger, entering her room at night, and by the window?'

'That has been thought of,' was the answer. He turned to the King of Navarre, who, after a moment's search, produced a small object from his pouch. This he gave to his companion, and the latter transferred it to me. I took it with curiosity. It was the half of a gold carolus, the broken edge of the coin being rough and jagged. 'Show that to Mademoiselle, my friend,' Du Mornay continued, 'and she will accompany you. She has the other half.'

'But be careful,' Henry added eagerly, 'to make no mention, even to her, of the King of Navarre. You mark me, M. de Marsac! If you have at any time occasion to speak of me, you may have the honour of calling me *your friend*, and referring to me always in the same manner.'

This he said with so gracious an air that I was charmed, and thought myself happy indeed to be addressed in this wise by a prince whose name was already so glorious. Nor was my satisfaction diminished when his companion drew out a bag containing, as he told me, three hundred crowns in gold, and placed it in my hands, bidding me defray therefrom the cost of the journey. 'Be careful, however,' he added earnestly, 'to avoid, in hiring your men, any appearance of wealth, lest the adventure seem to be suggested by some outside person; instead of being dictated by the desperate state of your own fortunes. Promise rather than give, so far as that will avail. And for what you must give, let each livre seem to be the last in your pouch.'

Henry nodded assent. 'Excellent advice!' he muttered, rising and drawing on his cloak, 'such as you ever give me, Mornay, and I as seldom take—more's the pity! But, after all, of little avail without this.' He lifted my sword from the table as he spoke, and weighed it in his hand. 'A pretty tool,' he continued, turning suddenly and looking me very closely in the face. 'A very pretty tool. Were I in your place, M. de Marsac, I would see that it hung loose in the scabbard. Ay, and more, man, use it!' he added, sinking his voice and sticking out his chin, while his grey eyes, looking ever closer into mine, seemed to grow cold and hard as steel. 'Use it to the last, for if you fall into Turenne's hands, God help you! I cannot!'

'If I am taken, sire,' I answered, trembling, but not with fear, 'my fate be on my own head.'

I saw the king's eyes soften at that, and his face change so swiftly that I scarce knew him for the same man. He let the weapon drop with a clash on the table. '*Ventre Saint Gris!*' he exclaimed with a strange thrill of yearning in his tone. 'I swear by God, I would I were in your shoes, sir. To strike a blow or two with no care what came of it. To take the road with a good horse and a good sword, and see what fortune would send. To be rid of all this statecraft and protocolling, and never to issue another declaration in this world, but just to be for once a Gentleman of France, with all to win and nothing to lose save the love of my lady! Ah! Mornay, would it not be sweet to leave all this fret and fume, and ride away to the green woods by Coarraze?'

'Certainly, if you prefer them to the Louvre, sire,' Du Mornay answered drily; while I stood, silent and amazed, before this strange man, who could so suddenly change from grave to gay, and one moment spoke so sagely, and the next like any wild lad in his teens. 'Certainly,' he answered, 'if that be your choice, sire; and if you think that even there the Duke of Guise will leave you in peace. Turenne, I am sure, will be glad to hear of your decision. Doubtless he will be elected Protector of the Churches. Nay, sire, for shame!' Du Mornay continued, almost with sternness. 'Would you leave France, which at odd times I have heard you say you loved, to shift for herself? Would you deprive her of the only man who does love her for her own sake?'

'Well, well, but she is such a fickle sweetheart, my friend,' the king answered, laughing, the side glimpse of his eye on me. 'Never was one so coy or so hard to clip! And, besides, has not the Pope divorced us?'

'The Pope! A fig for the Pope!' Du Mornay rejoined with impatient heat. 'What has he to do with France? An impertinent meddler, and an Italian to boot! I would he and all the brood of them were sunk a hundred fathoms deep in the sea. But, meantime, I would send him a text to digest.'

'*Exemplum*?' said the king.

'Whom God has joined together let no man put asunder.'

'Amen!' quoth Henry softly. 'And France is a fair and comely bride.'

After that he kept such a silence, falling as it seemed to me into a brown study, that he went away without so much as bidding me farewell, or being conscious, as far as I could tell, of my presence. Du Mornay exchanged a few words with me, to assure himself that I understood what I had to do, and then, with many kind expressions, which I did not fail to treasure up and con over in the times that were coming, hastened downstairs after his master.

My joy when I found myself alone may be conceived. Yet was it no ecstasy, but a sober exhilaration; such as stirred my pulses indeed, and bade me once more face the world with a firm eye and an assured brow, but was far from holding out before me a troubadour's palace or any dazzling prospect. The longer I dwelt on the interview, the more clearly I saw the truth. As the glamour which Henry's presence and singular kindness had cast over me began to lose some of its power, I recognised more and more surely why he had come to me. It was not out of any special favour for one whom he knew by report only, if at all by name; but because he had need of a man poor, and therefore reckless, middle-aged (of which comes discretion), obscure—therefore a safe instrument; to crown all, a gentleman, seeing that both a secret and a woman were in question.

Withal I wondered too. Looking from the bag of money on the table to the broken coin in my hand, I scarcely knew which to admire more: the confidence which entrusted the one to a man broken and beggared, or the courage of the gentlewoman who should accompany me on the faith of the other.

# 3
# Boot and Saddle

As was natural, I meditated deeply and far into the night on the difficulties of the task entrusted to me. I saw that it fell into two parts: the release of the lady, and her safe conduct to Blois, a distance of sixty leagues. The release I thought it probable I could effect single-handed, or with one companion only; but in the troubled condition of the country at this time, more particularly on both sides of the Loire, I scarcely saw how I could ensure a lady's safety on the road northwards unless I had with me at least five swords.

To get these together at a few hours' notice promised to be no easy task; although the presence of the Court of Navarre had filled Saint-Jean with a crowd of adventurers. Yet the king's command was urgent, and at some sacrifice, even at some risk, must be obeyed. Pressed by these considerations, I could think of no better man to begin with than Fresnoy.

His character was bad, and he had long forfeited such claim as he had ever possessed—I believe it was a misty one, on the distaff side—to gentility. But the same cause which had rendered me destitute—I mean the death of the Prince of Condé—had stripped him to the last rag; and this, perhaps, inclining me to serve him, I was the more quick to see his merits. I knew him already for a hardy, reckless man, very capable of striking a shrewd blow. I gave him credit for being trusty, as long as his duty jumped with his interest.

Accordingly, as soon as it was light, having fed and groomed the Cid, which was always the first employment of

35

my day, I set out in search of Fresnoy, and was presently lucky enough to find him taking his morning draught outside the 'Three Pigeons,' a little inn not far from the north gate. It was more than a fortnight since I had set eyes on him, and the lapse of time had worked so great a change for the worse in him that, forgetting my own shabbiness, I looked at him askance, as doubting the wisdom of enlisting one who bore so plainly the marks of poverty and dissipation. His great face—he was a large man—had suffered recent ill-usage, and was swollen and discoloured, one eye being as good as closed. He was unshaven, his hair was ill-kempt, his doublet unfastened at the throat, and torn and stained besides. Despite the cold—for the morning was sharp and frosty, though free from wind—there were half a dozen packmen drinking and squabbling before the inn, while the beasts they drove quenched their thirst at the trough. But these men seemed with one accord to leave him in possession of the bench at which he sat; nor did I wonder much at this when I saw the morose and savage glance which he shot at me as I approached. Whether he read my first impressions in my face, or for some other reason felt distaste for my company, I could not determine. But, undeterred by his behaviour, I sat down beside him and called for wine.

He nodded sulkily in answer to my greeting, and cast a half-shamed, half-angry look at me out of the corners of his eyes. 'You need not look at me as though I were a dog,' he muttered presently. 'You are not so very spruce yourself, my friend. But I suppose you have grown proud since you got that fat appointment at Court!' And he laughed out loud, so that I confess I was in two minds whether I should not force the jest down his ugly throat.

However I restrained myself, though my cheeks burned. 'You have heard about it, then,' I said, striving to speak indifferently.

'Who has not?' he said, laughing with his lips, though his eyes were far from merry. 'The Sieur de Marsac's appointment! Ha! ha! Why, man—'

'Enough of it now!' I exclaimed. And I dare say I writhed on my seat. 'As far as I am concerned the jest is a stale one, sir, and does not amuse me.'

'But it amuses me,' he rejoined with a grin.

'Let it be, nevertheless,' I said; and I think he read a warning in my eyes. 'I have come to speak to you upon another matter.'

He did not refuse to listen, but threw one leg over the other, and looking up at the inn-sign began to whistle in a rude, offensive manner. Still, having an object in view, I controlled myself and continued. 'It is this, my friend: money is not very plentiful at present with either of us.'

Before I could say any more he turned on me savagely, and with a loud oath thrust his bloated face, flushed with passion, close to mine. 'Now look here, M. de Marsac!' he cried violently, 'once for all, it is no good! I have not got the money, and I cannot pay it. I said a fortnight ago, when you lent it, that you should have it this week. Well,' slapping his hand on the bench, 'I have not got it, and it is no good beginning upon me. You cannot have it, and that is flat!'

'Damn the money!' I cried.

'What?' he exclaimed, scarcely believing his ears.

'Let the money be!' I repeated fiercely. 'Do you hear? I have not come about it. I am here to offer you work—good, well-paid work—if you will enlist with me and play me fair, Fresnoy.'

'Play fair!' he cried with an oath.

'There, there,' I said, 'I am willing to let bygones be bygones if you are. The point is, that I have an adventure on hand, and, wanting help, can pay you for it.'

He looked at me cunningly, his eye travelling over each rent and darn in my doublet. 'I will help you fast enough,' he said at last. 'But I should like to see the money first.'

'You shall,' I answered.

'Then I am with you, my friend. Count on me till death!' he cried, rising and laying his hand in mine with a boisterous

37

frankness which did not deceive me into trusting him far. 'And now, whose is the affair, and what is it?'

'The affair is mine,' I said coldly. 'It is to carry off a lady.'

He whistled and looked me over again, an impudent leer in his eyes. 'A lady?' he exclaimed. 'Umph! I could understand a young spark going in for such—but that's your affair. Who is it?'

'That is my affair, too,' I answered coolly, disgusted by the man's venality and meanness, and fully persuaded that I must trust him no farther than the length of my sword. 'All I want you to do, M. Fresnoy,' I continued stiffly, 'is to place yourself at my disposal and under my orders for ten days. I will find you a horse and pay you—the enterprise is a hazardous one, and I take that into account—two gold crowns a day, and ten more if we succeed in reaching a place of safety.'

'Such a place as—'

'Never mind that,' I replied. 'The question is, do you accept?'

He looked down sullenly, and I could see he was greatly angered by my determination to keep the matter to myself. 'Am I to know no more than that?' he asked, digging the point of his scabbard again and again into the ground.

'No more,' I answered firmly. 'I am bent on a desperate attempt to mend my fortunes before they fall as low as yours; and that is as much as I mean to tell living man. If you are loth to risk your life with your eyes shut, say so, and I will go to someone else.'

But he was not in a position, as I well knew, to refuse such an offer, and presently he accepted it with a fresh semblance of heartiness. I told him I should want four troopers to escort us, and these he offered to procure, saying that he knew just the knaves to suit me. I bade him hire two only, however, being too wise to put myself altogether in his hands; and then, having given him money to buy himself a horse—I made it a term that the men should bring

38

their own—and named a rendezvous for the first hour after noon, I parted from him and went rather sadly away.

For I began to see that the king had not underrated the dangers of an enterprise on which none but desperate men and such as were down in the world could be expected to embark. Seeing this, and also a thing which followed clearly from it—that I should have as much to fear from my own company as from the enemy—I looked forward with little hope to a journey during every day and every hour of which I must bear a growing weight of fear and responsibility.

It was too late to turn back, however, and I went about my preparations, if with little cheerfulness, at least with stead-fast purpose. I had my sword ground and my pistols put in order by the cutler over whom I lodged, and who performed this last office for me with the same goodwill which had characterised all his dealings with me. I sought out and hired a couple of stout fellows whom I believed to be indifferently honest, but who possessed the advantage of having horses; and besides bought two led horses myself for mademoiselle and her woman. Such other equipments as were absolutely necessary I purchased, reducing my stock of money in this way to two hundred and ten crowns. How to dispose of this sum so that it might be safe and yet at my command was a question which greatly exercised me. In the end I had recourse to my friend the cutler, who suggested hiding a hundred crowns of it in my cap, and deftly contrived a place for the purpose. This, the cap being lined with steel, was a matter of no great difficulty. A second hundred I sewed up in the stuffing of my saddle, placing the remainder in my pouch for present necessities.

A small rain was falling in the streets when, a little after noon, I started with my two knaves behind me and made for the north gate. So many were moving this way and the other that we passed unnoticed, and might have done so had we numbered six swords instead of three. When we reached the rendezvous, a mile beyond the gate, we found Fresnoy already there, taking shelter in the lee of a big holly-tree. He had four horsemen with him, and on our appearance rode forward to meet us, crying heartily, 'Welcome, M. le Capitaine!'

'Welcome, certainly,' I answered, pulling the Cid up sharply, and holding off from him. 'But who are these, M. Fresnoy?' and I pointed with my riding-cane to his four companions.

He tried to pass the matter off with a laugh. 'Oh! these?' he said. 'That is soon explained. The Evangelists would not be divided, so I brought them all—Matthew, Mark, Luke, and John—thinking it likely you might fail to secure your men. And I will warrant them for four as gallant boys as you will ever find behind you!'

They were certainly four as arrant ruffians as I had ever seen before me, and I saw I must not hesitate. 'Two or none, M. Fresnoy,' I said firmly. 'I gave you a commission for two, and two I will take—Matthew and Mark, or Luke and John, as you please.'

''Tis a pity to break the party,' said he, scowling.

'If that be all,' I retorted, 'one of my men is called John. And we will dub the other Luke, if that will mend the matter.'

'The Prince of Condé,' he muttered sullenly, 'employed these men.'

'The Prince of Condé employed some queer people sometimes, M. Fresnoy,' I answered, looking him straight between the eyes, 'as we all must. A truce to this, if you please. We will take Matthew and Mark. The other two be good enough to dismiss.'

He seemed to waver for a moment, as if he had a mind to disobey, but in the end, thinking better of it, he bade the men return; and as I complimented each of them with a piece of silver, they went off, after some swearing, in tolerably good humour. Thereon Fresnoy was for taking the road at once, but having no mind to be followed, I gave the word to wait until the two were out of sight.

I think, as we sat our horses in the rain, the holly-bush not being large enough to shelter us all, we were as sorry a band as ever set out to rescue a lady; nor was it without pain that I looked round and saw myself reduced to command such people. There was scarcely one whole unpatched garment among us, and three of my squires had but a spur apiece. To make up for this deficiency we mustered two black eyes, Fresnoy's included, and a broken nose. Matthew's nag lacked a tail, and, more remarkable still, its rider, as I presently discovered, was stone-deaf, while Mark's sword was innocent of a scabbard, and his bridle was plain rope. One thing, indeed, I observed with pleasure. The two men who had come with me looked askance at the two who had come with Fresnoy, and these returned the stare with interest. On this division and on the length of my sword I based all my hopes of safety and of something more. On it I was about to stake, not my own life only—which was no great thing, seeing what my prospects were—but the life and honour of a woman, young, helpless, and as yet unknown to me.

Weighed down as I was by these considerations, I had to bear the additional burden of hiding my fears and suspicions under a cheerful demeanour. I made a short speech to my following, who one and all responded by swearing to stand by me to death. I then gave the word, and we started, Fresnoy and I leading the way, Luke and John with the led horses following, and the other two bringing up the rear.

The rain continuing to fall and the country in this part being dreary and monotonous, even in fair weather, I felt my spirits sink still lower as the day advanced. The responsibility I was going to incur assumed more serious proportions each time I scanned my following; while Fresnoy, plying me with perpetual questions respecting my plans, was as uneasy a companion as my worst enemy could have wished me.

'Come!' he grumbled presently, when we had covered four leagues or so, 'you have not told me yet, sieur, where we stay tonight. You are travelling so slowly that—'

'I am saving the horses,' I answered shortly. 'We shall do a long day tomorrow.'

'Yours looks fit for a week of days,' he sneered, with an evil look at my Sardinian, which was, indeed, in better case than its master. 'It is sleek enough, any way!'

'It is as good as it looks,' I answered, a little nettled by his tone.

'There is a better here,' he responded.

'I don't see it,' I said. I had already eyed the nags all round, and assured myself that, ugly and blemished as they were, they were up to their work. But I had discerned no special merit among them. I looked them over again now, and came to the same conclusion—that, except the led horses, which I had chosen with some care, there was nothing among them to vie with the Cid, either in speed or looks. I told Fresnoy so.

'Would you like to try?' he said tauntingly.

I laughed, adding, 'If you think I am going to tire our horses by racing them, with such work as we have before us, you are mistaken, Fresnoy. I am not a boy, you know.'

'There need be no question of racing,' he answered more quietly. 'You have only to get on that rat-tailed bay of Matthew's to feel its paces and say I am right.'

I looked at the bay, a bald-faced, fiddle-headed horse, and saw that, with no signs of breeding, it was still a big-boned animal with good shoulders and powerful hips. I thought it possible Fresnoy might be right, and if so, and the bay's manners were tolerable, it might do for mademoiselle better than the horse I had chosen. At any rate, if we had a fast horse among us, it was well to know the fact, so bidding Matthew change with me, and be careful of the Cid, I mounted the bay, and soon discovered that its paces were easy and promised speed, while its manners seemed as good as even a timid rider could desire.

Our road at the time lay across a flat desolate heath, dotted here and there with thorn-bushes; the track being broken and stony, extended more than a score of yards in width, through travellers straying to this side and that to escape the worst places. Fresnoy and I, in making the change, had fallen slightly behind the other three, and were riding abreast of Matthew on the Cid.

'Well,' he said, 'was I not right?'

'In part,' I answered. 'The horse is better than its looks.'

'Like many others,' he rejoined, a spark of resentment in his tone—'men as well as horses, M. de Marsac. But what do you say? Shall we canter on a little and overtake the others?'

Thinking it well to do so, I assented readily, and we started together. We had ridden, however, no more than a hundred yards, and I was only beginning to extend the bay, when Fresnoy, slightly drawing rein, turned in his saddle and looked back. The next moment he cried, 'Hallo! what is this? Those fellows are not following us, are they?'

I turned sharply to look. At that moment, without falter or warning, the bay horse went down under me as if shot dead, throwing me half a dozen yards over its head; and that so suddenly that I had no time to raise my arms, but, falling heavily on my head and shoulder, lost consciousness.

I have had many falls, but no other to vie with that in utter unexpectedness. When I recovered my senses I found myself leaning, giddy and sick, against the bole of an old thorn-tree. Fresnoy and Matthew supported me on either side, and asked me how I found myself; while the other three men, their forms black against the stormy evening sky, sat their horses a few paces in front of me. I was too much dazed at first to see more, and this only in a mechanical fashion; but gradually, my brain grew clearer, and I advanced from wondering who the strangers round me were to recognising them, and finally to remembering what had happened to me.

'Is the horse hurt?' I muttered as soon as I could speak.

'Not a whit,' Fresnoy answered, chuckling, or I was much mistaken. 'I am afraid you came off the worse of the two, captain.'

He exchanged a look with the men on horseback as he spoke, and in a dull fashion I fancied I saw them smile. One even laughed, and another turned in his saddle as if to hide his face. I had a vague general sense that there was

43

some joke on foot in which I had no part. But I was too much shaken at the moment to be curious, and gratefully accepted the offer of one of the men to fetch me a little water. While he was away the rest stood round me, the same look of ill-concealed drollery on their faces. Fresnoy alone talked, speaking volubly of the accident, pouring out expressions of sympathy and cursing the road, the horse, and the wintry light until the water came; when, much refreshed by the draught, I managed to climb to the Cid's saddle and plod slowly onwards with them.

'A bad beginning,' Fresnoy said presently, stealing a sly glance at me as we jogged along side by side, Chizé half a league before us, and darkness not far off.

By this time, however, I was myself again, save for a little humming in the head, and, shrugging my shoulders, I told him so. 'All's well that ends well,' I added. 'Not that it was a pleasant fall, or that I wish to have such another.'

'No, I should think not,' he answered. His face was turned from me, but I fancied I heard him snigger.

Something, which may have been a vague suspicion, led me a moment later to put my hand into my pouch. Then I understood. I understood too well. The sharp surprise of the discovery was such that involuntarily I drove my spurs into the Cid, and the horse sprang forward.

'What is the matter?' Fresnoy asked.

'The matter?' I echoed, my hand still at my belt, feeling— feeling hopelessly.

'Yes, what is it?' he asked, a brazen smile on his rascally face.

I looked at him, my brow as red as fire. 'Oh! nothing— nothing,' I said. 'Let us trot on.'

In truth I had discovered that, taking advantage of my helplessness, the scoundrels had robbed me, while I lay insensible, of every gold crown in my purse! Nor was this all, or the worst, for I saw at once that in doing so they had effected something which was a thousandfold more ominous and formidable—established against me that secret understanding which it was my especial aim to prevent, and on the absence of which I had been counting. Nay, I saw that for my very life I had only my friend the cutler and my own prudence to thank, seeing that these rogues would certainly have murdered me without scruple had they succeeded in finding the bulk of my money. Baffled in this, while still persuaded that I had other resources, they had stopped short of that villainy—or this memoir had never been written. They had kindly permitted me to live until a more favourable opportunity of enriching themselves at my expense should put them in possession of my last crown!

Though I was sufficiently master of myself to refrain from complaints which I felt must be useless, and from menaces which it has never been my habit to utter unless I had also the power to put them into execution, it must not be imagined that I did not, as I rode on by Fresnoy's side, feel my position acutely or see how absurd a figure I cut in my dual character of leader and dupe. Indeed, the reflection that, being in this perilous position, I was about to stake another's safety as well as my own, made me feel the need of a few minutes' thought so urgent that I determined to gain them, even at the risk of leaving my men at liberty to plot further mischief. Coming almost immediately afterwards within sight of the turrets of the Château of Chizé, I told Fresnoy that we should lie the night at the village; and bade him take the men on and secure quarters at the inn. Attacked instantly by suspicion and curiosity, he demurred stoutly to leaving me, and might have persisted in his refusal had I not pulled up, and clearly shown him that I would have my own way in this case or come to an open breach. He shrank, as I expected, from the latter alternative, and, bidding me a sullen adieu, trotted on with his troop. I waited until they were out of sight, and then, turning the Cid's head, crossed a small brook which divided the road from the chase, and choosing a ride which seemed to pierce the wood in the direction of the Château, proceeded down it, keeping a sharp look-out on either hand.

It was then, my thoughts turning to the lady who was now so near, and who, noble, rich, and a stranger, seemed, as I approached her, not the least formidable of the embarrassments before me—it was then that I made a discovery which sent a cold shiver through my frame, and in a moment swept all memory of my paltry ten crowns from my head. Ten crowns! Alas! I had lost that which was worth all my crowns put together—the broken coin which the King of Navarre had entrusted to me, and which formed my sole credential, my only means of persuading Mademoiselle de la Vire that I came from him. I had put it in my pouch, and of course, though the loss of it only came home to my mind now, it had disappeared with the rest.

I drew rein and sat for some time motionless, the image of despair. The wind which stirred the naked boughs overhead, and whirled the dead leaves in volleys past my feet, and died away at last among the whispering bracken, met nowhere with wretchedness greater, I believe, than was mine at that moment.

4

# Mademoiselle de la Vire

My first desperate impulse on discovering the magnitude of my loss was to ride after the knaves and demand the token at the sword's point. The certainty, however, of finding them united, and the difficulty of saying which of the five possessed what I wanted, led me to reject this plan as I grew cooler; and since I did not dream, even in this dilemma, of abandoning the expedition, the only alternative seemed to be to act as if I still had the broken coin, and essay what a frank explanation might effect when the time came.

After some wretched, very wretched, moments of debate, I resolved to adopt this course; and, for the present, thinking I might gain some knowledge of the surroundings while the light lasted, I pushed cautiously forward through the trees and came in less than five minutes within sight of a corner of the Château, which I found to be a modern building of the time of Henry II, raised, like the houses of that time, for pleasure rather than defence, and decorated with many handsome casements and tourelles. Despite this, it wore, as I saw it, a grey and desolate air, due in part to the loneliness of the situation and the lateness of the hour; and in part, I think, to the smallness of the household maintained, for no one was visible on the terrace or at the windows. The rain dripped from the trees, which on two sides pressed so closely on the house as almost to darken the rooms, and everything I saw encouraged me to hope that mademoiselle's wishes would second my entreaties, and incline her to lend a ready ear to my story.

The appearance of the house, indeed, was a strong inducement to me to proceed, for it was impossible to believe that a young lady, a kinswoman of the gay and vivacious Turenne, and already introduced to the pleasures of the Court, would elect of her own free will to spend the winter in so dreary a solitude.

Taking advantage of the last moments of daylight, I rode cautiously round the house, and, keeping in the shadow of the trees, had no difficulty in discovering at the north-west corner the balcony of which I had been told. It was semi-circular in shape, with a stone balustrade, and hung some fifteen feet above a terraced walk which ran below it, and was separated from the chase by a low sunk fence.

I was surprised to observe that, notwithstanding the rain and the coldness of the evening, the window which gave upon this balcony was open. Nor was this all. Luck was in store for me at last. I had not gazed at the window more than a minute, calculating its height and other particulars, when, to my great joy, a female figure, closely hooded, stepped out and stood looking up at the sky. I was too far off to be able to discern by that uncertain light whether this was Mademoiselle de la Vire or her woman; but the attitude was so clearly one

47

of dejection and despondency, that I felt sure it was either one or the other. Determined not to let the opportunity slip, I dismounted hastily and, leaving the Cid loose, advanced on foot until I stood within half-a-dozen paces of the window.

At that point the watcher became aware of me. She started back, but did not withdraw. Still peering down at me, she called softly to someone inside the chamber, and immediately a second figure, taller and stouter, appeared. I had already doffed my cap, and I now, in a low voice, begged to know if I had the honour of speaking to Mademoiselle de la Vire. In the growing darkness it was impossible to distinguish faces.

'Hush!' the stouter figure muttered in a tone of warning. 'Speak lower. Who are you, and what do you here?'

'I am here,' I answered respectfully, 'commissioned by a friend of the lady I have named, to convey her to a place of safety.'

'*Mon Dieu!*' was the sharp answer. 'Now? It is impossible.'

'No,' I murmured, 'not now, but tonight. The moon rises at half-past two. My horses need rest and food. At three I will be below this window with the means of escape, if mademoiselle choose to use them.'

I felt that they were staring at me through the dusk, as though they would read my breast. 'Your name, sir?' the shorter figure murmured at last, after a pause which was full of suspense and excitement.

'I do not think my name of much import at present, Mademoiselle,' I answered, reluctant to proclaim myself a stranger. 'When—'

'Your name, your name, sir!' she repeated imperiously, and I heard her little heel rap upon the stone floor of the balcony.

'Gaston de Marsac,' I answered unwillingly.

They both started, and cried out together. 'Impossible!' the last speaker exclaimed, amazement and anger in her tone. 'This is a jest, sir. This—'

What more she would have said I was left to guess, for at

that moment her attendant—I had no doubt now which was mademoiselle and which Fanchette—suddenly laid her hand on her mistress's mouth and pointed to the room behind them. A second's suspense, and with a warning gesture the two turned and disappeared through the window.

I lost no time in regaining the shelter of the trees; and concluding, though I was far from satisfied with the interview, that I could do nothing more now, but might rather, by loitering in the neighbourhood, awaken suspicion, I remounted and made for the highway and the village, where I found my men in noisy occupation of the inn, a poor place, with unglazed windows, and a fire in the middle of the earthen floor. My first care was to stable the Cid in a shed at the back, where I provided for its wants as far as I could with the aid of a half-naked boy, who seemed to be in hiding there.

This done, I returned to the front of the house, having pretty well made up my mind how I would set about the task before me. As I passed one of the windows, which was partially closed by a rude curtain made of old sacks, I stopped to look in. Fresnoy and his four rascals were seated on blocks of wood round the hearth, talking loudly and fiercely, and ruffling it as if the fire and the room were their own. A pedlar, seated on his goods in one corner, was eyeing them with evident fear and suspicion; in another corner two children had taken refuge under a donkey, which some fowls had chosen as a roosting-place. The inn-keeper, a sturdy fellow, with a great club in his fist, sat moodily at the foot of a ladder which led to the loft above, while a slatternly woman, who was going to and fro getting supper, seemed in equal terror of her guests and her good man.

Confirmed by what I saw, and assured that the villains were ripe for any mischief, and, if not checked, would speedily be beyond my control, I noisily flung the door open and entered. Fresnoy looked up with a sneer as I did so, and one of the men laughed. The others became silent; but no one moved or greeted me. Without a moment's hesitation I stepped to the nearest fellow and with a sturdy kick, sent his log from under him. 'Rise, you rascal, when I enter!' I cried, giving vent to the anger I had long felt. 'And you, too!' and with a second kick I sent his neighbour's stool flying also, and administered a couple of cuts with my riding-cane across the man's shoulders. 'Have you no manners, sirrah? Across with you, and leave this side to your betters.'

The two rose, snarling and feeling for their weapons, and for a moment stood facing me, looking now at me and now askance at Fresnoy. But as he gave no sign, and their comrades only laughed, the men's courage failed them at the pinch, and with a very poor grace they sneaked over to the other side of the fire and sat there scowling.

I seated myself beside their leader. 'This gentleman and I will eat here,' I cried to the man at the foot of the ladder. 'Bid your wife lay for us, and of the best you have; and do you give those knaves their provender where the smell of their greasy jackets will not come between us and our victuals.'

The man came forward, glad enough, as I saw, to discover anyone in authority, and very civilly began to draw wine and place a board for us, while his wife filled our platters from the black pot which hung over the fire. Fresnoy's face meanwhile wore the amused smile of one who comprehended my motives, but felt sufficiently sure of his position and influence with his followers to be indifferent to my proceedings. I presently showed him, however, that I had not yet done with him. Our table was laid in obedience to my orders at such a distance from the men that they could not overhear our talk, and by-and-by I leant over to him.

'M. Fresnoy,' I said, 'you are in danger of forgetting one thing, I fancy, which it behoves you to remember.'

'What?' he muttered, scarcely deigning to look up at me.

'That you have to do with Gaston de Marsac,' I answered quietly. 'I am making, as I told you this morning, a last attempt to recruit my fortunes, and I will let no man—no man, do you understand, M. Fresnoy?—thwart me and go harmless.'

'Who wishes to thwart you?' he asked impudently.

'You,' I answered unmoved, helping myself, as I spoke, from the roll of black bread which lay beside me. 'You robbed me this afternoon; I passed it over. You encouraged those men to be insolent; I passed it over. But let me tell you this. If you fail me tonight, on the honour of a gentleman, M. Fresnoy, I will run you through as I would spit a lark.'

'Will you? But two can play at that game,' he cried, rising nimbly from his stool. 'Still better six! Don't you think, M. de Marsac, you had better have waited—?'

'I think you had better hear one word more,' I answered coolly, keeping my seat, 'before you appeal to your fellows there.'

'Well,' he said, still standing, 'what is it?'

'Nay,' I replied, after once more pointing to his stool in vain, 'if you prefer to take my orders standing, well and good.'

'Your orders?' he shrieked, growing suddenly excited.

'Yes, my orders!' I retorted, rising as suddenly to my feet and hitching forward my sword. 'My orders, sir,' I repeated fiercely, 'or, if you dispute my right to command as well as to pay this party, let us decide the question here and now—you and I, foot to foot, M. Fresnoy.'

The quarrel flashed up so suddenly, though I had been preparing it all along, that no one moved. The woman, indeed, fell back to her children, but the rest looked on open-mouthed. Had they stirred, or had a moment's hurly-burly heated his blood, I doubt not Fresnoy would have taken up my challenge, for he did not lack hardihood. But as it was, face to face with me in the silence, his courage failed him. He paused, glowering at me uncertainly, and did not speak.

'Well,' I said, 'don't you think that if I pay I ought to give orders, sir?'

'Who wishes to oppose your orders?' he muttered, drinking off a bumper, and sitting down with an air of impudent bravado, assumed to hide his discomfiture.

'If you don't, no one else does,' I answered. 'So that is settled. Landlord, some more wine.'

51

He was very sulky with me for a while, fingering his glass in silence and scowling at the table. He had enough gentility to feel the humiliation to which he had exposed himself, and a sufficiency of wit to understand that that moment's hesitation had cost him the allegiance of his fellow-ruffians. I hastened, therefore, to set him at his ease by explaining my plans for the night, and presently succeeded beyond my hopes for when he heard who the lady was whom I proposed to carry off, and that she was lying that evening at the Château de Chizé, his surprise swept away the last trace of resentment. He stared at me as at a maniac.

'Mon Dieu!' he exclaimed. 'Do you know what you are doing, Sieur?'

'I think so,' I answered.

'Do you know to whom the château belongs?'

'To the Vicomte de Turenne.'

'And that Mademoiselle de la Vire is his relation?'

'Yes,' I said.

'Mon Dieu!' he exclaimed again. And he looked at me open-mouthed.

'What is the matter?' I asked, though I had an uneasy consciousness that I knew—that I knew very well.

'Man, he will crush you as I crush this hat!' he answered in great excitement. 'As easily. Who do you think will protect you from him in a private quarrel of this kind? Navarre? France? our good man? Not one of them. You had better steal the king's crown jewels—he is weak; or Guise's last plot—he is generous at times; or Navarre's last sweetheart—he is as easy as an old shoe. You had better have to do with all these together, I tell you, than touch Turenne's ewe-lambs, unless your aim be to be broken on the wheel! Mon Dieu, yes!'

'I am much obliged to you for your advice,' I said stiffly, 'but the die is cast. My mind is made up. On the other hand, if you are afraid, M. Fresnoy—'

'I am afraid; very much afraid,' he answered frankly.

'Still your name need not be brought into the matter,' I

replied, 'I will take the responsibility. I will let them know my name here at the inn, where, doubtless, inquiries will be made.'

'To be sure, that is something,' he answered thoughtfully. 'Well, it is an ugly business, but I am in for it. You want me to go with you a little after two, do you? and the others to be in the saddle at three? Is that it?'

I assented, pleased to find him so far acquiescent; and in this way, talking the details over more than once, we settled our course, arranging to fly by way of Poitiers and Tours. Of course I did not tell him why I selected Blois as our refuge, nor what was my purpose there; though he pressed me more than once on the point, and grew thoughtful and somewhat gloomy when I continually evaded it. A little after eight we retired to the loft to sleep; our men remaining below round the fire and snoring so merrily as almost to shake the crazy old building. The host was charged to sit up and call us as soon as the moon rose, but, as it turned out, I might as well have taken this office on myself, for between excitement and distrust I slept little, and was wide awake when I heard his step on the ladder and knew it was time to rise.

I was up in a moment, and Fresnoy was little behind me; so that, losing no time in talk, we were mounted and on the road, each with a spare horse at his knee, before the moon was well above the trees. Once in the chase we found it necessary to proceed on foot, but, the distance being short, we presently emerged without misadventure and stood opposite to the château, the upper part of which shone cold and white in the moon's rays.

There was something so solemn in the aspect of the place, the night being fine and the sky without a cloud, that I stood for a minute awed and impressed, the sense of the responsibility I was here to accept strong upon me. In that short space of time all the dangers before me, as well the common risks of the road as the vengeance of Turenne and the turbulence of my own men, presented themselves to my mind, and made a last appeal to me to turn back from an enterprise so foolhardy. The blood in a man's veins runs low and slow at that hour, and mine was chilled by lack of sleep and the wintry air. It needed the remembrance of my solitary condition, of my past spent in straits and failure, of the grey hairs which swept my cheek, of the sword which I had long used honourably, if with little profit to myself; it needed the thought of all these things to restore me to courage and myself.

I judged at a later period that my companion was affected in somewhat the same way; for, as I stooped to press home the pegs which I had brought to tether the horses, he laid his hand on my arm. Glancing up to see what he wanted, I was struck by the wild look in his face (which the moonlight invested with a peculiar mottled pallor), and particularly in his eyes, which glittered like a madman's. He tried to speak, but seemed to find a difficulty in doing so; and I had to question him roughly before he found his tongue. When he did speak, it was only to implore me in an odd, excited manner to give up the expedition and return.

'What, now?' I said, surprised. 'Now we are here, Fresnoy?'

'Ay, give it up!' he cried, shaking me almost fiercely by the arm. 'Give it up, man! It will end badly, I tell you! In God's name, give it up, and go home before worse comes of it.'

'Whatever comes of it,' I answered coldly, shaking his grasp from my arm, and wondering much at this sudden fit of cowardice, 'I go on. You, M. Fresnoy, may do as you please!'

He started and drew back from me; but he did not reply, nor did he speak again. When I presently went off to fetch a ladder, of the position of which I had made a note during the afternoon, he accompanied me, and followed me back in the same dull silence to the walk below the balcony. I had looked more than once and eagerly at mademoiselle's window without any light or movement in that quarter rewarding my vigilance; but, undeterred by this, which might mean either that my plot was known, or that Mademoiselle de la Vire distrusted me, I set the ladder softly against the balcony, which was in deep shadow, and paused only to give Fresnoy his last instructions. These were simply to stand on guard at the foot of the ladder and defend it in case of surprise; so that, whatever happened inside the château, my retreat by the window might not be cut off.

Then I went cautiously up the ladder, and, with my sheathed sword in my left hand, stepped over the balustrade. Taking one pace forward, with fingers outstretched, I felt the leaded panes of the window and tapped softly.

As softly the casement gave way, and I followed it. A hand which I could see but not feel was laid on mine. All was darkness in the room, and before me, but the hand guided me two paces forward, then by a sudden pressure bade me stand. I heard the sound of a curtain being drawn behind me, and the next moment the cover of a rushlight was removed, and a feeble but sufficient light filled the chamber.

I comprehended that the drawing of that curtain over the window had cut off my retreat as effectually as if a door had been closed behind me. But distrust and suspicion gave way the next moment to the natural embarrassment of the man who finds himself in a false position and knows he can escape from it only by an awkward explanation.

The room in which I found myself was long, narrow, and low in the ceiling; and being hung with some dark stuff which swallowed up the light, terminated funereally at the farther end in the still deeper gloom of an alcove. Two or three huge chests, one bearing the remnants of a meal, stood against the walls. The middle of the floor was covered with a strip of coarse matting, on which a small table, a chair and foot-rest, and a couple of stools had place, with some smaller articles which lay scattered round a pair of half-filled saddle-bags. The slighter and smaller of the two figures I had seen stood beside the table, wearing a mask and riding cloak, and by her silent manner of gazing at me, as well as by a cold, disdainful bearing, which neither her mask nor cloak could hide, did more to chill and discomfit me than even my own knowledge that I had lost the pass-key which should have admitted me to her confidence.

The stouter figure of the afternoon turned out to be a red-cheeked, sturdy woman of thirty, with bright black eyes and a manner which lost nothing of its fierce impatience when she came a little later to address me. All my ideas of Fanchette were upset by the appearance of this woman, who, rustic in her speech and ways, seemed more like a duenna than the waiting-maid of a court beauty, and better fitted to guard a wayward damsel than to aid her in such an escapade as we had in hand.

She stood slightly behind her mistress, her coarse red hand resting on the back of the chair from which mademoiselle had apparently risen on my entrance. For a few seconds, which seemed minutes to me, we stood gazing at one another in silence, mademoiselle acknowledging my bow by a slight movement of the head. Then, seeing that they waited for me to speak, I did so.

'Mademoiselle de la Vire?' I murmured doubtfully.

She bent her head again; that was all.

I strove to speak with confidence. 'You will pardon me, mademoiselle,' I said, 'if I seem to be abrupt, but time is everything. The horses are standing within a hundred yards of the house, and all the preparations for your flight are made. If we leave now, we can do so without opposition. The delay even of an hour may lead to discovery.'

For answer she laughed behind her mask—laughed coldly and ironically. 'You go too fast, sir,' she said, her low clear voice matching the laugh and rousing a feeling almost of anger in my heart. 'I do not know you; or, rather, I know nothing of you which should entitle you to interfere in my affairs. You are too quick to presume, sir. You say you come from a friend. From whom?'

'From one whom I am proud to call by that title,' I answered with what patience I might.

'His name!'

I answered firmly that I could not give it. And I eyed her steadily as I did so.

This for the moment seemed to baffle and confuse her, but

after a pause she continued: 'Where do you propose to take me, sir?'

'To Blois; to the lodging of a friend of my friend.'

'You speak bravely,' she replied with a faint sneer. 'You have made some great friends lately it seems! But you bring me some letter, no doubt; at least some sign, some token, some warranty, that you are the person you pretend to be, M. de Marsac?'

'The truth is, mademoiselle,' I stammered, 'I must explain. I should tell you—'

'Nay, sir,' she cried impetuously, 'there is no need of telling. If you have what I say, show it me! It is you who lose time. Let us have no more words!'

I had used very few words, and, God knows, was not in the mind to use many; but, being in the wrong, I had no answer to make except the truth, and that humbly. 'I had such a token as you mention, mademoiselle,' I said, 'no farther back than this afternoon, in the shape of half a gold coin, entrusted to me by my friend. But, to my shame I say it, it was stolen from me a few hours back.'

'Stolen from you!' she exclaimed.

'Yes, mademoiselle; and for that reason I cannot show it,' I answered.

'You cannot show it? And you dare to come to me without it!' she cried, speaking with a vehemence which fairly startled me, prepared as I was for reproaches. 'You come to me! You!' she continued. And with that, scarcely stopping to take breath, she loaded me with abuse; calling me impertinent, a meddler, and a hundred other things, which I now blush to recall, and displaying in all a passion which even in her attendant would have surprised me, but in one so slight and seemingly delicate, overwhelmed and confounded me. In fault as I was, I could not understand the peculiar bitterness she displayed, or the contemptuous force of her language, and I stared at her in silent wonder until, of her own accord, she supplied the key to her feelings. In a fresh outburst of rage she snatched off her mask, and to my astonishment I

57

saw before me the young maid of honour whom I had encountered in the King of Navarre's ante-chamber, and whom I had been so unfortunate as to expose to the raillery of Mathurine.

'Who has paid you, sir,' she continued, clenching her small hands and speaking with tears of anger in her eyes, 'to make me the laughing-stock of the Court? It was bad enough when I thought you the proper agent of those to whom I have a right to look for aid! It was bad enough when I thought myself forced, through their inconsiderate choice, to decide between an odious imprisonment and the ridicule to which your intervention must expose me! But that you should have dared, of your own notion, to follow me, you, the butt of the Court—'

'Mademoiselle!' I cried.

'A needy, out-at-elbows adventurer!' she persisted, triumphing in her cruelty. 'It exceeds all bearing! It is not to be suffered! It—'

'Nay, mademoiselle; you *shall* hear me!' I cried, with a sternness which at last stopped her. 'Granted I am poor, I am still a gentleman; yes, mademoiselle,' I continued, firmly, 'a gentleman, and the last of a family which has spoken with yours on equal terms. And I claim to be heard. I swear that when I came here tonight I believed you to be a perfect stranger! I was unaware that I had ever seen you, unaware that I had ever met you before.'

'Then why did you come?' she said viciously.

'I was engaged to come by those whom you have mentioned, and there, and there only am I in fault. They entrusted to me a token which I have lost. For that I crave your pardon.'

'You have need to,' she answered bitterly, yet with a changed countenance, or I was mistaken, 'if your story be true, sir.'

'Ay, that you have!' the woman beside her echoed. 'Hoity toity, indeed! Here is a fuss about nothing. You call yourself a gentleman, and wear such a doublet as—'

'Peace, Fanchette!' mademoiselle said imperiously. And

then for a moment she stood silent, eyeing me intently, her lips trembling with excitement and two red spots burning in her cheeks. It was clear from her dress and other things that she had made up her mind to fly had the token been forthcoming; and seeing this, and knowing how unwilling a young girl is to forgo her own way, I still had some hopes that she might not persevere in her distrust and refusal. And so it turned out.

Her manner had changed to one of quiet scorn when she next spoke. 'You defend yourself skilfully, sir,' she said, drumming with her fingers on the table and eyeing me steadfastly. 'But can you give me any reason for the person you name making choice of such a messenger?'

'Yes,' I answered, boldly. 'That he may not be suspected of conniving at your escape.'

'Oh!' she cried, with a spark of her former passion. 'Then it is to be put about that Mademoiselle de la Vire had fled from Chizé with M. de Marsac, is it? I thought that!'

'Through the assistance of M. de Marsac,' I retorted, correcting her coldly. 'It is for you, mademoiselle,' I continued, 'to weigh that disadvantage against the unpleasantness of remaining here. It only remains for me to ask you to decide quickly. Time presses, and I have stayed here too long already.'

The words had barely passed my lips when they received unwelcome confirmation in the shape of a distant sound—the noisy closing of a door, which, clanging through the house at such an hour—judged it to be after three o'clock—could scarcely mean anything but mischief. This noise was followed immediately, even while we stood listening with raised fingers, by other sounds—a muffled cry, and the tramp of heavy footsteps in a distant passage. Mademoiselle looked at me, and I at her woman. 'The door!' I muttered. 'Is it locked?'

'And bolted!' Fanchette answered; 'and a great chest set against it. Let them ramp; they will do no harm for a bit.'

'Then you have still time, mademoiselle,' I whispered, retreating a step and laying my hand on the curtain before the window. Perhaps I affected greater coolness than I felt.

'It is not too late. If you choose to remain, well and good. I cannot help it. If, on the other hand, you decide to trust yourself to me, I swear, on the honour of a gentleman, to be worthy of the trust—to serve you truly and protect you to the last! I can say no more.'

She trembled, looking from me to the door, on which some one had just begun to knock loudly. That seemed to decide her Her lips apart, her eyes full of excitement, she turned hastily to Fanchette.

'Ay, go if you like,' the woman answered doggedly, reading the meaning of her look. 'There cannot be a greater villain than the one we know of. But once started, heaven help us, for if he overtakes us we'll pay dearly for it!'

The girl did not speak herself, but it was enough. The noise at the door increased each second, and began to be mingled with angry appeals to Fanchette to open, and with threats in case she delayed. I cut the matter short by snatching up one of the saddle-bags—the other we left behind—and flung back the curtain which covered the window. At the same time the woman dashed out the light—a timely precaution—and throwing open the casement I stepped on to the balcony, the others following me closely.

The moon had risen high, and flooding with light the small open space about the house enabled me to see clearly all round the foot of the ladder. To my surprise Fresnoy was not at his post, nor was he to be seen anywhere; but as, at the moment I observed this, an outcry away to my left, at the rear of the château, came to my ears, and announced that the danger was no longer confined to the interior of the house, I concluded that he had gone that way to intercept the attack. Without more ado, therefore, I began to descend as quickly as I could, my sword under one arm and the bag under the other.

I was half-way down, and mademoiselle was already stepping on to the ladder to follow, when I heard footsteps below, and saw him run up, his sword in his hand.

'Quick, Fresnoy!' I cried. 'To the horses and unfasten them! Quick!'

I slid down the rest of the way, thinking he had gone to do my bidding. But my feet were scarcely on the ground when a tremendous blow in the side sent me staggering three paces from the ladder. The attack was so sudden, so unexpected, that but for the sight of Fresnoy's scowling face, wild with rage, at my shoulder, and the sound of his fierce breathing as he strove to release his sword, which had passed through my saddle-bag, I might never have known who struck the blow, or how narrow had been my escape.

Fortunately the knowledge did come to me in time, and before he freed his blade; and it nerved my hand. To draw my blade at such close quarters was impossible, but, dropping the bag which had saved my life, I dashed my hilt twice in his face with such violence that he fell backwards and lay on the turf, a dark stain growing and spreading on his upturned face.

It was scarcely done before the women reached the foot of the ladder and stood beside me. 'Quick!' I cried to them, 'or they will be upon us.' Seizing mademoiselle's hand, just as half-a-dozen men came running round the corner of the house, I jumped with her down the haha, and, urging her to her utmost speed, dashed across the open ground which lay between us and the belt of trees. Once in the shelter of the latter, where our movements were hidden from view, I had still to free the horses and mount mademoiselle and her woman, and this in haste. But my companions' admirable coolness and presence of mind, and the objection which our pursuers, who did not know our numbers, felt to leaving the open ground, enabled us to do all with comparative ease. I sprang on the Cid (it has always been my habit to teach my horse to stand for me, nor do I know any accomplishment more serviceable at a pinch), and giving Fresnoy's grey a cut over the flanks which despatched it ahead, led the way down the ride by which I had gained the château in the afternoon. I knew it to be level and clear of trees, and the fact that we chose it might throw our pursuers off the track for a time, by leading them to think we had taken the south road instead of that through the village.

# The Road to Blois

We gained the road without let or hindrance, whence a sharp burst in the moonlight soon brought us to the village. Through this we swept on to the inn, almost running over the four evangelists, whom we found standing at the door ready for the saddle. I bade them, in a quick peremptory tone, to get to horse, and was overjoyed to see them obey without demur or word of Fresnoy. In another minute, with a great clatter of hoofs, we sprang clear of the hamlet, and were well on the road to Melle, with Poitiers some thirteen leagues before us. I looked back, and thought I discerned lights moving in the direction of the château; but the dawn was still two hours off, and the moonlight left me in doubt whether these were real or the creatures of my own fearful fancy.

I remember, three years before this time, on the occasion of the famous retreat from Angers—when the Prince of Condé had involved his army beyond the Loire, and saw himself, in the impossibility of recrossing the river, compelled to take ship for England, leaving every one to shift for himself —I well remember on that occasion riding, alone and pistol in hand, through more than thirty miles of the enemy's country without drawing rein. But my anxieties were then confined to the four shoes of my horse. The dangers to which I was exposed at every ford and crossroad were such as are inseparable from a campaign, and breed in generous hearts only a fierce pleasure, rarely to be otherwise enjoyed. And though I then rode warily, and where I could not carry terror, had all to fear myself, there was nothing secret or underhand in my business.

It was very different now. During the first few hours of our flight from Chizé I experienced a painful excitement, an alarm, a feverish anxiety to get forward, which was new to me; which oppressed my spirits to the very ground; which led me to take every sound borne to us on the wind for the sound of pursuit, transforming the clang of a hammer on the anvil into the ring of swords, and the voices of my own men into those of the pursuers. It was in vain mademoiselle rode with a free hand, and leaping such obstacles as lay in our way, gave promise of courage and endurance beyond my expectations. I could think of nothing but the three long days before us, with twenty-four hours to every day, and each hour fraught with a hundred chances of disaster and ruin.

In fact, the longer I considered our position—and as we pounded along, now splashing through a founderous hollow, now stumbling as we wound over a stony shoulder, I had ample time to reflect upon it—the greater seemed the difficulties before us. The loss of Fresnoy, while it freed me from some embarrassment, meant also the loss of a good sword, and we had mustered only too few before. The country which lay between us and the Loire, being the borderland between our party and the League, had been laid desolate so often as to be abandoned to pillage and disorder of every kind. The peasants had flocked into the towns. Their places had been taken by bands of robbers and deserters from both parties, who haunted the ruined villages about Poitiers, and preyed upon all who dared to pass. To add to our perils, the royal army under the Duke of Nevers was reported to be moving slowly southward, not very far to the left of our road; while a Huguenot expedition against Niort was also in progress within a few leagues of us.

With four staunch and trustworthy comrades at my back, I might have faced even this situation with a smile and a light heart; but the knowledge that my four knaves might mutiny at any moment, or, worse still, rid themselves of me and all restraint by a single treacherous blow such as Fresnoy had aimed at me, filled me with an ever-present dread; which it taxed my utmost energies to hide from them, and which

I strove in vain to conceal from mademoiselle's keener vision.

Whether it was this had an effect upon her, giving her a meaner opinion of me than that which I had for a while hoped she entertained, or that she began, now it was too late, to regret her flight and resent my part in it, I scarcely know; but from daybreak onwards she assumed an attitude of cold suspicion towards me, which was only less unpleasant than the scornful distance of her manner when she deigned, which was seldom, to address me.

Not once did she allow me to forget that I was in her eyes a needy adventurer, paid by her friends to escort her to a place of safety, but without any claim to the smallest privilege of intimacy or equality. When I would have adjusted her saddle, she bade her woman come and hold up her skirt, that my hands might not touch its hem even by accident. And when I would have brought wine to her at Melle, where we stayed for twenty minutes, she called Fanchette to hand it to her. She rode for the most part in her mask; and with her woman. One good effect only her pride and reserve had; they impressed our men with a strong sense of her importance, and the danger to which any interference with her might expose them.

The two men whom Fresnoy had enlisted I directed to ride a score of paces in advance. Luke and John I placed in the rear. In this manner I thought to keep them somewhat apart. For myself, I proposed to ride abreast of mademoiselle, but she made it so clear that my neighbourhood displeased her that I fell back, leaving her to ride with Fanchette; and contented myself with plodding at their heels, and striving to attach the later evangelists to my interests.

We were so fortunate, despite my fears, as to find the road nearly deserted—as, alas, was much of the country on either side—and to meet none but small parties travelling along it; who were glad enough, seeing the villainous looks of our outriders, to give us a wide berth, and be quit of us for the fright. We skirted Lusignan, shunning the streets, but passing near enough for me to point out to mademoiselle the site of the famous tower built, according to tradition, by the fairy Melusina, and rased thirteen years back by the Leaguers. She received my information so frigidly, however, that I offered no more, but fell back shrugging my shoulders, and rode in silence, until, some two hours after noon, the city of Poitiers came into sight, lying within its circle of walls and towers on a low hill in the middle of a country clothed in summer with rich vineyards, but now brown and bare and cheerless to the eye.

Fanchette turned and asked me abruptly if that were Poitiers.

I answered that it was, but added that for certain reasons I proposed not to halt, but to lie at a village a league beyond the city, where there was a tolerable inn.

'We shall do very well here,' the woman answered rudely. 'Anyway, my lady will go no farther. She is tired and cold, and wet besides, and has gone far enough.'

'Still,' I answered, nettled by the woman's familiarity, 'I think mademoiselle will change her mind when she hears my reasons for going farther.'

'Mademoiselle does not wish to hear them, sir,' the lady replied herself, and very sharply.

'Nevertheless, I think you had better hear them,' I persisted, turning to her respectfully. 'You see, mademoiselle—'

'I see only one thing, sir,' she exclaimed, snatching off her mask and displaying a countenance beautiful indeed, but flushed for the moment with anger and impatience, 'that, whatever betides, I stay at Poitiers tonight.'

'If it would content you to rest an hour?' I suggested gently.

'It will not content me!' she rejoined with spirit. 'And let me tell you, sir,' she went on impetuously, 'once for all, that you take too much upon yourself. You are here to escort me, and to give orders to these ragamuffins, for they are nothing better, with whom you have thought fit to disgrace our company; but not to give orders to me or to control my

65

movements. Confine yourself for the future, sir, to your duties, if you please.'

'I desire only to obey you,' I answered, suppressing the angry feelings which rose in my breast, and speaking as coolly as lay in my power. 'But, as the first of my duties is to provide for your safety, I am determined to omit nothing which can conduce to that end. You have not considered that, if a party in pursuit of us reaches Poitiers tonight, search will be made for us in the city, and we shall be taken. If, on the other hand, we are known to have passed through, the hunt may go no farther; certainly will go no farther tonight. Therefore we must not, mademoiselle,' I added firmly, 'lie in Poitiers tonight.'

'Sir,' she exclaimed, looking at me, her face crimson with wonder and indignation, 'do you dare to—?'

'I dare do my duty, mademoiselle,' I answered, plucking up a spirit, though my heart was sore. 'I am a man old enough to be your father, and with little to lose, or I had not been here. I care nothing what you think or what you say of me, provided I can do what I have undertaken to do and place you safely in the hands of your friends. But enough, mademoiselle, we are at the gate. If you will permit me, I will ride through the streets beside you. We shall so attract less attention.'

Without waiting for a permission which she was very unlikely to give, I pushed my horse forward, and took my place beside her, signing to Fanchette to fall back. The maid obeyed, speechless with indignation; while mademoiselle flashed a scathing glance at me and looked round in helpless anger, as though it was in her mind to appeal against me even to the passers-by. But she thought better of it, and contenting herself with muttering the word 'Impertinent' put on her mask with fingers which trembled, I fancy, not a little.

A small rain was falling and the afternoon was well advanced when we entered the town, but I noticed that, notwithstanding this, the streets presented a busy and animated appearance, being full of knots of people engaged in earnest talk. A bell was tolling somewhere, and near the cathedral a crowd of no little size was standing, listening to a man who seemed to be reading a placard or manifesto attached to the wall. In another place a soldier, wearing the crimson colours of the League, but splashed and stained as with recent travel, was holding forth to a breathless circle who seemed to hang upon his lips. A neighbouring corner sheltered a handful of priests who whispered together with gloomy faces. Many stared at us as we passed, and some would have spoken; but I rode steadily on, inviting no converse. Nevertheless at the north gate I got a rare fright; for, though it wanted a full half-hour of sunset, the porter was in the act of closing it. Seeing us, he waited grumbling until we came up, and then muttered, in answer to my remonstrance, something about queer times and wilful people having their way. I took little notice of what he said, however, being anxious only to get through the gate and leave as few traces of our passage as might be.

As soon as we were outside the town I fell back, permitting Fanchette to take my place. For another league, a long and dreary one, we plodded on in silence, horses and men alike jaded and sullen, and the women scarcely able to keep their saddles for fatigue. At last, much to my relief, seeing that I began to fear I had taxed mademoiselle's strength too far, the long low buildings of the inn at which I proposed to stay came in sight, at the crossing of the road and river. The place looked blank and cheerless, for the dusk was thickening; but as we trailed one by one into the courtyard a stream of fire-light burst on us from doors and windows, and a dozen sounds of life and comfort greeted our ears.

Noticing that mademoiselle was benumbed and cramped with long sitting, I would have helped her to dismount; but she fiercely rejected my aid, and I had to content myself with requesting the landlord to assign the best accommodation he had to the lady and her attendant, and secure as much privacy for them as possible. The man assented very civilly and said all should be done; but I noticed that his eyes wandered while I talked, and that he seemed to have something on his mind. When he returned, after disposing of them, it came out.

67

'Did you ever happen to see him, sir?' he asked with a sigh; yet was there a smug air of pleasure mingled with his melancholy.

'See whom?' I answered, staring at him, for neither of us had mentioned anyone.

'The Duke, sir.'

I stared again between wonder and suspicion. 'The Duke of Nevers is not in this part, is he?' I said slowly. 'I heard he was on the Brittany border, away to the westward.'

'Mon Dieu!' my host exclaimed, raising his hands in astonishment. 'You have not heard, sir?'

'I have heard nothing,' I answered impatiently.

'You have not heard, sir, that the most puissant and illustrious lord the Duke of Guise is dead?'

'M. de Guise dead? It is not true!' I cried astonished.

He nodded, however, several times with an air of great importance, and seemed as if he would have gone on to give me some particulars. But, remembering, as I fancied, that he spoke in the hearing of half-a-dozen guests who sat about the great fire behind me, and had both eyes and ears open, he contented himself with shifting his towel to his other arm and adding only, 'Yes, sir, dead as any nail. The news came through here yesterday, and made a pretty stir. It happened at Blois the day but one before Christmas, if all be true.'

I was thunderstruck. This was news which might change the face of France. 'How did it happen?' I asked.

My host covered his mouth with his hand and coughed, and, privily twitching my sleeve, gave me to understand with some shamefacedness that he could not say more in public. I was about to make some excuse to retire with him, when a harsh voice, addressed apparently to me, caused me to turn sharply. I found at my elbow a tall thin-faced monk in the habit of the Jacobin order. He had risen from his seat beside the fire, and seemed to be labouring under great excitement.

'Who asked how it happened?' he cried, rolling his eyes in a kind of frenzy, while still observant, or I was much

68

mistaken, of his listeners. 'Is there a man in France to whom the tale has not been told? Is there?'

'I will answer for one,' I replied, regarding him with little favour. 'I have heard nothing.'

'Then you shall! Listen!' he exclaimed, raising his right hand and brandishing it as though he denounced a person then present. 'Hear my accusation, made in the name of Mother Church and the saints against the arch hypocrite, the perjurer and assassin sitting in high places! He shall be Anathema Maranatha, for he has shed the blood of the holy and the pure, the chosen of Heaven! He shall go down to the pit, and that soon. The blood that he has shed shall be required of him, and that before he is one year older.'

'Tut-tut. All that sounds very fine, good father,' I said, waxing impatient, and a little scornful; for I saw that he was one of those wandering and often crazy monks in whom the League found their most useful emissaries. 'But I should profit more by your gentle words, if I knew whom you were cursing.'

'The man of blood!' he cried; 'through whom the last but not the least of God's saints and martyrs entered into glory on the Friday before Christmas.'

Moved by such profanity, and judging him, notwithstanding the extravagance of his words and gestures, to be less mad than he seemed, and at least as much knave as fool, I bade him sternly have done with his cursing, and proceed to his story if he had one.

He glowered at me for a moment, as though he were minded to launch his spiritual weapons at my head; but as I returned his glare with an unmoved eye—and my four rascals, who were as impatient as myself to learn the news, and had scarce more reverence for a shaven crown, began to murmur—he thought better of it, and cooling as suddenly as he had flamed up, lost no more time in satisfying our curiosity.

It would ill become me, however, to set down the extravagant and often blasphemous harangue in which, styling M. de Guise the martyr of God, he told the story now so familiar—the story of that dark wintry morning at Blois, when the king's messenger, knocking early at the duke's door, bade him hurry, for the king wanted him. The story is trite enough now. When I heard it first in the inn on the Clain, it was all new and all marvellous.

The monk, too, telling the story as if he had seen the events with his own eyes, omitted nothing which might impress his hearers. He told us how the duke received warning after warning, and answered in the very ante-chamber, 'He dare not!' How his blood, mysteriously advised of coming dissolution, grew chill, and his eye, wounded at Château Thierry, began to run, so that he had to send for the handkerchief he had forgotten to bring. He told us, even, how the duke drew his assassins up and down the chamber, how he cried for mercy, and how he died at last at the foot of the king's bed, and how the king, who had never dared to face him living, came and spurned him dead!

There were pale faces round the fire when he ceased, and bent brows and lips hard pressed together. When he stood and cursed the King of France—cursing him openly by the name of Henry of Valois, a thing I had never looked to hear in France—though no one said 'Amen,' and all glanced over their shoulders, and our host pattered from the room as if he had seen a ghost, it seemed to be no man's duty to gainsay him.

For myself, I was full of thoughts which it would have been unsafe to utter in that company or so near the Loire. I looked back sixteen years. Who but Henry of Guise had spurned the corpse of Coligny? And who but Henry of Valois had backed him in the act? Who but Henry of Guise had drenched Paris with blood, and who but Henry of Valois had ridden by his side? One 23rd of the month—a day never to be erased from France's annals—had purchased for him a term of greatness. A second 23rd saw him pay the price—saw his ashes cast secretly and by night no man knows where!

Moved by such thoughts, and observing that the priest was going the round of the company collecting money for masses for the duke's soul, to which object I could neither give with a good conscience nor refuse without exciting suspicion, I slipped out; and finding a man of decent appearance talking with the landlord in a small room beside the kitchen, I called for a flask of the best wine, and by means of that introduction obtained my supper in their company.

The stranger was a Norman horse-dealer, returning home after disposing of his string. He seemed to be in a large way of business, and being of a bluff, independent spirit, as many of those Norman townsmen are, was inclined at first to treat me with more familiarity than respect; the fact of my nag, for which he would have chaffered, excelling my coat in quality, leading him to set me down as a steward or intendant. The pursuit of his trade, however, had brought him into connection with all classes of men, and he quickly perceived his mistake; and as he knew the provinces between the Seine and Loire to perfection, and made it part of his business to foresee the chances of peace and war, I obtained a great amount of information from him, and indeed conceived no little liking for him. He believed that the assassination of M. de Guise would alienate so much of France from the king that his majesty would have little left save the towns on the Loire, and some other places lying within easy reach of his Court at Blois.

'But,' I said, 'things seem quiet now. Here, for instance.'

'It is the calm before the storm,' he answered. 'There is a monk in there. Have you heard him?'

I nodded.

'He is only one among a hundred—a thousand,' the horse-dealer continued, looking at me and nodding with meaning. He was a brown-haired man with shrewd grey eyes, such as many Normans have. 'They will get their way too, you will see,' he went on. 'Well, horses will go up, so I have no cause to grumble; but, if I were on my way to Blois with women or gear of that kind, I should not choose this time for picking posies on the road. I should see the inside of the gates as soon as possible.'

I thought there was much in what he said; and when he

went on to maintain that the king would find himself between the hammer and the anvil—between the League holding all the north and the Huguenots holding all the south—and must needs in time come to terms with the latter, seeing that the former would rest content with nothing short of his deposition, I began to agree with him that we should shortly see great changes and very stirring times.

'Still if they depose the king,' I said, 'the King of Navarre must succeed him. He is the heir of France.'

'Bah!' my companion replied somewhat contemptuously. 'The League will see to that. He goes with the other.'

'Then the kings are in one cry, and you are right,' I said with conviction. 'They must unite.'

'So they will. It is only a question of time,' he said.

In the morning, having only one man with him, and, as I guessed, a considerable sum of money, he volunteered to join our party as far as Blois. I assented gladly, and he did so, this addition to our numbers ridding me at once of the greater part of my fears. I did not expect any opposition on the part of mademoiselle, who would gain in consequence as well as in safety. Nor did she offer any. She was content, I think, to welcome any addition to our party which would save her from the necessity of riding in the company of my old cloak.

6

# My Mother's Lodging

Travelling by way of Châtellerault and Tours, we reached the neighbourhood of Blois a little after noon on the third day without misadventure or any intimation of pursuit. The Norman proved himself a cheerful companion on the road, as I already knew him to be a man of sense and shrewdness; while his presence rendered the task of keeping my men in

order an easy one. I began to consider the adventure as practically achieved; and regarding Mademoiselle de la Vire as
already in effect transferred to the care of M. de Rosny, I
ventured to turn my thoughts to the development of my own
plans and the choice of a haven in which I might rest secure
from the vengeance of M. de Turenne.

For the moment I had evaded his pursuit, and, assisted by
the confusion caused everywhere by the death of Guise, had
succeeded in thwarting his plans and affronting his authority
with seeming ease. But I knew too much of his power and
had heard too many instances of his fierce temper and resolute will to presume on short impunity or to expect the future
with anything but diffidence and dismay.

The exclamations of my companions on coming within
sight of Blois aroused me from these reflections. I joined
them, and fully shared their emotion as I gazed on the stately
towers which had witnessed so many royal festivities, and,
alas! one royal tragedy; which had sheltered Louis the Well-
beloved and Francis the Great, and rung with the laughter of
Diana of Poitiers and the second Henry. The play of fancy
wreathed the sombre building with a hundred memories
grave and gay. But, though the rich plain of the Loire still
swelled upward as of old in gentle homage at the feet of the
gallant town, the shadow of crime seemed to darken all, and
dim even the glories of the royal standard which hung idly in
the air.

We had heard so many reports of the fear and suspicion
which reigned in the city and of the strict supervision which
was exercised over all who entered—the king dreading a
repetition of the day of the Barricades—that we halted at a
little inn a mile short of the gate and broke up our company.
I parted from my Norman friend with mutual expressions of
esteem, and from my own men, whom I had paid off in the
morning, complimenting each of them with a handsome
present, with a feeling of relief equally sincere. I hoped—but
the hope was not fated to be gratified—that I might never see
the knaves again.

It wanted less than an hour of sunset when I rode up to the gate, a few paces in front of mademoiselle and her woman; as if I had really been the intendant for whom the horse-dealer had mistaken me. We found the guardhouse lined with soldiers, who scanned us very narrowly as we approached, and whose stern features and ordered weapons showed that they were not there for mere effect. The fact, however, that we came from Tours, a city still in the king's hands, served to allay suspicion, and we passed without accident.

Once in the streets, and riding in single file between the houses, to the windows of which the townsfolk seemed to be attracted by the slightest commotion, so full of terror was the air, I experienced a moment of huge relief. This was Blois— Blois at last. We were within a few score yards of the Bleeding Heart. In a few minutes I should receive a quittance, and be free to think only of myself. Nor was my pleasure much lessened by the fact that I was so soon to part from Mademoiselle de la Vire. Frankly, I was far from liking her. Exposure to the air of a court had spoiled, it seemed to me, whatever graces of disposition the young lady had ever possessed. She still maintained, and had maintained throughout the journey, the cold and suspicious attitude assumed at starting; nor had she ever expressed the least solicitude on my behalf, or the slightest sense that we were incurring danger in her service. She had not scrupled constantly to prefer her whims to the common advantage, and even safety; while her sense of self-importance had come to be so great, that she seemed to hold herself exempt from the duty of thanking any human creature. I could not deny that she was beautiful—indeed, I often thought, when watching her, of the day when I had seen her in the King of Navarre's antechamber in all the glory of her charms. But I felt none the less that I could turn my back on her—leaving her in safety—without regret; and be thankful that her path would never again cross mine.

With such thoughts in my breast I turned the corner of the Rue Saint-Denys and came at once upon the Bleeding Heart, a small but decent-looking hostelry situate near the end of the street and opposite a church. A bluff, grey-haired man, who was standing in the doorway, came forward as we halted, and looking curiously at mademoiselle asked what I lacked; adding civilly that the house was full and they had no sleeping room, the late events having drawn a great assemblage to Blois.

'I want only an address,' I answered, leaning from the saddle and speaking in a low voice that I might not be overheard by the passers-by. 'The Baron de Rosny is in Blois, is he not?'

The man started at the name of the Huguenot leader, and looked round him nervously. But, seeing that no one was very near us, he answered: 'He was, sir; but he left town a week ago and more. There have been strange doings here, and M. de Rosny thought that the climate suited him ill.'

He said this with so much meaning, as well as concern that he should not be overheard, that, though I was taken aback and bitterly disappointed, I succeeded in restraining all exclamations and even show of feeling. After a pause of dismay, I asked whither M. de Rosny had gone.

'To Rosny,' was the answer.

'And Rosny?'

'Is beyond Chartres, pretty well all the way to Mantes,' the man answered, stroking my horse's neck. 'Say thirty leagues.'

I turned my horse, and hurriedly communicated what he said to mademoiselle, who was waiting a few paces away. Unwelcome to me, the news was still less welcome to her. Her chagrin and indignation knew no bounds. For a moment words failed her, but her flashing eyes said more than her tongue as she cried to me: 'Well, sir, and what now? Is this the end of your fine promises? Where is your Rosny, if all be not a lying invention of your own?'

Feeling that she had some excuse I suppressed my choler, and humbly repeating that Rosny was at his house, two days farther on, and that I could see nothing for it but to go to him, I asked the landlord where we could find a lodging for the night.

75

'Indeed, sir, that is more than I can say,' he answered, looking curiously at us, and thinking, I doubt not, that with my shabby cloak and fine horse, and mademoiselle's mask and spattered riding-coat, we were an odd couple. 'There is not an inn which is not full to the garrets—nay, and the stables; and, what is more, people are chary of taking strangers in. These are strange times. They say,' he continued in a lower tone, 'that the old queen is dying up there, and will not last the night.'

I nodded. 'We must go somewhere,' I said.

'I would help you if I could,' he answered, shrugging his shoulders. 'But there it is! Blois is full from the tiles to the cellars.'

My horse shivered under me, and mademoiselle, whose patience was gone, cried harshly to me to do something. 'We cannot spend the night in the streets,' she said fiercely.

I saw that she was worn out and scarcely mistress of herself. The light was falling, and with it some rain. The reek of the kennels and the close air from the houses seemed to stifle us. The bell at the church behind us was jangling out vespers. A few people, attracted by the sight of our horses standing before the inn, had gathered round and were watching us.

Something I saw must be done, and done quickly. In despair, and seeing no other resort, I broached a proposal of which I had not hitherto even dreamed. 'Mademoiselle,' I said bluntly, 'I must take you to my mother's.'

'To your mother's, sir?' she cried, rousing herself. Her voice rang with haughty surprise.

'Yes,' I replied brusquely; 'since, as you say, we cannot spend the night in the streets, and I do not know where else I can dispose of you. From the last advices I had I believe her to have followed the Court hither. My friend,' I continued, turning to the landlord, 'do you know by name a Madame de Bonne, who should be in Blois?'

'A Madame de Bonne?' he muttered, reflecting. 'I have heard the name lately. Wait a moment.' Disappearing into the house, he returned almost immediately, followed by a lanky pale-faced youth wearing a tattered black soutane. 'Yes,' he said nodding, 'there is a worthy lady of that name lodging in the next street, I am told. As it happens, this young man lives in the same house, and will guide you, if you like.'

I assented, and, thanking him for his information, turned my horse and requested the youth to lead the way. We had scarcely passed the corner of the street, however, and entered one somewhat more narrow and less frequented, when mademoiselle, who was riding behind me, stopped and called to me. I drew rein, and, turning, asked what it was.

'I am not coming,' she said, her voice trembling slightly, but whether with alarm or anger I could not determine. 'I know nothing of you, and I—I demand to be taken to M. de Rosny.'

'If you cry that name aloud in the streets of Blois, mademoiselle,' I retorted, 'you are like enough to be taken whither you will not care to go! As for M. de Rosny, I have told you that he is not here. He has gone to his seat at Mantes.'

'Then take me to him!'

'At this hour of the night?' I said drily. 'It is two days' journey from here.'

'Then I will go to an inn,' she replied sullenly.

'You have heard that there is no room in the inns,' I rejoined with what patience I could. 'And to go from inn to inn at this hour might lead us into trouble. I can assure you that I am as much taken aback by M. de Rosny's absence as you are. For the present, we are close to my mother's lodging, and—'

'I know nothing of your mother!' she exclaimed passionately, her voice raised. 'You have enticed me hither by false pretences, sir, and I will endure it no longer. I will—'

'What you will do, I do not know then, mademoiselle,' I replied, quite at my wits' end; for what with the rain and the darkness, the unknown streets—in which our tarrying might at any moment collect a crowd—and this stubborn girl's opposition, I knew not whither to turn. 'For my part I can suggest nothing else. It does not become me to speak of my mother,' I continued, 'or I might say that even Mademoiselle

77

de la Vire need not be ashamed to accept the hospitality of Madame de Bonne. Nor are my mother's circumstances,' I added proudly, 'though narrow, so mean as to deprive her of the privileges of her birth.'

My last words appeared to make some impression upon my companion. She turned and spoke to her woman, who replied in a low voice, tossing her head the while and glaring at me in speechless indignation. Had there been anything else for it, they would doubtless have flouted my offer still; but apparently Fanchette could suggest nothing, and presently mademoiselle, with a sullen air, bade me lead on.

Taking this for permission, the lanky youth in the black soutane, who had remained at my bridle throughout the discussion, now listening and now staring, nodded and resumed his way; and I followed. After proceeding a little more than fifty yards he stopped before a mean-looking doorway, flanked by grated windows, and fronted by a lofty wall which I took to be the back of some nobleman's garden. The street at this point was unlighted, and little better than an alley; nor was the appearance of the house, which was narrow and ill-looking, though lofty, calculated, as far as I could make it out in the darkness, to allay mademoiselle's suspicions. Knowing, however, that people of position are often obliged in towns to lodge in poor houses, I thought nothing of this, and only strove to get mademoiselle dismounted as quickly as possible. The lad groped about and found two rings beside the door, and to these I tied up the horses. Then, bidding him lead the way, and begging mademoiselle to follow, I plunged into the darkness of the passage and felt my way to the foot of the staircase, which was entirely unlighted, and smelled close and unpleasant.

'Which floor?' I asked my guide.

'The fourth,' he answered quietly.

'Morbleu!' I muttered, as I began to ascend, my hand on the wall. 'What is the meaning of this?'

For I was perplexed. The revenues of Marsac, though small, should have kept my mother, whom I had last seen in

Paris before the Nemours edict, in tolerable comfort  such modest comfort, at any rate, as could scarcely be looked for in such a house as this  obscure, ill-tended, unlighted. To my perplexity was added, before I reached the top of the stairs, disquietude  disquietude on her account as well as on mademoiselle's. I felt that something was wrong, and would have given much to recall the invitation I had pressed on the latter.

What the young lady thought herself I could pretty well guess, as I listened to her hurried breathing at my shoulder. With every step I expected her to refuse to go farther. But, having once made up her mind, she followed me stubbornly, though the darkness was such that involuntarily I loosened my dagger, and prepared to defend myself should this turn out to be a trap.

We reached the top, however, without accident. Our guide knocked softly at a door and immediately opened it without waiting for an answer. A feeble light shone out on the stair-head, and bending my head, for the lintel was low, I stepped into the room.

I advanced two paces and stood looking about me in angry bewilderment. The bareness of extreme poverty marked everything on which my eyes rested. A cracked earthenware lamp smoked and sputtered on a stool in the middle of the rotting floor. An old black cloak nailed to the wall, and flapping to and fro in the draught like some dead gallowsbird, hung in front of the unglazed window. A jar in a corner caught the drippings from a hole in the roof. An iron pot and a second stool—the latter casting a long shadow across the floor—stood beside the handful of wood ashes, which smouldered on the hearth. And that was all the furniture I saw, except a bed which filled the farther end of the long narrow room, and was curtained off so as to form a kind of miserable alcove.

A glance sufficed to show me all this, and that the room was empty, or apparently empty. Yet I looked again and again, stupefied. At last finding my voice, I turned to the young man who had brought us hither, and with a fierce oath demanded of him what he meant.

He shrank back behind the open door, and yet answered with a kind of sullen surprise that I had asked for Madame de Bonne's, and this was it.

'Madame de Bonne's!' I muttered. 'This Madame de Bonne's!'

He nodded.

'Of course it is! And you know it!' mademoiselle hissed in my ear, her voice, as she interposed, hoarse with passion. 'Don't think that you can deceive us any longer. We know all! This,' she continued, looking round, her cheeks scarlet, her eyes ablaze with scorn, 'is your mother's, is it! Your mother who has followed the Court hither—whose means are narrow, but not so small as to deprive her of the privileges of her rank! This is your mother's hospitality, is it? You are a cheat, sir! and a detected cheat! Let us begone! Let me go, sir, I say!'

Twice I had tried to stop the current of her words; but in vain. Now with anger which surpassed hers a hundredfold—for who, being a man, would hear himself misnamed before his mother?—I succeeded. 'Silence, mademoiselle!' I cried, my grasp on her wrist. 'Silence, I say! This *is* my mother!'

And running forward to the bed, I fell on my knees beside it. A feeble hand had half withdrawn the curtain, and through the gap my mother's stricken face looked out, a great fear stamped upon it.

7

# Simon Fleix

For some minutes I forgot mademoiselle in paying those assiduous attentions to my mother which her state and my duty demanded; and which I offered the more anxiously that I recognised, with a sinking heart, the changes which age and illness had made in her since my last visit. The shock of mademoiselle's words had thrown her into a syncope, from which she did not recover for some time; and then rather through the assistance of our strange guide, who seemed well aware what to do, than through my efforts. Anxious as I was to learn what had reduced her to such straits and such a place, this was not the time to satisfy my curiosity, and I prepared myself instead for the task of effacing the painful impression which mademoiselle's words had made on her mind.

On first coming to herself she did not remember them, but, content to find me by her side—for there is something so alchemic in a mother's love that I doubt not my presence changed her garret to a palace—she spent herself in feeble caresses and broken words. Presently, however, her eye falling on mademoiselle and her maid, who remained standing by the hearth, looking darkly at us from time to time, she recalled, first the shock which had prostrated her, and then its cause, and raising herself on her elbow, looked about her wildly. 'Gaston!' she cried, clutching my hand with her thin fingers, 'what was it I heard? It was of you someone spoke— a woman! She called you— or did I dream it?—a cheat! You!'

'Madame, madame,' I said, striving to speak carelessly, though the sight of her grey hair, straggling and dishevelled, moved me strangely, 'was it likely? Would anyone dare to use such expressions of me in your presence? You must indeed have dreamed it!'

The words, however, returning more and more vividly to her mind, she looked at me very pitifully, and in great agitation laid her arm on my neck, as though she would shelter me with the puny strength which just enabled her to rise in bed. 'But someone,' she muttered, her eyes on the strangers, 'said it, Gaston? I heard it. What did it mean?'

'What you heard, madame,' I answered, with an attempt at gaiety, though the tears stood in my eyes, 'was, doubtless, mademoiselle here scolding our guide from Tours, who demanded three times the proper *pourboire*. The impudent rascal deserved all that was said to him, I assure you.'

'Was that it?' she murmured doubtfully.

'That must have been what you heard, madame,' I answered, as if I felt no doubt.

She fell back with a sigh of relief, and a little colour came into her wan face. But her eyes still dwelt curiously, and with apprehension, on mademoiselle, who stood looking sullenly into the fire; and seeing this my heart misgave me sorely that I had done a foolish thing in bringing the girl there. I foresaw a hundred questions which would be asked, and a hundred complications which must ensue, and felt already the blush of shame mounting to my cheek.

'Who is that?' my mother asked softly. 'I am ill. She must excuse me.' She pointed with her fragile finger to my companions.

I rose, and still keeping her hand in mine, turned so as to face the hearth. 'This, madame,' I answered formally, 'is Mademoiselle ——, but her name I will commit to you later, and in private. Suffice it to say that she is a lady of rank, who has been committed to my charge by a high personage.'

'A high personage?' my mother repeated gently, glancing at me with a smile of gratification.

'One of the highest,' I said. 'Such a charge being a great honour to me, I felt that I could not better execute it, madame, since we must lie in Blois one night, than by requesting your hospitality on her behalf.'

I dared mademoiselle as I spoke—I dared her with my eye to contradict or interrupt me. For answer, she looked at me once, inclining her head a little, and gazing at us from under her long eyelashes. Then she turned back to the fire, and her foot resumed its angry tapping on the floor.

'I regret that I cannot receive her better,' my mother answered feebly. 'I have had losses of late. I—but I will speak of that at another time. Mademoiselle doubtless knows,' she continued with dignity, 'you and your position in the South too well to think ill of the momentary straits to which she finds me reduced.'

I saw mademoiselle start, and I writhed under the glance

of covert scorn, of amazed indignation, which she shot at me. But my mother gently patting my hand, I answered patiently, 'Mademoiselle will think only what is kind, madame—of that I am assured. And lodgings are scarce tonight in Blois.'

'But tell me of yourself, Gaston,' my mother cried eagerly; and I had not the heart, with her touch on my hand, her eyes on my face, to tear myself away, much as I dreaded what was coming, and longed to end the scene. 'Tell me of yourself. You are still in favour with the king of —— I will not name him here?'

'Still, madame,' I answered, looking steadily at mademoiselle, though my face burned.

'You are still—he consults you, Gaston?'

'Still, madame.'

My mother heaved a happy sigh, and sank lower in the bed. 'And your employments?' she murmured, her voice trembling with gratification. 'They have not been reduced? You still retain them, Gaston?'

'Still, madame,' I answered, the perspiration standing on my brow, my shame almost more than I could bear.

'Twelve thousand livres a year, I think?'

'The same, madame.'

'And your establishment? How many do you keep now? Your valet, of course? And lackeys—how many at present?' She glanced, with an eye of pride, while she waited for my answer, first at the two silent figures by the fire, then at the poverty-stricken room; as if the sight of its bareness heightened for her the joy of my prosperity.

She had no suspicion of my trouble, my misery, or that the last question almost filled the cup too full. Hitherto all had been easy, but this seemed to choke me. I stammered and lost my voice. Mademoiselle, her head bowed, was gazing into the fire. Fanchette was staring at me, her black eyes round as saucers, her mouth half-open. 'Well, madame,' I muttered at length, 'to tell you the truth, at present, you must understand, I have been forced to— '

'What, Gaston?' Madame de Bonne half rose in bed. Her

voice was sharp with disappointment and apprehension; the grasp of her fingers on my hand grew closer.

I could not resist that appeal. I flung away the last rag of shame. 'To reduce my establishment somewhat,' I answered, looking a miserable defiance at mademoiselle's averted figure. She had called me a liar and a cheat—here in the room! I must stand before her a liar and a cheat confessed. 'I keep but three lackeys now, madame.'

'Still it is creditable,' my mother muttered thoughtfully, her eyes shining. 'Your dress, however, Gaston—only my eyes are weak—seems to me—'

'Tut, tut! It is but a disguise,' I answered quickly.

'I might have known that,' she rejoined, sinking back with a smile and a sigh of content. 'But when I first saw you I was almost afraid that something had happened to you. And I have been uneasy lately,' she went on, releasing my hand, and beginning to play with the coverlet, as though the remembrance troubled her. 'There was a man here a while ago—a friend of Simon Fleix there—who had been south to Pau and Nerac, and he said there was no M. de Marsac about the Court.'

'He probably knew less of the Court than the wine-tavern,' I answered with a ghastly smile.

'That was just what I told him,' my mother responded quickly and eagerly. 'I warrant you I sent him away ill-satisfied.'

'Of course,' I said, 'there will always be people of that kind. But now, if you will permit me, madame, I will make such arrangements for mademoiselle as are necessary.'

Begging her accordingly to lie down and compose herself—for even so short a conversation, following on the excitement of our arrival, had exhausted her to a painful degree—I took the youth, who had just returned from stabling our horses, a little aside, and learning that he lodged in a smaller chamber on the farther side of the landing, secured it for the use of mademoiselle and her woman. In spite of a certain excitability which marked him at times, he seemed to be a quick, ready

84

fellow, and he willingly undertook to go out, late as it was, and procure some provisions and a few other things which were sadly needed, as well for my mother's comfort as for our own. I directed Fanchette to aid him in the preparation of the other chamber, and thus for a while I was left alone with mademoiselle. She had taken one of the stools, and sat cowering over the fire, the hood of her cloak drawn about her head; in such a manner that even when she looked at me, which she did from time to time, I saw little more than her eyes, bright with contemptuous anger.

'So, sir,' she presently began, speaking in a low voice, and turning slightly towards me, 'you practise lying even here?'

I felt so strongly the futility of denial or explanation that I shrugged my shoulders and remained silent under the sneer. Two more days—two more days would take us to Rosny, and my task would be done, and mademoiselle and I would part for good and all. What would it matter then what she thought of me? What did it matter now?

For the first time in our intercourse my silence seemed to disconcert and displease her. 'Have you nothing to say for yourself?' she muttered sharply, crushing a fragment of charcoal under her foot, and stooping to peer at the ashes. 'Have you not another lie in your quiver, M. de Marsac? De Marsac!' And she repeated the title, with a scornful laugh, as if she put no faith in my claim to it.

But I would answer nothing—nothing; and we remained silent until Fanchette, coming in to say that the chamber was ready, held the light for her mistress to pass out. I told the woman to come back and fetch mademoiselle's supper, and then, being left alone with my mother, who had fallen asleep, with a smile on her thin, worn face, I began to wonder what had happened to reduce her to such dire poverty.

I feared to agitate her by referring to it; but later in the evening, when her curtains were drawn and Simon Fleix and I were left together, eyeing one another across the embers like dogs of different breeds—with a certain strangeness and suspicion—my thoughts recurred to the question; and determining first to learn something about my companion, whose pale, eager face and tattered, black dress gave him a certain individuality, I asked him whether he had come from Paris with Madame de Bonne.

He nodded without speaking.

I asked him if he had known her long.

'Twelve months,' he answered. 'I lodged on the fifth, madame on the second, floor of the same house in Paris.'

I leaned forward and plucked the hem of his black robe. 'What is this?' I said, with a little contempt. 'You are not a priest, man.'

'No,' he answered, fingering the stuff himself, and gazing at me in a curious, vacant fashion. 'I am a student of the Sorbonne.'

I drew off from him with a muttered oath, wondering— while I looked at him with suspicious eyes—how he came to be here, and particularly how he came to be in attendance on my mother, who had been educated from childhood in the Religion, and had professed it in private all her life. I could think of no one who, in old days, would have been less welcome in her house than a Sorbonnist, and began to fancy that here should lie the secret of her miserable condition.

'You don't like the Sorbonne?' he said, reading my thoughts; which were, indeed, plain enough.

'No more than I love the devil!' I said bluntly.

He leaned forward and, stretching out a thin, nervous hand, laid it on my knee. 'What if they are right, though?' he muttered, his voice hoarse. 'What if they are right, M. de Marsac?'

'Who right?' I asked roughly, drawing back afresh.

'The Sorbonne,' he repeated, his face red with excitement, his eyes peering uncannily into mine. 'Don't you see,' he continued, pinching my knee in his earnestness, and thrusting his face nearer and nearer to mine, 'it all turns on that? It all turns on that—salvation or damnation! Are they right? Are you right? You say yes to this, no to that, you white-coats; and you say it lightly, but are you right? Are you right? Mon

86

Dieu!' he continued, drawing back abruptly and clawing the air with impatience, 'I have read, read, read! I have listened to sermons, theses, disputations, and I know nothing. I know no more than when I began.'

He sprang up and began to pace the floor, while I gazed at him with a feeling of pity. A very learned person once told me that the troubles of these times bred four kinds of men, who were much to be compassionated: fanatics on the one side or the other, who lost sight of all else in the intensity of their faith; men who, like Simon Fleix, sought desperately after something to believe, and found it not; and lastly, scoffers, who, believing in nothing, looked on all religion as a mockery.

He presently stopped walking—in his utmost excitement I remarked that he never forgot my mother, but trod more lightly when he drew near the alcove—and spoke again.

'You are a Huguenot?' he said.

'Yes,' I replied.

'So is she,' he rejoined, pointing towards the bed. 'But do you feel no doubts?'

'None,' I said quietly.

'Nor does she,' he answered again, stopping opposite me. 'You made up your mind—how?'

'I was born in the Religion,' I said.

'And you have never questioned it?'

'Never.'

'Nor thought much about it?'

'Not a great deal,' I answered.

'Saint Gris!' he exclaimed in a low tone. 'And do you never think of hell-fire—of the worm which dieth not, and the fire which shall not be quenched? Do you never think of that, M. de Marsac?'

'No, my friend, never!' I answered, rising impatiently; for at that hour, and in that silent, gloomy room I found his conversation dispiriting. 'I believe what I was taught to believe, and I strive to hurt no one but the enemy. I think little; and if I were you I would think less. I would do

87

something, man—fight, play, work, anything but think! Leave that to clerks.'

'I am a clerk,' he answered.

'A poor one, it seems,' I retorted, with a little scorn in my tone. 'Leave it, man. Work! Fight! Do something!'

'Fight?' he said, as if the idea were a novel one. 'Fight? But there, I might be killed; and then hell-fire, you see!'

'Zounds, man!' I cried, out of patience with a folly which, to tell the truth, the lamp burning low, and the rain pattering on the roof, made the skin of my back feel cold and creepy. 'Enough of this! Keep your doubts and your fire to yourself! And answer me,' I continued, sternly. 'How came Madame de Bonne so poor? How did she come down to this place?'

He sat down on his stool, the excitement dying quickly out of his face. 'She gave away all her money,' he said slowly and reluctantly. It may be imagined that this answer surprised me. 'Gave it away?' I exclaimed. 'To whom? And when?'

He moved uneasily on his seat and avoided my eye, his altered manner filling me with suspicions which the insight I had just obtained into his character did not altogether preclude. At last he said, 'I had nothing to do with it, if you mean that; nothing. On the contrary, I have done all I could to make it up to her. I followed her here. I swear that is so, M. de Marsac.'

'You have not told me yet to whom she gave it,' I said sternly.

'She gave it,' he muttered, 'to a priest.'

'To what priest?'

'I do not know his name. He is a Jacobin.'

'And why?' I asked, gazing incredulously at the student. 'Why did she give it to him? Come, come! have a care. Let me have none of your Sorbonne inventions!'

He hesitated a moment, looking at me timidly, and then seemed to make up his mind to tell me. 'He found out—it was when we lived in Paris, you understand, last June—that she was a Huguenot. It was about the time they burned the Foucards, and he frightened her with that, and made her pay him money, a little at first, and then more and more, to keep her secret. When the king came to Blois she followed his Majesty, thinking to be safer here; but the priest came too, and got money, and more, until he left her—this.'

'This!' I said. And I set my teeth together.

Simon Fleix nodded.

I looked round the wretched garret to which my mother had been reduced, and pictured the days and hours of fear and suspense through which she had lived; through which she must have lived with the caitiff's threat hanging over her grey head! I thought of her birth and her humiliation; of her frail form and patient, undying love for me; and solemnly, and before heaven, I swore that night to punish the man. My anger was too great for words, and for tears I was too old. I asked Simon Fleix no more questions, save when the priest might be looked for again—which he could not tell me—and whether he would know him again—to which he answered, 'Yes.' But, wrapping myself in my cloak, I lay down by the fire and pondered long and sadly.

So, while I had been pinching there, my mother had been starving here. She had deceived me, and I her. The lamp flickered, throwing uncertain shadows as the draught tossed the strange window-curtain to and fro. The leakage from the roof fell drop by drop, and now and again the wind shook the crazy building, as though it would lift it up bodily and carry it away.

8

# An Empty Room

Desiring to start as early as possible, that we might reach Rosny on the second evening, I roused Simon Fleix before it was light, and learning from him where the horses were stabled, went out to attend to them; preferring to do this myself, that I might have an opportunity of seeking out a tailor, and providing myself with clothes better suited to my rank than those to which I had been reduced of late. I found that I still had ninety crowns left of the sum which the King of Navarre had given me, and twelve of these I laid out on a doublet of black cloth with russet points and ribands, a dark cloak lined with the same sober colour, and a new cap and feather. The tradesman would fain have provided me with a new scabbard also, seeing my old one was worn-out at the heel; but this I declined, having a fancy to go with my point bare until I should have punished the scoundrel who had made my mother's failing days a misery to her; a business which, the King of Navarre's once done, I promised myself to pursue with energy and at all costs.

The choice of my clothes, and a few alterations which it was necessary to make in them, detained me some time, so that it was later than I could have wished when I turned my face towards the house again, bent on getting my party to horse as speedily as possible. The morning, I remember, was bright, frosty, and cold; the kennels were dry, the streets comparatively clean. Here and there a ray of early sunshine, darting between the overhanging eaves, gave promise of glorious travelling-weather. But the faces, I remarked in my walk, did not reflect the surrounding cheerfulness. Moody looks met me everywhere and on every side; and while courier after courier galloped by me bound for the castle, the townsfolk stood aloof in doorways listless and inactive, or, gathering in groups in corners, talked what I took to be treason under the breath. The Queen-mother still lived, but Orleans had revolted, and Sens and Mans, Chartres and Melun. Rouen was said to be wavering, Lyons in arms, while Paris had deposed her king, and cursed him daily from a hundred altars. In fine, the great rebellion which followed the death of Guise, and lasted so many years, was already in progress; so that on this first day of the new year the king's writ scarce ran farther than he could see, peering anxiously out from the towers above my head.

Reaching the house, I climbed the long staircase hastily, abusing its darkness and foulness, and planning as I went how my mother might most easily and quickly be moved to a better lodging. Gaining the top of the last flight, I saw that mademoiselle's door on the left of the landing was open, and concluding from this that she was up, and ready to start, I entered my mother's room with a brisk step and spirits reinforced by the crisp morning air.

But on the threshold I stopped, and stood silent and amazed. At first I thought the room was empty. Then, at a second glance, I saw the student. He was on his knees beside the bed in the alcove, from which the curtain had been partially dragged away. The curtain before the window had been torn down also, and the cold light of day, pouring in on the unsightly bareness of the room, struck a chill to my heart. A stool lay overturned by the fire, and above it a grey cat, which I had not hitherto noticed, crouched on a beam and eyed me with stealthy fierceness. Mademoiselle was not to be seen, nor was Fanchette, and Simon Fleix did not hear me. He was doing something at the bed—for my mother it seemed.

'What is it, man?' I cried softly, advancing on tiptoe to the bedside. 'Where are the others?'

The student looked round and saw me. His face was pale and gloomy. His eyes burned, and yet there were tears in them, and on his cheeks. He did not speak, but the chilliness, the bareness, the emptiness of the room spoke for him, and my heart sank.

I took him by the shoulders. 'Find your tongue, man!' I said angrily. 'Where are they?'

He rose from his knees and stood staring at me. 'They are gone!' he said stupidly.

'Gone?' I exclaimed. 'Impossible! When? Whither?'

'Half an hour ago. Whither—I do not know.'

Confounded and amazed, I glared at him between fear and rage. 'You do not know?' I cried. 'They are gone, and you do not know?'

He turned suddenly on me and gripped my arm. 'No, I do not know! I do not know!' he cried, with a complete change of manner and in a tone of fierce excitement. 'Only, may the fiend go with them! But I do know this. I know this, M. de Marsac, with whom they went, these friends of yours! A fop came, a dolt, a fine spark, and gave them fine words and fine speeches and a gold token, and, hey presto! they went, and forgot you!'

'What!' I cried, beginning to understand, and snatching fiercely at the one clue in his speech. 'A gold token? They have been decoyed away then! There is no time to be lost. I must follow.'

'No, for that is not all!' he replied, interrupting me sternly, while his grasp on my arm grew tighter and his eyes flashed as they looked into mine. 'You have not heard all. They have gone with one who called you an impostor, and a thief, and a beggar, and that to your mother's face—and killed her! Killed her as surely as if he had taken a sword to her, M. de Marsac! Will you, after that, leave her for them?'

He spoke plainly. And yet, God forgive me, it was some time before I understood him: before I took in the meaning of his words, or could transfer my thoughts from the absent to my mother lying on the bed before me. When I did do so, and turned to her, and saw her still face and thin hair straggling over the coarse pillow, then, indeed, the sight overcame me. I thought no more of others—for I thought her dead; and with a great and bitter cry I fell on my knees beside her and hid my face. What, after all, was this head-strong girl to me? what were even kings and king's com-missions to me beside her—beside the one human being who loved me still, the one being of my blood and name left, the one ever-patient, ever-constant heart which for years had beaten only for me? For a while, for a few moments, I was worthy of her; for I forgot all others.

Simon Fleix roused me at last from my stupor, making me understand that she was not dead, but in a deep swoon, the result of the shock she had undergone. A leech, for whom he had despatched a neighbour, came in as I rose, and taking my place, presently restored her to consciousness. But her extreme feebleness warned me not to hope for more than a temporary recovery; nor had I sat by her long before I discerned that this last blow, following on so many fears and privations, had reached a vital part, and that she was even now dying.

She lay for a while with her hand in mine and her eyes closed, but about noon, the student contriving to give her some broth, she revived, and, recognising me, lay for more than an hour gazing at me with unspeakable content and satisfaction. At the end of that time, and when I thought she was past speaking, she signed to me to bend over her, and whispered something, which at first I could not catch. Presently I made it out to be, 'She is gone—The girl you brought?'

Much troubled, I answered yes, begging her not to think about the matter. I need not have feared, however, for when she spoke again she did so without emotion, and rather as one seeing clearly something before her.

'When you find her, Gaston,' she murmured, 'do not be angry with her. It was not her fault. She—he deceived her. See!'

I followed the direction rather of her eyes than her hand, and found beneath the pillow a length of gold chain. 'She left that?' I murmured, a strange tumult of emotions in my breast.

'She laid it there,' my mother whispered. 'And she would have stopped him saying what he did'—a shudder ran through my mother's frame at the remembrance of the man's words, though her eyes still gazed into mine with faith and confidence—'she would have stopped him, but she could not, Gaston. And then he hurried her away.'

'He showed her a token, madame, did he not?' I could not for my life repress the question, so much seemed to turn on the point.

'A bit of gold,' my mother whispered, smiling faintly.

93

'Now let me sleep.' And, clinging always to my hand, she closed her eyes.

The student came back soon afterwards with some comforts for which I had despatched him, and we sat by her until the evening fell, and far into the night. It was a relief to me to learn from the leech that she had been ailing for some time, and that in any case the end must have come soon. She suffered no pain and felt no fears, but meeting my eyes whenever she opened her own, or came out of the drowsiness which possessed her, thanked God, I think, and was content. As for me, I remember that room became, for the time, the world. Its stillness swallowed up all the tumults which filled the cities of France, and its one interest—the coming and going of a feeble breath—eclipsed the ambitions and hopes of a lifetime.

Before it grew light Simon Fleix stole out to attend to the horses. When he returned he came to me and whispered in my ear that he had something to tell me; and my mother lying in a quiet sleep at the time, I disengaged my hand, and, rising softly, went with him to the hearth.

Instead of speaking, he held his fist before me and suddenly unclosed the fingers. 'Do you know it?' he said, glancing at me abruptly.

I took what he held, and looking at it, nodded. It was a knot of velvet of a peculiar dark red colour, and had formed, as I knew the moment I set eyes on it, part of the fastening of mademoiselle's mask. 'Where did you find it?' I muttered, supposing that he had picked it up on the stairs.

'Look at it!' he answered impatiently. 'You have not looked.'

I turned it over, and then saw something which had escaped me at first—that the wider part of the velvet was disfigured by a fantastic stitching, done very roughly and rudely with a thread of white silk. The stitches formed letters, the letters words. With a start I read, '*A moi*!' and saw in a corner, in smaller stitches, the initials 'C. d. l. V.'

I looked eagerly at the student. 'Where did you find this?' I said.

'I picked it up in the street,' he answered quietly, 'not three hundred paces from here.'

I thought a moment. 'In the gutter, or near the wall?' I asked.

'Near the wall, to be sure.'

'Under a window?'

'Precisely,' he said. 'You may be easy; I am not a fool. I marked the place, M. de Marsac, and shall not forget it.'

Even the sorrow and solicitude I felt on my mother's behalf—feelings which had seemed a minute before to secure me against all other cares or anxieties whatever—were not proof against this discovery. For I found myself placed in a strait so cruel I must suffer either way. On the one hand, I could not leave my mother; I were a heartless ingrate to do that. On the other, I could not, without grievous pain, stand still and inactive while Mademoiselle de la Vire, whom I had sworn to protect, and who was now suffering through my laches and mischance, appealed to me for help. For I could not doubt that this was what the bow of velvet meant; still less that it was intended for me, since few save myself would be likely to recognise it, and she would naturally expect me to make some attempt at pursuit.

And I could not think little of the sign. Remembering mademoiselle's proud and fearless spirit, and the light in which she had always regarded me, I augured the worst from it. I felt assured that no imaginary danger and no emergency save the last would have induced her to stoop so low; and this consideration, taken with the fear I felt that she had fallen into the hands of Fresnoy, whom I believed to be the person who had robbed me of the gold coin, filled me with a horrible doubt which way my duty lay. I was pulled, as it were, both ways. I felt my honour engaged both to go and to stay, and while my hand went to my hilt, and my feet trembled to be gone, my eyes sought my mother, and my ears listened for her gentle breathing.

Perplexed and distracted, I looked at the student, and he at me. 'You saw the man who took her away,' I muttered.

Hitherto, in my absorption on my mother's account, I had put few questions, and let the matter pass as though it moved me little and concerned me less. 'What was he like? Was he a big, bloated man, Simon, with his head bandaged, or perhaps a wound on his face?'

'The gentleman who went away with mademoiselle, do you mean?' he asked.

'Yes, yes, gentleman if you like!'

'Not at all,' the student answered. 'He was a tall young gallant, very gaily dressed, dark-haired, and with a rich complexion. I heard him tell her that he came from a friend of hers too high to be named in public or in Blois. He added that he brought a token from him; and when mademoiselle mentioned you—she had just entered madame's room with her woman when he appeared—'

'He had watched me out, of course.'

'Just so. Well, when she mentioned you, he swore you were an adventurer, and a beggarly impostor, and what not, and bade her say whether she thought it likely that her friend would have entrusted such a mission to such a man.'

'And then she went with him?'

The student nodded.

'Readily? Of her own free-will?'

'Certainly,' he answered. 'It seemed so to me. She tried to prevent him speaking before your mother, but that was all.'

On the impulse of the moment I took a step towards the door; recollecting my position, I turned back with a groan. Almost beside myself, and longing for any vent for my feelings, I caught the lad by the shoulder, where he stood on the hearth, and shook him to and fro.

'Tell me, man, what am I to do?' I said between my teeth. 'Speak! think! invent something!'

But he shook his head.

I let him go with a muttered oath, and sat down on a stool by the bed and took my head between my hands. At that very moment, however, relief came—came from an unexpected quarter. The door opened and the leech entered.

He was a skilful man, and, though much employed about the Court, a Huguenot—a fact which had emboldened Simon Fleix to apply to him through the landlord of the Bleeding Heart, the secret rendezvous of the Religion in Blois. When he had made his examination he was for leaving, being a grave and silent man, and full of business, but at the door I stopped him.

'Well, sir?' I said in a low tone, my hand on his cloak.

'She has rallied, and may live three days,' he answered quietly. 'Four, it may be, and as many more as God wills.'

Pressing two crowns into his hand, I begged him to call daily, which he promised to do; and then he went. My mother was still dozing peacefully, and I turned to Simon Fleix, my doubts resolved and my mind made up.

'Listen,' I said, 'and answer me shortly. We cannot both leave; that is certain. Yet I must go, and at once, to the place where you found the velvet knot. Do you describe the spot exactly, so that I may find it, and make no mistake.'

He nodded, and after a moment's reflection answered.

'You know the Rue Saint-Denys, M. de Marsac? Well, go down it, keeping the Bleeding Heart on your left. Take the second turning on the same side after passing the inn. The third house from the corner, on the left again, consists of a gateway leading to the Hospital of the Holy Cross. Above the gateway are two windows in the lower storey, and above them two more. The knot lay below the first window you come to. Do you understand?'

'Perfectly,' I said. 'It is something to be a clerk, Simon.'

He looked at me thoughtfully, but added nothing; and I was busy tightening my sword-hilt, and disposing my cloak about the lower part of my face. When I had arranged this to my satisfaction, I took out and counted over the sum of thirty-five crowns, which I gave to him, impressing on him the necessity of staying beside my mother should I not return; for though I proposed to reconnoitre only, and learn if possible whether mademoiselle was still in Blois, the future was uncertain, and whereas I was known to my enemies, they were strangers to me.

Having enjoined this duty upon him, I bade my mother a silent farewell, and, leaving the room, went slowly down the stairs, the picture of her worn and patient face going with me, and seeming, I remember, to hallow the purpose I had in my mind.

The clocks were striking the hour before noon as I stepped from the doorway, and, standing a moment in the lane, looked this way and that for any sign of espionage. I could detect none, however. The lane was deserted; and feeling assured that any attempt to mislead my opponents, who probably knew Blois better than I did, must fail, I made none, but deliberately took my way towards the Bleeding Heart, in the Rue Saint-Denys. The streets presented the same appearance of gloomy suspense which I had noticed on the previous day. The same groups stood about in the same corners, the same suspicious glances met me in common with all other strangers who showed themselves; the same listless inaction characterised the townsfolk, the same anxious hurry those who came and went with news. I saw that even here, under the walls of the palace, the bonds of law and order were strained almost to bursting, and judged that if there ever was a time in France when right counted for little, and the strong hand for much, it was this. Such a state of things was not unfavourable to my present design, and caring little for suspicious looks, I went resolutely on my way.

I had no difficulty in finding the gateway of which Simon had spoken, or in identifying the window beneath which he had picked up the velvet knot. An alley opening almost opposite, I took advantage of this to examine the house at my leisure, and remarked at once, that whereas the lower window was guarded only by strong shutters, now open, that in the storey above was heavily barred. Naturally I concentrated my attention on the latter. The house, an old building of stone, seemed sufficiently reputable, nor could I discern anything about it which would have aroused my distrust had the knot been found elsewhere. It bore the arms of a religious brotherhood, and had probably at one time formed the principal entrance to the hospital, which still stood behind it, but it had now come, as I judged, to be used as a dwelling of the better class. Whether the two floors were separately inhabited or not I failed to decide.

After watching it for some time without seeing anyone pass in or out, or anything occurring to enlighten me one way or the other, I resolved to venture in, the street being quiet and the house giving no sign of being strongly garrisoned. The entrance lay under the archway, through a door on the right side. I judged from what I saw that the porter was probably absent, busying himself with his gossips in matters of State.

And this proved to be the case, for when I had made the passage of the street with success, and slipped quietly in through the half-open door, I found only his staff and charcoal-pan there to represent him. A single look satisfied me on that point; forthwith, without hesitation, I turned to the stairs and began to mount, assured that if I would effect anything single-handed I must trust to audacity and surprise rather than to caution or forethought.

The staircase was poorly lighted by loopholes looking towards the rear, but it was clean and well-kept. Silence, broken only by the sound of my footsteps, prevailed throughout the house, and all seemed so regular and decent and orderly that the higher I rose the lower fell my hopes of success. Still, I held resolutely on until I reached the second floor and stood before a closed door. The moment had come to put all to the touch. I listened for a few seconds, but hearing nothing, cautiously lifted the latch. Somewhat to my surprise the door yielded to my hand, and I entered.

A high settle stood inside, interrupting my view of the room, which seemed to be spacious and full of rich stuffs and furniture, but low in the roof, and somewhat dimly lighted by two windows rather wide than high. The warm glow of a fire shone on the woodwork of the ceiling, and as I softly closed the door a log on the hearth gave way, with a crackling of sparks, which pleasantly broke the luxurious silence. The next moment a low, sweet voice asked, 'Alphonse, is that you?'

I walked round the settle and came face to face with a beautiful woman reclining on a couch. On hearing the door open she had raised herself on her elbow. Now, seeing a stranger before her, she sprang up with a low cry, and stood gazing at me, her face expressing both astonishment and anger. She was of middling height, her features regular though somewhat childlike, her complexion singularly fair. A profusion of golden hair hung in disorder about her neck, and matched the deep blue of her eyes, wherein it seemed to me, there lurked more spirit and fire than the general cast of her features led one to expect.

After a moment's silence, during which she scanned me from head to foot with great haughtiness—and I her with curiosity and wonder—she spoke. 'Sir!' she said slowly, 'to what am I to attribute this—visit?'

For the moment I was so taken aback by her appearance and extraordinary beauty, as well as by the absence of any sign of those I sought, that I could not gather my thoughts to reply, but stood looking vaguely at her. I had expected, when I entered the room, something so different from this!

'Well, sir?' she said again, speaking sharply, and tapping her foot on the floor.

'This visit, madame?' I stammered.

'Call it intrusion, sir, if you please!' she cried imperiously. 'Only explain it, or begone.'

'I crave leave to do both, madame,' I answered, collecting myself by an effort. 'I ascended these stairs and opened your door in error—that is the simple fact—hoping to find a friend of mine here. I was mistaken, it seems, and it only remains for me to withdraw, offering at the same time the humblest apologies.' And as I spoke I bowed low and prepared to retire.

'One moment, sir!' she said quickly, and in an altered tone.

'You are, perhaps, a friend of M. de Bruhl—of my husband. In that case, if you desire to leave any message I will—I shall be glad to deliver it.'

She looked so charming that, despite the tumult of my feelings, I could not but regard her with admiration. 'Alas! madame, I cannot plead that excuse,' I answered. 'I regret that I have not the honour of his acquaintance.'

She eyed me with some surprise. 'Yet still, sir,' she answered, smiling a little, and toying with a gold brooch which clasped her habit, 'you must have had some ground, some reason, for supposing you would find a friend here?'

'True, madame,' I answered, 'but I was mistaken.'

I saw her colour suddenly. With a smile and a faint twinkle of the eye she said, 'It is not possible, sir, I suppose —you have not come here, I mean, out of any reason connected with a—a knot of velvet, for instance?'

I started, and involuntarily advanced a step towards her. 'A knot of velvet!' I exclaimed, with emotion. 'Mon Dieu! Then I was not mistaken! I have come to the right house, and you—you know something of this! Madame,' I continued impulsively, 'that knot of velvet? Tell me what it means, I implore you!'

She seemed alarmed by my violence, retreating a step or two, and looking at me haughtily, yet with a kind of shame-facedness. 'Believe me, it means nothing,' she said hurriedly. 'I beg you to understand that, sir. It was a foolish jest.'

'A jest?' I said. 'It fell from this window.'

'It was a jest, sir,' she answered stubbornly. But I could see that, with all her pride, she was alarmed; her face was troubled, and there were tears in her eyes. And this rendered me under the circumstances only the more persistent.

'I have the velvet here, madame,' I said. 'You must tell me more about it.'

She looked at me with a weightier impulse of anger than she had yet exhibited. 'I do not think you know to whom you are speaking,' she said, breathing fast. 'Leave the room, sir, and at once! I have told you it was a jest. If you are a gentleman you will believe me and go.' And she pointed to the door.

But I held my ground, with an obstinate determination to pierce the mystery. 'I am a gentleman, madame,' I said, 'and yet I must know more. Until I know more I cannot go.'

'Oh, this is insufferable!' she cried, looking round as if for a way of escape; but I was between her and the only door. 'This is unbearable! The knot was never intended for you, sir. And what is more, if M. de Bruhl come and find you here, you will repent it bitterly.'

I saw that she was at least as much concerned on her own account as on mine, and thought myself justified under the circumstances in taking advantage of her fears. I deliberately laid my cap on the table which stood beside me. 'I will go, madame,' I said, looking at her fixedly, 'when I know all that you know about this knot I hold, and not before. If you are unwilling to tell me, I must wait for M. de Bruhl, and ask him.'

She cried out 'Insolent!' and looked at me as if in her rage and dismay she would gladly have killed me; being, I could see, a passionate woman. But I held my ground, and after a moment she spoke. 'What do you want to know?' she said, frowning darkly.

'This knot—how did it come to lie in the street below your window? I want to know that first.'

'I dropped it,' she answered sullenly.

'Why?' I said.

'Because—' And then she stopped and looked at me, and then again looked down, her face crimson. 'Because, if you must know,' she continued hurriedly, tracing a pattern on the table with her finger, 'I saw it bore the words "*A moi.*" I have been married only two months, and I thought my husband might find it—and bring it to me. It was a silly fancy.'

'But where did you get it?' I asked, and I stared at her in growing wonder and perplexity. For the more questions I put, the further, it seemed to me, I strayed from my object.

'I picked it up in the Ruelle d'Arcy,' she answered, tapping her foot on the floor resentfully. 'It was the silly thing put it into my head to—to do what I did. And now, have you any more questions, sir?'

'One only,' I said, seeing it all clearly enough. 'Will you tell me, please, exactly where you found it?'

'I have told you. In the Ruelle d'Arcy, ten paces from the Rue de Valois. Now, sir, will you go?'

'One word, madame. Did—'

But she cried, 'Go, sir, go! go!' so violently, that after making one more attempt to express my thanks, I thought it better to obey her. I had learned all she knew; I had solved the puzzle. But, solving it, I found myself no nearer to the end I had in view, no nearer to mademoiselle. I closed the door with a silent bow, and began to descend the stairs, my mind full of anxious doubts and calculations. The velvet knot was the only clue I possessed, but was I right in placing any dependence on it? I knew now that, wherever it had originally lain, it had been removed once. If once, why not twice? why not three times?

# 9

# The House in the Ruelle d'Arcy

I had not gone down half a dozen steps before I heard a man enter the staircase from the street, and begin to ascend. It struck me at once that this might be M. de Bruhl; and I realised that I had not left madame's apartment a moment too soon. The last thing I desired, having so much on my hands, was to embroil myself with a stranger, and accordingly I quickened my pace, hoping to meet him so near the foot of the stairs as to leave him in doubt whether I had been visiting the upper or lower part of the house. The staircase was dark, however, and being familiar with it, he had the advantage over me. He came leaping up two steps at a time, and turning the angle abruptly, surprised me before I was clear of the upper flight.

On seeing me, he stopped short and stared; thinking at first, I fancy, that he ought to recognise me. When he did not, he stood back a pace. 'Umph!' he said. 'Have you been—have you any message for me, sir?'

'No,' I said, 'I have not.'

He frowned. 'I am M. de Bruhl,' he said.

'Indeed?' I muttered, not knowing what else to say.

'You have been—'

'Up your stairs, sir? Yes. In error,' I answered bluntly.

He gave a kind of grunt at that, and stood aside, incredulous and dissatisfied, yet uncertain how to proceed. I met his black looks with a steady countenance, and passed by him, becoming aware, however, as I went down the stairs that he had turned and was looking after me. He was a tall, handsome man, dark, and somewhat ruddy of complexion, and was dressed in the extreme of Court fashion, in a suit of myrtle-green trimmed with sable. He carried also a cloak lined with the same on his arm. Beyond looking back when I reached the street, to see that he did not follow me, I thought no more of him. But we were to meet again, and often. Nay, had I then known all that was to be known I would have gone back and— But of that in another place.

The Rue de Valois, to which a tradesman, who was peering cautiously out of his shop, directed me, proved to be one of the main streets of the city, narrow and dirty, and darkened by overhanging eaves and signboards, but full of noise and bustle. One end of it opened on the *parvis* of the Cathedral. the other and quieter end appeared to abut on the west gate of the town. Feeling the importance of avoiding notice in the neighbourhood of the house I sought, I strolled into the open space in front of the Cathedral, and accosting two men who stood talking there, learned that the Ruelle d'Arcy was the third lane on the right of the Rue de Valois, and some little distance along it. Armed with this information I left them, and with my head bent down, and my cloak drawn about the lower part of my face, as if I felt the east wind, I proceeded down the street until I reached the opening of the lane. Without looking up I turned briskly into it.

When I had gone ten paces past the turning, however, I stopped and, gazing about me, began to take in my surroundings as fast as I could. The lane, which seemed little frequented, was eight or nine feet wide, unpaved, and full of ruts. The high blank wall of a garden rose on one side of it, on the other the still higher wall of a house; and both were completely devoid of windows, a feature which I recognised with the utmost dismay. For it completely upset all my calculations. In vain, I measured with my eye the ten paces I had come; in vain I looked up, looked this way and that. I was nonplussed. No window opened on the lane at that point, nor, indeed, throughout its length. For it was bounded to the end, as far as I could see, by dead-walls as of gardens.

Recognising, with a sinking heart, what this meant, I saw in a moment that all hopes I had raised on Simon Fleix's discovery were baseless. Mademoiselle had dropped the velvet bow, no doubt, but not from a window. It was still a clue, but one so slight and vague as to be virtually useless, proving only that she was in trouble and in need of help; perhaps that she had passed through this lane on her way from one place of confinement to another.

Thoroughly baffled and dispirited, I leant for awhile against the wall, brooding over the ill-luck which seemed to attend me in this, as in so many previous adventures. Nor was the low voice of conscience, suggesting that such failures arose from mismanagement rather than from ill-luck, slow to make itself heard. I reflected that if I had not allowed myself to be robbed of the gold token, mademoiselle would have trusted me; that if I had not brought her to so poor an abode as my mother's, she would not have been cajoled into following a stranger; finally, that if I had remained with her, and sent Simon to attend to the horses in my place, no stranger would have gained access to her.

But it has never been my way to accept defeat at the first offer, and though I felt these self-reproaches to be well deserved, a moment's reflection persuaded me that in the singular and especial providence which had brought the velvet knot safe to my hands I ought to find encouragement. Had Madame de Bruhl not picked it up it would have continued to lie in this by-path, through which neither I nor Simon Fleix would have been likely to pass. Again, had madame not dropped it in her turn, we should have sought in vain for any, even the slightest, clue to Mademoiselle de la Vire's fate and position.

Cheered afresh by this thought, I determined to walk to the end of the lane; and forthwith did so, looking sharply about me as I went, but meeting no one. The bare upper branches of a tree rose here and there above the walls, which were pierced at intervals by low, strong doors. These doors I carefully examined, but without making any discovery; all were securely fastened, and many seemed to have been rarely opened. Emerging at last and without result on the inner side of the city ramparts, I turned, and moodily retraced my steps through the lane, proceeding more slowly as I drew near to the Rue de Valois. This time, being a little farther from the street, I made a discovery.

The corner house, which had its front on the Rue de Valois, presented, as I have said, a dead, windowless wall to the lane; but from my present standpoint I could see the upper part of the back of this house—that part of the back, I mean, which rose above the lower garden-wall that abutted on it—and in this there were several windows. The whole of two and a part of a third were within the range of my eyes; and suddenly in one of these I discovered something which made my heart beat high with hope and expectation. The window in question was heavily grated; that which I saw was tied to one of the bars. It was a small knot of some white stuff—linen apparently —and it seemed a trifle to the eye; but it was looped, as far as I could see from a distance, after the same fashion as the scrap of velvet I had in my pouch.

The conclusion was obvious, at the same time that it inspired me with the liveliest admiration of mademoiselle's wit and resources. She was confined in that room; the odds were that she was behind those bars. A bow dropped thence would fall, the wind being favourable, into the lane, not ten, but twenty paces from the street. I ought to have been prepared for a slight inaccuracy in a woman's estimate of distance.

It may be imagined with what eagerness I now scanned the house, with what minuteness I sought for a weak place. The longer I looked, however, the less comfort I derived from my inspection. I saw before me a gloomy stronghold of brick, four-square, and built in the old Italian manner, with battlements at the top, and a small machicolation, little more than a string-course, above each storey; this serving at once to lessen the monotony of the dead-walls, and to add to the frowning weight of the upper part. The windows were few and small, and the house looked damp and mouldy; lichen clotted the bricks, and moss filled the string-courses. A low door opening from the lane into the garden naturally attracted my attention; but it proved to be of abnormal strength, and bolted both at the top and bottom.

Assured that nothing could be done on that side, and being unwilling to remain longer in the neighbourhood, lest I should attract attention, I returned to the street, and twice walked past the front of the house, seeing all I could with as little appearance of seeing anything as I could compass. The front retreated somewhat from the line of the street, and was flanked on the farther side by stables. Only one chimney smoked, and that sparely. Three steps led up to imposing double doors, which stood half open, and afforded a glimpse of a spacious hall and a state staircase. Two men, apparently servants, lounged on the steps, eating chestnuts, and jesting with one another; and above the door were three shields blazoned in colours. I saw with satisfaction, as I passed the second time, that the middle coat was that of Turenne impaling one which I could not read—which thoroughly satisfied me that the bow of velvet had not lied; so that, without more ado, I turned homewards, formulating my plans as I went.

I found all as I had left it; and my mother still lying in a half-conscious state, I was spared the pain of making excuses for past absence, or explaining that which I designed. I communicated the plan I had formed to Simon Fleix, who saw no difficulty in procuring a respectable person to stay with Madame de Bonne. But for some time he would come no farther into the business. He listened, his mouth open and his eyes glittering, to my plan until I came to his share in it; and then he fell into a violent fit of trembling.

'You want me to fight, monsieur,' he cried reproachfully, shaking all over like one in the palsy. 'You said so the other night. You want to get me killed! That's it.'

'Nonsense!' I answered sharply. 'I want you to hold the horses!'

He looked at me wildly, with a kind of resentment in his face, and yet as if he were fascinated.

'You will drag me into it!' he persisted. 'You will!'

'I won't,' I said.

'You will! You will! And the end I know. I shall have no chance. I am a clerk, and not bred to fighting. You want to be the death of me!' he cried excitedly.

'I don't want you to fight,' I answered with some contempt. 'I would rather that you kept out of it for my mother's sake. I only want you to stay in the lane and hold the horses. You will run little more risk than you do sitting by the hearth here.'

And in the end I persuaded him to do what I wished; though still, whenever he thought of what was in front of him, he fell a-trembling again, and many times during the afternoon got up and walked to and fro between the window and the hearth, his face working and his hands clenched like those of a man in a fever. I put this down at first to sheer chicken-heartedness, and thought it augured ill for my enterprise; but generally remarking that he made no attempt to draw back, and that though the sweat stood on his brow he set about such preparations as were necessary —remembering also how long and kindly, and without pay or guerdon, he had served my mother, I began to see that here was something phenomenal; a man strange and beyond the ordinary, of whom it was impossible to predicate what he would do when he came to be tried.

For myself, I passed the afternoon in a state almost of apathy. I thought it my duty to make this attempt to free mademoiselle, and to make it at once, since it was impossible to say what harm might come of delay, were she in such hands as Fresnoy's; but I had so little hope of success that I regarded the enterprise as desperate. The certain loss of my mother, however, and the low ebb of my fortunes, with the ever-present sense of failure, contributed to render me indifferent to risks; and even when we were on our way, through by-streets known to Simon, to the farther end of the Ruelle d'Arcy, and the red and frosty sunset shone in our faces, and gilded for a moment the dull eaves and grey towers above us, I felt no softening. Whatever the end, there was but one in the world whom I should regret, or who would regret me; and she hung, herself, on the verge of eternity.

So that I was able to give Simon Fleix his last directions with as much coolness as I ever felt in my life. I stationed him with the three horses in the lane—which seemed as quiet and little frequented as in the morning—near the end of it, and about a hundred paces or more from the house.

'Turn their heads towards the ramparts,' I said, wheeling them round myself, 'and then they will be ready to start. They are all quiet enough. You can let the Cid loose. And now listen to me, Simon,' I continued. 'Wait here until you see me return, or until you see you are going to be attacked. In the first case, stay for me, of course; in the second, save yourself as you please. Lastly, if neither event occurs before half-past five—you will hear the convent-bell yonder ring at the half-hour—begone, and take the horses; they are yours. And one word more,' I added hurriedly. 'If you can only get away with one horse, Simon, take the Cid. It is worth more than most men, and will not fail you at a pinch.'

As I turned away, I gave him one look to see if he understood. It was not without hesitation that after that look I left him. The lad's face was flushed, he was breathing hard, his eyes seemed to be almost starting from his head. He sat his horse shaking in every limb, and had all the air of a man in a fit. I expected him to call me back, but he did not; reflecting that I must trust him, or give up the attempt, I went up the lane with my sword under my arm, and my cloak loose on my shoulders. I met a man driving a donkey laden with faggots. I saw no one else. It was already dusk between the walls, though light enough in the open country; but that was in my favour, my only regret being that as the town gates closed shortly after half-past five, I could not defer my attempt until a still later hour.

Pausing in the shadow of the house while a man might count ten, I impressed on my memory the position of the particular window which bore the knot; then I passed quickly into the street, which was still full of movement, and for a second, feeling myself safe from observation in the crowd, I stood looking at the front of the house. The door was shut. My heart sank when I saw this, for I had looked to find it still open.

The feeling, however, that I could not wait, though time might present more than one opportunity, spurred me on. What I could do I must do now, at once. The sense that this was so being heavy upon me, I saw nothing for it but to use the knocker and gain admission, by fraud if I could and if not, by force. Accordingly I stepped briskly across the kennel, and made for the entrance.

When I was within two paces of the steps, however, someone abruptly threw the door open and stepped out. The man did not notice me, and I stood quickly aside, hoping that at the last minute my chance had come. Two men, who had apparently attended this first person downstairs, stood respectfully behind him, holding lights. He paused a moment on the steps to adjust his cloak, and with more than a little surprise I recognised my acquaintance of the morning, M. de Bruhl.

I had scarcely time to identify him before he walked down the steps swinging his cane, brushed carelessly past me, and was gone. The two men looked after him awhile, shading their lights from the wind, and one saying something, the other laughed coarsely. The next moment they threw the door to and went, as I saw by the passage of their light, into the room on the left of the hall.

Now was my time. I could have hoped for, prayed for, expected no better fortune than this. The door had rebounded slightly from the jamb, and stood open an inch or more. In a second I pushed it from me gently, slid into the hall, and closed it behind me.

The door of the room on the left was wide open, and the light which shone through the doorway—otherwise the hall was dark—as well as the voices of the two men I had seen warned me to be careful. I stood, scarcely daring to breathe, and looked about me. There was no matting on the floor, no fire on the hearth. The hall felt cold, damp, and uninhabited. The state staircase rose in front of me, and presently bifurcating, formed a gallery round the place. I looked up, and up, and far above me, in the dim heights of the second floor, I espied a faint light—perhaps, the reflection of a light.

A movement in the room on my left warned me that I had no time to lose, if I meant to act. At any minute one of the men might come out and discover me. With the utmost care I started my journey. I stole across the stone floor of the hall easily and quietly enough, but I found the real difficulty begin when I came to the stairs. They were of wood, and creaked and groaned under me to such an extent that, with each step I trod, I expected the men to take the alarm. Fortunately all went well until I passed the first corner—I chose, of course, the left-hand flight—then a board jumped under my foot with a crack which sounded in the empty hall,

and to my excited ears, as loud as a pistol-shot. I was in two
minds whether I should not on the instant make a rush
for it, but happily I stood still. One of the men came out and
listened, and I heard the other ask, with an oath, what it was.
I leant against the wall, holding my breath.

'Only that wench in one of her tantrums!' the man who
had come out answered, applying an epithet to her which
I will not set down, but which I carried to his account in the
event of our coming face to face presently. 'She is quiet now.
She may hammer and hammer, but—'

The rest I lost, as he passed through the doorway and
went back to his place by the fire. But in one way his words
were of advantage to me. I concluded that I need not be so
very cautious now, seeing that they would set down anything
they heard to the same cause; and I sped on more quickly.
I had just gained the second floor landing when a loud noise
below—the opening of the street door and the heavy tread of
feet in the hall—brought me to a temporary standstill. I
looked cautiously over the balustrade, and saw two men go
across to the room on the left. One of them spoke as he
entered, chiding the other knaves, I fancied, for leaving the
door unbarred; and the tone, though not the words, echoing
sullenly up the staircase, struck a familiar chord in my
memory.

10

# The Fight on the Stairs

The certainty, which this sound gave me, that I was in the
right house, and that it held also the villain to whom I owed
all my misfortunes—for who but Fresnoy could have
furnished the broken coin which had deceived mademoiselle?
—had a singularly inspiriting effect upon me. I felt every

muscle in my body grow on the instant hard as steel, my eyes more keen, my ears sharper—all my senses more apt and vigorous. I stole off like a cat from the balustrade, over which I had been looking, and without a second's delay began the search for mademoiselle's room; reflecting that though the garrison now amounted to four, I had no need to despair. If I could release the prisoners without noise—which would be easy were the key in the lock—we might hope to pass through the hall by a *tour de force* of one kind or another. And a church-clock at this moment striking five, and reminding me that we had only half an hour in which to do all and reach the horses, I was the more inclined to risk something.

The light which I had seen from below hung in a flat-bottomed lantern just beyond the head of the stairs, and outside the entrance to one of two passages which appeared to lead to the back part of the house. Suspecting that M. de Bruhl's business had lain with mademoiselle, I guessed that the light had been placed for his convenience. With this clue and the position of the window to guide me, I fixed on a door on the right of this passage, and scarcely four paces from the head of the stairs. Before I made any sign, however, I knelt down and ascertained that there was a light in the room, and also that the key was not in the lock.

So far satisfied, I scratched on the door with my finger-nails, at first softly, then with greater force, and presently I heard someone in the room rise. I felt sure that the person, whoever it was, had taken the alarm and was listening, and putting my lips to the keyhole I whispered mademoiselle's name.

A footstep crossed the room sharply, and I heard muttering just within the door. I thought I detected two voices. But I was impatient, and, getting no answer, whispered in the same manner as before, 'Mademoiselle de la Vire, are you there?'

Still no answer. The muttering, too, had stopped, and all was still—in the room, and in the silent house. I tried again. 'It is I, Gaston de Marsac,' I said. 'Do you hear? I am come to release you.' I spoke as loudly as I dared, but most of the sound seemed to come back on me and wander in suspicious murmurings down the staircase.

This time, however, an exclamation of surprise rewarded me, and a voice, which I recognised at once as mademoiselle's, answered softly:

'What is it? Who is there?'

'Gaston de Marsac,' I answered. 'Do you need my help?'

The very brevity of her reply; the joyful sob which accompanied it, and which I detected even through the door; the wild cry of thankfulness—almost an oath—of her companion—all these assured me at once that I was welcome —welcome as I had never been before—and, so assuring me, braced me to the height of any occasion which might befall.

'Can you open the door?' I muttered. All the time I was on my knees, my attention divided between the inside of the room and the stray sounds which now and then came up to me from the hall below. 'Have you the key?'

'No; we are locked in,' mademoiselle answered.

I expected this. 'If the door is bolted inside,' I whispered, 'unfasten it, if you please.'

They answered that it was not, so bidding them stand back a little from it, I rose and set my shoulders against it. I hoped to be able to burst it in with only one crash, which by itself, a single sound, might not alarm the men downstairs. But my weight made no impression upon the lock, and the opposite wall being too far distant to allow me to get any purchase for my feet, I presently desisted. The closeness of the door to the jambs warned me that an attempt to prise it open would be equally futile; and for a moment I stood gazing in perplexity at the solid planks, which bid fair to baffle me to the end.

The position was, indeed, one of great difficulty, nor can I now think of any way out of it better or other than that which I adopted. Against the wall near the head of the stairs I had noticed, as I came up, a stout wooden stool. I stole out and fetched this, and setting it against the opposite wall, endeavoured in this way to get sufficient purchase for my feet. The lock still held; but, as I threw my whole weight on the door, the panel against which I leaned gave way and broke inwards with a loud, crashing sound, which echoed through the empty house, and might almost have been heard in the street outside.

It reached the ears, at any rate, of the men sitting below, and I heard them troop noisily out and stand in the hall, now talking loudly, and now listening. A minute of breathless suspense followed—it seemed a long minute; and then, to my relief, they tramped back again, and I was free to return to my task. Another thrust, directed a little lower, would, I hoped, do the business; but to make this the more certain I knelt down and secured the stool firmly against the wall. As I rose after settling it, something else, without sound or warning, rose also, taking me completely by surprise—a man's head above the top stair, which, as it happened, faced me. His eyes met mine, and I knew I was discovered.

He turned and bundled downstairs again with a scared face, going so quickly that I could not have caught him if I would, or had had the wit to try. Of silence there was no longer need. In a few seconds the alarm would be raised. I had small time for thought. Laying myself bodily against the door, I heaved and pressed with all my strength; but whether I was careless in my haste, or the cause was other, the lock did not give. Instead the stool slipped, and I fell with a crash on the floor at the very moment the alarm reached the men below.

I remember that the crash of my unlucky fall seemed to release all the prisoned noises of the house. A faint scream within the room was but a prelude, lost the next moment in the roar of dismay, the clatter of weapons, and volley of oaths and cries and curses which, rolling up from below, echoed hollowly about me, as the startled knaves rushed to their weapons, and charged across the flags and up the staircase. I had space for one desperate effort. Picking myself up, I seized the stool by two of its legs and dashed it twice against the door, driving in the panel I had before splintered.

But that was all. The lock held, and I had no time for a third blow. The men were already half-way up the stairs. In a breath almost they would be upon me. I flung down the useless stool and snatched up my sword, which lay unsheathed beside me. So far the matter had gone against us, but it was time for a change of weapons now, and the end was not yet. I sprang to the head of the stairs and stood there, my arm by my side and my point resting on the floor, in such an attitude of preparedness as I could compass at the moment.

For I had not been in the house all this time, as may well be supposed, without deciding what I would do in case of surprise, and exactly where I could best stand on the defensive. The flat bottom of the lamp which hung outside the passage threw a deep shadow on the spot immediately below it, while the light fell brightly on the steps beyond. Standing in the shadow I could reach the edge of the stairs with my point, and swing the blade freely, without fear of the balustrade; and here I posted myself with a certain grim satisfaction as Fresnoy, with his three comrades behind him, came bounding up the last flight.

They were four to one, but I laughed to see how, not abruptly, but shamefacedly and by degrees, they came to a stand half-way up the flight, and looked at me, measuring the steps and the advantage which the light shining in their eyes gave me. Fresnoy's ugly face was rendered uglier by a great strip of plaster which marked the place where the hilt of my sword had struck him in our last encounter at Chizé; and this and the hatred he bore to me gave a peculiar malevolence to his look. The deaf man, Matthew, whose savage stolidity had more than once excited my anger on our journey, came next to him, the two strangers whom I had seen in the hall bringing up the rear. Of the four, these last seemed the most anxious to come to blows, and had Fresnoy not barred the way with his hand we should have crossed swords without parley.

'Halt, will you!' he cried, with an oath, thrusting one of

them back. And then to me he said, 'So, so, my friend! It is you, is it?'

I looked at him in silence, with a scorn which knew no bounds, and did not so much as honour him by raising my sword, though I watched him heedfully.

'What are you doing here?' he continued, with an attempt at bluster.

Still I would not answer him, or move, but stood looking down at him. After a moment of this, he grew restive, his temper being churlish and impatient at the best. Besides, I think he retained just so much of a gentleman's feelings as enabled him to understand my contempt and smart under it. He moved a step upward, his brow dark with passion.

'You beggarly son of a scarecrow!' he broke out on a sudden, adding a string of foul imprecations, 'will you speak, or are you going to wait to be spitted where you stand? If we once begin, my bantam, we shall not stop until we have done your business! If you have anything to say, say it, and—' But I omit the rest of his speech, which was foul beyond the ordinary.

Still I did not move or speak, but looked at him unwavering, though it pained me to think the women heard. He made a last attempt. 'Come, old friend,' he said, swallowing his anger again, or pretending to do so, and speaking with a vile *bonhomie* which I knew to be treacherous, 'if we come to blows we shall give you no quarter. But one chance you shall have, for the sake of old days when we followed Condé. Go! Take the chance, and go. We will let you pass, and that broken door shall be the worst of it. That is more,' he added with a curse, 'than I would do for any other man in your place, M. de Marsac.'

A sudden movement and a low exclamation in the room behind me showed that his words were heard there; and these sounds being followed immediately by a noise as of riving wood, mingled with the quick breathing of someone hard at work. I judged that the women were striving with the door—enlarging the opening it might be. I dared not look round, however, to see what progress they made, nor did I answer Fresnoy, save by the same silent contempt, but stood watching the men before me with the eye of a fencer about to engage. And I know nothing more keen, more vigilant, more steadfast than that.

It was well I did, for without signal or warning the group wavered a moment, as though retreating, and the next instant precipitated itself upon me. Fortunately, only two could engage me at once, and Fresnoy, I noticed, was not of the two who dashed forward up the steps. One of the strangers forced himself to the front, and, taking the lead, pressed me briskly, Matthew seconding him in appearance, while really watching for an opportunity of running in and stabbing me at close quarters, a manoeuvre I was not slow to detect.

That first bout lasted half a minute only. A fierce exultant joy ran through me as the steel rang and grated, and I found that I had not mistaken the strength of wrist or position. The men were mine. They hampered one another on the stairs, and fought in fetters, being unable to advance or retreat, to lunge with freedom, or give back without fear. I apprehended greater danger from Matthew than from my actual opponent, and presently, watching my opportunity, disarmed the latter by a strong parade, and sweeping Matthew's sword aside by the same movement, slashed him across the forehead; then, drawing back a step, gave my first opponent the point. He fell in a heap on the floor, as good as dead, and Matthew, dropping his sword, staggered backwards and downwards into Fresnoy's arms.

'Bonne Foi! France et Bonne Foi!' It seemed to me that I had not spoken, that I had plied steel in grimmest silence; and yet the cry still rang and echoed in the roof as I lowered my point, and stood looking grimly down at them. Fresnoy's face was disfigured with rage and chagrin. They were now but two to one, for Matthew, though his wound was slight, was disabled by the blood which ran down into his eyes and blinded him. 'France et Bonne Foi!'

'Bonne Foi and good sword!' cried a voice behind me. And

looking swiftly round, I saw mademoiselle's face thrust through the hole in the door. Her eyes sparkled with a fierce light, her lips were red beyond the ordinary, and her hair, loosened and thrown into disorder by her exertions, fell in thick masses about her white cheeks, and gave her the aspect of a war-witch, such as they tell of in my country of Brittany. 'Good sword!' she cried again, and clapped her hands.

'But better board, mademoiselle!' I answered gaily. Like most of the men of my province, I am commonly melancholic, but I have the habit of growing witty at such times as these. 'Now, M. Fresnoy,' I continued, 'I am waiting your convenience. Must I put on my cloak to keep myself warm?'

He answered by a curse, and stood looking at me irresolutely. 'If you will come down,' he said.

'Send your man away and I will come,' I answered briskly. 'There is space on the landing, and a moderate light. But I must be quick. Mademoiselle and I are due elsewhere, and we are late already.'

Still he hesitated. Still he looked at the man lying at his feet—who had stretched himself out and passed, quietly enough, a minute before—and stood dubious, the most pitiable picture of cowardice and malice—he being ordinarily a stout man—I ever saw. I called him poltroon and white-feather, and was considering whether I had not better go down to him, seeing that our time must be up, and Simon would be quitting his post, when a cry behind me caused me to turn, and I saw that mademoiselle was no longer looking through the opening in the door.

Alarmed on her behalf, as I reflected that there might be other doors to the room, and the men have other accomplices in the house, I sprang to the door to see, but had barely time to send a single glance round the interior— which showed me only that the room was still occupied—before Fresnoy, taking advantage of my movement and of my back being turned, dashed up the stairs, with his comrade at his heels, and succeeded in penning me into the narrow passage where I stood.

I had scarcely time, indeed, to turn and put myself on

guard before he thrust at me. Nor was that all. The superiority in position no longer lay with me. I found myself fighting between walls close to the opening in the door, through which the light fell athwart my eyes, baffling and perplexing me. Fresnoy was not slow to see the aid this gave him, and pressed me hard and desperately; so that we played for a full minute at close quarters, thrusting and parrying, neither of us having room to use the edge, or time to utter word or prayer.

At this game we were so evenly matched that for a time the end was hard to tell. Presently, however, there came a change. My opponent's habit of wild living suited ill with a prolonged bout, and as his strength and breath failed and he began to give ground I discerned I had only to wear him out to have him at my mercy. He felt this himself, and even by that light I saw the sweat spring in great drops to his forehead, saw the terror grow in his eyes. Already I was counting him a dead man and the victory mine, when something flashed behind his blade, and his comrade's poniard, whizzing past his shoulder, struck me fairly on the chin, staggering me and hurling me back dizzy and half-stunned, uncertain what had happened to me.

Sped an inch lower it would have done its work and finished mine. Even as it was, my hand going up as I reeled back gave Fresnoy an opening, of which he was not slow to avail himself. He sprang forward, lunging at me furiously, and would have run me through there and then, and ended the matter, had not his foot, as he advanced, caught in the stool, which still lay against the wall. He stumbled, his point missed my hip by a hair's breadth, and he himself fell all his length on the floor, his rapier breaking off short at the hilt.

His one remaining backer stayed to cast a look at him, and that was all. The man fled, and I chased him as far as the head of the stairs; where I left him, assured by the speed and agility he displayed in clearing flight after flight that I had nothing to fear from him. Fresnoy lay, apparently stunned, and completely at my mercy. I stood an instant looking down at him, in two minds whether I should not run him through.

But the memory of old days, when he had played his part in more honourable fashion and shown a coarse good-fellowship in the field, held my hand; and flinging a curse at him, I turned in anxious haste to the door, the centre of all this bloodshed and commotion. The light still shone through the breach in the panel, but for some minutes—since Fresnoy's rush up the stairs, indeed—I had heard no sound from this quarter. Now, looking in with apprehensions which grew with the continuing silence, I learned the reason. The room was empty!

Such a disappointment in the moment of triumph was hard to bear. I saw myself, after all done, and won, on the point of being again outwitted, distanced, it might be fooled. In frantic haste and excitement I snatched up the stool beside me, and, dashing it twice against the lock, forced it at last to yield. The door swung open, and I rushed into the room, which, abandoned by those who had so lately occupied it, presented nothing to detain me. I cast a single glance round, saw that it was squalid, low-roofed, unfurnished, a mere prison; then swiftly crossing the floor, I made for a door at the farther end, which my eye had marked from the first. A candle stood flaring and guttering on a stool, and as I passed I took it up.

Somewhat to my surprise the door yielded to my touch. In trembling haste—for what might not befall the women while I fumbled with doors or wandered in passages?—I flung it wide, and passing through it, found myself at the head of a narrow, mean staircase, leading doubtless, to the servants' offices. At this, and seeing no hindrance before me, I took heart of grace, reflecting that mademoiselle might have escaped from the house this way. Though it would now be too late to quit the city, I might still overtake her, and all end well. Accordingly I hurried down the stairs, shading my candle as I went from a cold draught of air which met me, and grew stronger as I descended; until reaching the bottom at last, I came abruptly upon an open door, and an old, wrinkled, shrivelled woman.

The hag screamed at sight of me, and crouched down on the floor; and doubtless, with my drawn sword, and the blood dripping from my chin and staining all the front of my doublet, I looked fierce and uncanny enough. But I felt it was no time for sensibility—I was panting to be away—and I demanded of her sternly where they were. She seemed to have lost her voice—through fear, perhaps—and for answer only stared at me stupidly; but on my handling my weapon with some readiness she so far recovered her senses as to utter two loud screams, one after the other, and point to the door beside her. I doubted her; and yet I thought in her terror she must be telling the truth, the more as I saw no other door. In any case I must risk it, so, setting the candle down on the step beside her, I passed out.

For a moment the darkness was so intense that I felt my way with my sword before me, in absolute ignorance where I was or on what my foot might next rest. I was at the mercy of anyone who chanced to be lying in wait for me; and I shivered as the cold damp wind struck my cheek and stirred my hair. But by-and-by, when I had taken two or three steps, my eyes grew accustomed to the gloom, and I made out the naked boughs of trees between myself and the sky, and guessed that I was in a garden. My left hand, touching a shrub, confirmed me in this belief, and in another moment I distinguished something like the outline of a path stretching away before me. Following it rapidly—as rapidly as I dared —I came to a corner, as it seemed to me, turned it blindly, and stopped short, peering into a curtain of solid blackness which barred my path, and overhead mingled confusedly with the dark shapes of trees. But this, too, after a brief hesitation, I made out to be a wall. Advancing to it with outstretched hands, I felt the woodwork of a door, and, groping about, lit presently on a loop of cord. I pulled at this, the door yielded, and I went out.

I found myself in a narrow, dark lane, and looking up and down discovered, what I might have guessed before, that it was the Ruelle d'Arcy. But mademoiselle? Fanchette? Simon?

Where were they? No one was to be seen. Tormented by doubts, I lifted up my voice and called on them in turn; first on mademoiselle, then on Simon Fleix. In vain; I got no answer. High up above me I saw, as I stood back a little, lights moving in the house I had left; and the suspicion that, after all, the enemy had foiled me grew upon me. Somehow they had decoyed mademoiselle to another part of the house, and then the old woman had misled me!

I turned fiercely to the door, which I had left ajar, resolved to re-enter by the way I had come, and have an explanation whether or no. To my surprise—for I had not moved six paces from the door nor heard the slightest sound—I found it not only closed but bolted—bolted both at top and bottom, as I discovered on trying it.

I fell on that to kicking it furiously, desperately; partly in a tempest of rage and chagrin, partly in the hope that I might frighten the old woman, if it was she who had closed it, into opening it again. In vain, of course; and presently I saw this and desisted, and, still in a whirl of haste and excitement, set off running towards the place where I had left Simon Fleix and the horses. It was fully six o'clock as I judged; but some faint hope that I might find him there with mademoiselle and her woman still lingered in my mind. I reached the end of the lane, I ran to the very foot of the ramparts, I looked right and left. In vain. The place was dark, silent, deserted.

I called 'Simon! Simon! Simon Fleix!' but my only answer was the soughing of the wind in the eaves, and the slow tones of the convent-bell striking six.

# II

# The Man at the Door

There are some things, not shameful in themselves, which it shames one to remember, and among these I count the succeeding hurry and perturbation of that night: the vain search, without hope or clue, to which passion impelled me, and the stubborn persistence with which I rushed frantically from place to place long after the soberness of reason would have had me desist. There was not, it seems to me, looking back now, one street or alley, lane or court, in Blois which I did not visit again and again in my frantic wanderings; not a beggar skulking on foot that night whom I did not hunt down and question; not a wretched woman sleeping in arch or doorway whom I did not see and scrutinise. I returned to my mother's lodging again and again, always fruitlessly. I rushed to the stables and rushed away again, or stood and listened in the dark, empty stalls, wondering what had happened, and torturing myself with suggestions of this or that. And everywhere, not only at the North-gate, where I interrogated the porters and found that no party resembling that which I sought had passed out, but on the Parvis of the Cathedral, where a guard was drawn up, and in the common streets, where I burst in on one group and another with my queries, I ran the risk of suspicion and arrest, and all that might follow thereon.

It was strange indeed that I escaped arrest. The wound in my chin still bled at intervals, staining my doublet; and as I was without my cloak, which I had left in the house in the Rue de Valois, I had nothing to cover my disordered dress. I was keenly, fiercely anxious. Stray passers meeting me in the glare of a torch, or seeing me hurry by the great braziers

which burned where four streets met, looked askance at me
and gave me the wall; while men in authority cried to me to
stay and answer their questions. I ran from the one and the
other with the same savage impatience, disregarding everything in the feverish anxiety which spurred me on and
impelled me to a hundred imprudences, such as at my age I
should have blushed to commit. Much of this feeling was due,
no doubt, to the glimpse I had had of mademoiselle, and the
fiery words she had spoken; more, I fancy, to chagrin and
anger at the manner in which the cup of success had been
dashed at the last moment from my lips.

For four hours I wandered through the streets, now hot
with purpose, now seeking aimlessly. It was ten o'clock
when at length I gave up the search, and, worn out both in
body and mind, climbed the stairs at my mother's lodgings
and entered her room. An old woman sat by the fire, crooning
softly to herself, while she stirred something in a black pot.
My mother lay in the same heavy, deep sleep in which I had
left her. I sat down opposite the nurse (who cried out at my
appearance) and asked her dully for some food. When I had
eaten it, sitting in a kind of stupor the while, the result
partly of my late exertions, and partly of the silence which
prevailed round me, I bade the woman call me if any change
took place; and then going heavily across to the garret Simon
had occupied, I lay down on his pallet, and fell into a sound,
dreamless sleep.

The next day and the next night I spent beside my
mother, watching the life ebb fast away, and thinking with
grave sorrow of her past and my future. It pained me
beyond measure to see her die thus, in a garret, without
proper attendance or any but bare comforts; the existence
which had once been bright and prosperous ending in penury
and gloom, such as my mother's love and hope and self-
sacrifice little deserved. Her state grieved me sharply on my
own account too, seeing that I had formed none of those
familiar relations which men of my age have commonly
formed, and which console them for the loss of parents and

forebears; Nature so ordering it, as I have taken note, that men look forward rather than backward, and find in the ties they form with the future full compensation for the parting strands behind them. I was alone, poverty-stricken, and in middle life, seeing nothing before me except danger and hardship, and these unrelieved by hope or affection. This last adventure, too, despite all my efforts, had sunk me deeper in the mire; by increasing my enemies and alienating from me some to whom I might have turned at the worst. In one other respect also it had added to my troubles not a little; for the image of mademoiselle wandering alone and unguarded through the streets, or vainly calling on me for help, persisted in thrusting itself on my imagination when I least wanted it, and came even between my mother's patient face and me.

I was sitting beside Madame de Bonne a little after sunset on the second day, the woman who attended her being absent on an errand, when I remarked that the lamp, which had been recently lit, and stood on a stool in the middle of the room, was burning low and needed snuffing. I went to it softly, and while stooping over it, trying to improve the light, heard a slow, heavy step ascending the stairs. The house was quiet, and the sound attracted my full attention. I raised myself and stood listening, hoping that this might be the doctor, who had not been that day.

The footsteps passed the landing below, but at the first stair of the next flight the person, whoever it was, stumbled, and made a considerable noise. At that, or it might be a moment later, the step still ascending, I heard a sudden rustling behind me, and, turning quickly with a start, saw my mother sitting up in bed. Her eyes were open, and she seemed fully conscious; which she had not been for days, nor indeed since the last conversation I have recorded. But her face, though it was now sensible, was pinched and white, and so drawn with mortal fear that I believed her dying, and sprang to her, unable to construe otherwise the pitiful look in her straining eyes.

'Madame,' I said, hastily passing my arm round her, and

speaking with as much encouragement as I could infuse into my voice, 'take comfort. I am here. Your son.'

'Hush!' she muttered in answer, laying her feeble hand on my wrist and continuing to look, not at me, but at the door. 'Listen, Gaston! Don't you hear? There it is again. Again!'

For a moment I thought her mind still wandered, and I shivered, having no fondness for hearing such things. Then I saw she was listening intently to the sound which had attracted my notice. The step had reached the landing by this time. The visitor, whoever it was, paused there a moment, being in darkness, and uncertain, perhaps, of the position of the door; but in a little while I heard him move forward again, my mother's fragile form, clasped as it was in my embrace, quivering with each step he took, as though his weight stirred the house. He tapped at the door.

I had thought, while I listened and wondered, of more than one whom this might be: the leech, Simon Fleix, Madame de Bruhl, Fresnoy even. But as the tap came, and I felt my mother tremble in my arms, enlightenment came with it, and I pondered no more. I knew as well as if she had spoken and told me. There could be only one man whose presence had such power to terrify her, only one whose mere step, sounding through the veil, could drag her back to consciousness and fear! And that was the man who had beggared her, who had traded so long on her terrors.

I moved a little, intending to cross the floor softly, that when he opened the door he might find me face to face with him; but she detected the movement, and, love giving her strength, she clung to my wrist so fiercely that I had not the heart, knowing how slender was her hold on life and how near the brink she stood, to break from her. I constrained myself to stand still, though every muscle grew tense as a drawn bowstring, and I felt the strong rage rising in my throat and choking me as I waited for him to enter.

A log on the hearth gave way with a dull sound startling in the silence. The man tapped again, and getting no answer, for neither of us spoke, pushed the door slowly open, uttering before he showed himself the words, '*Dieu vous bénisse!*' in a voice so low and smooth I shuddered at the sound. The next moment he came in and saw me, and, starting, stood at gaze, his head thrust slightly forward, his shoulders bent, his hand still on the latch, amazement and frowning spite in turn distorting his lean face. He had looked to find a weak, defenceless woman, whom he could torture and rob at his will; he saw instead a strong man armed, whose righteous anger he must have been blind indeed had he failed to read.

Strangest thing of all, we had met before! I knew him at once—he me. He was the same Jacobin monk whom I had seen at the inn on the Clain, and who had told me the news of Guise's death.

I uttered an exclamation of surprise on making this discovery, and my mother, freed suddenly, as it seemed, from the spell of fear, which had given her unnatural strength, sank back on her bed. Her grasp relaxed, and her breath came and went with so loud a rattle that I removed my gaze from him, and bent over her, full of concern and solicitude. Our eyes met. She tried to speak, and at last gasped, 'Not now, Gaston! Let him—let him—'

Her lips framed the word 'go,' but she could not give it sound. I understood, however, and in impotent wrath I waved my hand to him to begone. When I looked up he had already obeyed me. He had seized the first opportunity to escape. The door was closed, the lamp burned steadily, and we were alone.

I gave her a little Armagnac, which stood beside the bed for such an occasion, and she revived, and presently opened her eyes. But I saw at once a great change in her. The look of fear had passed altogether from her face, and one of sorrow, yet content, had taken its place. She laid her hand in mine, and looked up at me, being too weak, as I thought, to speak. But by-and-by, when the strong spirit had done its work, she signed to me to lower my head to her mouth.

'The King of Navarre,' she murmured—'you are sure, Gaston—he will retain you in your—employments?'

Her pleading eyes were so close to mine, I felt no scruples such as some might have felt, seeing her so near death; but I answered firmly and cheerfully, 'Madame, I am assured of it. There is no prince in Europe so trustworthy or so good to his servants.'

She sighed with infinite content, and blessed him in a feeble whisper. 'And if you live,' she went on, 'you will rebuild the old house, Gaston. The walls are sound yet. And the oak in the hall was not burned. There is a chest of linen at Gil's, and a chest with your father's gold lace—but that is pledged,' she added dreamily. 'I forgot.'

'Madame,' I answered solemnly, 'it shall be done—it shall be done as you wish, if the power lie with me.'

She lay for some time after that murmuring prayers, her head supported on my shoulder. I longed impatiently for the nurse to return, that I might despatch her for the leech; not that I thought anything could be done, but for my own comfort and greater satisfaction afterwards, and that my mother might not die without some fitting attendance. The house remained quiet, however, with that impressive quietness which sobers the heart at such times, and I could not do this. And about six o'clock my mother opened her eyes again.

'This is not Marsac,' she murmured abruptly, her eyes roving from the ceiling to the wall at the foot of the bed.

'No, Madame,' I answered, leaning over her, 'you are in Blois. But I am here—Gaston, your son.'

She looked at me, a faint smile of pleasure stealing over her pinched face. 'Twelve thousand livres a year,' she whispered, rather to herself than to me, 'and an establishment, reduced a little, yet creditable, very creditable.' For a moment she seemed to be dying in my arms, but again opened her eyes quickly and looked me in the face. 'Gaston?' she said, suddenly and strangely. 'Who said Gaston? He is with the King—I have blessed him; and his days shall be long in the land!' Then, raising herself in my arms with a last effort of strength, she cried loudly, 'Way there! Way for my son, the Sieur de Marsac!'

They were her last words. When I laid her down on the bed a moment later, she was dead, and I was alone.

Madame de Bonne, my mother, was seventy at the time of her death, having survived my father eighteen years. She was Marie de Roche de Loheac, third daughter of Raoul, Sieur de Loheac, on the Vilaine, and by her great-grandmother, a daughter of Jean de Laval, was descended from the ducal family of Rohan, a relationship which in after-times, and under greatly altered circumstances, Henry Duke of Rohan condescended to acknowledge, honouring me with his friendship on more occasions than one. Her death, which I have here recorded, took place on the fourth of January, the Queen-mother of France, Catherine de Medicis, dying a little after noon on the following day.

In Blois, as in every other town, even Paris itself, the Huguenots possessed at this time a powerful organisation; and with the aid of the surgeon, who showed me much respect in my bereavement, and exercised in my behalf all the influence which skilful and honest men of his craft invariably possess, I was able to arrange for my mother's burial in a private ground about a league beyond the walls and near the village of Chaverny. At the time of her death I had only thirty crowns in gold remaining, Simon Fleix, to whose fate I could obtain no clue, having carried off thirty-five with the horses. The whole of this residue, however, with the exception of a handsome gratuity to the nurse and a trifle spent on my clothes, I expended on the funeral, desiring that no stain should rest on my mother's birth or my affection. Accordingly, though the ceremony was of necessity private, and indeed secret, and the mourners were few, it lacked nothing, I think, of the decency and propriety which my mother loved; and which she preferred, I have often heard her say, to the vulgar show that is equally at the command of the noble and the farmer of taxes.

Until she was laid in her quiet resting-place I stood in constant fear of some interruption on the part either of Bruhl, whose connection with Fresnoy and the abduction I did not doubt, or of the Jacobin monk. But none came; and nothing happening to enlighten me as to the fate of Mademoiselle de la Vire, I saw my duty clear before me. I disposed of the furniture of my mother's room, and indeed of everything which was saleable, and raised in this way enough money to buy myself a new cloak—without which I could not travel in the wintry weather—and to hire a horse. Sorry as the animal was, the dealer required security, and I had none to offer. It was only at the last moment I bethought me of the fragment of gold chain which mademoiselle had left behind her, and which, as well as my mother's rings and vinaigrette, I had kept back from the sale. This I was forced to lodge with him. Having thus, with some pain and more humiliation, provided means for the journey, I lost not an hour in beginning it. On the eighth of January I set out for Rosny, to carry the news of my ill-success and of mademoiselle's position whither I had looked a week before to carry herself.

# 12

# Maximilian de Bethune, Baron de Rosny

I looked to make the journey to Rosny in two days. But the heaviness of the roads and the sorry condition of my hackney hindered me so greatly that I lay the second night at Dreux, and, hearing the way was still worse between that place and my destination, began to think that I should be fortunate if I reached Rosny by the following noon. The country in this part seemed devoted to the League, the feeling increasing in violence as I approached the Seine. I heard nothing save abuse of the King of France and praise of the Guise princes, and had much ado, keeping a still tongue and riding modestly, to pass without molestation or inquiry.

Drawing near to Rosny, on the third morning, through a low marshy country covered with woods and alive with game of all kinds, I began to occupy myself with thoughts of the reception I was likely to encounter; which, I conjectured, would be none of the most pleasant. The daring and vigour of the Baron de Rosny, who had at this time the reputation of being in all parts of France at once, and the familiar terms on which he was known to live with the King of Navarre, gave me small reason to hope that he would listen with indulgence to such a tale as I had to tell. The nearer I came to the hour of telling it, indeed, the more improbable seemed some of its parts, and the more glaring my own carelessness in losing the token, and in letting mademoiselle out of my sight in such a place as Blois. I saw this so clearly now, and more clearly as the morning advanced, that I do not know that I ever anticipated anything with more fear than this explanation; which it yet seemed my duty to offer with all reasonable speed. The morning was warm, I remember; cloudy, yet not dark; the air near at hand full of moisture and very clear, with a circle of mist rising some way off, and filling the woods with blue distances. The road was deep and founderous, and as I was obliged to leave it from time to time in order to pass the worst places, I presently began to fear that I had strayed into a by-road. After advancing some distance, in doubt whether I should persevere or turn back, I was glad to see before me a small house placed at the junction of several woodland paths. From the bush which hung over the door, and a water-trough which stood beside it, I judged the place to be an inn; and determining to get my horse fed before I went farther, I rode up to the door and rapped on it with my riding-switch.

The position of the house was so remote that I was surprised to see three or four heads thrust immediately out of a window. For a moment I thought I should have done better to have passed by; but the landlord coming out very civilly, and leading the way to a shed beside the house, I reflected that I had little to lose, and followed him. I found, as I expected, four horses tied up in the shed, the bits hanging round their necks and their girths loosed; while my surprise was not lessened by the arrival, before I had fastened up my own horse, of a sixth rider, who, seeing us by the shed, rode up to us, and saluted me as he dismounted.

He was a tall, strong man in the prime of youth, wearing a plain, almost mean suit of dust-coloured leather, and carrying no weapons except a hunting-knife, which hung in a sheath at his girdle. He rode a powerful silver-roan horse, and was splashed to the top of his high untanned boots, as if he had come by the worst of paths, if by any.

He cast a shrewd glance at the landlord as he led his horse into the shed; and I judged from his brown complexion and quick eyes that he had seen much weather and lived an out-of-door life.

He watched me somewhat curiously while I mixed the fodder for my horse; and when I went into the house and sat down in the first room I came to, to eat a little bread-and-cheese which I had in my pouch, he joined me almost immediately. Apparently he could not stomach my poor fare, however, for after watching me for a time in silence, switching his boot with his whip the while, he called the landlord, and asked him, in a masterful way, what fresh meat he had, and particularly if he had any lean collops, or a fowl.

The fellow answered that there was nothing. His honour could have some Lisieux cheese, he added, or some stewed lentils.

'His honour does not want cheese,' the stranger answered peevishly, 'nor lentil porridge. And what is this I smell, my friend?' he continued, beginning suddenly to sniff with vigour. 'I swear I smell cooking.'

'It is the hind-quarter of a buck, which is cooking for the four gentlemen of the Robe; with a collop or two to follow,' the landlord explained; and humbly excused himself on the ground that the gentlemen had strictly engaged it for their own eating.

'What? A whole quarter! *and* a collop or two to

follow!' the stranger retorted, smacking his lips. 'Who are they?'

'Two advocates and their clerks from the Parliament of Paris. They have been viewing a boundary near here, and are returning this afternoon,' the landlord answered.

'No reason why they should cause a famine!' ejaculated the stranger with energy. 'Go to them and say a gentleman, who has ridden far, and fasted since seven this morning, requests permission to sit at their table. A quarter of venison and a collop or two among four!' he continued, in a tone of extreme disgust. 'It is intolerable! And advocates! Why, at that rate, the King of France should eat a whole buck, and rise hungry! Don't you agree with me, sir?' he continued, turning on me and putting the question abruptly.

He was so comically and yet so seriously angry, and looked so closely at me as he spoke, that I hastened to say I agreed with him perfectly.

'Yet you eat cheese, sir!' he retorted irritably.

I saw that, notwithstanding the simplicity of his dress, he was a gentleman, and so, forbearing to take offence, I told him plainly that my purse being light I travelled rather as I could than as I would.

'Is it so?' he answered hastily. 'Had I known that, I would have joined you in the cheese! After all, I would rather fast with a gentleman, than feast with a churl. But it is too late now. Seeing you mix the fodder, I thought your pockets were full.'

'The nag is tired, and has done its best,' I answered.

He looked at me curiously, and as though he would say more. But the landlord returning at that moment, he turned to him instead.

'Well!' he said briskly. 'Is it all right?'

'I am sorry, your honour,' the man answered, reluctantly, and with a very downcast air, 'but the gentlemen beg to be excused.'

'Zounds!' cried my companion roundly. 'They do, do they?'

'They say they have no more, sir,' the landlord continued,

faltering, 'than enough for themselves and a little dog they have with them.'

A shout of laughter which issued at that moment from the other room seemed to show that the quartet were making merry over my companion's request. I saw his cheek redden, and looked for an explosion of anger on his part; but instead he stood a moment in thought in the middle of the floor, and then, much to the innkeeper's relief, pushed a stool towards me, and called for a bottle of the best wine. He pleasantly begged leave to eat a little of my cheese, which he said looked better than the Lisieux, and, filling my glass with wine, fell to as merrily as if he had never heard of the party in the other room.

I was more than a little surprised, I remember; for I had taken him to be a passionate man, and not one to sit down under an affront. Still I said nothing, and we conversed very well together. I noticed, however, that he stopped speaking more than once, as though to listen; but conceiving that he was merely reverting to the party in the other room, who grew each moment more uproarious, I said nothing, and was completely taken by surprise when he rose on a sudden, and, going to the open window, leaned out, shading his eyes with his hand.

'What is it?' I said, preparing to follow him.

He answered by a quiet chuckle. 'You shall see,' he added the next instant.

I rose, and going to the window looked out over his shoulder. Three men were approaching the inn on horseback. The first, a great burly, dark-complexioned man with fierce black eyes and a feathered cap, had pistols in his holsters and a short sword by his side. The other two, with the air of servants, were stout fellows, wearing green doublets and leather bree-ches. All three rode good horses, while a footman led two hounds after them in a leash. On seeing us they cantered forward, the leader waving his bonnet.

'Halt, there!' cried my companion, lifting up his voice when they were within a stone's throw of us. 'Maignan!'

'My lord?' answered he of the feather, pulling up on the instant.

'You will find six horses in the shed there,' the stranger cried in a voice of command. 'Turn out the four to the left as you go in. Give each a cut, and send it about its business!'

The man wheeled his horse before the words were well uttered, and crying obsequiously that 'it was done,' flung his reins to one of the other riders and disappeared in the shed, as if the order given him were the most commonplace one in the world.

The party in the other room, however, by whom all could be heard, were not slow to take the alarm. They broke into a shout of remonstrance, and one of their number, leaping from the window, asked with a very fierce air what the devil we meant. The others thrust out their faces, swollen and flushed with the wine they had drunk, and with many oaths backed up the question. Not feeling myself called upon to interfere, I prepared to see something diverting.

My companion, whose coolness surprised me, had all the air of being as little concerned as myself. He even persisted for a time in ignoring the angry lawyer, and, turning a deaf ear to all the threats and abuse with which the others assailed him, continued to look calmly at the prospect. Seeing this, and that nothing could move him, the man who had jumped through the window, and who seemed the most enterprising of the party, left us at last and ran towards the stalls. The aspect of the two serving-men, however, who rode up grinning, and made as if they would ride him down, determined him to return; which he did, pale with fury, as the last of the four horses clattered out, and after a puzzled look round trotted off at its leisure into the forest.

On this, the man grew more violent, as I have remarked frightened men do; so that at last the stranger condescended to notice him. 'My good sir,' he said coolly, looking at him through the window as if he had not seen him before, 'you annoy me. What is the matter?'

The fellow retorted with a vast amount of bluster, asking what the devil we meant by turning out his horses.

'Only to give you and the gentlemen with you a little exercise,' my companion answered, with grim humour, and in a severe tone strange in one so young—'than which nothing is more wholesome after a full meal. That, and a lesson in good manners. Maignan,' he continued, raising his voice, 'if this person has anything more to say, answer him. He is nearer your degree than mine.'

And leaving the man to slink away like a whipped dog—for the mean are ever the first to cringe—my friend turned from the window. Meeting my eyes as he went back to his seat, he laughed. 'Well,' he said, 'what do you think?'

'That the ass in the lion's skin is very well till it meets the lion,' I answered.

He laughed again, and seemed pleased, as I doubt not he was. 'Pooh, pooh!' he said. 'It passed the time, and I think I am quits with my gentlemen now. But I must be riding. Possibly our roads may lie for a while in the same direction, sir?' And he looked at me irresolutely.

I answered cautiously that I was going to the town of Rosny.

'You are not from Paris?' he continued, still looking at me.

'No,' I answered. 'I am from the south.'

'From Blois, perhaps?'

I nodded.

'Ah!' he said, making no comment, which somewhat surprised me, all men at this time desiring news, and looking to Blois for it. 'I am riding towards Rosny also. Let us be going.'

But I noticed that as we got to horse, the man he called Maignan holding his stirrup with much formality, he turned and looked at me more than once with an expression in his eye which I could not interpret; so that, being in an enemy's country, where curiosity was a thing to be deprecated, I began to feel somewhat uneasy. However, as he presently gave way to a fit of laughter, and seemed to be digesting his late diversion at the inn, I thought no more of it, finding him excellent company and a man of surprising information.

Notwithstanding this my spirits began to flag as I approached Rosny; and as on such occasions nothing is more trying than the well-meant rallying of a companion ignorant of our trouble, I felt rather relief than regret when he drew rein at four cross-roads a mile or so short of the town, and, announcing that here our paths separated, took a civil leave of me, and went his way with his servants.

I dismounted at an inn at the extremity of the town, and, stopping only to arrange my dress and drink a cup of wine, asked the way to the château, which was situate, I learned, no more than a third of a mile away. I went thither on foot by way of an avenue of trees leading up to a drawbridge and gateway. The former was down, but the gates were closed, and all the formalities of a fortress in time of war were observed on my admission, though the garrison appeared to consist only of two or three serving-men and as many foresters. I had leisure after sending in my name to observe that the house was old and partly ruinous, but of great strength, covered in places with ivy, and closely surrounded by woods. A staid-looking page came presently to me, and led me up a narrow staircase to a parlour lighted by two windows, looking, one on to the courtyard, the other towards the town. Here a tall man was waiting to receive me, who rose on my entrance and came forward. Judge of my surprise when I recognised my acquaintance of the afternoon! 'M. de Rosny?' I exclaimed, standing still and looking at him in confusion.

'The same, sir,' he said, with a quiet smile. 'You come from the King of Navarre, I believe, and on an errand to me. You may speak openly. The king has no secrets from me.'

There was something in the gravity of his demeanour as he waited for me to speak which strongly impressed me; notwithstanding that he was ten years younger than myself, and I had seen him so lately in a lighter mood. I felt that his reputation had not belied him—that here was a great man;

and reflecting with despair on the inadequacy of the tale I had to tell him, I paused to consider in what terms I should begin. He soon put an end to this, however. 'Come, sir,' he said with impatience. 'I have told you that you may speak out. You should have been here four days ago, as I take it. Now you are here, where is the lady?'

'Mademoiselle de la Vire?' I stammered, rather to gain time than with any other object.

'Tut, tut!' he rejoined, frowning. 'Is there any other lady in the question? Come, sir, speak out. Where have you left her? This is no affair of gallantry,' he continued, the harshness of his demeanour disagreeably surprising me, 'that you need beat about the bush. The king entrusted to you a lady, who, I have no hesitation in telling you now, was in possession of certain State secrets. It is known that she escaped safely from Chizé and arrived safely at Blois. Where is she?'

'I would to Heaven I knew, sir!' I exclaimed in despair, feeling the painfulness of my position increased a hundredfold by his manner. 'I wish to God I did.'

'What is this?' he cried in a raised voice. 'You do not know where she is? You jest, M. de Marsac.'

'It were a sorry jest,' I answered, summoning up a rueful smile. And on that, plunging desperately into the story which I have here set down, I narrated the difficulties under which I had raised my escort, the manner in which I came to be robbed of the gold token, how mademoiselle was trepanned, the lucky chance by which I found her again, and the final disappointment. He listened, but listened throughout with no word of sympathy—rather with impatience, which grew at last into derisive incredulity. When I had done he asked me bluntly what I called myself.

Scarcely understanding what he meant, I repeated my name.

He answered, rudely and flatly, that it was impossible. 'I do not believe it, sir!' he repeated, his brow dark. 'You are not the man. You bring neither the lady nor the token, nor anything else by which I can test your story. Nay, sir, do not scowl at me,' he continued sharply. 'I am the mouthpiece of the King of Navarre, to whom this matter is of the highest importance. I cannot believe that the man whom he would choose would act so. This house you prate of in Blois, for instance, and the room with the two doors? What were you doing while mademoiselle was being removed?'

'I was engaged with the men of the house,' I answered, striving to swallow the anger which all but choked me. 'I did what I could. Had the door given way, all would have been well.'

He looked at me darkly. 'That is fine talking!' he said with a sneer. Then he dropped his eyes and seemed for a time to fall into a brown study, while I stood before him, confounded by this new view of the case, furious, yet not knowing how to vent my fury, cut to the heart by his insults, yet without hope or prospect of redress.

'Come!' he said harshly, after two or three minutes of gloomy reflection on his part and burning humiliation on mine, 'is there anyone here who can identify you, or in any other way confirm your story, sir? Until I know how the matter stands I can do nothing.'

I shook my head in sullen shame. I might protest against his brutality and this judgment of me, but to what purpose while he sheltered himself behind his master?

'Stay!' he said presently, with an abrupt gesture of remembrance. 'I had nearly forgotten. I have some here who have been lately at the King of Navarre's Court at Saint-Jean d'Angely. If you still maintain that you are the M. de Marsac to whom this commission was entrusted, you will doubtless have no objection to seeing them?'

On this I felt myself placed in a most cruel dilemma. If I refused to submit my case to the proposed ordeal, I stood an impostor confessed. If I consented to see these strangers, it was probable they would not recognise me, and possible that they might deny me in terms calculated to make my position even worse, if that might be. I hesitated; but, Rosny standing inexorable before me awaiting an answer, I finally consented.

'Good!' he said curtly. 'This way, if you please. They are here. The latch is tricky. Nay, sir, it is my house.'

Obeying the stern motion of his hand, I passed before him into the next room, feeling myself more humiliated than I can tell by this reference to strangers. For a moment I could see no one. The day was waning, the room I entered was long and narrow, and illuminated only by a glowing fire. Besides I was myself, perhaps, in some embarrassment. I believed that my conductor had made a mistake, or that his guests had departed, and I turned towards him to ask for an explanation. He merely pointed onwards, however, and I advanced; whereupon a young and handsome lady, who had been seated in the shadow of the great fireplace, rose suddenly, as if startled, and stood looking at me, the glow of the burning wood falling on one side of her face and turning her hair to gold.

'Well!' M. de Rosny said, in a voice which sounded a little odd in my ears. 'You do not know madame, I think?'

I saw that she was a complete stranger to me, and bowed to her without speaking. The lady saluted me in turn ceremoniously and in silence.

'Is there no one else here who should know you?' M. de Rosny continued, in a tone almost of persiflage, and with the same change in his voice which had struck me before; but now it was more marked. 'If not, M. de Marsac, I am afraid — But first look round, look round, sir; I would not judge any man hastily.'

He laid his hand on my shoulder as he finished in a manner so familiar and so utterly at variance with his former bearing that I doubted if I heard or felt aright. Yet I looked mechanically at the lady, and seeing that her eyes glistened in the firelight, and that she gazed at me very kindly, I wondered still more; falling, indeed, into a very confusion of amazement. This was not lessened but augmented a hundredfold when, turning in obedience to the pressure of de Rosny's hand, I saw beside me, as if she had risen from the floor, another lady—no other than Mademoiselle de la Vire herself! She had that moment stepped out of the shadow of the great fireplace, which had hitherto hidden her, and stood before me curtseying prettily, with the same look on her face and in her eyes which madame's wore.

'Mademoiselle!' I muttered, unable to take my eyes from her.

'Mais oui, monsieur, mademoiselle,' she answered, curtseying lower, with the air of a child rather than a woman.

'Here?' I stammered, my mouth open, my eyes staring.

'Here, sir—thanks to the valour of a brave man,' she answered, speaking in a voice so low I scarcely heard her. And then, dropping her eyes, she stepped back into the shadow, as if either she had said too much already, or doubted her composure were she to say more. She was so radiantly dressed, she looked in the firelight more like a fairy than a woman, being of small and delicate proportions; and she seemed in my eyes so different a person, particularly in respect of the softened expression of her features, from the Mademoiselle de la Vire whom I had known and seen plunged in sloughs and bent to the saddle with fatigue, that I doubted still if I had seen aright, and was as far from enlightenment as before.

It was M. de Rosny himself who relieved me from the embarrassment I was suffering. He embraced me in the most kind and obliging manner, and this more than once; begging me to pardon the deception he had practised upon me, and to which he had been impelled partly by the odd nature of our introduction at the inn, and partly by his desire to enhance the joyful surprise he had in store for me. 'Come,' he said presently, drawing me to the window, 'let me show you some more of your old friends.'

I looked out, and saw below me in the courtyard my three horses drawn up in a row, the Cid being bestridden by Simon Fleix, who, seeing me, waved a triumphant greeting. A groom stood at the head of each horse, and on either side was a man with a torch. My companion laughed gleefully. 'It was Maignan's arrangement,' he said. 'He has a quaint taste in such things.'

After greeting Simon Fleix a hundred times, I turned back into the room, and, my heart overflowing with gratitude and wonder, I begged M. de Rosny to acquaint me with the details of mademoiselle's escape.

'It was the most simple thing in the world,' he said, taking me by the hand and leading me back to the hearth. 'While you were engaged with the rascals, the old woman who daily brought mademoiselle's food grew alarmed at the uproar, and came into the room to learn what it was. Mademoiselle, unable to help you, and uncertain of your success, thought the opportunity too good to be lost. She forced the old woman to show her and her maid the way out through the garden. This done, they ran down a lane, as I understand, and came immediately upon the lad with the horses, who recognised them and helped them to mount. They waited some minutes for you, and then rode off.'

'But I inquired at the gate,' I said.

'At which gate?' inquired M de Rosny, smiling.

'The North-gate, of course,' I answered.

'Just so,' he rejoined with a nod. 'But they went out through the West-gate and made a circuit. He is a strange lad, that of yours below there. He has a head on his shoulder, M. de Marsac. Well, two leagues outside the town they halted, scarcely knowing how to proceed. By good fortune, however, a horse-dealer of my acquaintance was at the inn. He knew Mademoiselle de la Vire, and, hearing whither she was bound, brought her hither without let or hindrance.'

'Was he a Norman?' I asked.

M. de Rosny nodded, smiling at me shrewdly. 'Yes,' he said, 'he told me much about you. And now let me introduce you to my wife, Madame de Rosny.'

He led me up to the lady who had risen at my entrance, and who now welcomed me as kindly as she had before looked on me, paying me many pleasant compliments. I gazed at her with interest, having heard much of her beauty and of the strange manner in which M. de Rosny, being enamoured of two young ladies, and chancing upon both while lodging in different apartments at an inn, had decided which he should visit and make his wife. He appeared to read what was in my mind, for as I bowed before her, thanking her for the obliging things which she had uttered, and which for ever bound me to her service, he gaily pinched her ear, and said, 'When you want a good wife, M. de Marsac, be sure you turn to the right.'

He spoke in jest, and having his own case only in his mind. But I, looking mechanically in the direction he indicated, saw mademoiselle standing a pace or two to my right in the shadow of the great chimney-piece. I know not whether she frowned more or blushed more; but this for certain, that she answered my look with one of sharp displeasure, and, turning her back on me, swept quickly from the room, with no trace in her bearing of that late tenderness and gratitude which I had remarked.

# 13

# At Rosny

The morning brought only fresh proofs of the kindness which M. de Rosny had conceived for me. Awaking early I found on a stool beside my clothes, a purse of gold containing a hundred crowns; and a youth presently entering to ask me if I lacked anything, I had at first some difficulty in recognising Simon Fleix, so sprucely was the lad dressed, in a mode resembling Maignan's. I looked at the student more than once before I addressed him by his name; and was as much surprised by the strange change I observed in him— for it was not confined to his clothes—as by anything which had happened since I entered the house. I rubbed my eyes, and asked what he had done with his soutane.

'Burned it, M. de Marsac,' he answered briefly.

I saw that he had burned much, metaphorically speaking,

beside his soutane. He was less pale, less lank, less woebegone than formerly, and went more briskly. He had lost the air of crack-brained disorder which had distinguished him, and was smart, sedate, and stooped less. Only the odd sparkle remained in his eyes, and bore witness to the same nervous, eager spirit within.

'What are you going to do, then, Simon?' I asked, noting these changes curiously.

'I am a soldier,' he answered, 'and follow M. de Marsac.'

I laughed. 'You have chosen a poor service, I am afraid,' I said, beginning to rise; 'and one, too, Simon, in which it is possible you may be killed. I thought that would not suit you,' I continued, to see what he would say. But he answered nothing, and I looked at him in great surprise. 'You have made up your mind, then, at last?' I said.

'Perfectly,' he answered.

'And solved all your doubts?'

'I have no doubts.'

'You are a Huguenot?'

'That is the only true and pure religion,' he replied gravely. And with apparent sincerity and devotion he repeated Beza's Confession of Faith.

This filled me with profound astonishment, but I said no more at the time, though I had my doubts. I waited until I was alone with M. de Rosny, and then I unbosomed myself on the matter; expressing my surprise at the suddenness of the conversion, and at such a man, as I had found the student to be, stating his views so firmly and steadfastly, and with so little excitement. Observing that M. de Rosny smiled but answered nothing, I explained myself farther.

'I am surprised,' I said, 'because I have always heard it maintained that clerkly men, becoming lost in the mazes of theology, seldom find any sure footing; that not one in a hundred returns to his old faith, or finds grace to accept a new one. I am speaking only of such, of course, as I believe this lad to be—eager, excitable brains, learning much, and without judgment to digest what they learn.'

'Of such I also believe it to be true,' M. de Rosny answered, still smiling. 'But even on them a little influence, applied at the right moment, has much effect, M. de Marsac.'

'I allow that,' I said. 'But my mother, of whom I have spoken to you, saw much of this youth. His fidelity to her was beyond praise. Yet her faith, though grounded on a rock, had no weight with him.'

M. de Rosny shook his head, still smiling.

'It is not our mothers who convert us,' he said.

'What!' I cried, my eyes opened. 'Do you mean—do you mean that mademoiselle has done this?'

'I fancy so,' he answered, nodding. 'I think my lady cast her spell over him by the way. The lad left Blois with her, if what you say be true, without faith in the world. He came to my hands two days later the stoutest of Huguenots. It is not hard to read this riddle.'

'Such conversions are seldom lasting,' I said.

He looked at me queerly; and, the smile still hovering about his lips, answered, 'Tush, man! Why so serious? Theodore Beza himself could not look dryer. The lad is in earnest, and there is no harm done.'

And, Heaven knows, I was in no mood to suspect harm; nor inclined just then to look at the dark side of things. It may be conceived how delightful it was to me to be received as an equal and honoured guest by a man, even then famous, and now so grown in reputation as to overshadow all Frenchmen save his master; how pleasant to enjoy the comforts and amiabilities of home, from which I had been long estranged; to pour my mother's story into madame's ears and find comfort in her sympathy; to feel myself, in fine, once more a gentleman with an acknowledged place in the world. Our days we spent in hunting, or excursions of some kind, our evenings in long conversations, which impressed me with an ever-growing respect for my lord's powers.

For there seemed to be no end either to his knowledge of France, or to the plans for its development, which even then filled his brain, and have since turned wilderness into fruitful lands, and squalid towns into great cities. Grave and formal, he could yet unbend; the most sagacious of counsellors, he was a soldier also, and loved the seclusion in which we lived the more that it was not devoid of danger; the neighbouring towns being devoted to the League, and the general disorder alone making it possible for him to lie unsuspected in his own house.

One thing only rendered my ease and comfort imperfect, and that was the attitude which Mademoiselle de la Vire assumed towards me. Of her gratitude in the first blush of the thing I felt no doubt, for not only had she thanked me very prettily, though with reserve, on the evening of my arrival, but the warmth of M. de Rosny's kindness left me no choice, save to believe that she had given him an exaggerated idea of my merits and services. I asked no more than this. Such good offices left me nothing to expect or desire; my age and ill-fortune placing me at so great a disadvantage that, far from dreaming of friendship or intimacy with her, I did not even assume the equality in our daily intercourse to which my birth, taken by itself, entitled me. Knowing that I must appear in her eyes old, poor, and ill-dressed, and satisfied with having asserted my conduct and honour, I was careful not to trespass on her gratitude; and while forward in such courtesies as could not weary her, I avoided with equal care every appearance of pursuing her, or inflicting my company upon her. I addressed her formally and upon formal topics only, such, I mean, as we shared with the rest of our company; and reminded myself often that though we now met in the same house and at the same table, she was still the Mademoiselle de la Vire who had borne herself so loftily in the King of Navarre's ante-chamber. This I did, not out of pique or wounded pride, which I no more, God knows, harboured against her than against a bird; but that I might not in my new prosperity forget the light in which such a woman, young, spoiled, and beautiful, must still regard me.

Keeping to this inoffensive posture, I was the more hurt

when I found her gratitude fade with the hour. After the first two days, during which I remarked that she was very silent, seldom speaking to me or looking at me, she resumed much of her old air of disdain. For that I cared little; but she presently went farther, and began to rake up the incidents which had happened at Saint-Jean d'Angely, and in which I had taken part. She continually adverted to my poverty while there, to the odd figure I had cut, and the many jests her friends had made at my expense. She seemed to take a pleasure positively savage in these, gibing at me sometimes so bitterly as to shame and pain me, and bring the colour to Madame de Rosny's cheeks.

To the time we had spent together, on the other hand, she never or rarely referred. One afternoon, however, a week after my arrival at Rosny, I found her sitting alone in the parlour. I had not known she was there, and I was for withdrawing at once with a bow and a muttered apology. But she stopped me with an angry gesture. 'I do not bite,' she said, rising from her stool and meeting my eyes, a red spot in each cheek. 'Why do you look at me like that? Do you know, M. de Marsac, that I have no patience with you.' And she stamped her foot on the floor.

'But, mademoiselle,' I stammered humbly, wondering what in the world she meant, 'what have I done?'

'Done?' she repeated angrily. 'Done? It is not what you have done, it is what you are. I have no patience with you. Why are you so dull, sir? Why are you so dowdy? Why do you go about with your doublet awry, and your hair lank? Why do you speak to Maignan as if he were a gentleman? Why do you look always solemn and polite, and as if all the world were a prêche? Why? Why? Why, I say?'

She stopped from sheer lack of breath, leaving me as much astonished as ever in my life. She looked so beautiful in her fury and fierceness too, that I could only stare at her and wonder dumbly what it all meant.

'Well!' she cried impatiently, after bearing this as long as she could, 'have you not a word to say for yourself? Have you no tongue? Have you no will of your own at all, M. de Marsac?'

'But, mademoiselle,' I began, trying to explain.

'Chut!' she exclaimed, cutting me short before I could get farther, as the way of women is. And then she added, in a changed tone, and very abruptly, 'You have a velvet knot of mine, sir. Give it me.'

'It is in my room,' I answered, astonished beyond measure at this sudden change of subject, and equally sudden demand.

'Then fetch it, sir, if you please,' she replied, her eyes flashing afresh. 'Fetch it. Fetch it, I say! It has served its turn, and I prefer to have it. Who knows but that some day you may be showing it for a love-knot?'

'Mademoiselle!' I cried, hotly. And I think that for the moment I was as angry as she was.

'Still, I prefer to have it,' she answered sullenly, casting down her eyes.

I was so much enraged, I went without a word and fetched it, and, bringing it to her where she stood, in the same place, put it into her hands. When she saw it some recollection, I fancy, of the day when she had traced the cry for help on it, came to her in her anger; for she took it from me with all her bearing altered. She trembled, and held it for a moment in her hands, as if she did not know what to do with it. She was thinking, doubtless, of the house in Blois and the peril she had run there; and, being for my part quite willing that she should think and feel how badly she had acted, I stood looking at her, sparing her no whit of my glance.

'The gold chain you left on my mother's pillow,' I said coldly, seeing she continued silent, 'I cannot return to you at once, for I have pledged it. But I will do so as soon as I can.'

'You have pledged it?' she muttered, with her eyes averted.

'Yes, mademoiselle, to procure a horse to bring me here,' I replied drily. 'However, it shall be redeemed. In return, there is something I too would ask.'

'What?' she murmured, recovering herself with an effort,

and looking at me with something of her old pride and defiance.

'The broken coin you have,' I said. 'The token, I mean. It is of no use to you, for your enemies hold the other half. It might be of service to me.'

'How?' she asked curtly.

'Because some day I may find its fellow, mademoiselle.'

'And then?' she cried. She looked at me, her lips parted, her eyes flashing. 'What then, when you have found its fellow, M. de Marsac?'

I shrugged my shoulders.

'Bah!' she exclaimed, clenching her little hand, and stamping her foot on the floor, in a passion I could not understand. 'That is you! That is M. de Marsac all over. You say nothing, and men think nothing of you. You go with your hat in your hand, and they tread on you. They speak, and you are silent! Why, if I could use a sword as you can, I would keep silence before no man, nor let any man save the King of France cock his hat in my presence! But you! There! Go, leave me. Here is your coin. Take it and go. Send me that lad of yours to keep me awake. At any rate he has brains, he is young, he is a man, he has a soul, he can feel—if he were anything but a clerk.'

She waved me off in such a wind of passion as might have amused me in another, but in her smacked so strongly of ingratitude as to pain me not a little. I went, however, and sent Simon to her; though I liked the errand very ill, and no better when I saw the lad's face light up at the mention of her name. But apparently she had not recovered her temper when he reached her, for he fared no better than I had done; coming away presently with the air of a whipped dog, as I saw from the yew-tree walk where I was strolling.

Still, after that she made it a habit to talk to him more and more; and, Monsieur and Madame de Rosny being much taken up with one another, there was no one to check her fancy or speak a word of advice. Knowing her pride, I had no fears for her; but it grieved me to think that the lad's head should be turned. A dozen times I made up my mind to speak to her on his behalf; but for one thing it was not my business, and for another I soon discovered that she was aware of my displeasure, and valued it not a jot. For venturing one morning, when she was in a pleasant humour, to hint that she treated those beneath her too inhumanly, and with an unkindness as little becoming noble blood as familiarity, she asked me scornfully if I did not think she treated Simon Fleix well enough. To which I had nothing to answer.

I might here remark on the system of secret intelligence by means of which M. de Rosny, even in this remote place, received news of all that was passing in France. But it is common fame. There was no coming or going of messengers, which would quickly have aroused suspicion in the neighbouring town, nor was it possible for me to say exactly by what channels news came. But come it did, and at all hours of the day. In this way we heard of the danger of La Ganache and of the effort contemplated by the King of Navarre for its relief. M. de Rosny not only communicated these matters to me without reserve, but engaged my affections by farther proofs of confidence such as might well have flattered a man of greater importance.

I have said that, as a rule, there was no coming or going of messengers. But one evening, returning from the chase with one of the keepers, who had prayed my assistance in hunting down a crippled doe, I was surprised to find a strange horse, which had evidently been ridden hard and far, standing smoking in the yard. Inquiring whose it was, I learned that a man believed by the grooms to be from Blois had just arrived and was closeted with the baron. An event so far out of the ordinary course of things naturally aroused my wonder; but desiring to avoid any appearance of curiosity, which, if indulged, is apt to become the most vulgar of vices, I refrained from entering the house, and repaired instead to the yew-walk. I had scarcely, however, heated my blood, a little chilled with riding, before the page came to me to fetch me to his master.

I found M. de Rosny striding up and down his room, his manner so disordered and his face disfigured by so much grief and horror that I started on seeing him. My heart sinking in a moment, I did not need to look at Madame, who sat weeping silently in a chair, to assure myself that something dreadful had happened. The light was failing, and a lamp had been brought into the room. M. de Rosny pointed abruptly to a small piece of paper which lay on the table beside it, and, obeying his gestures, I took this up and read its contents, which consisted of less than a score of words.

'He is ill and like to die,' the message ran, 'twenty leagues south of La Ganache. Come at all costs. P. M.'

'Who?' I said stupidly—stupidly, for already I began to understand. 'Who is ill and like to die?'

M. de Rosny turned to me, and I saw that the tears were trickling unbidden down his cheeks. 'There is but one *he* for me,' he cried. 'May God spare that one! May He spare him to France, which needs him, to the Church, which hangs on him, and to me, who love him! Let him not fall in the hour of fruition. O Lord, let him not fall!' And he sank on to a stool, and remained in that posture with his face in his hands, his broad shoulders shaken with grief.

'Come, sir,' I said, after a pause sacred to sorrow and dismay; 'let me remind you that while there is life there is hope.'

'Hope?'

'Yes, M. de Rosny, hope,' I replied more cheerfully. 'He has work to do. He is elected, called, and chosen; the Joshua of his people, as M. d'Amours rightly called him. God will not take him yet. You shall see him and be embraced by him, as has happened a hundred times. Remember, sir, the King of Navarre is strong, hardy, and young, and no doubt in good hands.'

'Mornay's,' M. de Rosny cried, looking up with contempt in his eye.

Yet from that moment he rallied, spurred, I think, by the

thought that the King of Navarre's recovery depended under God on M. du Mornay; whom he was ever inclined to regard as his rival. He began to make instant preparations for departure from Rosny, and bade me do so also, telling me, somewhat curtly and without explanation, that he had need of me. The danger of so speedy a return to the South, where the full weight of the Vicomte de Turenne's vengeance awaited me, occurred to me strongly; and I ventured, though with a little shame, to mention it. But M. de Rosny, after gazing at me a moment in apparent doubt, put the objection aside with a degree of peevishness unusual in him, and continued to press on his arrangements as earnestly as though they did not include separation from a wife equally loving and beloved

Having few things to look to myself, I was at leisure, when the hour of departure came, to observe both the courage with which Madame de Rosny supported her sorrow, 'for the sake of France,' and the unwonted tenderness which Mademoiselle de la Vire, lifted for once above herself, lavished on her. I seemed to stand—happily in one light, and yet the feeling was fraught with pain—outside their familiar relations; yet, having made my adieux as short and formal as possible, that I might not encroach on other and more sacred ones, I found at the last moment something in waiting for me. I was surprised as I rode under the gateway a little ahead of the others, by something small and light falling on the saddle-bow before me. Catching it before it could slide to the ground, I saw, with infinite astonishment, that I held in my hand a tiny velvet bow.

To look up at the window of the parlour, which I have said was over the archway, was my first impulse. I did so, and met mademoiselle's eyes for a second, and a second only. The next moment she was gone. M. de Rosny clattered through the gate at my heels, the servants behind him. And we were on the road.

# 14

# M. de Rambouillet

For a while we were but a melancholy party. The incident I have last related—which seemed to admit of more explanations than one—left me in a state of the greatest perplexity; and this prevailed with me for a time, and was only dissipated at length by my seeing my own face, as it were, in a glass. For, chancing presently to look behind me, I observed that Simon Fleix was riding, notwithstanding his fine hat and feather and his new sword, in a posture and with an air of dejection difficult to exaggerate; whereon the reflection that master and man had the same object in their minds—nay, the thought that possibly he bore in his bosom a like token to that which lay warm in mine—occurring to me, I roused myself as from some degrading dream, and, shaking up the Cid, cantered forward to join Rosny, who, in no cheerful mood himself, was riding steadily forward, wrapped to his eyes in his cloak.

The news of the King of Navarre's illness had fallen on him, indeed, in the midst of his sanguine scheming with the force of a thunderbolt. He saw himself in danger of losing at once the master he loved and the brilliant future to which he looked forward; and amid the imminent crash of his hopes and the destruction of the system in which he lived, he had scarcely time to regret the wife he was leaving at Rosny or the quiet from which he was so suddenly called. His heart was in the South, at La Ganache, by Henry's couch. His main idea was to get there quickly at all risks. The name of the King of Navarre's physician was constantly on his lips. 'Dortoman is a good man. If anyone can save him, Dortoman will,' was his perpetual cry. And whenever he met anyone who had the least appearance of bearing news, he would have me stop and interrogate him, and by no means let the traveller go until he had given us the last rumour from Blois—the channel through which all the news from the South reached us.

An incident which occurred at the inn that evening cheered him somewhat; the most powerful minds being prone, I have observed, to snatch at omens in times of uncertainty. An elderly man, of strange appearance, and dressed in an affected and bizarre fashion, was seated at table when we arrived. Though I entered first in my assumed capacity of leader of the party, he let me pass before him without comment, but rose and solemnly saluted M. de Rosny, albeit the latter walked behind me and was much more plainly dressed. Rosny returned his greeting and would have passed on; but the stranger, interposing with a still lower bow, invited him to take his seat, which was near the fire and sheltered from the draught, at the same time making as if he would himself remove to another place.

'Nay,' said my companion, surprised by such an excess of courtesy, 'I do not see why I should take your place, sir.'

'Not mine only,' the old man rejoined, looking at him with a particularity and speaking with an emphasis which attracted our attention, 'but those of many others, who I can assure you will very shortly yield them up to you, whether they will or not.'

M. de Rosny shrugged his shoulders and passed on, affecting to suppose the old man wandered. But privately he thought much of his words, and more when he learned that he was an astrologer from Paris, who had the name, at any rate in this country, of having studied under Nostradamus. And whether he drew fresh hopes from this, or turned his attention more particularly as we approached Blois to present matters, certainly he grew more cheerful, and began again to discuss the future, as though assured of his master's recovery.

'You have never been to the king's Court?' he said presently, following up, as I judged, a train of thought in his own mind. 'At Blois, I mean.'

'No; nor do I feel anxious to visit it,' I answered. 'To tell you the truth, M. le Baron,' I continued with some warmth, 'the sooner we are beyond Blois, the better I shall be pleased. I think we run some risk there, and, besides, I do not fancy a shambles. I do not think I could see the king without thinking of the Bartholomew, nor his chamber without thinking of Guise.'

'Tut, tut!' he said, 'you have killed a man before now.'

'Many,' I answered.

'Do they trouble you?'

'No, but they were killed in fair fight,' I replied. 'That makes a difference.'

'To you,' he said drily. 'But you are not the King of France, you see. Should you ever come across him,' he continued, flicking his horse's ears, a faint smile on his lips, 'I will give you a hint. Talk to him of the battles at Jarnac and Moncontour, and praise your Condé's father! As Condé lost the fight and he won it, the compliment comes home to him. The more hopelessly a man has lost his powers, my friend, the more fondly he regards them, and the more highly he prizes the victories he can no longer gain.'

'Ugh!' I muttered.

'Of the two parties at Court,' Rosny continued, calmly overlooking my ill-humour, 'trust D'Aumont and Biron and the French clique. They are true to France at any rate. But whomsoever you see consort with the two Retzs—the King of Spain's jackals as men name them—avoid him for a Spaniard and a traitor.'

'But the Retzs are Italians,' I objected peevishly.

'The same thing,' he answered curtly. 'They cry, "*Vive le Roi!*" but privately they are for the League, or for Spain, or for whatever may most hurt us; who are better Frenchmen than themselves, and whose leader will some day, if God spare his life, be King of France.'

'Well, the less I have to do with the one or the other of them, save at the sword's point, the better I shall be pleased,' I rejoined.

On that he looked at me with a queer smile; as was his way when he had more in his mind than appeared. And this, and something special in the tone of his conversation, as well, perhaps, as my own doubts about my future and his intentions regarding me, gave me an uneasy feeling; which lasted through the day, and left me only when more immediate peril presently rose to threaten us.

It happened in this way. We had reached the outskirts of Blois, and were just approaching the gate, hoping to pass through it without attracting attention, when two travellers rode slowly out of a lane, the mouth of which we were passing. They eyed us closely as they reined in to let us go by; and M. de Rosny, who was riding with his horse's head at my stirrup, whispered me to press on. Before I could comply, however, the strangers cantered by us, and turning in the saddle when abreast of us looked us in the face. A moment later one of them cried loudly, 'It is he!' and both pulled their horses across the road, and waited for us to come up.

Aware that if M. de Rosny were discovered he would be happy if he escaped with imprisonment, the king being too jealous of his Catholic reputation to venture to protect a Huguenot, however illustrious, I saw that the situation was desperate; for, though we were five to two, the neighbourhood of the city—the gate being scarcely a bow-shot off—rendered flight or resistance equally hopeless. I could think of nothing for it save to put a bold face on the matter, and, M. de Rosny doing the same, we advanced in the most innocent way possible.

'Halt, there!' cried one of the strangers sharply. 'And let me tell you, sir, you are known.'

'What if I am?' I answered impatiently, still pressing on. 'Are you highwaymen, that you stop the way?'

The speaker on the other side looked at me keenly, but in a moment retorted, 'Enough trifling, sir! Who *you* are I do not know. But the person riding at your rein is M. de Rosny. Him I do know, and I warn him to stop.'

I thought the game was lost, but to my surprise my

companion answered at once and almost in the same words I had used. 'Well, sir, and what of that?' he said.

'What of that?' the stranger exclaimed, spurring his horse so as still to bar the way. 'Why, only this, that you must be a madman to show yourself on this side of the Loire.'

'It is long since I have seen the other,' was my companion's unmoved answer.

'You are M. de Rosny? You do not deny it?' the man cried in astonishment.

'Certainly I do not deny it,' M. de Rosny answered bluntly. 'And more, the day has been, sir,' he continued with sudden fire, 'when few at his Majesty's Court would have dared to chop words with Solomon de Bethune, much less to stop him on the highway within a mile of the palace. But times are changed with me, sir, and it would seem with others also, if true men rallying to his Majesty in his need are to be challenged by every passer on the road.'

'What! Are you Solomon de Bethune?' the man cried incredulously. Incredulously, but his countenance fell, and his voice was full of chagrin and disappointment.

'Who else, sir?' M. de Rosny replied haughtily. 'I am, and, as far as I know, I have as much right on this side of the Loire as any other man.'

'A thousand pardons.'

'If you are not satisfied—'

'Nay, M. de Rosny, I am perfectly satisfied.'

The stranger repeated this with a very crestfallen air, adding, 'A thousand pardons'; and fell to making other apologies, doffing his hat with great respect. 'I took you, if you will pardon me saying so, for your Huguenot brother, M. Maximilian,' he explained. 'The saying goes that he is at Rosny.'

'I can answer for that being false,' M. de Rosny answered peremptorily, 'for I have just come from there, and I will answer for it he is not within ten leagues of the place. And now, sir, as we desire to enter before the gates shut, perhaps you will excuse us.' With which he bowed, and I bowed, and they bowed, and we separated. They gave us the road, which M. de Rosny took with a great air, and we trotted to the gate, and passed through it without misadventure.

The first street we entered was a wide one, and my companion took advantage of this to ride up abreast of me. 'That is the kind of adventure our little prince is fond of,' he muttered. 'But for my part, M. de Marsac, the sweat is running down my forehead. I have played the trick more than once before, for my brother and I are as like as two peas. And yet it would have gone ill with us if the fool had been one of his friends.'

'All's well that ends well,' I answered in a low voice, thinking it an ill time for compliments. As it was, the remark was unfortunate, for M. de Rosny was still in the act of reining back when Maignan called out to us to say we were being followed.

I looked behind, but could see nothing except gloom and rain and overhanging eaves and a few figures cowering in doorways. The servants, however, continued to maintain that it was so, and we held, without actually stopping, a council of war. If detected, we were caught in a trap, without hope of escape; and for the moment I am sure M. de Rosny regretted that he had chosen this route by Blois — that he had thrust himself, in his haste and his desire to take with him the latest news, into a snare so patent. The castle—huge, dark, and grim—loomed before us at the end of the street in which we were, and, chilled as I was myself by the sight, I could imagine how much more appalling it must appear to him, the chosen counsellor of his master, and the steadfast opponent of all which it represented.

Our consultation came to nothing, for no better course suggested itself than to go as we had intended to the lodging commonly used by my companion. We did so, looking behind us often, and saying more than once that Maignan must be mistaken. As soon as we had dismounted, however, and gone in, he showed us from the window a man loitering near; and this confirmation of our alarm sending us to our expedients again, while Maignan remained watching in a room without a light, I suggested that I might pass myself off, though ten years older, for my companion.

'Alas!' he said, drumming with his fingers on the table, 'there are too many here who know me to make that possible. I thank you all the same.'

'Could you escape on foot? Or pass the wall anywhere, or slip through the gates early?' I suggested.

'They might tell us at the Bleeding Heart,' he answered. 'But I doubt it. I was a fool, sir, to put my neck into Mendoza's halter, and that is a fact. But here is Maignan. What is it, man?' he continued eagerly.

'The watcher is gone, my lord,' the equerry answered.

'And has left no one?'

'No one that I can see.'

We both went into the next room and looked from the windows. The man was certainly not where we had seen him before. But the rain was falling heavily, the eaves were dripping, the street was a dark cavern with only here and there a spark of light, and the fellow might be lurking elsewhere. Maignan, being questioned, however, believed he had gone off of set purpose.

'Which may be read half a dozen ways,' I remarked.

'At any rate, we are fasting,' M. de Rosny answered. 'Give me a full man in a fight. Let us sit down and eat. It is no good jumping in the dark, or meeting troubles half way.'

We were not through our meal, however, Simon Fleix waiting on us with a pale face, when Maignan came in again from the dark room. 'My lord,' he said quietly, 'three men have appeared. Two of them remain twenty paces away. The third has come to the door.'

As he spoke we heard a cautious summons below. Maignan was for going down, but his master bade him stand. 'Let the woman of the house go,' he said.

I remarked and long remembered M. de Rosny's *sangfroid* on this occasion. His pistols he had already laid on a chair beside him, throwing his cloak over them; and now, while we waited, listening in breathless silence, I saw him hand a large slice of bread-and-meat to his equerry, who, standing behind his chair, began eating it with the same coolness. Simon Fleix, on the other hand, stood gazing at the door, trembling in every limb, and with so much of excitement and surprise in his attitude that I took the precaution of bidding him, in a low voice, do nothing without orders. At the same moment it occurred to me to extinguish two of the four candles which had been lighted; and I did so, M. de Rosny nodding assent, just as the muttered conversation which was being carried on below ceased, and a man's tread sounded on the stairs.

It was followed immediately by a knock on the outside of our door. Obeying my companion's look, I cried, 'Enter!'

A slender man of middle height, booted and wrapped up, with his face almost entirely hidden by a fold of his cloak, came in quickly, and, closing the door behind him, advanced towards the table. 'Which is M. de Rosny?' he said.

Rosny had carefully turned his face from the light, but at the sound of the other's voice he sprang up with a cry of relief. He was about to speak, when the new-comer, raising his hand peremptorily, continued, 'No names, I beg. Yours, I suppose, is known here. Mine is not, nor do I desire it should be. I want speech of you, that is all.'

'I am greatly honoured,' M. de Rosny replied, gazing at him eagerly. 'Yet, who told you I was here?'

'I saw you pass under a lamp in the street,' the stranger answered. 'I knew your horse first, and you afterwards, and bade a groom follow you. Believe me,' he added, with a gesture of the hand, 'you have nothing to fear from me.'

'I accept the assurance in the spirit in which it is offered,' my companion answered with a graceful bow, 'and think myself fortunate in being recognised'—he paused a moment and then continued—'by a Frenchman and a man of honour.'

The stranger shrugged his shoulders. 'Your pardon, then,' he said, 'if I seem abrupt. My time is short. I want to do the best with it I can. Will you favour me?'

I was for withdrawing, but M. de Rosny ordered Maignan

to place lights in the next room, and, apologising to me very graciously, retired thither with the stranger, leaving me relieved indeed by these peaceful appearances, but full of wonder and conjectures who this might be, and what the visit portended. At one moment I was inclined to identify the stranger with M. de Rosny's brother; at another with the English ambassador; and then, again, a wild idea that he might be M. de Bruhl occurred to me. The two remained together about a quarter of an hour and then came out, the stranger leading the way, and saluting me politely as he passed through the room. At the door he turned to say, 'At nine o'clock, then?'

'At nine o'clock,' M. de Rosny replied, holding the door open. 'You will excuse me if I do not descend, Marquis?'

'Yes, go back, my friend,' the stranger answered. And, lighted by Maignan, whose face on such occasions could assume the most stolid air in the world, he disappeared down the stairs, and I heard him go out.

M. de Rosny turned to me, his eyes sparkling with joy, his face and mien full of animation. 'The King of Navarre is better,' he said. 'He is said to be out of danger. What do you think of that, my friend?'

'That is the best news I have heard for many a day,' I answered. And I hastened to add, that France and the Religion had reason to thank God for His mercy.

'Amen to that,' my patron replied reverently. 'But that is not all—that is not all.' And he began to walk up and down the room humming the 118th Psalm a little above his breath—

> *La voici l'heureuse journée*
> *Que Dieu a faite à plein désir;*
> *Par nous soit joie démenée,*
> *Et prenons en elle plaisir.*

He continued, indeed, to walk up and down the floor so long, and with so joyful a countenance and demeanour, that I ventured at last to remind him of my presence, which he had clearly forgotten. 'Ha! to be sure,' he said, stopping short and looking at me with the utmost good-humour. 'What time is it? Seven. Then until nine o'clock, my friend, I crave your indulgence. In fine, until that time I must keep counsel. Come, I am hungry still. Let us sit down, and this time I hope we may not be interrupted. Simon, set us on a fresh bottle. Ha! ha! *Vivent le Roi et le Roi de Navarre!*' And again he fell to humming the same psalm—

> *O Dieu éternel, je te prie,*
> *Je te prie, ton roi maintiens:*
> *O Dieu, je te prie reprie,*
> *Sauve ton roi et l'entretiens!*

doing so with a light in his eyes and a joyous emphasis, which impressed me the more in a man ordinarily so calm and self-contained. I saw that something had occurred to gratify him beyond measure, and, believing his statement that this was not the good news from La Ganache only, I waited with the utmost interest and anxiety for the hour of nine, which had no sooner struck than our former visitor appeared with the same air of mystery and disguise which had attended him before.

M. de Rosny, who had risen on hearing his step and had taken up his cloak, paused with it half on and half off, to cry anxiously, 'All is well, is it not?'

'Perfectly,' the stranger replied, with a nod.

'And my friend?'

'Yes, on condition that you answer for his discretion and fidelity.' And the stranger glanced involuntarily at me, who stood uncertain whether to hold my ground or retire.

'Good,' M. de Rosny cried. Then he turned to me with a mingled air of dignity and kindness, and continued: 'This is the gentleman. M. de Marsac, I am honoured with permission to present you to the Marquis de Rambouillet, whose interest and protection I beg you to deserve, for he is a true Frenchman and a patriot whom I respect.'

M. de Rambouillet saluted me politely. 'Of a Brittany family, I think?' he said.

I assented; and he replied with something complimentary. But afterwards he continued to look at me in silence with a keenness and curiosity I did not understand. At last, when M. de Rosny's impatience had reached a high pitch, the marquis seemed impelled to add something. 'You quite understand, M. de Rosny?' he said. 'Without saying anything disparaging of M. de Marsac, who is, no doubt, a man of honour'—and he bowed to me very low—'this is a delicate matter, and you will introduce no one into it, I am sure, whom you cannot trust as yourself.'

'Precisely,' M. de Rosny replied, speaking drily, yet with a grand air which fully matched his companion's. 'I am prepared to trust this gentleman not only with my life but with my honour.'

'Nothing more remains to be said then,' the marquis rejoined, bowing to me again. 'I am glad to have been the occasion of a declaration so flattering to you, sir.'

I returned his salute in silence, and obeying M. de Rosny's muttered direction put on my cloak and sword. M. de Rosny took up his pistols.

'You will have no need of those,' the marquis said with a high glance.

'Where we are going, no,' my companion answered, calmly continuing to dispose them about him. 'But the streets are dark and not too safe.'

M. de Rambouillet laughed. 'That is the worst of you Huguenots,' he said. 'You never know when to lay suspicion aside.'

A hundred retorts sprang to my lips. I thought of the Bartholomew, of the French fury of Antwerp, of half a dozen things which make my blood boil to this day. But M. de Rosny's answer was the finest of all. 'That is true, I am afraid,' he said quietly. 'On the other hand, you Catholics— take the late M. de Guise for instance—have the habit of erring on the other side, I think, and sometimes trust too far.'

The marquis, without making any answer to this home-thrust, led the way out, and we followed, being joined at the door of the house by a couple of armed lackeys, who fell in behind us. We went on foot. The night was dark, and the prospect out of doors was not cheering. The streets were wet and dirty, and notwithstanding all our care we fell continually into pitfalls or over unseen obstacles. Crossing the Parvis of the Cathedral, which I remembered, we plunged in silence into an obscure street near the river, and so narrow that the decrepit houses shut out almost all view of the sky. The gloom of our surroundings, no less than my ignorance of the errand on which we were bound, filled me with anxiety and foreboding. My companions keeping strict silence, however, and taking every precaution to avoid being recognised, I had no choice but to do likewise.

I could think, and no more. I felt myself borne along by an irresistible current, whither and for what purpose I could not tell; and experienced to an extent strange at my age the influence of the night and the weather. Twice we stood aside to let a party of roisterers go by, and the excessive care M. de Rambouillet evinced on these occasions to avoid recognition did not tend to reassure me or make me think more lightly of the unknown business on which I was bound.

Reaching at last an open space, our leader bade us in a low voice be careful and follow him closely. We did so, and crossed in this way and in single file a narrow plank or wooden bridge; but whether water ran below or a dry ditch only, I could not determine. My mind was taken up at the moment with the discovery which I had just made, that the dark building, looming huge and black before us with a single light twinkling here and there at great heights, was the Castle of Blois.

# 15

# Vilain Herodes

All the distaste and misliking I had expressed earlier in the day for the Court of Blois recurred with fresh force in the darkness and gloom; and though, booted and travel-stained as we were, I did not conceive it likely that we should be obtruded on the circle about the king, I felt nonetheless an oppressive desire to be through with our adventure, and away from the ill-omened precincts in which I found myself. The darkness prevented me seeing the faces of my companions; but on M. de Rosny, who was not quite free himself, I think, from the influences of the time and place, twitching my sleeve to enforce vigilance, I noted that the lackeys had ceased to follow us, and that we three were beginning to ascend a rough staircase cut in the rock. I gathered, though the darkness limited my view behind as well as in front to a few twinkling lights, that we were mounting the scarp from the moat to the side wall of the castle; and I was not surprised when the marquis muttered to us to stop, and knocked softly on the wood of a door.

M. de Rosny might have spared the touch he had laid on my sleeve, for by this time I was fully and painfully sensible of the critical position in which we stood, and was very little likely to commit an indiscretion. I trusted he had not done so already! No doubt—it flashed across me while we waited— he had taken care to safeguard himself. But how often, I reflected, had all safeguards been set aside and all precautions eluded by those to whom he was committing himself! Guise had thought himself secure in this very building, which we were about to enter. Coligny had received the most absolute of safe-conducts from those to whom we were apparently bound. The end in either case had been the same—the confidence of the one proving of no more avail than the wisdom of the other. What if the King of France thought to make his peace with his Catholic subjects—offended by the murder of Guise—by a second murder of one as obnoxious to them as he was precious to their arch-enemy in the South? Rosny was sagacious indeed; but then I reflected with sudden misgiving that he was young, ambitious, and bold.

The opening of the door interrupted without putting an end to this train of apprehension. A faint light shone out; so feebly as to illuminate little more than the stairs at our feet. The marquis entered at once, M. de Rosny followed, I brought up the rear; and the door was closed by a man who stood behind it. We found ourselves crowded together at the foot of a very narrow staircase, which the doorkeeper—a stolid pikeman in a grey uniform, with a small lanthorn swinging from the crosspiece of his halberd—signed to us to ascend. I said a word to him, but he only stared in answer, and M. de Rambouillet, looking back and seeing what I was about, called to me that it was useless, as the man was a Swiss and spoke no French.

This did not tend to reassure me; any more than did the chill roughness of the wall which my hand touched as I groped upwards, or the smell of bats which invaded my nostrils and suggested that the staircase was little used and belonged to a part of the castle fitted for dark and secret doings.

We stumbled in the blackness up the steps, passing one door and then a second before M. de Rambouillet whispered to us to stand, and knocked gently at a third.

The secrecy, the darkness, and above all the strange arrangements made to receive us, filled me with the wildest conjectures. But when the door opened and we passed one by one into a bare, unfurnished, draughty gallery, immediately, as I judged, under the tiles, the reality agreed with no one of my anticipations. The place was a mere garret, without a hearth, without a single stool. Three windows, of which one was roughly glazed, while the others were filled with oiled paper, were set in one wall; the others displaying the stones and mortar without disguise or ornament. Beside the door through which we had entered stood a silent figure in the grey uniform I had seen below, his lanthorn on the floor at his feet. A second door at the farther end of the gallery, which was full twenty paces long, was guarded in like manner. A couple of lanthorns stood in the middle of the floor, and that was all.

Inside the door, M. de Rambouillet with his finger on his lip stopped us, and we stood a little group of three a pace in front of the sentry, and with the empty room before us. I looked at M. de Rosny, but he was looking at Rambouillet. The marquis had his back towards me, the sentry was gazing into vacancy; so that baffled in my attempt to learn anything from the looks of the other actors in the scene, I fell back on my ears. The rain dripped outside and the moaning wind rattled the casements; but mingled with these melancholy sounds—which gained force, as such things always do, from the circumstances in which we were placed and our own silence—I fancied I caught the distant hum of voices and music and laughter. And that, I know not why, brought M. de Guise again to my mind.

The story of his death, as I had heard it from that accursed monk in the inn on the Clain, rose up in all its freshness, with all its details. I started when M. de Rambouillet coughed. I shivered when Rosny shifted his feet. The silence grew oppressive. Only the stolid men in grey seemed unmoved, unexpectant; so that I remember wondering whether it was their nightly duty to keep guard over an empty garret, the floor strewn with scraps of mortar and ends of tiles.

The interruption, when it came at last, came suddenly. The sentry at the farther end of the gallery started and fell back a pace. Instantly the door beside him opened and a man came in, and closing it quickly behind him, advanced up the room with an air of dignity, which even his strange appearance and attire could not wholly destroy.

He was of good stature and bearing, about forty years old as I judged, his wear a dress of violet velvet with black points cut in the extreme of the fashion. He carried a sword but no ruff, and had a cup and ball of ivory—a strange toy much in vogue among the idle—suspended from his wrist by a ribbon. He was lean and somewhat narrow, but so far I found little fault with him. It was only when my eye reached his face, and saw it rouged like a woman's and surmounted by a little turban, that a feeling of scarcely understood disgust seized me, and I said to myself, 'This is the stuff of which kings' minions are made!'

To my surprise, however, M. de Rambouillet went to meet him with the utmost respect, sweeping the dirty floor with his bonnet, and bowing to the very ground. The new-comer acknowledged his salute with negligent kindness. Remarking pleasantly 'You have brought a friend, I think?' he looked towards us with a smile.

'Yes, sire, he is here,' the marquis answered, stepping aside a little. And with the word I understood that this was no minion, but the king himself: Henry, the Third of the name, and the last of the great House of Valois, which had ruled France by the grace of God for two centuries and a half! I stared at him, and stared at him, scarcely believing what I saw. For the first time in my life I was in the presence of the king!

Meanwhile M. de Rosny, to whom he was, of course, no marvel, had gone forward and knelt on one knee. The king raised him graciously, and with an action which, viewed apart from his woman's face and silly turban, seemed royal and fitting. 'This is good of you, Rosny,' he said. 'But it is only what I expected of you.'

'Sire,' my companion answered, 'your Majesty has no more devoted servant than myself, unless it be the king my master.'

'By my faith,' Henry answered with energy—'and if I am not a good churchman, whatever those rascally Parisians say, I am nothing—by my faith, I think I believe you!'

'If your Majesty would believe me in that and in some other things also,' M. de Rosny answered, 'it would be very well for France.' Though he spoke courteously, he threw so much weight and independence into his words that I thought of the old proverb, 'A good master, a bold servant.'

'Well, that is what we are here to see,' the king replied. 'But one tells me one thing,' he went on fretfully, 'and one another, and which am I to believe?'

'I know nothing of others, sire,' Rosny answered with the same spirit. 'But my master has every claim to be believed. His interest in the royalty of France is second only to your Majesty's. He is also a king and a kinsman, and it irks him to see rebels beard you, as has happened of late.'

'Ay, but the chief of them?' Henry exclaimed, giving way to sudden excitement and stamping furiously on the floor. 'He will trouble me no more. Has my brother heard of *that*? Tell me, sir, has that news reached him?'

'He has heard it, sire.'

'And he approved? He approved, of course?'

'Beyond doubt the man was a traitor,' M. de Rosny answered delicately. 'His life was forfeit, sire. Who can question it?'

'And he has paid the forfeit,' the king rejoined, looking down at the floor and immediately falling into a moodiness as sudden as his excitement. His lips moved. He muttered something inaudible, and began to play absently with his cup and ball, his mind occupied apparently with a gloomy retrospect. 'M. de Guise, M. de Guise,' he murmured at last, with a sneer and an accent of hate which told of old humiliations long remembered. 'Well, damn him, he is dead now. He is dead. But being dead he yet troubles us. Is not that the verse, father? Ha!' with a start, 'I was forgetting. But that is the worst wrong he has done me,' he continued, looking up and growing excited again. 'He has cut me off from Mother Church. There is hardly a priest comes near me now, and presently they will excommunicate me. And, as I hope for salvation, the Church has no more faithful son than me.'

I believe he was on the point, forgetting M. de Rosny's presence there and his errand, of giving way to unmanly tears, when M. de Rambouillet, as if by accident, let the heel of his scabbard fall heavily on the floor. The king started, and passing his hand once or twice across his brow, seemed to recover himself. 'Well,' he said, 'no doubt we shall find a way out of our difficulties.'

'If your Majesty,' Rosny answered respectfully, 'would accept the aid my master proffers, I venture to think that they would vanish the quicker.'

'You think so,' Henry rejoined. 'Well, give me your shoulder. Let us walk a little.' And, signing to Rambouillet to leave him, he began to walk up and down with M. de Rosny, talking familiarly with him in an undertone. Only such scraps of the conversation as fell from them when they turned at my end of the gallery now reached me. Patching these together, however, I managed to understand somewhat. At one turn I heard the king say, 'But then Turenne offers—' At the next, 'Trust him? Well, I do not know why I should not. He promises—' Then 'A Republic, Rosny? That his plan? Pooh! he dare not. He could not. France is a kingdom by the ordinance of God in my family.'

I gathered from these and other chance words, which I have since forgotten, that M. de Rosny was pressing the king to accept the help of the King of Navarre, and warning him against the insidious offers of the Vicomte de Turenne. The mention of a Republic, however, seemed to excite his Majesty's wrath rather against Rosny for presuming to refer to such a thing than against Turenne, to whom he refused to credit it. He paused near my end of the promenade.

'Prove it!' he said angrily. 'But can you prove it? Can you prove it? Mind you, I will take no hearsay evidence, sir. Now, there is Turenne's agent here—you did not know, I dare say, that he had an agent here?'

'You refer, sire, to M. de Bruhl,' Rosny answered, without hesitation. 'I know him, sire.'

'I think you are the devil,' Henry answered, looking

171

curiously at him. 'You seem to know most things. But mind you, my friend, he speaks me fairly, and I will not take this on hearsay even from your master. Though,' he added after pausing a moment, 'I love him.'

'And he, your Majesty. He desires only to prove it.'

'Yes, I know, I know,' the king answered fretfully. 'I believe he does. I believe he does wish me well. But there will be a devil of an outcry among my people. And Turenne gives fair words too. And I do not know,' he continued, fidgeting with his cup and ball, 'that it might not suit me better to agree with him, you see.'

I saw M. de Rosny draw himself up. 'Dare I speak openly to you, sire,' he said, with less respect and more energy than he had hitherto used. 'As I should to my master?'

'Ay, say what you like,' Henry answered. But he spoke sullenly, and it seemed to me that he looked less pleasantly at his companion.

'Then I will venture to utter what is in your Majesty's mind,' my patron answered steadfastly. 'You fear, sire, lest, having accepted my master's offer and conquered your enemies, you should not be easily rid of him.'

Henry looked relieved. 'Do you call that diplomacy?' he said with a smile. 'However, what if it be so? What do you say to it? Methinks I have heard an idle tale about a horse which would hunt a stag; and for the purpose set a man upon its back.'

'This I say, sire, first,' Rosny answered very earnestly. 'That the King of Navarre is popular only with one-third of the kingdom, and is only powerful when united with you. Secondly, sire, it is his interest to support the royal power, to which he is heir. And, thirdly, it must be more to your Majesty's honour to accept help from a near kinsman than from an ordinary subject, and one who, I still maintain, sire, has no good designs in his mind.'

'The proof?' Henry said sharply. 'Give me that!'

'I can give it in a week from this day.'

'It must be no idle tale, mind you,' the king continued suspiciously.

'You shall have Turenne's designs, sire, from one who had them from his own mouth.'

The king looked startled, but after a pause turned and resumed his walk. 'Well,' he said, 'if you do that, I on my part—'

The rest I lost, for the two passing to the farther end of the gallery, came to a standstill there, balking my curiosity and Rambouillet's also. The marquis, indeed, began to betray his impatience, and the great clock immediately over our heads presently striking the half-hour after ten, he started and made as if he would have approached the king. He checked the impulse, however, but still continued to fidget uneasily, losing his reserve by-and-by so far as to whisper to me that his Majesty would be missed.

I had been, up to this point, a silent and inactive spectator of a scene which appealed to my keenest interests and aroused my most ardent curiosity. Surprise following surprise, I had begun to doubt my own identity; so little had I expected to find myself first in the presence of the Most Christian King— and that under circumstances as strange and bizarre as could well be imagined—and then an authorised witness at a negotiation upon which the future of all the great land of France stretching for so many hundred leagues on every side of us, depended. I say I could scarcely believe in my own identity; or that I was the same Gaston de Marsac who had slunk, shabby and out-at-elbows, about Saint-Jean d'Angely. I tasted the first sweetness of secret power, which men say is the sweetest of all and the last relinquished; and, the hum of distant voices and laughter still reaching me at intervals, I began to understand why we had been admitted with so much precaution, and to comprehend the gratification of M. de Rosny when the promise of this interview first presented to him the hope of effecting so much for his master and for France.

Now I was to be drawn into the whirlpool itself. I was still travelling back over the different stages of the adventure which had brought me to this point, when I was rudely awakened by M. de Rosny calling my name in a raised voice. Seeing, somewhat late, that he was beckoning to me to approach, I went forward in a confused and hasty fashion; kneeling before the king as I had seen him kneel, and then rising to give ear to his Majesty's commands. Albeit, having expected nothing less than to be called upon, I was not in the clearest mood to receive them. Nor was my bearing such as I could have wished it to be.

'M. de Rosny tells me that you desire a commission at Court, sir,' the king said quickly.

'I, sire?' I stammered, scarcely able to believe my ears. I was so completely taken aback that I could say no more, and I stopped there with my mouth open.

'There are few things I can deny M. de Rosny,' Henry continued, speaking very rapidly, 'and I am told that you are a gentleman of birth and ability. Out of kindness to him, therefore, I grant you a commission to raise twenty men for my service. Rambouillet,' he continued, raising his voice slightly, 'you will introduce this gentleman to me publicly tomorrow, that I may carry into effect my intention on his behalf. You may go now, sir. No thanks. And M. de Rosny,' he added, turning to my companion and speaking with energy, 'have a care for my sake that you are not recognised as you go. Rambouillet must contrive something to enable you to leave without peril. I should be desolated if anything happened to you, my friend, for I could not protect you. I give you my word if Mendoza or Retz found you in Blois I could not save you from them unless you recanted.'

'I will not trouble either your Majesty or my conscience,' M. de Rosny replied, bowing low, 'if my wits can help me.'

'Well, the saints keep you,' the king answered piously, going towards the door by which he had entered; 'for your master and I have both need of you. Rambouillet, take care of him as you love me. And come early in the morning to my closet and tell me how it has fared with him.'

We all stood bowing while he withdrew, and only turned to retire when the door closed behind him. Burning with

174

indignation and chagrin as I was at finding myself disposed of in the way I have described, and pitchforked, whether I would or no, into a service I neither fancied nor desired, I still managed for the present to restrain myself; and, permitting my companions to precede me, followed in silence, listening sullenly to their jubilations. The marquis seemed scarcely less pleased than M. de Rosny; and as the latter evinced a strong desire to lessen any jealousy the former might feel, and a generous inclination to attribute to him a full share of the credit gained, I remained the only person dissatisfied with the evening's events. We retired from the château with the same precautions which had marked our entrance, and parting with M. de Rambouillet at the door of our lodging—not without many protestations of esteem on his part and of gratitude on that of M. de Rosny—mounted to the first-floor in single file and in silence, which I was determined not to be the first to break.

Doubtless M. de Rosny knew my thoughts, for, speedily dismissing Maignan and Simon who were in waiting, he turned to me without preface. 'Come, my friend,' he said, laying his hand on my shoulder and looking me in the face in a way which all but disarmed me at once, 'do not let us misunderstand one another. You think you have cause to be angry with me. I cannot suffer that, for the King of Navarre had never greater need of your services than now.'

'You have played me an unworthy trick, sir,' I answered, thinking he would cozen me with fair speeches.

'Tut, tut!' he replied. 'You do not understand.'

'I understand well enough,' I answered, with bitterness, 'that, having done the King of Navarre's work, he would now be rid of me.'

'Have I not told you,' M. de Rosny replied, betraying for the first time some irritation, 'that he has greater need of your services than ever? Come, man, be reasonable, or, better still, listen to me.' And turning from me, he began to walk up and down the room, his hands behind him. 'The King of France—I want to make it as clear to you as possible—' he said, 'cannot make head against the League without help, and, willy-nilly, must look for it to the Huguenots whom he has so long persecuted. The King of Navarre, their acknowledged leader, has offered that help; and so, to spite my master, and prevent a combination so happy for France, has M. de Turenne, who would fain raise the faction he commands to eminence, and knows well how to make his profit out of the dissensions of his country. Are you clear so far, sir?'

I assented. I was becoming absorbed in spite of myself.

'Very well,' he resumed. 'This evening—never did anything fall out more happily than Rambouillet's meeting with me—he is a good man!—I have brought the king to this: that if proof of the selfish nature of Turenne's designs be laid before him he will hesitate no longer. That proof exists. A fortnight ago it was here; but it is not here now.'

'That is unlucky!' I exclaimed. I was so much interested in his story, as well as flattered by the confidence he was placing in me, that my ill-humour vanished. I went and stood with my shoulder against the mantelpiece, and he, passing to and fro between me and the light, continued his tale.

'A word about this proof,' he said. 'It came into the King of Navarre's hands before its full value was known to us, for that only accrued to it on M. de Guise's death. A month ago it—this piece of evidence I mean—was at Chizé. A fortnight or so ago it was here in Blois. It is now, M. de Marsac,' he continued, facing me suddenly as he came opposite me, 'in my house at Rosny.'

I started. 'You mean Mademoiselle de la Vire?' I cried.

'I mean Mademoiselle de la Vire!' he answered, 'who some month or two ago, overheard M. de Turenne's plans, and contrived to communicate with the King of Navarre. Before the latter could arrange a private interview, however, M. de Turenne got wind of her dangerous knowledge, and swept her off to Chizé. The rest you know, M. de Marsac, if any man knows it.'

'But what will you do?' I asked. 'She is at Rosny.'

'Maignan, whom I trust implicitly, as far as his lights go, will start to fetch her tomorrow. At the same hour I start southwards. You, M. de Marsac, will remain here as my agent, to watch over my interests, to receive Mademoiselle on her arrival, to secure for her a secret interview with the king, to guard her while she remains here. Do you understand?'

Did I understand? I could not find words in which to thank him. My remorse and gratitude, my sense of the wrong I had done him, and of the honour he was doing me, were such that I stood mute before him as I had stood before the king. 'You accept, then?' he said, smiling. 'You do not deem the adventure beneath you, my friend?'

'I deserve your confidence so little, sir,' I answered, stricken to the ground, 'that I beg you to speak, while I listen. By attending exactly to your instructions I may prove worthy of the trust reposed in me. And only so.'

He embraced me again and again, with a kindness which moved me almost to tears. 'You are a man after my own heart,' he said, 'and if God wills I will make your fortune. Now listen, my friend. Tomorrow at Court, as a stranger and a man introduced by Rambouillet, you will be the cynosure of all eyes. Bear yourself bravely. Pay court to the women, but attach yourself to no one in particular. Keep aloof from Retz and the Spanish faction, but beware especially of Bruhl. He alone will have your secret, and may suspect your design. Mademoiselle should be here in a week; while she is with you, and until she has seen the king, trust no one, suspect everyone, fear all things. Consider the battle won only when the king says, "I am satisfied." '

Much more he told me, which served its purpose and has been forgotten. Finally he honoured me by bidding me share his pallet with him, that we might talk without restraint, and that if anything occurred to him in the night he might communicate it to me.

'But will not Bruhl denounce me as a Huguenot?' I asked him.

'He will not dare to do so,' M. de Rosny answered, 'both
as a Huguenot himself, and as his master's representative;
and, further, because it would displease the king. No, but
whatever secret harm one man can do another, that you have
to fear. Maignan, when he returns with mademoiselle, will
leave two men with you; until they come I should borrow a
couple of stout fellows from Rambouillet. Do not go out
alone after dark, and beware of doorways, especially your
own.'

A little later, when I thought him asleep, I heard him
chuckle; and rising on my elbow I asked him what it was.
'Oh, it is your affair,' he answered, still laughing silently, so
that I felt the mattress shake under him. 'I don't envy you
one part of your task, my friend.'

'What is that?' I said suspiciously.

'Mademoiselle,' he answered, stifling with difficulty a
burst of laughter. And after that he would not say another
word, bad, good, or indifferent, though I felt the bed shake
more than once, and knew that he was digesting his
pleasantry.

16

# In the King's Chamber

M. de Rosny had risen from my side and started on his
journey when I opened my eyes in the morning, and awoke
to the memory of the task which had been so strangely
imposed upon me; and which might, according as the events
of the next fortnight shaped themselves, raise me to high
position or put an end to my career. He had not forgotten
to leave a souvenir behind him, for I found beside my pillow
a handsome silver-mounted pistol, bearing the letter 'R' and
a coronet; nor had I more than discovered this instance of

his kindness before Simon Fleix came in to tell me that M. de Rosny had left two hundred crowns in his hands for me.

'Any message with it?' I asked the lad.

'Only that he had taken a keepsake in exchange,' Simon answered, opening the window as he spoke.

In some wonder I began to search, but I could not discover that anything was missing until I came to put on my doublet, when I found that the knot of ribbon which mademoiselle had flung to me at my departure from Rosny was gone from the inside of the breast, where I had pinned it for safety with a long thorn. The discovery that M. de Rosny had taken this was displeasing to me on more than one account. In the first place, whether mademoiselle had merely wished to plague me (as was most probable) or not, I was loth to lose it, my day for ladies' favours being past and gone; in the second, I misdoubted the motive which had led him to purloin it, and tormented myself with thinking of the different constructions he might put upon it, and the disparaging view of my trustworthiness which it might lead him to take. I blamed myself much for my carelessness in leaving it where a chance eye might rest upon it; and more when, questioning Simon further, I learned that M. de Rosny had added, while mounting at the door, 'Tell your master, safe bind, safe find; and a careless lover makes a loose mistress.'

I felt my cheek burn in a manner unbecoming my years while Simon with some touch of malice repeated this; and I made a vow on the spot, which I kept until I was tempted to break it, to have no more to do with such trifles. Meanwhile, I had to make the best of it; and brisking up, and bidding Simon, who seemed depressed by the baron's departure brisk up also, I set about my preparations for making such a figure at Court as became me: procuring a black velvet suit, and a cap and feather to match; item, a jewelled clasp to secure the feather; with a yard or two of lace and two changes of fine linen.

Simon had grown sleek at Rosny, and losing something of the wildness which had marked him, presented in the dress M. de Rosny had given him a very creditable appearance; being also, I fancy, the only equerry in Blois who could write. A groom I engaged on the recommendation of M. de Rambouillet's master of the horse; and I gave out also that I required a couple of valets. It needed only an hour under the barber's hands and a set of new trappings for the Cid to enable me to make a fair show, such as might be taken to indicate a man of ten or twelve thousand livres a year.

In this way I expended a hundred and fifteen crowns. Reflecting that this was a large sum, and that I must keep some money for play, I was glad to learn that in the crowded state of the city even men with high rank were putting up with poor lodging; I determined, therefore, to combine economy with a scheme which I had in my head by taking the rooms in which my mother died, with one room below them. This I did, hiring such furniture as I needed, which was not a great deal. To Simon Fleix, whose assistance in these matters was invaluable, I passed on much of M. de Rosny's advice, bidding him ruffle it with the best in his station, and inciting him to labour for my advancement by promising to make his fortune whenever my own should be assured. I hoped, indeed, to derive no little advantage from the quickness of wit which had attracted M. de Rosny's attention; although I did not fail to take into account at the same time that the lad was wayward and fitful, prone at one time to depression, and at another to giddiness, and equally uncertain in either mood.

M. de Rambouillet being unable to attend the *levée*, had appointed me to wait upon him at six in the evening; at which hour I presented myself at his lodgings, attended by Simon Fleix. I found him in the midst of half a dozen gentlemen whose habit it was to attend him upon all public occasions; and these gallants, greeting me with the same curious and suspicious glances which I have seen hounds bestow on a strange dog introduced into their kennel, I was speedily made to feel that it is one thing to have business at Court, and another to be well received there.

M. de Rambouillet, somewhat to my surprise, did nothing to remove this impression. On all ordinary occasions a man of stiff and haughty bearing, and thoroughly disliking, though he could not prevent, the intrusion of a third party into a transaction which promised an infinity of credit, he received me so coldly and with so much reserve as for the moment to dash my spirits and throw me back on myself.

During the journey to the Castle, however, which we performed on foot, attended by half a dozen armed servants bearing torches, I had time to recall M. de Rosny's advice, and to bethink me of the intimacy which that great man had permitted me; with so much effect in the way of heartening me, that as we crossed the courtyard of the castle I advanced myself, not without some murmuring on the part of others, to Rambouillet's elbow, considering that as I was attached to him by the king's command, this was my proper place. I had no desire to quarrel, however, and persisted for some time in disregarding the nudges and muttered words which were exchanged round me, and even the efforts which were made as we mounted the stairs to oust me from my position. But a young gentleman, who showed himself very forward in these attempts, presently stumbling against me, I found it necessary to look at him.

'Sir,' he said, in a small and lisping voice, 'you trod on my toe.'

Though I had not done so, I begged his pardon very politely. But as his only acknowledgment of this courtesy consisted in an attempt to get his knee in front of mine—we were mounting very slowly, the stairs being cumbered with a multitude of servants, who stood on either hand—I did tread on his toe, with a force and directness which made him cry out.

'What is the matter?' Rambouillet asked, looking back hastily.

'Nothing, M. le Marquis,' I answered, pressing on steadfastly.

'Sir,' my young friend said again, in the same lisping voice, 'you trod on my toe.'

'I believe I did, sir,' I answered.

'You have not yet apologised,' he murmured gently in my ear.

'Nay, there you are wrong,' I rejoined bluntly, 'for it is always my habit to apologise first and tread afterwards.'

He smiled as at a pleasant joke; and I am bound to say that his bearing was so admirable that if he had been my son I could have hugged him. 'Good!' he answered. 'No doubt your sword is as sharp as your wits, sir. I see,' he continued, glancing naively at my old scabbard—he was himself the very gem of a courtier, a slender youth with a pink-and-white complexion, a dark line for a moustache, and a pearl-drop in his ear—'it is longing to be out. Perhaps you will take a turn in the tennis-court tomorrow?'

'With pleasure, sir,' I answered, 'if you have a father, or your elder brother is grown up.'

What answer he would have made to this gibe I do not know, for at that moment we reached the door of the antechamber; and this being narrow, and a sentry in the grey uniform of the Swiss Guard compelling all to enter in single file, my young friend was forced to fall back, leaving me free to enter alone, and admire at my leisure a scene at once brilliant and sombre.

The Court being in mourning for the Queen-mother, black predominated in the dresses of those present, and set off very finely the gleaming jewels and gemmed sword-hilts which were worn by the more important personages. The room was spacious and lofty, hung with arras, and lit by candles burning in silver sconces; it rang as we entered with the shrill screaming of a parrot, which was being teased by a group occupying the farther of the two hearths. Near them play was going on at one table, and primero at a second. In a corner were three or four ladies, in a circle about a red-faced, plebeian-looking man, who was playing at forfeits with one of their number; while the middle of the room seemed dominated by a middle-sized man with a peculiarly inflamed and passionate countenance, who, seated on a table, was inveighing against someone or something in the most violent terms, his language being interlarded with all kinds of strange and forcible oaths. Two or three gentlemen, who had the air of being his followers, stood about him, listening between submission and embarrassment; while beside the nearer fireplace, but at some distance from him, lounged a nobleman, very richly dressed, and wearing on his breast the Cross of the Holy Ghost; who seemed to be the object of his invective, but affecting to ignore it was engaged in conversation with a companion. A bystander muttering that Crillon had been drinking, I discovered with immense surprise that the declaimer on the table was that famous soldier; and I was still looking at him in wonder—for I had been accustomed all my life to associate courage with modesty—when, the door of the chamber suddenly opening, a general movement in that direction took place. Crillon, disregarding all precedency, sprang from his table and hurried first to the threshold. The Baron de Biron, on the other hand—for the gentleman by the fire was no other—waited, in apparent ignorance of the slight which was being put upon him, until M. de Rambouillet came up; then he went forward with him. Keeping close to my patron's elbow, I entered the chamber immediately behind him.

Crillon had already seized upon the king, and, when we entered, was stating his grievance in a voice not much lower than that which he had used outside. M. de Biron, seeing this, parted from the marquis, and, going aside with his former companion, sat down on a trunk against the wall; while Rambouillet, followed by myself and three or four gentlemen of his train, advanced to the king, who was standing near the alcove. His Majesty seeing him, and thankful, I think, for the excuse, waved Crillon off. 'Tut, tut! You told me all that this morning,' he said good-naturedly.

'And here is Rambouillet, who has, I hope, something fresh to tell. Let him speak to me. Sanctus! Don't look at me as if you would run me through, man. Go and quarrel with someone of your own size.'

Crillon at this retired grumbling, and Henry, who had just risen from primero with the Duke of Nevers, nodded to Rambouillet. 'Well, my friend, anything fresh?' he cried. He was more at his ease and looked more cheerful than at our former interview; yet still care and suspicion lurked about his peevish mouth, and in the hollows under his gloomy eyes. 'A new guest, a new face, or a new game—which have you brought?'

'In a sense, sire, a new face,' the marquis answered, bowing, and standing somewhat aside that I might have place.

'Well, I cannot say much for the pretty baggage,' quoth the king quickly. And amid a general titter he extended his hand to me. 'I'll be sworn, though,' he continued, as I rose from my knee, 'that you want something, my friend?'

'Nay, sire,' I answered, holding up my head boldly—for Crillon's behaviour had been a further lesson to me—'I have, by your leave, the advantage. For your Majesty has supplied me with a new jest. I see many new faces round me, and I have need only of a new game. If your Majesty would be pleased to grant me—'

'There! Said I not so?' cried the king, raising his hand with a laugh. 'He does want something. But he seems not undeserving. What does he pray, Rambouillet?'

'A small command,' M. de Rambouillet answered, readily playing his part. 'And your Majesty would oblige me if you could grant the Sieur de Marsac's petition. I will answer for it he is a man of experience.'

'Chut! A small command?' Henry ejaculated, sitting down suddenly in apparent ill-humour. 'It is what everyone wants —when they do not want big ones. Still, I suppose,' he continued, taking up a comfit-box, which lay beside him, and opening it, 'if you do not get what you want for him you will sulk like the rest, my friend.'

'Your Majesty has never had cause to complain of me,' quoth the marquis, forgetting his rôle, or too proud to play it.

'Tut, tut, tut, tut! Take it, and trouble me no more,' the king rejoined. 'Will pay for twenty men do for him? Very well then. There, M. de Marsac,' he continued, nodding at me and yawning, 'your request is granted. You will find some other pretty baggages over there. Go to them. And now, Rambouillet,' he went on, resuming his spirits as he turned to matters of more importance, 'here is a new sweetmeat Zamet has sent me. I have made Zizi sick with it. Will you try it? It is flavoured with white mulberries.'

Thus dismissed, I fell back; and stood for a moment, at a loss whither to turn, in the absence of either friends or acquaintances. His Majesty, it is true, had bidden me go to certain pretty baggages, meaning, apparently, five ladies who were seated at the farther end of the room, diverting themselves with as many cavaliers; but the compactness of this party, the beauty of the ladies, and the merry peals of laughter which proceeded from them, telling of a wit and vivacity beyond the ordinary, sapped the resolution which had borne me well hitherto. I felt that to attack such a phalanx, even with a king's good will, was beyond the daring of a Crillon, and I looked round to see whether I could not amuse myself in some more modest fashion.

The material was not lacking. Crillon, still mouthing out his anger, strode up and down in front of the trunk on which M. de Biron was seated; but the latter was, or affected to be, asleep. 'Crillon is for ever going into rages now,' a courtier beside me whispered.

'Yes,' his fellow answered, with a shrug of the shoulder; 'it is a pity there is no one to tame him. But he has such a long reach, morbleu!'

'It is not that so much as the fellow's fury,' the first speaker rejoined under his breath. 'He fights like a mad thing; fencing is no use against him.'

The other nodded. For a moment the wild idea of winning renown by taming M. de Crillon occurred to me as I stood alone in the middle of the floor; but it had not more than passed through my brain when I felt my elbow touched, and turned to find the young gentleman whom I had encountered on the stairs standing by my side.

'Sir,' he lisped, in the same small voice, 'I think you trod on my toe a while ago?'

I stared at him, wondering what he meant by this absurd repetition. 'Well, sir,' I answered drily, 'and if I did?'

'Perhaps,' he said, stroking his chin with his jewelled fingers, 'pending our meeting tomorrow, you would allow me to consider it as a kind of introduction?'

'If it please you,' I answered, bowing stiffly, and wondering what he would be at.

'Thank you,' he answered. 'It does please me, under the circumstances; for there is a lady here who desires a word with you. I took up her challenge. Will you follow me?'

He bowed, and turned in his languid fashion. I, turning too, saw, with secret dismay, that the five ladies, referred to above, were all now gazing at me, as expecting my approach; and this with such sportive glances as told only too certainly of some plot already in progress or some trick to be presently played me. Yet I could not see that I had any choice save to obey, and, following my leader with as much dignity as I could compass, I presently found myself bowing before the lady who sat nearest, and who seemed to be the leader of these nymphs.

'Nay, sir,' she said, eyeing me curiously, yet with a merry face, 'I do not need you; I do not look so high!'

Turning in confusion to the next, I was surprised to see before me the lady whose lodging I had invaded in my search for Mademoiselle de la Vire—she, I mean, who, having picked up the velvet knot, had dropped it so providentially where Simon Fleix found it. She looked at me, blushing and laughing, and the young gentleman, who had done her errand, presenting me by name, she asked me, while the others listened, whether I had found my mistress.

Before I could answer, the lady to whom I had first

addressed myself interposed. 'Stop, sir!' she cried. 'What is this—a tale, a jest, a game, or a forfeit?'

'An adventure, madam,' I answered, bowing low.

'Of gallantry, I'll be bound,' she exclaimed. 'Fie, Madame de Bruhl, and you but six months married!'

Madame de Bruhl protested, laughing, that she had no more to do with it than Mercury. 'At the worst,' she said, 'I carried the *poulets*! But I can assure you, duchess, this gentleman should be able to tell us a very fine story, if he would.'

The duchess and all the other ladies clapping their hands at this, and crying out that the story must and should be told, I found myself in a prodigious quandary; and one wherein my wits derived as little assistance as possible from the bright eyes and saucy looks which environed me. Moreover, the commotion attracting other listeners, I found my position, while I tried to extricate myself, growing each moment worse, so that I began to fear that as I had little imagination I should perforce have to tell the truth. The mere thought of this threw me into a cold perspiration, lest I should let slip something of consequence, and prove myself unworthy of the trust which M. de Rosny had reposed in me.

At the moment when, despairing of extricating myself, I was stooping over Madame de Bruhl begging her to assist me, I heard, amid the babel of laughter and raillery which surrounded me—certain of the courtiers having already formed hands in a circle and sworn I should not depart without satisfying the ladies—a voice which struck a chord in my memory. I turned to see who the speaker was, and encountered no other than M. de Bruhl himself; who, with a flushed and angry face, was listening to the explanation which a friend was pouring into his ear. Standing at the moment with my knee on Madame de Bruhl's stool, and remembering very well the meeting on the stairs, I conceived in a flash that the man was jealous; but whether he had yet heard my name, or had any clue to link me with the person who had rescued Mademoiselle de la Vire from his clutches, I could not tell. Nevertheless his presence led my thoughts into a new channel. The determination to punish him began to take form in my mind, and very quickly I regained my composure. Still I was for giving him one chance. Accordingly I stooped once more to Madame de Bruhl's ear, and begged her to spare me the embarrassment of telling my tale. But then, finding her pitiless, as I expected, and the rest of the company growing more and more insistent, I hardened my heart to go through with the fantastic notion which had occurred to me.

Indicating by a gesture that I was prepared to obey, and the duchess crying for a hearing, this was presently obtained, the sudden silence adding the king himself to my audience. 'What is it?' he asked, coming up effusively, with a lap-dog in his arms. 'A new scandal, eh?'

'No, sire, a new tale-teller,' the duchess answered pertly. 'If your Majesty will sit, we shall hear him the sooner.'

He pinched her ear and sat down in the chair which a page presented. 'What is it? Rambouillet's *grison* again?' he said with some surprise. 'Well, fire away, man. But who brought you forward as a Rabelais?'

There was a general cry of 'Madame de Bruhl!' whereat that lady shook her fair hair about her face, and cried out for someone to bring her a mask.

'Ha, I see!' said the king drily, looking pointedly at M. de Bruhl, who was as black as thunder. 'But go on, man.'

The king's advent, by affording me a brief respite, had enabled me to collect my thoughts, and, disregarding the ribald interruptions, which at first were frequent, I began as follows: 'I am no Rabelais, sire,' I said, 'but droll things happen to the most unlikely. Once upon a time it was the fortune of a certain swain, whom I will call Dromio, to arrive in a town not a hundred miles from Blois, having in his company a nymph of great beauty, who had been entrusted to his care by her parents. He had not more than lodged her in his apartments, however, before she was decoyed away by a trick, and borne off against her will by a young gallant, who had seen her and been smitten by her charms. Dromio, returning, and finding his mistress gone, gave way to the most poignant grief. He ran up and down the city, seeking her in every place, and filling all places with his lamentations; but for a time in vain, until chance led him to a certain street, where, in an almost incredible manner, he found a clue to her by discovering underfoot a knot of velvet, bearing Phyllida's name wrought on it in delicate needlework, with the words, "A moi!"'

'Sanctus!' cried the king, amid a general murmur of surprise, 'that is well devised! Proceed, sir. Go on like that, and we will make your twenty men twenty-five.'

'Dromio,' I continued, 'at sight of this trifle experienced the most diverse emotions, for while he possessed in it a clue to his mistress's fate, he had still to use it so to discover the place whither she had been hurried. It occurred to him at last to begin his search with the house before which the knot had lain. Ascending accordingly to the second-floor, he found there a fair lady reclining on a couch, who started up in affright at his appearance. He hastened to reassure her, and to explain the purpose of his coming and learned after a conversation with which I will not trouble your Majesty, though it was sufficiently diverting, that the lady had found the velvet knot in another part of the town, and had herself dropped it again in front of her own house.'

'Pourquoi?' the king asked, interrupting me.

'The swain, sire,' I answered, 'was too much taken up with his own troubles to bear that in mind, even if he learned it. But this delicacy did not save him from misconception, for as he descended from the lady's apartment he met her husband on the stairs.'

'Good!' the king exclaimed, rubbing his hands in glee. 'The husband!' And under cover of the gibe and the courtly laugh which followed it M. de Bruhl's start of surprise passed unnoticed save by me.

'The husband,' I resumed, 'seeing a stranger descending his staircase, was for stopping him and learning the reason of his presence; but Dromio, whose mind was with Phyllida, refused to stop, and, evading his questions, hurried to the part of the town where the lady had told him she found the velvet knot. Here, sire, at the corner of a lane running between garden-walls, he found a great house, barred and gloomy, and well adapted to the abductor's purpose. Moreover, scanning it on every side, he presently discovered, tied about the bars of an upper window, a knot of white linen, the very counterpart of that velvet one which he bore in his breast. Thus he knew that the nymph was imprisoned in that room!'

'I will make it twenty-five, as I am a good Churchman!' his Majesty exclaimed, dropping the little dog he was nursing into the duchess's lap, and taking out his comfit-box. 'Rambouillet,' he added languidly, 'your friend is a treasure!'

I bowed my acknowledgments, and took occasion as I did so to step a pace aside, so as to command a view of Madame de Bruhl, as well as her husband. Hitherto madame, willing to be accounted a part in so pretty a romance, and ready enough also, unless I was mistaken, to cause her husband a little mild jealousy, had listened to the story with a certain sly demureness. But this I foresaw would not last long; and I felt something like compunction as the moment for striking the blow approached. But I had now no choice. 'The best is yet to come, sire,' I went on, 'as I think you will acknowledge in a moment. Dromio, though he had discovered his mistress, was still in the depths of despair. He wandered round and round the house, seeking ingress and finding none, until at length, sunset approaching, and darkness redoubling his fears for the nymph, fortune took pity on him. As he stood in front of the house he saw the abductor come out, lighted by two servants. Judge of his surprise, sire,' I continued, looking round and speaking slowly, to give full effect to my words, 'when he recognised in him no other than the husband of the lady who, by picking up and again dropping the velvet knot, had contributed so much to the success of his search!'

'Ha! these husbands!' cried the king. And slapping his knee in an ecstasy at his own acuteness, he laughed in his seat till he rolled again. 'These husbands! Did I not say so?'

The whole Court gave way to like applause, and clapped their hands as well, so that few save those who stood nearest took notice of Madame de Bruhl's faint cry, and still fewer understood why she rose up suddenly from her stool and stood gazing at her husband with burning cheeks and clenched hands. She took no heed of me, much less of the laughing crowd round her, but looked only at him with her soul in her eyes. He, after uttering one hoarse curse, seemed to have no thought for any but me. To have the knowledge that his own wife had baulked him brought home to him in this mocking fashion, to find how little a thing had tripped him that day, to learn how blindly he had played into the hands of fate, above all to be exposed at once to his wife's resentment and the ridicule of the Court—for he could not be sure that I should not the next moment disclose his name—all so wrought on him that for a moment I thought he would strike me in the presence.

His rage, indeed, did what I had not meant to do. For the king, catching sight of his face, and remembering that Madame de Bruhl had elicited the story, screamed suddenly, 'Haro!' and pointed ruthlessly at him with his finger. After that I had no need to speak, the story leaping from eye to eye, and every eye settling on Bruhl, who sought in vain to compose his features. Madame, who surpassed him, as women commonly do surpass men, in self-control, was the first to recover herself, and sitting down as quickly as she had risen, confronted alike her husband and her rivals with a pale smile.

For a moment curiosity and excitement kept all breathless, the eye alone busy. Then the king laughed mischievously. 'Come, M. de Bruhl,' he cried, 'perhaps you will finish the tale for us?' And he threw himself back in his chair, a sneer on his lips.

'Or why not Madame de Bruhl?' said the duchess, with her head on one side and her eyes glittering over her fan. 'Madame would, I am sure, tell it so well.'

But madame only shook her head, smiling always that forced smile. For Bruhl himself, glaring from face to face like a bull about to charge, I have never seen a man more out of countenance, or more completely brought to bay. His discomposure, exposed as he was to the ridicule of all present, was such that the presence in which he stood scarcely hindered him from some violent attack; and his eyes, which had wandered from me at the king's word, presently returning to me again, he so far forgot himself as to raise his hand furiously, uttering at the same time a savage oath.

The king cried out angrily, 'Have a care, sir!' But Bruhl only heeded this so far as to thrust aside those who stood round him and push his way hurriedly through the circle.

'Arnidieu!' cried the king, when he was gone. 'This is fine conduct! I have half a mind to send after him and have him put where his hot blood would cool a little. Or—'

He stopped abruptly, his eyes resting on me. The relative positions of Bruhl and myself as the agents of Rosny and Turenne occurred to him for the first time, I think, and suggested the idea, perhaps, that I had laid a trap for him, and that he had fallen into it. At any rate his face grew darker and darker, and at last, 'A nice kettle of fish this is you have prepared for us, sir!' he muttered, gazing at me gloomily.

The sudden change in his humour took even courtiers by surprise. Faces a moment before broad with smiles grew long again. The less important personages looked uncomfortably at one another, and with one accord frowned on me. 'If your Majesty would please to hear the end of the story at another time?' I suggested humbly, beginning to wish with all my heart that I had never said a word.

'Chut!' he answered, rising, his face still betraying his perturbation. 'Well, be it so. For the present you may go, sir. Duchess, give me Zizi, and come to my closet. I want you to

see my puppies. Retz, my good friend, do you come too. I
have something to say to you. Gentlemen, you need not wait.
It is likely I shall be late.'

And, with the utmost abruptness, he broke up the circle.

# 17

# The Jacobin Monk

Had I needed any reminder of the uncertainty of Court
favour, or an instance whence I might learn the lesson of
modesty, and so stand in less danger of presuming on my
new and precarious prosperity, I had it in this episode, and
in the demeanour of the company round me. On the circle
breaking up in confusion, I found myself the centre of
general regard, but regard of so dubious a character, the
persons who would have been the first to compliment me
had the king retired earlier, standing farthest aloof now, that
I felt myself rather insulted than honoured by it. One or two,
indeed, of the more cautious spirits did approach me; but it
was with the air of men providing against a danger particularly remote, their half-hearted speeches serving only to
fix them in my memory as belonging to a class, especially
abhorrent to me—the class, I mean, of those who would run
at once with the hare and the hounds.

I was rejoiced to find that on one person, and that the one
whose disposition towards me was, next to the king's, of first
importance, this episode had produced a different impression.
Feeling, as I made for the door, a touch on my arm, I turned
to find M. de Rambouillet at my elbow, regarding me with a
glance of mingled esteem and amusement; in fine, with a very
different look from that which had been my welcome earlier
in the evening. I was driven to suppose that he was too great
a man, or too sure of his favour with the king, to be swayed

by the petty motives which actuated the Court generally, for he laid his hand familiarly on my shoulder, and walked on beside me.

'Well, my friend,' he said, 'you have distinguished yourself finely! I do not know that I ever remember a pretty woman making more stir in one evening. But if you are wise you will not go home alone tonight.'

'I have my sword, M. le Marquis,' I answered, somewhat proudly.

'Which will avail you little against a knife in the back!' he retorted drily. 'What attendance have you?'

'My equerry, Simon Fleix, is on the stairs.'

'Good, so far, but not enough,' he replied, as we reached the head of the staircase. 'You had better come home with me now, and two or three of my fellows shall go on to your lodging with you. Do you know, my friend,' he continued, looking at me keenly, 'you are either a very clever or a very foolish man?'

I made answer modestly. 'Neither the one, I fear, nor the other, I hope, sir,' I said.

'Well, you have done a very pertinent thing,' he replied, 'for good or evil. You have let the enemy know what he has to expect, and he is not one, I warn you, to be despised. But whether you have been very wise or very foolish in declaring open war remains to be seen.'

'A week will show,' I answered.

He turned and looked at me. 'You take it coolly,' he said.

'I have been knocking about the world for forty years, Marquis,' I rejoined.

He muttered something about Rosny having a good eye, and then stopped to adjust his cloak. We were by this time in the street. Making me go hand in hand with him, he requested the other gentlemen to draw their swords; and the servants being likewise armed and numbering half a score or more, with pikes and torches, we made up a very formidable party, and caused, I think, more alarm as we passed through the streets to Rambouillet's lodging than we had any reason to feel. Not that we had it all to ourselves, for the attendance at Court that evening being large, and the circle breaking up as I have described more abruptly than usual, the vicinity of the Castle was in a ferment, and the streets leading from it were alive with the lights and laughter of parties similar to our own.

At the door of the Marquis's lodging I prepared to take leave of him with many expressions of gratitude, but he would have me enter and sit down with him to a light refection, which it was his habit to take before retiring. Two of his gentlemen sat down with us, and a valet, who was in his confidence, waiting on us, we made very merry over the scene in the presence. I learned that M. de Bruhl was far from popular at Court; but being known to possess some kind of hold over the king, and enjoying besides a great reputation for recklessness and skill with the sword, he had played a high part for a length of time, and attached to himself, especially since the death of Guise, a considerable number of followers.

'The truth is,' one of the Marquis's gentlemen, who was a little heated with wine, observed, 'there is nothing at this moment which a bold and unscrupulous man may not win in France!'

'Nor a bold and Christian gentleman for France!' replied M. de Rambouillet with some asperity. 'By the way,' he continued, turning abruptly to the servant, 'where is M. François?'

The valet answered that he had not returned with us from the castle. The Marquis expressed himself annoyed at this, and I gathered, firstly, that the missing man was his near kinsman, and, secondly, that he was also the young spark who had been so forward to quarrel with me earlier in the evening. Determining to refer the matter, should it become pressing, to Rambouillet for adjustment, I took leave of him, and attended by two of his servants, whom he kindly transferred to my service for the present, I started towards my lodging a little before midnight.

The moon had risen while we were at supper, and its light,

which whitened the gables on one side of the street, diffused a glimmer below sufficient to enable us to avoid the kennel. Seeing this, I bade the men put out our torch. Frost had set in, and a keen wind was blowing, so that we were glad to hurry on at a good pace; and the streets being quite deserted at this late hour, or haunted only by those who had come to dread the town marshal, we met no one and saw no lights. I fell to thinking, for my part, of the evening I had spent searching Blois for mademoiselle, and of the difference between then and now. Nor did I fail while on this track to retrace it still farther to the evening of our arrival at my mother's; whence, as a source, such kindly and gentle thoughts welled up in my mind as were natural, and the unfailing affection of that gracious woman required. These, taking the place for the moment of the anxious calculations and stern purposes which had of late engrossed me, were only ousted by something which, happening under my eyes, brought me violently and abruptly to myself.

This was the sudden appearance of three men, who issued one by one from an alley a score of yards in front of us, and after pausing a second to look back the way they had come, flitted on in single file along the street, disappearing, as far as the darkness permitted me to judge, round a second corner. I by no means liked their appearance, and as a scream and the clash of arms rang out next moment from the direction in which they had gone, I cried lustily to Simon Fleix to follow and ran on, believing from the rascals' movements that they were after no good, but that rather some honest man was like to be sore beset.

On reaching the lane down which they had plunged, however, I paused a moment, considering not so much its blackness, which was intense, the eaves nearly meeting overhead, as the small chance I had of distinguishing between attackers and attacked. But Simon and the men overtaking me, and the sounds of a sharp tussle still continuing, I decided to venture, and plunged into the alley, my left arm well advanced, with the skirt of my cloak thrown over it, and my sword drawn back. I shouted as I ran, thinking that the knaves might desist on hearing me; and this was what happened, for as I arrived on the scene of action—the farther end of the alley—two men took to their heels, while of two who remained, one lay at length in the kennel, and another rose slowly from his knees.

'You are just in time, sir,' the latter said, breathing hard, but speaking with a preciseness which sounded familiar. 'I am obliged to you, sir, whoever you are. The villains had got me down, and in a few minutes more would have made my mother childless. By the way, you have no light, have you?' he continued, lisping like a woman.

One of M. de Rambouillet's men, who had by this time come up, cried out that it was M. François.

'Yes, blockhead!' the young gentleman answered with the utmost coolness. 'But I asked for a light, not for my name.'

'I trust you are not hurt, sir?' I said, putting up my sword.

'Scratched only,' he answered, betraying no surprise on learning who it was had come up so opportunely; as he no doubt did learn from my voice, for he continued with a bow, 'A slight price to pay for the knowledge that M. de Marsac is as forward on the field as on the stairs.'

I bowed my acknowledgments.

'This fellow,' I said, 'is he much hurt?'

'Tut, tut! I thought I had saved the marshal all trouble,' M. François replied. 'Is he not dead, Gil?'

The poor wretch made answer for himself, crying out piteously and in a choking voice, for a priest to shrive him. At that moment Simon Fleix returned with our torch, which he had lighted at the nearest cross-streets, where there was a brazier, and we saw by this light that the man was coughing up blood, and might live perhaps half an hour.

'Mordieu! That comes of thrusting too high!' M. François muttered, regretfully. 'An inch lower, and there would have been none of this trouble! I suppose somebody must fetch one. Gil,' he continued, 'run, man, to the sacristy in the Rue Saint-Denys, and get a Father. Or—stay! Help to lift him under the lee of the wall there. The wind cuts like a knife here.'

The street being on the slope of the hill, the lower part of the house nearest us stood a few feet from the ground, on wooden piles, and the space underneath it, being enclosed at the back and sides, was used as a cart-house. The servants moved the dying man into this rude shelter, and I accompanied them, being unwilling to leave the young gentleman alone. Not wishing, however, to seem to interfere, I walked to the farther end, and sat down on the shaft of a cart, whence I idly admired the strange aspect of the group I had left, as the glare of the torch brought now one and now another into prominence, and sometimes shone on M. François' jewelled fingers toying with his tiny moustache, and sometimes on the writhing features of the man at his feet.

On a sudden, and before Gil had started on his errand, I saw there was a priest among them. I had not seen him enter, nor had I any idea whence he came. My first impression was only that here was a priest, and that he was looking at me— not at the man craving his assistance on the floor, or at those who stood round him, but at me, who sat away in the shadow beyond the ring of light!

This was surprising; but a second glance explained it, for then I saw that he was the Jacobin monk who had haunted my mother's dying hours. And, amazed as much at this strange *rencontre* as at the man's boldness, I sprang up and strode forwards, forgetting, in an impulse of righteous anger, the office he came to do. And this the more as his face, still turned to me, seemed instinct to my eyes with triumphant malice. As I moved towards him, however, with a fierce exclamation on my lips, he suddenly dropped his eyes and knelt. Immediately M. François cried 'Hush!' and the men turned to me with scandalised faces. I fell back. Yet even then, whispering on his knees by the dying man, the knave was thinking, I felt sure, of me, glorying at once in his immunity and the power it gave him to tantalise me without fear.

I determined, whatever the result, to intercept him when all was over; and on the man dying a few minutes later, I walked resolutely to the open side of the shed, thinking it likely he might try to slip away as mysteriously as he had come. He stood a moment speaking to M. François, however, and then, accompanied by him, advanced boldly to meet me, a lean smile on his face.

'Father Antoine,' M. d'Agen said politely, 'tells me that he knows you, M. de Marsac, and desires to speak to you, *mal-à-propos* as is the occasion.'

'And I to him,' I answered, trembling with rage, and only restraining by an effort the impulse which would have had me dash my hand in the priest's pale, smirking face. 'I have waited long for this moment,' I continued, eyeing him steadily, as M. François withdrew out of hearing, 'and had you tried to avoid me, I would have dragged you back, though all your tribe were here to protect you.'

His presence so maddened me that I scarcely knew what I said. I felt my breath come quickly, I felt the blood surge to my head, and it was with difficulty I restrained myself when he answered with well-affected sanctity, 'Like mother, like son, I fear, sir. Huguenots both.'

I choked with rage. 'What!' I said, 'you dare to threaten me as you threatened my mother? Fool! know that only today for the purpose of discovering and punishing you I took the rooms in which my mother died.'

'I know it,' he answered quietly. And then in a second, as by magic, he altered his demeanour completely, raising his head and looking me in the face. 'That, and so much besides, I know,' he continued, giving me, to my satisfaction, frown for frown, 'that if you will listen to me for a moment, M. de Marsac, and listen quietly, I will convince you that the folly is not on my side.'

Amazed at his new manner, in which there was none of the madness that had marked him at our first meeting, but a strange air of authority, unlike anything I had associated with him before, I signed to him to proceed.

'You think that I am in your power?' he said, smiling.

'I think,' I retorted swiftly, 'that, escaping me now, you will have at your heels henceforth a worse enemy than even your own sins.'

'Just so,' he answered, nodding. 'Well, I am going to show you that the reverse is the case; and that you are as completely in my hands, to spare or to break, as this straw. In the first place, you are here in Blois, a Huguenot!'

'Chut!' I exclaimed contemptuously, affecting a confidence I was far from feeling. 'A little while back that might have availed you. But we are in Blois, not Paris. It is not far to the Loire, and you have to deal with a man now, not with a woman. It is you who have cause to tremble, not I.'

'You think to be protected,' he answered with a sour smile, 'even on this side of the Loire, I see. But one word to the Pope's Legate, or to the Duke of Nevers, and you would see the inside of a dungeon, if not worse. For the king—'

'King or no king!' I answered, interrupting him with more assurance than I felt, seeing that I remembered only too well Henry's remark that Rosny must not look to him for protection, 'I fear you not a whit! And that reminds me. I have heard you talk treason—rank, black treason, priest, as ever sent man to rope, and I will give you up. By heaven I will!' I cried, my rage increasing, as I discerned, more and more clearly, the dangerous hold he had over me. 'You have threatened me! One word, and I will send you to the gallows!'

'Sh!' he answered, indicating M. François by a gesture of the hand. 'For your own sake, not mine. This is fine talking, but you have not yet heard all I know. Would you like to hear how you have spent the last month? Two days after Christmas, M. de Marsac, you left Chizé with a young lady— I can give you her name, if you please. Four days afterwards you reached Blois, and took her to your mother's lodgings. Next morning she left you for M. de Bruhl. Two days later you tracked her to a house in the Ruelle d'Arcy, and freed her, but lost her in the moment of victory. Then you stayed in Blois until your mother's death, going a day or two later to

M. de Rosny's house by Mantes, where mademoiselle still is. Yesterday you arrived in Blois with M. de Rosny; you went to his lodging; you—'

'Proceed, sir,' I muttered, leaning forward. Under cover of my cloak I drew my dagger half-way from its sheath. 'Proceed, sir, I pray,' I repeated with dry lips.

'You slept there,' he continued, holding his ground, but shuddering slightly, either from cold or because he perceived my movement and read my design in my eyes. 'This morning you remained here in attendance on M. de Rambouillet.'

For the moment I breathed freely again, perceiving that though he knew much, the one thing on which M. de Rosny's design turned had escaped him. The secret interview with the king, which compromised alike Henry himself and M. de Rambouillet, had apparently passed unnoticed and unsuspected. With a sigh of intense relief I slid back the dagger, which I had fully made up my mind to use had he known all, and drew my cloak round me with a shrug of feigned indifference. I sweated to think what he did know, but our interview with the king having escaped him, I breathed again.

'Well, sir,' I said curtly, 'I have listened. And now, what is the purpose of all this?'

'My purpose?' he answered, his eyes glittering. 'To show you that you are in my power. You are the agent of M. de Rosny. I, the agent, however humble, of the Holy Catholic League. Of your movements I know all. What do you know of mine?'

'Knowledge,' I made grim answer, 'is not everything, sir priest.'

'It is more than it was,' he said, smiling his thin-lipped smile. 'It is going to be more than it is. And I know much—about you, M. de Marsac.'

'You know too much!' I retorted, feeling his covert threats close round me like the folds of some great serpent. 'But you are imprudent, I think. Will you tell me what is to prevent me striking you through where you stand, and ridding myself at a blow of so much knowledge?'

'The presence of three men, M. de Marsac,' he answered lightly, waving his hand towards M. François and the others, 'every one of whom would give you up to justice. You forget that you are north of the Loire, and that priests are not to be massacred here with impunity, as in your lawless south-country. However, enough. The night is cold, and M. d'Agen grows suspicious as well as impatient. We have, perhaps, spoken too long already. Permit me'—he bowed and drew back a step—'to resume this discussion tomorrow.'

Despite his politeness and the hollow civility with which he thus sought to close the interview, the light of triumph which shone in his eyes, as the glare of the torch fell athwart them, no less than the assured tone of his voice, told me clearly that he knew his power. He seemed, indeed, trans-formed: no longer a slinking, peaceful clerk, preying on a woman's fears, but a bold and crafty schemer, skilled and unscrupulous, possessed of hidden knowledge and hidden resources; the personification of evil intellect. For a moment, knowing all I knew, and particularly the responsibilities which lay before me, and the interests committed to my hands, I quailed, confessing myself unequal to him. I forgot the righteous vengeance I owed him; I cried out helplessly against the ill-fortune which had brought him across my path. I saw myself enmeshed and fettered beyond hope of escape, and by an effort only controlled the despair I felt.

'Tomorrow?' I muttered hoarsely. 'At what time?'

He shook his head with a cunning smile. 'A thousand thanks, but I will settle that myself!' he answered. 'Au revoir!' And muttering a word of leave-taking to M. François d'Agen, he blessed the two servants, and went out into the night.

## 18

# The Offer of the League

When the last sound of his footsteps died away, I awoke as from an evil dream, and becoming conscious of the presence of M. François and the servants, recollected mechanically that I owed the former an apology for my discourtesy in keeping him standing in the cold. I began to offer it; but my distress and confusion of mind were such that in the middle of a set phrase I broke off, and stood looking fixedly at him, my trouble so plain that he asked me civilly if anything ailed me.

'No,' I answered, turning from him impatiently; 'nothing, nothing, sir. Or tell me,' I continued, with an abrupt change of mind, 'who is that who has just left us?'

'Father Antoine, do you mean?'

'Ay, Father Antoine, Father Judas, call him what you like,' I rejoined bitterly.

'Then if you leave the choice to me,' M. François answered with grave politeness, 'I would rather call him something more pleasant, M. de Marsac—James or John, let us say. For there is little said here which does not come back to him. If walls have ears, the walls of Blois are in his pay. But I thought you knew him,' he continued. 'He is secretary, confidant, chaplain, what you will, to Cardinal Retz, and one of those whom—in your ear—greater men court and more powerful men lean on. If I had to choose between them, I would rather cross M. de Crillon.'

'I am obliged to you,' I muttered, checked as much by his manner as his words.

'Not at all,' he answered more lightly. 'Any information I have is at your disposal.'

However, I saw the imprudence of venturing farther, and hastened to take leave of him, persuading him to allow one of M. de Rambouillet's servants to accompany him home. He said that he should call on me in the morning; and forcing myself to answer him in a suitable manner, I saw him depart one way, and myself, accompanied by Simon Fleix, went off another. My feet were frozen with long standing—I think the corpse we left was scarce colder—but my head was hot with feverish doubts and fears. The moon had sunk and the streets were dark. Our torch had burned out, and we had no light. But where my followers saw only blackness and vacancy, I saw an evil smile and a lean visage fraught with menace and exultation.

For the more closely I directed my mind to the position in which I stood, the graver it seemed. Pitted against Bruhl alone, amid strange surroundings and in an atmosphere of Court intrigue, I had thought my task sufficiently difficult and the disadvantages under which I laboured sufficiently serious before this interview. Conscious of a certain rustiness and a distaste for finesse, with resources so inferior to Bruhl's that even M. de Rosny's liberality had not done much to make up the difference, I had accepted the post offered me rather readily than sanguinely; with joy, seeing that it held out the hope of high reward, but with no certain expectation of success. Still, matched with a man of violent and headstrong character, I had seen no reason to despair; nor any why I might not arrange the secret meeting between the king and mademoiselle with safety, and conduct to its end an intrigue simple and unsuspected, and requiring for its execution rather courage and caution than address or experience.

Now, however, I found that Bruhl was not my only or my most dangerous antagonist. Another was in the field—or, to speak more correctly, was waiting outside the arena, ready to snatch the prize when we should have disabled one another. From a dream of Bruhl and myself as engaged in a competition for the king's favour, wherein neither could expose the other nor appeal even in the last resort to the joint-enemies of his Majesty and ourselves, I awoke to a very different state of things; I awoke to find those enemies the masters of the situation, possessed of the clue to our plans, and permitting them only as long as they seemed to threaten no serious peril to themselves.

No discovery could be more mortifying or more fraught with terror. The perspiration stood on my brow as I recalled the warning which M. de Rosny had uttered against Cardinal Retz, or noted down the various points of knowledge which were in Father Antoine's possession. He knew every event of the last month, with one exception, and could tell, I verily believed, how many crowns I had in my pouch. Conceding this, and the secret sources of information he must possess, what hope had I of keeping my future movements from him? Mademoiselle's arrival would be known to him before she had well passed the gates; nor was it likely, or even possible, that I should again succeed in reaching the king's presence untraced and unsuspected. In fine, I saw myself, equally with Bruhl, a puppet in this man's hands, my goings out and my comings in watched and reported to him, his mercy the only bar between myself and destruction. At any moment I might be arrested as a Huguenot, the enterprise in which I was engaged ruined, and Mademoiselle de la Vire exposed to the violence of Bruhl or the equally dangerous intrigues of the League.

Under these circumstances I fancied sleep impossible; but habit and weariness are strong persuaders, and when I reached my lodging I slept long and soundly, as became a man who had looked danger in the face more than once. The morning light too brought an accession both of courage and hope. I reflected on the misery of my condition at Saint-Jean d'Angely, without friends or resources, and driven to herd with such a man as Fresnoy. And telling myself that the gold crowns which M. de Rosny had lavished upon me were not for nothing, nor the more precious friendship with which he had honoured me a gift that called for no return, I rose with new spirit and a countenance which drew Simon Fleix—

who had seen me lie down the picture of despair—into the utmost astonishment.

'You have had good dreams,' he said, eyeing me jealously and with a disturbed air.

'I had a very evil one last night,' I answered lightly, wondering a little why he looked at me so, and why he seemed to resent my return to hopefulness and courage. I might have followed this train of thought farther with advantage, since I possessed a clue to his state of mind; but at that moment a summons at the door called him away to it, and he presently ushered in M. d'Agen, who, saluting me with punctilious politeness, had not said fifty words before he introduced the subject of his toe—no longer, however, in a hostile spirit, but as the happy medium which had led him to recognise the worth and sterling qualities—so he was pleased to say—of his preserver.

I was delighted to find him in this frame of mind, and told him frankly that the friendship with which his kinsman, M. de Rambouillet, honoured me would prevent me giving him satisfaction save in the last resort. He replied that the service I had done him was such as to render this immaterial, unless I had myself cause of offence; which I was forward to deny.

We were paying one another compliments after this fashion, while I regarded him with the interest which the middle-aged bestow on the young and gallant in whom they see their own youth and hopes mirrored, when the door was again opened, and after a moment's pause admitted, equally, I think, to the disgust of M. François and myself, the form of Father Antoine.

Seldom have two men more diverse stood, I believe, in a room together; seldom has any greater contrast been presented to a man's eyes than that opened to mine on this occasion. On the one side the gay young spark, with his short cloak, his fine suit of black-and-silver, his trim limbs and jewelled hilt and chased comfit-box; on the other, the tall, stooping monk, lean-jawed and bright-eyed, whose gown hung about him in coarse, ungainly folds. And M. François' sentiment on first seeing the other was certainly dislike. In spite of this, however, he bestowed a greeting on the new-comer which evidenced a secret awe, and in other ways showed so plain a desire to please that I felt my fears of the priest return in force. I reflected that the talents which in such a garb could win the respect of M. François d'Agen— a brilliant star among the younger courtiers, and one of a class much given to thinking scorn of their fathers' roughness —must be both great and formidable; and, so considering, I received the monk with a distant courtesy which I had once little thought to extend to him. I put aside for the moment the private grudge I bore him with so much justice, and remembered only the burden which lay on me in my contest with him.

I conjectured without difficulty that he chose to come at this time, when M. François was with me, out of a cunning regard to his own safety; and I was not surprised when M. François, beginning to make his adieux, Father Antoine begged him to wait below, adding that he had something of importance to communicate. He advanced his request in terms of politeness bordering on humility; but I could clearly see that, in assenting to it, M. d'Agen bowed to a will stronger than his own, and would, had he dared to follow his own bent, have given a very different answer. As it was he retired—nominally to give an order to his lackey—with a species of impatient self-restraint which it was not difficult to construe.

Left alone with me, and assured that we had no listeners, the monk was not slow in coming to the point.

'You have thought over what I told you last night?' he said brusquely, dropping in a moment the suave manner which he had maintained in M. François' presence.

I replied coldly that I had.

'And you understand the position?' he continued quickly, looking at me from under his brows as he stood before me, with one clenched fist on the table. 'Or shall I tell you more?

Shall I tell you how poor and despised you were some weeks ago, M. de Marsac—you who now go in velvet, and have three men at your back? Or whose gold it is has brought you here, and made you this? Chut! Do not let us trifle. You are here as the secret agent of the King of Navarre. It is my business to learn your plans and his intentions, and I propose to do so.'

'Well?' I said.

'I am prepared to buy them,' he answered; and his eyes sparkled as he spoke, with a greed which set me yet more on my guard.

'For whom?' I asked. Having made up my mind that I must use the same weapons as my adversary, I reflected that to express indignation, such as might become a young man new to the world, could help me not a whit. 'For whom?' I repeated, seeing that he hesitated.

'That is my business,' he replied slowly.

'You want to know too much and tell too little,' I retorted, yawning.

'And you are playing with me,' he cried, looking at me suddenly, with so piercing a gaze and so dark a countenance that I checked a shudder with difficulty. 'So much the worse for you, so much the worse for you!' he continued fiercely. 'I am here to buy the information you hold, but if you will not sell, there is another way. At an hour's notice I can ruin your plans, and send you to a dungeon! You are like a fish caught in a net not yet drawn. It thrusts its nose this way and that, and touches the mesh, but is slow to take the alarm until the net is drawn—and then it is too late. So it is with you, and so it is,' he added, falling into the ecstatic mood which marked him at times, and left me in doubt whether he were all knave or in part enthusiast, 'with all those who set themselves against Saint Peter and his Church!'

'I have heard you say much the same of the King of France,' I said derisively.

'You trust in him?' he retorted, his eyes gleaming. 'You have been up there, and seen his crowded chamber, and counted his forty-five gentlemen and his grey-coated Swiss? I tell you the splendour you saw was a dream, and will vanish as a dream. The man's strength and his glory shall go from him, and that soon. Have you no eyes to see that he is beside the question? There are but two powers in France—the Holy Union, which still prevails, and the accursed Huguenot; and between them is the battle.'

'Now you are telling me more,' I said.

He grew sober in a moment, looking at me with a vicious anger hard to describe.

'Tut, tut,' he said, showing his yellow teeth, 'the dead tell no tales. And for Henry of Valois, he so loves a monk that you might better accuse his mistress. But for you, I have only to cry "Ho! a Huguenot and a spy!" and though he loved you more than he loved Quélus or Maugiron, he dare not stretch out a finger to save you!'

I knew that he spoke the truth, and with difficulty maintained the air of indifference with which I had entered on the interview.

'But what if I leave Blois?' I ventured, merely to see what he would say.

He laughed 'You cannot,' he answered. 'The net is round you, M. de Marsac, and there are those at every gate who know you and have their instructions. I can destroy you, but I would fain have your information, and for that I will pay you five hundred crowns and let you go.'

'To fall into the hands of the King of Navarre?'

'He will disown you, in any case,' he answered eagerly. 'He had that in his mind, my friend, when he selected an agent so obscure. He will disown you. Ah, mon Dieu! had I been an hour quicker I had caught Rosny—Rosny himself!'

'There is one thing lacking still,' I replied. 'How am I to be sure that, when I have told you what I know, you will pay me the money or let me go?'

'I will swear to it!' he answered earnestly, deceived into thinking I was about to surrender. 'I will give you my oath, M. de Marsac!'

'I would as soon have your shoe-lace!' I exclaimed, the indignation I could not entirely repress finding vent in that phrase. 'A Churchman's vow is worth a candle—or a candle and a half, is it?' I continued ironically. 'I must have some security a great deal more substantial than that, father.'

'What?' he asked, looking at me gloomily.

Seeing an opening, I cudgelled my brains to think of any condition which, being fulfilled, might turn the table on him and place him in my power. But his position was so strong, or my wits so weak, that nothing occurred to me at the time, and I sat looking at him, my mind gradually passing from the possibility of escape to the actual danger in which I stood, and which encompassed also Simon Fleix, and, in a degree, doubtless, M. de Rambouillet. In four or five days, too, Mademoiselle de la Vire would arrive. I wondered if I could send any warning to her; and then, again, I doubted the wisdom of interfering with M. de Rosny's plans, the more as Maignan, who had gone to fetch mademoiselle, was of a kind to disregard any orders save his master's.

'Well!' said the monk, impatiently recalling me to myself, 'what security do you want?'

'I am not quite sure at this moment,' I made answer slowly 'I am in a difficult position. I must have some time to consider.'

'And to rid yourself of me, if it be possible,' he said with irony. 'I quite understand. But I warn you that you are watched; and that wherever you go and whatever you do, eyes which are mine are upon you.'

'I, too, understand,' I said coolly.

He stood awhile uncertain, regarding me with mingled doubt and malevolence, tortured on the one hand by fear of losing the prize if he granted delay, on the other of failing as utterly if he exerted his power and did not succeed in subduing my resolution. I watched him, too, and gauging his eagerness and the value of the stake for which he was striving by the strength of his emotions, drew small comfort from the sight. More than once it had occurred to me, and now it occurred to me again, to extricate myself by a blow. But a natural reluctance to strike an unarmed man, however vile and knavish, and the belief that he had not trusted himself in my power without taking the fullest precautions, withheld me. When he grudgingly, and with many dark threats, proposed to wait three days—and not an hour more—for my answer, I accepted; for I saw no other alternative open. And on these terms, but not without some short discussion, we parted, and I heard his stealthy footstep go sneaking down the stairs.

## 19

# Men Call it Chance

If I were telling more than the truth, or had it in my mind to embellish my adventures, I could, doubtless, by the exercise of a little ingenuity make it appear that I owed my escape from Father Antoine's meshes to my own craft; and tell, in fine, as pretty a story of plots and counterplots as M. de Brantôme has ever woven. Having no desire, however, to magnify myself, and, at this time of day, scarcely any reason, I am fain to confess that the reverse was the case; and that while no man ever did less to free himself than I did, my adversary retained his grasp to the end, and had surely, but for a strange interposition, effected my ruin. How relief came, and from what quarter, I might defy the most ingenious person, after reading my memoirs to this point, to say; and this not so much by reason of any subtle device, as because the hand of Providence was for once directly manifest.

The three days of grace which the priest had granted I passed in anxious but futile search for some means of escape, every plan I conceived dying stillborn, and not the least of my miseries lying in the fact that I could discern no better course than still to sit and think, and seemed doomed to perpetual inaction. M. de Rambouillet being a strict Catholic, though in all other respects a patriotic man, I knew better than to have recourse to him; and the priest's influence over M. d'Agen I had myself witnessed. For similar reasons I rejected the idea of applying to the king; and this exhausting the list of those on whom I had any claim, I found myself thrown on my own resources, which seemed limited—my wits failing me at this pinch—to my sword and Simon Fleix.

Assured that I must break out of Blois if I would save, not myself only, but others more precious because entrusted to my charge, I thought it no disgrace to appeal to Simon; describing in a lively fashion the danger which threatened us, and inciting the lad by every argument which I thought likely to have weight with him to devise some way of escape.

'Now is the time, my friend,' I said, 'to show your wits, and prove that M. de Rosny, who said you had a cunning above the ordinary, was right. If your brain can ever save your head, now is the time! For I tell you plainly, if you cannot find some way to outmanoeuvre this villain before tomorrow, I am spent. You can judge for yourself what chance you will have of going free.'

I paused at that, waiting for him to make some suggestion. To my chagrin he remained silent, leaning his head on his hand, and studying the table with his eyes in a sullen fashion; so that I began to regret the condescension I had evinced in letting him be seated, and found it necessary to remind him that he had taken service with me, and must do my bidding.

'Well,' he said morosely, and without looking up, 'I am ready to do it. But I do not like priests, and this one least of all. I know him, and I will not meddle with him!'

'You will not meddle with him?' I cried, almost beside myself with dismay.

'No, I won't,' he replied, retaining his listless attitude. 'I know him, and I am afraid of him. I am no match for him.'

'Then M. de Rosny was wrong, was he?' I said, giving way to my anger.

'If it please you,' he answered pertly.

This was too much for me. My riding-switch lay handy, and I snatched it up. Before he knew what I would be at, I fell upon him, and gave him such a sound wholesome drubbing as speedily brought him to his senses. When he cried for mercy—which he did not for a good space, being still possessed by the peevish devil which had ridden him ever since his departure from Rosny—I put it to him again whether M. de Rosny was not right. When he at last admitted this, but not till then, I threw the whip away and let him go, but did not cease to reproach him as he deserved.

'Did you think,' I said, 'that I was going to be ruined because you would not use your lazy brains? That I was going to sit still, and let you sulk, while mademoiselle walked blindfold into the toils? Not at all, my friend!'

'Mademoiselle!' he exclaimed, looking at me with a sudden change of countenance, and ceasing to rub himself and scowl, as he had been doing. 'She is not here, and is in no danger.'

'She will be here tomorrow, or the next day,' I said.

'You did not tell me that!' he replied, his eyes glittering. 'Does Father Antoine know it?'

'He will know it the moment she enters the town,' I answered.

Noting the change which the introduction of mademoiselle's name into the affair had wrought in him, I felt something like humiliation. But at the moment I had no choice; it was my business to use such instruments as came to my hand, and not, mademoiselle's safety being at stake, to pick and choose too nicely. In a few minutes our positions were reversed. The lad had grown as hot as I cold, as keenly excited as I critical. When he presently came to a stand in front of me, I saw a strange likeness between his face and the priest's; nor was I astonished when he presently made just such a proposal as I should have expected from Father Antoine himself.

'There is only one thing for it,' he muttered, trembling all over. 'He must be got rid of!'

'Fine talking!' I said, contemptuously. 'If he were a

soldier he might be brought to it. But he is a priest, my friend, and does not fight.'

'Fight? Who wants him to fight?' the lad answered, his face dark, his hands moving restlessly. 'It is the easier done. A blow in the back, and he will trouble us no more.'

'Who is to strike it?' I asked drily.

Simon trembled and hesitated; but presently, heaving a deep sigh, he said, 'I will.'

'It might not be difficult,' I muttered, thinking it over.

'It would be easy,' he answered under his breath. His eyes shone, his lips were white, and his long dark hair hung wet over his forehead.

I reflected; and the longer I did so the more feasible seemed the suggestion. A single word, and I might sweep from my path the man whose existence threatened mine; who would not meet me fairly, but, working against me darkly and treacherously, deserved no better treatment at my hands than that which a detected spy receives. He had wronged my mother; he would fain destroy my friends!

And, doubtless, I shall be blamed by some and ridiculed by more for indulging in scruples at such a time. But I have all my life long been prejudiced against that form of underhand violence which I have heard old men contend came into fashion in our country in modern times, and which certainly seems to be alien from the French character. Without judging others too harshly, or saying that the poniard is never excusable—for then might some wrongs done to women and the helpless go without remedy —I have set my face against its use as unworthy of a soldier. At the time, moreover, of which I am now writing the extent to which our enemies had lately resorted to it tended to fix this feeling with peculiar firmness in my mind; and, but for the very desperate dilemma in which I stood at the moment— and not I alone—I do not think that I should have entertained Simon's proposal for a minute.

As it was, I presently answered him in a way which left him in no doubt of my sentiments. 'Simon, my friend,' I said—and I remember I was a little moved—'you have something still to learn, both as a soldier and a Huguenot. Neither the one nor the other strikes at the back.'

'But if he will not fight?' the lad retorted rebelliously. 'What then?'

It was so clear that our adversary gained an unfair advantage in this way that I could not answer the question. I let it pass, therefore, and merely repeating my former injunction, bade Simon think out another way.

He promised reluctantly to do so, and, after spending some moments in thought, went out to learn whether the house was being watched.

When he returned, his countenance wore so new an expression that I saw at once that something had happened. He did not meet my eye, however, and did not explain, but made as if he would go out again, with something of confusion in his manner. Before finally disappearing, however, he seemed to change his mind once more; for, marching up to me where I stood eyeing him with the utmost astonishment, he stopped before me, and suddenly drawing out his hand, thrust something into mine.

'What is it, man?' I said mechanically.

'Look!' he answered rudely, breaking silence for the first time. 'You should know. Why ask me? What have I to do with it?'

I looked then, and saw that he had given me a knot of velvet precisely similar in shape, size, and material to that well-remembered one which had aided me so opportunely in my search for mademoiselle. This differed from that a little in colour, but in nothing else, the fashion of the bow being the same, and one lappet bearing the initials 'C. d. l. V.,' while the other had the words, '*A moi.*' I gazed at it in wonder. 'But, Simon,' I said, 'what does it mean? Where did you get it?'

'Where should I get it?' he answered jealously. Then, seeming to recollect himself, he changed his tone. 'A woman gave it to me in the street,' he said.

I asked him what woman.

'How should I know?' he answered, his eyes gleaming with anger. 'It was a woman in a mask.'

'Was it Fanchette?' I said sternly.

'It might have been. I do not know,' he responded.

I concluded at first that mademoiselle and her escort had arrived in the outskirts of the city, and that Maignan had justified his reputation for discretion by sending in to learn from me whether the way was clear before he entered. In this notion I was partly confirmed and partly shaken by the accompanying message; which Simon, from whom every scrap of information had to be dragged as blood from a stone, presently delivered.

'You are to meet the sender half an hour after sunset tomorrow evening,' he said, 'on the Parvis at the north-east corner of the Cathedral.'

'Tomorrow evening?'

'Yes, when else?' the lad answered ungraciously. 'I said tomorrow evening.'

I thought this strange. I could understand why Maignan should prefer to keep his charge outside the walls until he heard from me, but not why he should postpone a meeting so long. The message, too, seemed unnecessarily meagre, and I began to think Simon was still withholding something.

'Was that all?' I asked him.

'Yes, all,' he answered, 'except—'

'Except what?' I said sternly.

'Except that the woman showed me the gold token Mademoiselle de la Vire used to carry,' he answered reluctantly, 'and said, if you wanted further assurance that would satisfy you.'

'Did you see the coin?' I cried eagerly.

'To be sure,' he answered.

'Then, mon dieu!' I retorted, 'either you are deceiving me, or the woman you saw deceived you. For mademoiselle has not got the token! I have it; here, in my possession! Now, do you still say you saw it, man?'

'I saw one like it,' he answered, trembling, his face damp. 'That I will swear. And the woman told me what I have told you. And no more.'

'Then it is clear,' I answered, 'that mademoiselle has nothing to do with this, and is doubtless many a league away. This is one of M. de Bruhl's tricks. Fresnoy gave him the token he stole from me. And I told him the story of the velvet knot myself. This is a trap; and had I fallen into it, and gone to the Parvis tomorrow evening, I had never kept another assignation, my lad.'

Simon looked thoughtful. Presently he said, with a crest-fallen air, 'You were to go alone. The woman said that.'

Though I knew well why he had suppressed this item, I forbore to blame him. 'What was the woman like?' I said.

'She had very much of Fanchette's figure,' he answered. He could not go beyond that. Blinded by the idea that the woman was mademoiselle's attendant, and no one else, he had taken little heed of her, and could not even say for certain that she was not a man in woman's clothes.

I thought the matter over and discussed it with him; and was heartily minded to punish M. de Bruhl, if I could discover a way of turning his treacherous plot against himself. But the lack of any precise knowledge of his plans prevented me stirring in the matter; the more as I felt no certainty that I should be master of my actions when the time came.

Strange to say the discovery of this movement on the part of Bruhl, who had sedulously kept himself in the background since the scene in the king's presence, far from increasing my anxieties, had the effect of administering a fillip to my spirits; which the cold and unyielding pressure of the Jacobin had reduced to a low point. Here was something I could understand, resist, and guard against. The feeling that I had once more to do with a man of like aims and passions with myself quickly restored me to the use of my faculties; as I have heard that a swordsman opposed to the powers of evil regains his vigour on finding himself engaged with a mortal foe. Though I knew that the hours of grace were fast running to a close, and that on the morrow the priest would call for an answer, I experienced that evening an unreasonable lightness and cheerfulness. I retired to rest with confidence, and slept in comfort, supported in part, perhaps, by the assurance that in that room where my mother died her persecutor could have no power to harm me.

Upon Simon Fleix, on the other hand, the discovery that Bruhl was moving, and that consequently peril threatened us from a new quarter, had a different effect. He fell into a state of extreme excitement, and spent the evening and a great part of the night in walking restlessly up and down the room, wrestling with the fears and anxieties which beset us, and now talking fast to himself, now biting his nails in an agony of impatience. In vain I adjured him not to meet troubles half-way; or, pointing to the pallet which he occupied at the foot of my couch, bade him, if he could not devise a way of escape, at least to let the matter rest until morning. He had no power to obey, but, tortured by the vivid anticipations which it was his nature to entertain, he continued to ramble to and fro in a fever of the nerves, and had no sooner lain down than he was up again. Remembering, however, how well he had borne himself on the night of mademoiselle's escape from Blois, I refrained from calling him a coward; and contented myself instead with the reflection that nothing sits worse on a fighting-man than too much knowledge—except, perhaps, a lively imagination.

I thought it possible that mademoiselle might arrive next day before Father Antoine called to receive his answer. In this event I hoped to have the support of Maignan's experience. But the party did not arrive. I had to rely on myself and my own resources, and, this being so, determined to refuse the priest's offer, but in all other things to be guided by circumstances.

About noon he came, attended, as was his practice, by two friends, whom he left outside. He looked paler and more shadowy than before, I thought, his hands thinner, and his cheeks more transparent. I could draw no good augury, however, from these signs of frailty, for the brightness of his eyes and the unusual elation of his manner told plainly of a spirit assured of the mastery. He entered the room with an air of confidence, and addressed me in a tone of patronage which left me in no doubt of his intentions; the frankness with which he now laid bare his plans going far to prove that already he considered me no better than his tool.

I did not at once undeceive him, but allowed him to proceed, and even to bring out the five hundred crowns, which he had promised me, and the sight of which he doubtless supposed would clench the matter.

Seeing this he became still less reticent, and spoke so largely that I presently felt myself impelled to ask him if he would answer a question.

'That is as may be, M. de Marsac,' he answered lightly. 'You may ask it.'

'You hint at great schemes which you have in hand, father,' I said. 'You speak of France and Spain and Navarre, and kings and Leagues and cardinals! You talk of secret strings, and would have me believe that if I comply with your wishes I shall find you as powerful a patron as M. de Rosny. But—one moment, if you please,' I continued hastily, seeing that he was about to interrupt me with such eager assurances as I had already heard; 'tell me this. With so many irons in the fire, why did you interfere with one old gentlewoman— for the sake of a few crowns?'

'I will tell you even that,' he answered, his face flushing at my tone. 'Have you ever heard of an elephant? Yes. Well, it has a trunk, you know, with which it can either drag an oak from the earth or lift a groat from the ground. It is so with me. But again you ask,' he continued with an airy grimace, 'why I wanted a few crowns. Enough that I did. There are going to be two things in the world, and two only, M. de Marsac: brains and money. The former I have, and had: the latter I needed—and took.'

'Money and brains?' I said, looking at him thoughtfully.

'Yes,' he answered, his eyes sparkling, his thin nostrils

beginning to dilate. 'Give me these two, and I will rule France!'

'You will rule France?' I exclaimed, amazed beyond measure by his audacity. 'You, man?'

'Yes, I,' he answered, with abominable coolness. 'I, priest, monk, Churchman, clerk. You look surprised, but mark you, sir, there is a change going on. Our time is coming, and yours is going. What hampers our lord the king and shuts him up in Blois, while rebellions stalk through France? Lack of men? No; but lack of money. Who can get the money for him—you the soldier, or I the clerk? A thousand times, I! Therefore, my time is coming, and before you die you will see a priest rule France.'

'God forbid it should be you,' I answered scornfully.

'As you please,' he answered, shrugging his shoulders, and assuming in a breath a mask of humility which sat as ill on his monstrous conceit as ever nun's veil on a trooper. 'Yet it may even be I; by the favour of the Holy Catholic Church, whose humble minister I am.'

I sprang up with a great oath at that, having no stomach for more of the strange transformations, in which this man delighted, and whereof the last had ever the air of being the most hateful. 'You villain!' I cried, twisting my moustaches, a habit I have when enraged. 'And so you would make me a stepping-stone to your greatness. You would bribe me—a soldier and a gentleman. Go, before I do you a mischief. That is all I have to say to you. Go! You have your answer. I will tell you nothing—not a jot or a tittle. Begone from my room!'

He fell back a step in his surprise, and stood against the table biting his nails and scowling at me, fear and chagrin contending with half a dozen devils for the possession of his face. 'So you have been deceiving me,' he said slowly, and at last.

'I have let you deceive yourself,' I answered, looking at him with scorn, but with none of the fear with which he had for a while inspired me. 'Begone, and do your worst.'

'You know what you are doing,' he said. 'I have that will hang you, M. de Marsac—or worse.'

'Go!' I cried.

'You have thought of your friends,' he continued mock· ingly.

'Go!' I said.

'Of Mademoiselle de la Vire, if by any chance she fall into my hands? It will not be hanging for her. You remember the two Foucauds?'—and he laughed.

The vile threat, which I knew he had used to my mother, so worked upon me that I strode forward unable to control myself longer. In another moment I had certainly taken him by the throat and squeezed the life out of his miserable carcase, had not Providence in its goodness intervened to save me. The door, on which he had already laid his hand in terror, opened suddenly. It admitted Simon, who, closing it behind him, stood looking from one to the other of us in nervous doubt; divided between that respect for the priest which a training at the Sorbonne had instilled into him, and the rage which despair arouses in the weakest.

His presence, while it checked me in my purpose, seemed to give Father Antoine courage, for the priest stood his ground, and even turned to me a second time, his face dark with spite and disappointment. 'Good,' he said hoarsely. 'Destroy yourself if you will! I advise you to bar your door, for in an hour the guards will be here to fetch you to the question.'

Simon cried out at the threat, so that I turned and looked at the lad. His knees were shaking, his hair stood on end.

The priest saw his terror and his own opportunity. 'Ay, in an hour,' he continued slowly, looking at him with cruel eyes. 'In an hour, lad! You must be fond of pain to court it, and out of humour with life to throw it away. Or stay,' he continued abruptly, after considering Simon's agony for a moment, and doubtless deducing from it a last hope, 'I will be merciful. I will give you one more chance.'

'And yourself?' I said with a sneer.

'As you please,' he answered, declining to be diverted from the trembling lad, whom his gaze seemed to fascinate. 'I will give you until half an hour after sunset this evening to reconsider the matter. If you make up your minds to accept my terms, meet me then. I leave tonight for Paris, and I will give you until the last moment. But,' he continued grimly, 'if you do not meet me, or, meeting me, remain obstinate—God do so to me, and more also, if you see the sun rise thrice.'

Some impulse, I know not what, seeing that I had no thought of accepting his terms or meeting him, led me to ask briefly, 'Where?'

'On the Parvis of the Cathedral,' he answered after a moment's calculation. 'At the north-east corner, half an hour after sunset. It is a quiet spot.'

Simon uttered a stifled exclamation. And then for a moment there was silence in the room, while the lad breathed hard and irregularly, and I stood rooted to the spot, looking so long and so strangely at the priest that Father Antoine laid his hand again on the door and glanced uneasily behind him. Nor was he content until he had hit on, as he fancied, the cause of my strange regard.

'Ha!' he said, his thin lip curling in conceit at his astuteness, 'I understand. You think to kill me tonight? Let me tell you, this house is watched. If you leave here to meet me with any companion—unless it be M. d'Agen, whom I can trust— I shall be warned, and be gone before you reach the rendez-vous. And gone, mind you,' he added, with a grim smile, 'to sign your death-warrant.'

He went out with that, closing the door behind him; and we heard his step go softly down the staircase. I gazed at Simon, and he at me, with all the astonishment and awe which it was natural we should feel in presence of so remarkable a coincidence.

For by a marvel the priest had named the same spot and the same time as the sender of the velvet knot!

'He will go,' Simon said, his face flushed and his voice trembling, 'and they will go.'

'And in the dark they will not know him,' I muttered. 'He is about my height. They will take him for me!'

'And kill him!' Simon cried hysterically. 'They will kill him! He goes to his death, monsieur. It is the finger of God.'

## 20

# The King's Face

It seemed so necessary to bring home the crime to Bruhl should the priest really perish in the trap laid for me, that I came near to falling into one of those mistakes to which men of action are prone. For my first impulse was to follow the priest to the Parvis, closely enough, if possible, to detect the assassins in the act, and with sufficient force, if I could muster it, to arrest them. The credit of dissuading me from this course lies with Simon, who pointed out its dangers in so convincing a manner that I was brought with little difficulty to relinquish it.

Instead, acting on his advice, I sent him to M. d'Agen's lodging, to beg that young gentleman to call upon me before evening. After searching the lodging and other places in vain, Simon found M. d'Agen in the tennis-court at the Castle, and, inventing a crafty excuse, brought him to my lodging a full hour before the time.

My visitor was naturally surprised to find that I had nothing particular to say to him. I dared not tell him what occupied my thoughts, and for the rest invention failed me. But his gaiety and those pretty affectations on which he spent an infinity of pains, for the purpose, apparently, of hiding the sterling worth of a character deficient neither in courage nor backbone, were united to much good nature.

Believing at last that I had sent for him in a fit of the vapours, he devoted himself to amusing me and abusing Bruhl—a very favourite pastime with him. And in this way he made out a call of two hours.

I had not long to wait for proof of Simon's wisdom in taking this precaution. We thought it prudent to keep within doors after our guest's departure, and so passed the night in ignorance whether anything had happened or not. But about seven next morning one of the Marquis's servants, despatched by M. d'Agen, burst in upon us with the news—which was no news from the moment his hurried footstep sounded on the stairs—that Father Antoine had been set upon and killed the previous evening!

I heard this confirmation of my hopes with grave thankfulness; Simon with so much emotion that when the messenger was gone he sat down on a stool and began to sob and tremble as if he had lost his mother, instead of a mortal foe. I took advantage of the occasion to read him a sermon on the end of crooked courses; nor could I myself recall without a shudder the man's last words to me; or the lawless and evil designs in which he had rejoiced, while standing on the very brink of the pit which was to swallow up both him and them in everlasting darkness.

Naturally, the uppermost feeling in my mind was relief. I was free once more. In all probability the priest had kept his knowledge to himself, and without him his agents would be powerless. Simon, it is true, heard that the town was much excited by the event; and that many attributed it to the Huguenots. But we did not suffer ourselves to be depressed by this, nor had I any foreboding until the sound of a second hurried footstep mounting the stairs reached our ears.

I knew the step in a moment for M. d'Agen's, and something ominous in its ring brought me to my feet before he opened the door. Significant as was his first hasty look round the room, he recovered at sight of me all his habitual *sang-froid*. He saluted me, and spoke coolly, though rapidly. But he panted, and I noticed in a moment that he had lost his lisp.

'I am happy in finding you,' he said, closing the door carefully behind him, 'for I am the bearer of ill news, and there is not a moment to be lost. The king has signed an order for your instant consignment to prison, M. de Marsac, and, once there, it is difficult to say what may not happen.'

'My consignment?' I exclaimed. I may be pardoned if the news for a moment found me unprepared.

'Yes,' he replied quickly. 'The king has signed it at the instance of Marshal Retz.'

'But for what?' I cried in amazement.

'The murder of Father Antoine. You will pardon me,' he continued urgently, 'but this is no time for words. The Provost-Marshal is even now on his way to arrest you. Your only hope is to evade him, and gain an audience of the king. I have persuaded my uncle to go with you, and he is waiting at his lodgings. There is not a moment to be lost, however, if you would reach the king's presence before you are arrested.'

'But I am innocent!' I cried.

'I know it,' M. d'Agen answered, 'and can prove it. But if you cannot get speech of the king innocence will avail you nothing. You have powerful enemies. Come without more ado, M. de Marsac, I pray,' he added.

His manner, even more than his words, impressed me with a sense of urgency; and postponing for a time my own judgment, I hurriedly thanked him for his friendly offices. Snatching up my sword, which lay on a chair, I buckled it on; for Simon's fingers trembled so violently he could give me no help. This done I nodded to M. d'Agen to go first, and followed him from the room, Simon attending us of his own motion. It would be then about eleven o'clock in the fore-noon.

My companion ran down the stairs without ceremony, and so quickly it was all I could do to keep up with him. At the outer door he signed me to stand, and darting himself into the street, he looked anxiously in the direction of the Rue Saint-Denys. Fortunately the coast was still clear, and he beckoned to me to follow him. I did so and starting to walk in the opposite direction as fast as we could, in less than a minute we had put a corner between us and the house.

Our hopes of escaping unseen, however, were promptly dashed. The house, I have said, stood in a quiet by-street, which was bounded on the farther side by a garden-wall buttressed at intervals. We had scarcely gone a dozen paces from my door when a man slipped from the shelter of one of these buttresses, and after a single glance at us, set off to run towards the Rue Saint-Denys.

M. d'Agen looked back and nodded. 'There goes the news,' he said. 'They will try to cut us off, but I think we have the start of them.'

I made no reply, feeling that I had resigned myself entirely into his hands. But as we passed through the Rue de Valois, in part of which a market was held at this hour, attracting a considerable concourse of peasants and others, I fancied I detected signs of unusual bustle and excitement. It seemed unlikely that news of the priest's murder should affect so many people and to such a degree, and I asked M. d'Agen what it meant.

'There is a rumour abroad,' he answered, without slackening speed, 'that the king intends to move south to Tours at once.'

I muttered my surprise and satisfaction. 'He will come to terms with the Huguenots then?' I said.

'It looks like it,' M. d'Agen rejoined. 'Retz's party are in an ill-humour on that account, and will wreak it on you if they get a chance. On guard!' he added abruptly. 'Here are two of them!'

As he spoke we emerged from the crowd, and I saw, half a dozen paces in front of us, and coming to meet us, a couple of Court gallants, attended by as many servants. They espied us at the same moment, and came across the street, which was tolerably wide at that part, with the evident intention of stopping us. Simultaneously, however, we crossed to take their side, and so met them face to face in the middle of the way.

'M. d'Agen,' the foremost exclaimed, speaking in a haughty tone, and with a dark side glance at me, 'I am sorry to see you in such company! Doubtless you are not aware that this gentleman is the subject of an order which has even now been issued to the Provost-Marshal.'

'And if so, sir? What of that?' my companion lisped in his silkiest tone.

'What of that?' the other cried, frowning, and pushing slightly forward.

'Precisely,' M. d'Agen repeated, laying his hand on his hilt and declining to give back. 'I am not aware that his Majesty has appointed you Provost-Marshal, or that you have any warrant, M. Villequier, empowering you to stop gentlemen in the public streets.'

M. Villequier reddened with anger. 'You are young, M. d'Agen,' he said, his voice quivering, 'or I would make you pay dearly for that!'

'My friend is not young,' M. d'Agen retorted, bowing. 'He is a gentleman of birth, M. Villequier; by repute, as I learned yesterday, one of the best swordsmen in France, and no Gascon. If you feel inclined to arrest him, do so I pray. And I will have the honour of engaging your son.'

As we had all by this time our hands on our swords, there needed but a blow to bring about one of those street brawls which were more common then than now. A number of market-people, drawn to the spot by our raised voices, had gathered round, and were waiting eagerly to see what would happen. But Villequier, as my companion perhaps knew, was a Gascon in heart as well as by birth, and seeing our determined aspects, thought better of it. Shrugging his shoulders with an affectation of disdain which imposed on no one, he signalled to his servants to go on, and himself stood aside.

'I thank you for your polite offer,' he said with an evil smile, 'and will remember it. But as you say, sir, I am not the Provost-Marshal.'

Paying little heed to his words, we bowed, passed him, and hurried on. But the peril was not over. Not only had the *rencontre* cost us some precious minutes, but the Gascon, after letting us proceed a little way, followed us. And word being passed by his servants, as we supposed, that one of us was the murderer of Father Antoine, the rumour spread through the crowd like wildfire, and in a few moments we found ourselves attended by a troop of *canaille* who, hanging on our skirts, caused Simon Fleix no little apprehension. Not withstanding the contempt which M. d'Agen, whose bearing throughout was admirable, expressed for them, we might have found it necessary to turn and teach them a lesson had we not reached M. de Rambouillet's in the nick of time; where we found the door surrounded by half a dozen armed servants, at sight of whom our persecutors fell back with the cowardice which is usually found in that class.

If I had been tempted of late to think M. de Rambouillet fickle, I had no reason to complain now; whether his attitude was due to M. d'Agen's representations, or to the reflection that without me the plans he had at heart must miscarry. I found him waiting within, attended by three gentlemen, all cloaked and ready for the road; while the air of purpose which sat on his brow indicated that he thought the crisis no common one. Not a moment was lost, even in explanations. Waving me to the door again, and exchanging a few sentences with his nephew, he gave the word to start, and we issued from the house in a body. Doubtless the fact that those who sought to ruin me were his political enemies had some weight with him; for I saw his face harden as his eyes met those of M. de Villequier, who passed slowly before the door as we came out. The Gascon, however, was not the man to interfere with so large a party, and dropped back; while M. de Rambouillet, after exchanging a cold salute with him, led the way towards the Castle at a round pace. His nephew and I walked one on either side of him, and the others, to the number of ten or eleven, pressed on behind in a compact body, our cortège presenting so determined a front that the crowd, which had remained hanging about the door, fled every way. Even some peaceable folk who found themselves in our road took the precaution of slipping into doorways, or stood aside to give us the full width of the street.

I remarked—and I think it increased my anxiety—that our leader was dressed with more than usual care and richness, but, unlike his attendants, wore no arms. He took occasion, as we hurried along, to give me a word of advice. 'M. de Marsac,' he said, looking at me suddenly, 'my nephew has given me to understand that you place yourself entirely in my hands.'

I replied that I asked for no better fortune, and, whatever the event, thanked him from the bottom of my heart.

'Be pleased then to keep silence until I bid you speak,' he replied sharply, for he was one of those whom a sudden stress sours and exacerbates. 'And, above all, no violence without my orders. We are about to fight a battle, and a critical one, but it must be won with our heads. If we can we will keep you out of the Provost-Marshal's hands.'

And if not? I remembered the threats Father Antoine had used, and in a moment I lost sight of the street with all its light and life and movement. I felt no longer the wholesome stinging of the wind. I tasted instead a fetid air, and saw round me a narrow cell and masked figures, and in particular a swarthy man in a leather apron leaning over a brazier, from which came lurid flames. And I was bound. I experienced that utter helplessness which is the last test of courage. The man came forward, and then—then, thank God! the vision passed away. An exclamation to which M. d'Agen gave vent, brought me back to the present, and to the blessed knowledge that the fight was not yet over.

We were within a score of paces, I found, of the Castle gates; but so were also a second party, who had just debouched from a side-street, and now hurried on, pace for pace, with us, with the evident intention of forestalling us. The race ended in both companies reaching the entrance at the same time, with the consequence of some jostling taking place amongst the servants. This must have led to blows but for the strenuous commands which M. de Rambouillet had laid upon his followers. I found myself in a moment confronted by a row of scowling faces, while a dozen threatening hands were stretched out towards me, and as many voices, among which I recognised Fresnoy's, cried out tumultuously, 'That is he! That is the one!'

An elderly man in a quaint dress stepped forward, a paper in his hand, and, backed as he was by half a dozen halberdiers, would in a moment have laid hands on me if M. de Rambouillet had not intervened with a negligent air of authority, which sat on him the more gracefully as he held nothing but a riding-switch in his hands. 'Tut, tut! What is this?' he said lightly. 'I am not wont to have my people interfered with, M. Provost, without my leave. You know me, I suppose?'

'Perfectly, M. le Marquis,' the man answered with dogged respect; 'but this is by the king's special command.'

'Very good,' my patron answered, quietly eyeing the faces behind the Provost-Marshal, as if he were making a note of them; which caused some of the gentlemen manifest uneasiness. 'That is soon seen, for we are even now about to seek speech with his Majesty.'

'Not this gentleman,' the Provost-Marshal answered firmly, raising his hand again. 'I cannot let him pass.'

'Yes, this gentleman too, by your leave,' the Marquis retorted, lightly putting the hand aside with his cane.

'Sir,' said the other, retreating a step, and speaking with some heat, 'this is no jest with all respect. I hold the king's own order, and it may not be resisted.'

The nobleman tapped his silver comfit-box and smiled. 'I shall be the last to resist it—if you have it,' he said languidly.

'You may read it for yourself,' the Provost-Marshal answered, his patience exhausted.

M. de Rambouillet took the parchment with the ends of his fingers, glanced at it, and gave it back. 'As I thought,' he said, 'a manifest forgery.'

'A forgery!' cried the officer, crimson with indignation. 'And I had it from the hands of the king's own secretary!'

At this those behind murmured, some 'shame,' and some one thing, and some another—all with an air so threatening that the Marquis's gentlemen closed up behind him, and M. d'Agen laughed rudely.

But M. de Rambouillet remained unmoved. 'You may have had it from whom you please, sir,' he said. 'It is a forgery, and I shall resist its execution. If you choose to await me here, I will give you my word to render this gentleman to you within an hour, should the order hold good. If you will not wait, I shall command my servants to clear the way, and if ill happen, then the responsibility will lie with you.'

He spoke in so resolute a manner it was not difficult to see that something more was at stake than the arrest of a single man. This was so; the real issue was whether the king, with whose instability it was difficult to cope, should fall back into the hands of his old advisers or not. My arrest was a move in the game intended as a counterblast to the victory which M. de Rambouillet had gained when he persuaded the king to move to Tours; a city in the neighbourhood of the Huguenots, and a place of arms whence union with them would be easy.

The Provost-Marshal could, no doubt, make a shrewd guess at these things. He knew that the order he had would be held valid or not according as one party or the other gained the mastery; and, seeing M. de Rambouillet's resolute demeanour, he gave way. Rudely interrupted more than once by his attendants, among whom were some of Bruhl's men, he muttered an ungracious assent to our proposal; on which, and without a moment's delay, the Marquis took me by the arm and hurried me across the courtyard.

And so far, well. My heart began to rise. But, for the Marquis, as we mounted the staircase the anxiety he had dissembled while we faced the Provost-Marshal broke out in angry mutterings; from which I gathered that the crisis was yet to come. I was not surprised, therefore, when an usher rose on our appearance in the antechamber, and, quickly crossing the floor, interposed between us and the door of the chamber, informing the Marquis with a low obeisance that his Majesty was engaged.

'He will see me,' M. de Rambouillet cried, looking haughtily round on the sneering pages and lounging court-iers, who grew civil under his eye.

'I have particular orders, sir, to admit no one,' the man answered.

'Tut, tut, they do not apply to me,' my companion retorted, nothing daunted. 'I know the business on which the king is engaged, and I am here to assist him.' And raising his hand he thrust the startled official aside, and hardily pushed the doors of the chamber open.

The king, surrounded by half a dozen persons, was in the act of putting on his riding-boots. On hearing us, he turned his head with a startled air, and dropped in his confusion one of the ivory cylinders he was using; while his aspect, and that of the persons who stood round him, reminded me irresistibly of a party of schoolboys detected in a fault.

He recovered himself, it is true, almost immediately; and turning his back to us, continued to talk to the persons round him on such trifling subjects as commonly engaged him. He carried on this conversation in a very free way, studiously ignoring our presence; but it was plain he remained aware of it, and even that he was uneasy under the cold and severe gaze which the Marquis, who seemed in nowise affrighted by his reception, bent upon him.

I, for my part, had no longer any confidence. Nay, I came near to regretting that I had persevered in an attempt so useless. The warrant which awaited me at the gates seemed less formidable than his Majesty's growing displeasure; which I saw I was incurring by remaining where I was. It needed not the insolent glance of Marshal Retz, who lounged smiling by the king's hand, or the laughter of a couple of pages who stood at the head of the chamber, to deprive me of my last hope; while some things which might have cheered me—the uneasiness of some about the king, and the disquietude which underlay Marshal Retz's manner—escaped my notice altogether.

What I did see clearly was that the king's embarrassment was fast changing to anger. The paint which reddened his cheeks prevented any alteration in his colour being visible, but his frown and the nervous manner in which he kept taking off and putting on his jewelled cap betrayed him. At length, signing to one of his companions to follow, he moved a little aside to a window, whence, after a few moments, the gentleman came to us.

'M. de Rambouillet,' he said, speaking coldly and formally, 'his Majesty is displeased by this gentleman's presence, and requires him to withdraw forthwith.'

'His Majesty's word is law,' my patron answered, bowing low, and speaking in a clear voice audible throughout the chamber, 'but the matter which brings this gentleman here is of the utmost importance, and touches his Majesty's person.'

M. de Retz laughed jeeringly. The other courtiers looked grave. The king shrugged his shoulders with a peevish gesture, but after a moment's hesitation, during which he looked first at Retz and then at M. de Rambouillet, he signed to the Marquis to approach.

'Why have you brought him here?' he muttered sharply, looking askance at me. 'He should have been bestowed according to my orders.'

'He has information for your Majesty's private ear,' Rambouillet answered. And he looked so meaningly at the king that Henry, I think, remembered on a sudden his compact with Rosny, and my part in it; for he started with the air of a man suddenly awakened. 'To prevent that information reaching you, sire,' my patron continued, 'his enemies have practised on your Majesty's well-known sense of justice.'

'Oh, but stay, stay!' the king cried, hitching forward the scanty cloak he wore, which barely came down to his waist. 'The man has killed a priest! He has killed a priest, man!'

he repeated with confidence, as if he had now got hold of the right argument.

'That is not so, sire, craving your Majesty's pardon,' M. de Rambouillet replied with the utmost coolness.

'Tut! Tut! The evidence is clear,' the king said peevishly.

'As to that, sire,' my companion rejoined, 'if it is of the murder of Father Antoine he is accused, I say boldly that there is none.'

'Then there you are mistaken!' the king answered. 'I heard it with my own ears this morning.'

'Will you deign, sire, to tell me its nature?' M. de Rambouillet persisted.

But on that Marshal Retz thought it necessary to intervene. 'Need we turn his Majesty's chamber into a court of justice?' he said smoothly. Hitherto he had not spoken; trusting, perhaps, to the impression he had already made upon the king.

M. de Rambouillet took no notice of him.

'But Bruhl,' said the king, 'you see, Bruhl says—'

'Bruhl!' my companion replied, with so much contempt that Henry started. 'Surely your Majesty has not taken his word against this gentleman, of all people?'

Thus reminded, a second time, of the interests entrusted to me, and of the advantage which Bruhl would gain by my disappearance, the king looked first confused, and then angry. He vented his passion in one or two profane oaths, with the childish addition that we were all a set of traitors, and that he had no one whom he could trust. But my companion had touched the right chord at last; for when the king grew more composed, he waved aside Marshal Retz's protestations, and sullenly bade Rambouillet say what he had to say.

'The monk was killed, sire, about sunset,' he answered. 'Now my nephew, M. d'Agen, is without, and will tell your Majesty that he was with this gentleman at his lodgings from about an hour before sunset last evening until a full hour after. Consequently, M. de Marsac can hardly be the assassin, and M. le Maréchal must look elsewhere if he wants vengeance.'

'Justice, sir, not vengeance,' Marshal Retz said with a dark glance. His keen Italian face hid his trouble well, but a little pulse of passion beating in his olive cheek betrayed the secret to those who knew him. He had a harder part to play than his opponent; for while Rambouillet's hands were clean, Retz knew himself a traitor, and liable at any moment to discovery and punishment.

'Let M. d'Agen be called,' Henry said curtly.

'And if your Majesty pleases,' Retz added, 'M. de Bruhl also. If you really intend, sire, that is, to reopen a matter which I thought had been settled.'

The king nodded obstinately, his face furrowed with ill-temper. He kept his shifty eyes, which seldom met those of the person he addressed, on the floor; and this accentuated the awkward stooping carriage which was natural to him. There were seven or eight dogs of exceeding smallness in the room, and while we waited for the persons who had been summoned, he kicked, now one and now another of the baskets which held them, as if he found in this some vent for his ill-humour.

The witnesses presently appeared, followed by several persons, among whom were the Dukes of Nevers and Mercoeur, who came to ride out with the king, and M. de Crillon; so that the chamber grew passably full. The two dukes nodded formally to the Marquis, as they passed him, but entered into a muttered conversation with Retz, who appeared to be urging them to press his cause. They seemed to decline, however, shrugging their short cloaks as if the matter were too insignificant. Crillon on his part cried audibly, and with an oath, to know what the matter was; and being informed, asked whether all this fuss was being made about a damned shaveling monk.

Henry, whose tenderness for the cowl was well known, darted an angry glance at him, but contented himself with saying sharply to M. d'Agen, 'Now, sir, what do you know about the matter?'

'One moment, sire,' M. Rambouillet cried, interposing

before François could answer. 'Craving your Majesty's pardon, you have heard M. de Bruhl's account. May I, as a favour to myself, beg you, sire, to permit us also to hear it?'

'What?' Marshal Retz exclaimed angrily, 'are we to be the judges, then, or his Majesty? Arnidieu!' he continued hotly, 'what, in the fiend's name, have we to do with it? I protest 'fore Heaven—'

'Ay, sir, and what do you protest?' my champion retorted turning to him with stern disdain.

'Silence!' cried the king, who had listened almost bewildered. 'Silence! By God, gentlemen,' he continued, his eye travelling round the circle with a sparkle of royal anger in it not unworthy of his crown, 'you forget yourselves. I will have none of this quarrelling in my presence or out of it. I lost Quélus and Maugiron that way, and loss enough, and I will have none of it, I say! M. de Bruhl,' he added, standing erect, and looking for the moment, with all his paint and frippery, a king, 'M. de Bruhl, repeat your story.'

The feelings with which I listened to this controversy may be imagined. Devoured in turn by hope and fear as now one side and now the other seemed likely to prevail, I confronted at one moment the gloom of the dungeon, and at another tasted the air of freedom, which had never seemed so sweet before. Strong as these feelings were, however, they gave way to curiosity at this point, when I heard Bruhl called, and saw him come forward at the king's command. Knowing this man to be himself guilty, I marvelled with what face he would present himself before all those eyes, and from what depths of impudence he could draw supplies in such an emergency.

I need not have troubled myself, however, for he was fully equal to the occasion. His high colour and piercing black eyes met the gaze of friend and foe alike without flinching. Dressed well and elegantly, he wore his raven hair curled in the mode, and looked alike gay, handsome, and imperturbable. If there was a suspicion of coarseness about his bulkier figure, as he stood beside M. d'Agen, who was the courtier perfect and point devise, it went to the scale of sincerity, seeing that men naturally associate truth with strength.

'I know no more than this, sire,' he said easily; 'that, happening to cross the Parvis at the moment of the murder, I heard Father Antoine scream. He uttered four words only, in the tone of a man in mortal peril. They were'—and here the speaker looked for an instant at me—'Ha! Marsac! *A moi!*'

'Indeed!' M. de Rambouillet said, after looking to the king for permission. 'And that was all? You saw nothing?'

Bruhl shook his head. 'It was too dark,' he said.

'And heard no more?'

'No.'

'Do I understand, then,' the Marquis continued slowly, 'that M. de Marsac is arrested because the priest—God rest his soul!—cried to him for help?'

'For help?' M. de Retz exclaimed fiercely.

'For help?' said the king, surprised. And at that the most ludicrous change fell upon the faces of all. The king looked puzzled, the Duke of Nevers smiled, the Duke of Mercoeur laughed aloud. Crillon cried boisterously, 'Good hit!' and the majority, who wished no better than to divine the winning party, grinned broadly, whether they would or no.

To Marshal Retz, however, and Bruhl, that which to everyone else seemed an amusing retort had a totally different aspect; while the former turned yellow with chagrin and came near to choking, the latter looked as chapfallen and startled as if his guilt had been that moment brought home to him. Assured by the tone of the monk's voice—which must, indeed, have thundered in his ears—that my name was uttered in denunciation by one who thought me his assailant, he had chosen to tell the truth without reflecting that words, so plain to him, might bear a different construction when repeated.

'Certainly the words seem ambiguous,' Henry muttered.

'But it was Marsac killed him,' Retz cried in a rage.

'It is for some evidence of that we are waiting,' my champion answered suavely.

The Marshal looked helplessly at Nevers and Mercoeur, who commonly took part with him; but apparently those noblemen had not been primed for this occasion. They merely shook their heads and smiled. In the momentary silence which followed, while all looked curiously at Bruhl, who could not conceal his mortification, M. d'Agen stepped forward.

'If your Majesty will permit me,' he said, a malicious simper crossing his handsome face—I had often remarked his extreme dislike for Bruhl without understanding it—'I think I can furnish some evidence more to the point than that to which M. de Bruhl has with so much fairness restricted himself.' He then went on to state that he had had the honour of being in my company at the time of the murder; and he added, besides, so many details as to exculpate me to the satisfaction of any candid person.

The king nodded. 'That settles the matter,' he said, with a sigh of relief. 'You think so, Mercoeur, do you not? Precisely. Villequier, see that the order respecting M. de Marsac is cancelled.'

M. de Retz could not control his wrath on hearing this direction given. 'At this rate,' he cried recklessly, 'we shall have few priests left here! We have got a bad name at Blois, as it is!'

For a moment all in the circle held their breath, while the king's eyes flashed fire at this daring allusion to the murder of the Duke de Guise, and his brother the Cardinal. But it was Henry's misfortune to be ever indulgent in the wrong place, and severe when severity was either unjust or impolitic. He recovered himself with an effort, and revenged himself only by omitting to invite the Marshal, who was now trembling in his shoes, to join his riding-party.

The circle broke up amid some excitement. I stood on one side with M. d'Agen, while the king and his immediate following passed out, and, greatly embarrassed as I was by the civil congratulating of many who would have seen me hang with equal goodwill, I was sharp enough to see that something was brewing between Bruhl and Marshal Retz, who stood back conversing in low tones. I was not surprised, therefore, when the former made his way towards me through the press which filled the antechamber, and with a lowering brow requested a word with me.

'Certainly,' I said, watching him narrowly, for I knew him to be both treacherous and a bully. 'Speak on, sir.'

'You have balked me once and again,' he rejoined, in a voice which shook a little, as did the fingers with which he stroked his waxed moustache. "There is no need of words between us. I, with one sword besides, will tomorrow at noon keep the bridge at Chaverny, a league from here. It is an open country. Possibly your pleasure may lead you to ride that way with a friend?'

'You may depend upon me, sir,' I answered, bowing low, and feeling thankful that the matter was at length to be brought to a fair and open arbitration. 'I will be there—and in person. For my deputy last night,' I added, searching his face with a steadfast eye, 'seems to have been somewhat unlucky.'

# 21

# Two Women

Out of compliment, and to show my gratitude, I attended M. de Rambouillet home to his lodging, and found him as much pleased with himself, and consequently with me, as I was with him. For the time, indeed, I came near to loving him; and, certainly, he was a man of high and patriotic feeling, and of skill and conduct to match. But he lacked that touch of nature and that power of sympathising with others which gave to such men as M. de Rosny and the king, my master, their peculiar charm; though after what I have related of him in the last chapter it does not lie in my mouth to speak ill of him. And, indeed, he was a good man.

When I at last reached my lodging, I found a surprise awaiting me in the shape of a note which had just arrived no one knew how. If the manner of its delivery was mysterious, however, its contents were brief and sufficiently explicit; for it ran thus: '*Sir, by meeting me three hours after noon in the square before the House of the Little Sisters you will do a service at once to yourself and to the undersigned, Marie de Bruhl.*'

That was all, written in a feminine character, yet it was enough to perplex me. Simon, who had manifested the liveliest joy at my escape, would have had me treat it as I had treated the invitation to the Parvis of the Cathedral; ignore it altogether I mean. But I was of a different mind, and this for three reasons, among others: that the request was straightforward, the time early, and the place sufficiently public to be an unlikely theatre for violence, though well fitted for an interview to which the world at large was not invited. Then, too, the square lay little more than a bowshot from my lodging, though on the farther side of the Rue Saint-Denys.

Besides, I could conceive many grounds which Madame de Bruhl might have for seeing me; of which some touched me nearly. I disregarded Simon's warnings, therefore, and repaired at the time appointed to the place—a clean, paved square a little off the Rue Saint-Denys, and entered from the latter by a narrow passage. It was a spot pleasantly convenient for meditation, but overlooked on one side by the House of the Little Sisters; in which, as I guessed afterwards, madame must have awaited me, for the square when I entered it was empty, yet in a moment, though no one came in from the street, she stood beside me. She wore a mask and long cloak. The beautiful hair and perfect complexion, which had filled me with so much admiration at our first meeting in her house, were hidden, but I saw enough of her figure and carriage to be sure that it was Madame de Bruhl and no other.

She began by addressing me in a tone of bitterness, for which I was not altogether unprepared.

'Well, sir,' she exclaimed, her voice trembling with anger, 'you are satisfied, I hope, with your work?'

I expected this and had my answer ready. 'I am not aware, madame,' I said, 'that I have cause to reproach myself. But, however that may be, I trust you have summoned me for some better purpose than to chide me for another's fault; though it was my voice which brought it to light.'

'Why did you shame me publicly?' she retorted, thrusting her handkerchief to her lips and withdrawing it again with a passionate gesture.

'Madame,' I answered patiently—I was full of pity for her, 'consider for a moment the wrong your husband did me, and how small and inadequate was the thing I did to him in return.'

'To him!' she ejaculated so fiercely that I started. 'It was to me—to me you did it! What had I done that you should expose me to the ridicule of those who know no pity, and the anger of one as merciless? What had I done, sir?'

I shook my head sorrowfully. 'So far, madame,' I answered, 'I allow I owe you reparation, and I will make it should it ever be in my power. Nay, I will say more,' I continued, for the tone in which she spoke had wrung my heart. 'In one point I strained the case against your husband. To the best of my belief he abducted the lady who was in my charge, not for the love of her, but for political reasons, and as the agent of another.'

She gasped. 'What?' she cried. 'Say that again!'

As I complied she tore off her mask and gazed into my face with straining eyes and parted lips. I saw then how much she was changed, even in these few days—how pale and worn were her cheeks, how dark the circles round her eyes. 'Will you swear to it?' she said at last, speaking with uncontrollable eagerness, while she laid a hand which shook with excitement on my arm. 'Will you swear to it, sir?'

'It is true,' I answered steadfastly. I might have added that after the event her husband had so treated mademoiselle as to lead her to fear the worst. But I refrained, feeling that it was no part of my duty to come between husband and wife.

She clasped her hands, and for a moment looked passionately upwards, as though she were giving thanks to Heaven; while the flush of health and loveliness which I had so much admired returned, and illuminated her face in a wonderful manner. She seemed, in truth and for the moment, transformed. Her blue eyes filled with tears, her lips moved; nor have I ever seen anything bear so much a resemblance to those pictures of the Virgin Mary which Romans worship as madame did then.

The change, however, was as evanescent as it was admirable. In an instant she seemed to collapse. She struck her hands to her face and moaned, and I saw tears, which she vainly strove to restrain, dropping through her fingers. 'Too late!' she murmured, in a tone of anguish which wrung my heart. 'Alas, you robbed me of one man, you give me back another. I know him now for what he is. If he did not love then, he does now. It is too late!'

She seemed so much overcome that I assisted her to reach a bench which stood against the wall a few paces away; nor, I confess, was it without difficulty and much self-reproach that I limited myself to those prudent offices only which her state and my duty required. To console her on the subject of her husband was impossible; to ignore him, and so to console her, a task which neither my discretion nor my sense of honour, though sorely tried, permitted me to undertake.

She presently recovered and, putting on her mask, again said hurriedly that she had a word to say to me. 'You have treated me honestly,' she continued, 'and, though I have no cause to do anything but hate you, I say in return, look to yourself! You escaped last night—I know all, for it was my velvet knot—which I had made thinking to send it to you to procure this meeting—that he used as a lure. But he is not yet at the end of his resources. Look to yourself, therefore.'

I thought of the appointment I had made with him for the

morrow, but I confined myself to thanking her, merely saying, as I bowed over the hand she resigned to me in token of farewell, 'Madame, I am grateful. I am obliged to you both for your warning and your forgiveness.'

Bending her head coldly she drew away her hand. At that moment, as I lifted my eyes, I saw something which for an instant rooted me to the spot with astonishment. In the entrance of the passage which led to the Rue Saint-Denys two people were standing, watching us. The one was Simon Fleix, and the other, a masked woman, a trifle below the middle height, and clad in a riding-coat, was Mademoiselle de la Vire!

I knew her in a moment. But the relief I experienced on seeing her safe and in Blois was not unmixed with annoyance that Simon Fleix should have been so imprudent as to parade her unnecessarily in the street. I felt something of confusion also on my own account; for I could not tell how long she and her escort had been watching me. And these two feelings were augmented when, after turning to pay a final salute to Madame de Bruhl, I looked again towards the passage and discovered that mademoiselle and her squire were gone.

Impatient as I was, I would not seem to leave madame rudely or without feeling, after the consideration she had shown me in her own sorrow; and accordingly I waited uncovered until she disappeared within the Little Sisters. Then I started eagerly towards my lodging, thinking I might yet overtake mademoiselle before she entered. I was destined to meet, however, with another though very pertinent hindrance. As I passed from the Rue Saint-Denys into the quiet of my street I heard a voice calling my name, and, looking back, saw M. de Rambouillet's equerry, a man deep in his confidence, running after me. He brought a message from his master, which he begged me to consider of the first importance.

'The Marquis would not trust it to writing, sir,' he continued, drawing me aside into a corner where we were conveniently retired, 'but he made me learn it by heart.

"Tell M. de Marsac," said he, "that that which he was left in Blois to do must be done quickly, or not at all. There is something afoot in the other camp, I am not sure what. But now is the time to knock in the nail. I know his zeal, and I depend upon him."'

An hour before I should have listened to this message with serious doubts and misgivings. Now, acquainted with mademoiselle's arrival, I returned M. de Rambouillet an answer in the same strain, and parting civilly from Bertram, who was a man I much esteemed, I hastened on to my lodgings, exulting in the thought that the hour and the woman were come at last, and that before the dawn of another day I might hope, all being well, to accomplish with honour to myself and advantage to others the commission which M. de Rosny had entrusted to me.

I must not deny that, mingled with this, was some excitement at the prospect of seeing mademoiselle again. I strove to conjure up before me as I mounted the stairs the exact expression of her face as I had last seen it bending from the window at Rosny; to the end that I might have some guide for my future conduct, and might be less likely to fall into the snare of a young girl's coquetry. But I could come now, as then, to no satisfactory or safe conclusion, and only felt anew the vexation I had experienced on losing the velvet knot, which she had given me on that occasion.

I knocked at the door of the rooms which I had reserved for her, and which were on the floor below my own; but I got no answer. Supposing that Simon had taken her upstairs, I mounted quickly, not doubting I should find her there. Judge of my surprise and dismay when I found that room also empty, save for the lackey whom M. de Rambouillet had lent me!

'Where are they?' I asked the man, speaking sharply, and standing with my hand on the door.

'The lady and her woman, sir?' he answered, coming forward.

'Yes, yes!' I cried impatiently, a sudden fear at my heart.

'She went out immediately after her arrival with Simon Fleix, sir, and has not yet returned,' he answered.

The words were scarcely out of his mouth before I heard several persons enter the passage below and begin to ascend the stairs. I did not doubt that mademoiselle and the lad had come home another way and been somehow detained; and I turned with a sigh of relief to receive them. But when the persons whose steps I had heard appeared, they proved to be only M. de Rosny's equerry, stout, burly, and bright-eyed as ever, and two armed servants.

## 22

# 'La Femme Dispose'

The moment the equerry's foot touched the uppermost stair I advanced upon him. 'Where is your mistress, man?' I said. 'Where is Mademoiselle de la Vire? Be quick, tell me what you have done with her.'

His face fell amazingly. 'Where is she?' he answered, faltering between surprise and alarm at my sudden onslaught. 'Here, she should be. I left her here not an hour ago. Mon Dieu! Is she not here now ?'

His alarm increased mine tenfold. 'No!' I retorted, 'she is not! She is gone! And you—what business had you, in the fiend's name, to leave her here, alone and unprotected? Tell me that!'

He leaned against the balustrade, making no attempt to defend himself, and seemed, in his sudden terror, anything but the bold, alert fellow, who had ascended the stairs two minutes before. 'I was a fool,' he groaned. 'I saw your man Simon here; and Fanchette, who is as good as a man, was with her mistress. And I went to stable the horses. I thought no evil. And now—My God!' he added, suddenly straightening himself, while his face grew hard and grim, 'I am undone! My master will never forgive me!'

'Did you come straight here?' I said, considering that, after all, he was no more in fault than I had been on a former occasion.

'We went first to M. de Rosny's lodging,' he answered, 'where we found your message telling us to come here. We came on without dismounting.'

'Mademoiselle may have gone back, and be there,' I said.

'It is possible. Do you stay here and keep a good look-out, and I will go and see. Let one of your men come with me.'

He uttered a brief assent; being a man as ready to take as to give orders, and thankful now for any suggestion which held out a hope of mademoiselle's safety. Followed by the servant he selected, I ran down the stairs, and in a moment was hurrying along the Rue Saint-Denys. The day was waning. The narrow streets and alleys were already dark, but the air of excitement which I had noticed in the morning still marked the townsfolk, of whom a great number were strolling abroad, or standing in doorways talking to their gossips. Feverishly anxious as I was, I remarked the gloom which dwelt on all faces; but as I set it down to the king's approaching departure, and besides was intent on seeing that those we sought did not by any chance pass us in the crowd, I thought little of it. Five minutes' walking brought us to M. de Rosny's lodging. There I knocked at the door; impatiently, I confess, and with little hope of success. But, to my surprise, barely an instant elapsed before the door opened, and I saw before me Simon Fleix!

Discovering who it was, he cowered back, with a terrified face, retreated to the wall with his arm raised.

'You scoundrel!' I exclaimed, restraining myself with difficulty. 'Tell me this moment where Mademoiselle de la Vire is! Or, by Heaven, I shall forget what my mother owed to you, and do you a mischief!'

For an instant he glared at me viciously, with all his teeth exposed, as though he meant to refuse—and more. Then he thought better of it, and, raising his hand, pointed sulkily upwards.

'Go before me and knock at the door,' I said, tapping the hilt of my dagger with meaning.

Cowed by my manner, he obeyed, and led the way to the room in which M. de Rambouillet had surprised us on a former occasion. Here he stopped at the door and knocked gently; on which a sharp voice inside bade us enter. I raised the latch and did so, closing the door behind me.

Mademoiselle, still wearing her riding-coat, sat in a chair before the hearth, on which a newly kindled fire sputtered and smoked. She had her back to me, and did not turn on my entrance, but continued to toy in an absent manner with the strings of the mask which lay in her lap. Fanchette stood bolt upright behind her, with her elbows squared and her hands clasped; in such an attitude that I guessed the maid had been expressing her strong dissatisfaction with this latest whim of her mistress, and particularly with mademoiselle's imprudence in wantonly exposing herself, with so inadequate a guard as Simon, in a place where she had already suffered so much. I was confirmed in this notion on seeing the woman's harsh countenance clear at sight of me; though the churlish nod, which was all the greeting she bestowed on me, seemed to betoken anything but favour or good-will. She touched her mistress on the shoulder, however, and said, 'M. de Marsac is here.'

Mademoiselle turned her head and looked at me languidly, without stirring in her chair or removing the foot she was warming. 'Good evening,' she said.

The greeting seemed so brief and so commonplace, ignoring, as it did, both the pains and anxiety to which she had just put me and the great purpose for which we were here —to say nothing of that ambiguous parting which she must surely remember as well as I—that the words I had prepared died on my lips, and I looked at her in honest confusion. All her small face was pale except her lips. Her brow was dark, her eyes were hard as well as weary. And not words only failed me as I looked at her, but anger; having mounted the stairs hotfoot to chide, I felt on a sudden—despite my new cloak and scabbard, my appointment, and the name I had made at Court—the same consciousness of age and shabbiness and poverty which had possessed me in her presence from the beginning. I muttered, 'Good evening, mademoiselle,' and that was all I could say—I who had frightened the burly Maignan a few minutes before!

Seeing, I have no doubt, the effect she produced on me, she maintained for some time an embarrassing silence. At length she said, frigidly, 'Perhaps M. de Marsac will sit, Fanchette. Place a chair for him. I am afraid, however, that after his success at Court he may find our reception somewhat cold. But we are only from the country,' she added, looking at me askance, with a gleam of anger in her eyes.

I thanked her huskily, saying that I would not sit, as I could not stay. 'Simon Fleix,' I continued, finding my voice with difficulty, 'has, I am afraid, caused you some trouble by bringing you to this house instead of telling you that I had made preparation for you at my lodgings.'

'It was not Simon Fleix's fault,' she replied curtly. 'I prefer these rooms. They are more convenient.'

'They are, perhaps, more convenient,' I rejoined humbly, 'but I have to think of safety, mademoiselle, as you know. At my house I have a competent guard, and can answer for your being unmolested.'

'You can send your guard here,' she said with a royal air.

'But, mademoiselle—'

'Is it not enough that I have said that I prefer these rooms?' she replied sharply, dropping her mask on her lap and looking round at me in undisguised displeasure. 'Are you deaf, sir? Let me tell you, I am in no mood for arguments. I am tired with riding. I prefer these rooms, and that is enough!'

Nothing could exceed the determination with which she said these words, unless it were the malicious pleasure in thwarting my wishes which made itself seen through the veil of assumed indifference. I felt myself brought up with a vengeance, and in a manner the most provoking that could be conceived. But opposition so childish, so utterly wanton, by exciting my indignation, had presently the effect of banishing the peculiar bashfulness I felt in her presence, and recalling me to my duty.

'Mademoiselle,' I said firmly, looking at her with a fixed countenance, 'pardon me if I speak plainly. This is no time for playing with straws. The men from whom you escaped once are as determined and more desperate now. By this time they probably know of your arrival. Do, then, as I ask, I pray and beseech you. Or this time I may lack the power, though never the will, to save you.'

Wholly ignoring my appeal, she looked into my face—for by this time I had advanced to her side—with a whimsical smile. 'You are really much improved in manner since I last saw you,' she said.

'Mademoiselle!' I replied, baffled and repelled. 'What do you mean?'

'What I say,' she answered, flippantly. 'But it was to be expected.'

'For shame!' I cried, provoked almost beyond bearing by her ill-timed raillery, 'will you never be serious until you have ruined us and yourself? I tell you this house is not safe for you! It is not safe for me! I cannot bring my men to it, for there is not room for them. If you have any spark of consideration, of gratitude, therefore—'

'Gratitude!' she exclaimed, swinging her mask slowly to and fro by a ribbon, while she looked up at me as though my excitement amused her. 'Gratitude—'tis a very pretty phrase, and means much; but it is for those who serve us faithfully, M. de Marsac, and not for others. You receive so many favours, I am told, and are so successful at Court, that I should not be justified in monopolising your services.'

'But, mademoiselle—' I said in a low tone. And there I stopped. I dared not proceed.

'Well, sir,' she answered, looking up at me after a moment's silence, and ceasing on a sudden to play with her toy, 'what is it?'

'You spoke of favours,' I continued, with an effort. 'I never received but one from a lady. That was at Rosny, and from your hand.'

'From my hand?' she answered, with an air of cold surprise.

'It was so, mademoiselle.'

'You have fallen into some strange mistake, sir,' she replied, rousing herself, and looking at me indefinitely. 'I never gave you a favour.'

I bowed low. 'If you say you did not, mademoiselle, that is enough,' I answered.

'Nay, but do not let me do you an injustice, M. de Marsac,' she rejoined, speaking more quickly and in an altered tone. 'If you can show me the favour I gave you, I shall, of course, be convinced. Seeing is believing, you know,' she added, with a light nervous laugh, and a gesture of something like shyness.

If I had not sufficiently regretted my carelessness, and loss of the bow at the time, I did so now. I looked at her in silence, and saw her face, that had for a moment shown signs of feeling, almost of shame, grow slowly hard again.

'Well, sir?' she said impatiently. 'The proof is easy.'

'It was taken from me; I believe, by M. de Rosny,' I answered lamely, wondering what ill-luck had led her to put the question and press it to this point.

'It was taken from you!' she exclaimed, rising and confronting me with the utmost suddenness, while her eyes flashed, and her little hand crumpled the mask beyond future usefulness. 'It was taken from you, sir!' she repeated, her voice and her whole frame trembling with anger and disdain. 'Then I thank you, I prefer my version. Yours is impossible. For let me tell you, when Mademoiselle de la Vire does confer a favour, it will be on a man with the power and the wit—and the constancy, to keep it, even from M. de Rosny!'

Her scorn hurt, though it did not anger me. I felt it to be in a measure deserved, and raged against myself rather than against her. But aware through all of the supreme importance of placing her in safety, I subjected my immediate feelings to the exigencies of the moment and stooped to an argument which would, I thought, have weight though private pleading failed.

'Putting myself aside, mademoiselle,' I said, with more formality than I had yet used, 'there is one consideration which must weigh with you. The king—'

'The king!' she cried, interrupting me violently, her face hot with passion and her whole person instinct with stubborn self-will. 'I shall not see the king!'

'You will not see the king?' I repeated in amazement.

'No, I will not!' she answered, in a whirl of anger, scorn, and impetuosity. 'There! I will not! I have been made a toy and a tool long enough, M. de Marsac,' she continued, 'and I will serve others' ends no more. I have made up my mind. Do not talk to me; you will do no good, sir. I would to Heaven,' she added bitterly, 'I had stayed at Chizé and never seen this place!'

'But, mademoiselle,' I said, 'you have not thought—'

'Thought!' she exclaimed, shutting her small white teeth so viciously I all but recoiled. 'I have thought enough. I am sick of thought. I am going to act now. I will be a puppet no longer. You may take me to the Castle by force if you will; but you cannot make me speak.'

I looked at her in the utmost dismay and astonishment; being unable at first to believe that a woman who had gone through so much, had run so many risks, and ridden so many miles for a purpose, would, when all was done and the hour come, decline to carry out her plan. I could not believe it, I say, at first; and I tried arguments and entreaties without stint, thinking that she only asked to be entreated or coaxed.

But I found prayers and even threats breath wasted upon her; and beyond these I would not go. I know I have been blamed by some and ridiculed by others for not pushing the matter farther; but those who have stood face to face with a woman of spirit—a woman whose very frailty and weakness fought for her—will better understand the difficulties with which I had to contend and the manner in which conviction was at last borne in on my mind. I had never before confronted stubbornness of this kind. As mademoiselle said again and again, I might force her to Court, but I could not make her speak.

When I had tried every means of persuasion, and still found no way of overcoming her resolution—the while Fanchette looked on with a face of wood, neither aiding me nor taking part against me—I lost, I confess, in the chagrin of the moment that sense of duty which had hitherto animated me; and though my relation to mademoiselle should have made me as careful as ever of her safety, even in her own despite, I left her at last in anger and went out without saying another word about removing her—a thing which was still in my power. I believe a very brief reflection would have recalled me to myself and my duty; but the opportunity was not given me, for I had scarcely reached the head of the stairs before Fanchette came after me, and called to me in a whisper to stop.

She held a taper in her hand, and this she raised to my face, smiling at the disorder which she doubtless read there. 'Do you say that this house is not safe?' she asked abruptly, lowering the light as she spoke.

'You have tried a house in Blois before?' I replied with the same bluntness. 'You should know as well as I, woman.'

'She must be taken from here, then,' she answered, nodding her head, cunningly. 'I can persuade her. Do you send for your people, and be here in half an hour. It may take me that time to wheedle her. But I shall do it.'

'Then listen,' I said eagerly, seizing the opportunity and her sleeve and drawing her farther from the door. 'If you can persuade her to that, you can persuade to all I wish. Listen, my friend,' I continued, sinking my voice still lower. 'If she will see the king for only ten minutes, and tell him what she knows, I will give you—'

'What?' the woman asked suddenly and harshly, drawing at the same time her sleeve from my hand.

'Fifty crowns,' I replied, naming in my desperation a sum which would seem a fortune to a person in her position. 'Fifty crowns down, the moment the interview is over.'

'And for that you would have me sell her!' the woman cried with a rude intensity of passion which struck me like a blow. 'For shame! For shame, man! You persuaded her to leave her home and her friends, and the country where she was known; and now you would have me sell her! Shame on you! Go!' she added scornfully. 'Go this instant and get your men. The king, say you? The king! I tell you I would not have her finger ache to save all your kings!'

She flounced away with that, and I retired crestfallen; wondering much at the fidelity which Providence, doubtless for the well-being of the gentle, possibly for the good of all, has implanted in the humble. Finding Simon, to whom I had scarce patience to speak, waiting on the stairs below, I despatched him to Maignan, to bid him come to me with his men. Meanwhile I watched the house myself until their arrival, and then, going up, found that Fanchette had been as good as her word. Mademoiselle, with a sullen mien, and a red spot on either cheek, consented to descend, and, preceded by a couple of links, which Maignan had thoughtfully provided, was escorted safely to my lodgings; where I bestowed her in the rooms below my own, which I had designed for her.

At the door she turned and bowed to me, her face on fire.

'So far, sir, you have got your way,' she said, breathing quickly. 'Do not flatter yourself, however, that you will get it farther—even by bribing my woman!'

# 23

# The Last Valois

I stood for a few moments on the stairs, wondering what I should do in an emergency to which the Marquis's message of the afternoon attached so pressing a character. Had it not been for that I might have waited until morning, and felt tolerably certain of finding mademoiselle in a more reasonable mood then. But as it was I dared not wait. I dared not risk the delay, and I came quickly to the conclusion that the only course open to me was to go at once to M. de Rambouillet, and tell him frankly how the matter stood.

Maignan had posted one of his men at the open doorway leading into the street, and fixed his own quarters on the landing at the top, whence he could overlook an intruder without being seen himself. Satisfied with the arrangement, I left Rambouillet's man to reinforce him, and took with me Simon Fleix, of whose conduct in regard to mademoiselle I entertained the gravest doubts.

The night, I found on reaching the street, was cold, the sky where it was visible between the eaves being bright with stars. A sharp wind was blowing, too, compelling us to wrap our cloaks round us and hurry on at a pace which agreed well with the excitement of my thoughts. Assured that had mademoiselle been complaisant I might have seen my mission accomplished within the hour, it was impossible I should not feel impatient with one who, to gratify a whim, played with the secrets of a kingdom as if they were counters, and risked in passing ill-humour the results of weeks of preparation. And I was impatient, and with her. But my resentment fell so far short of the occasion that I wondered uneasily at my own easiness, and felt more annoyed with myself for failing to be properly annoyed with her, than inclined to lay the blame where it was due. It was in vain I told myself contemptuously that she was a woman, and that women were not accountable. I felt that the real secret and motive of my indulgence lay, not in this, but in the suspicion, which her reference to the favour given me on my departure from Rosny had converted almost into a certainty, that I was myself the cause of her sudden ill-humour.

I might have followed this train of thought farther, and to very pertinent conclusions. But on reaching M. de Rambouillet's lodging I was diverted from it by the abnormally quiet aspect of the house, on the steps of which half a dozen servants might commonly be seen lounging. Now the doors were closed, no lights shone through the windows, and the hall sounded empty and desolate when I knocked. Not a lackey hurried to receive me even then; but the slipshod tread of the old porter, as he came with a lantern to open, alone broke the silence. I waited eagerly wondering what all this could mean; and when the man at last opened, and, recognising my face, begged my pardon if he had kept me waiting I asked him impatiently what was the matter.

'And where is the Marquis?' I added, stepping inside to be out of the wind, and loosening my cloak.

'Have you not heard, sir?' the man asked, holding up his lantern to my face. He was an old, wizened, lean fellow. 'It is a break-up, sir, I am afraid, this time.'

'A break-up?' I rejoined, peevishly. 'Speak out, man! What is the matter? I hate mysteries.'

'You have not heard the news, sir? That the Duke of Mercoeur and Marshal Retz, with all their people, left Blois this afternoon?'

'No?' I answered, somewhat startled. 'Whither are they gone?'

'To Paris, it is said, sir,—to join the League.'

'But do you mean that they have deserted the king?' I asked.

'For certain, sir!' he answered.

'Not the Duke of Mercoeur?' I exclaimed. 'Why, man, he is the king's brother-in-law. He owes everything to him.'

'Well, he is gone, sir,' the old man answered positively. 'The news was brought to M. le Marquis about four o'clock or a little after. He got his people together, and started after them to try and persuade them to return. Or, so it is said.'

As quickly as I could, I reviewed the situation in my mind. If this strange news were true, and men like Mercoeur, who had every reason to stand by the king, as well as men like Retz, who had long been suspected of disaffection, were abandoning the Court, the danger must be coming close indeed. The king must feel his throne already tottering, and be eager to grasp at any means of supporting it. Under such circumstances it seemed to be my paramount duty to reach him; to gain his ear if possible, and at all risks; that I and not Bruhl, Navarre not Turenne, might profit by the first impulse of self-preservation.

Bidding the porter shut his door and keep close, I hurried to the Castle, and was presently more than confirmed in my resolution. For to my surprise I found the Court in much the same state as M. de Rambouillet's house. There were double guards indeed at the gates, who let me pass after scrutinising me narrowly; but the courtyard, which should have been at this hour ablaze with torches and crowded with lackeys and grooms, was a dark wilderness, in which half a dozen links trembled mournfully. Passing through the doors I found things within in the same state: the hall ill lit and desolate; the staircase manned only by a few whispering groups, who scanned me as I passed; the antechambers almost empty, or occupied by the grey uniforms of the Switzer guards. Where I had looked to see courtiers assembling to meet their sovereign and assure him of their fidelity, I found only gloomy faces, watchful eyes, and mouths ominously closed. An air of constraint and foreboding rested on all. A single footstep sounded hollowly. The long corridors, which had so lately rung with laughter and the rattle of dice, seemed already devoted to the silence and desolation which awaited them when the Court should depart. Where any spoke I caught the name of Guise; and I could have fancied that his mighty shadow lay upon the place and cursed it.

Entering the chamber, I found matters little better there. His Majesty was not present, nor were any of the Court ladies; but half a dozen gentlemen, among whom I recognised Revol, one of the king's secretaries, stood near the alcove. They looked up on my entrance, as though expecting news, and then, seeing who it was, looked away again impatiently. The Duke of Nevers was walking moodily to and fro before one of the windows, his hands clasped behind his back: while Biron and Crillon, reconciled by the common peril, talked loudly on the hearth. I hesitated a moment, uncertain how to proceed, for I was not yet so old at Court as to feel at home there. But, at last making up my mind, I walked boldly up to Crillon and requested his good offices to procure me an immediate audience of the king.

'An audience? Do you mean you want to see him alone?' he said, raising his eyebrows and looking whimsically at Biron.

'That is my petition, M. de Crillon,' I answered firmly, though my heart sank. 'I am here on M. de Rambouillet's business, and I need to see his Majesty forthwith.'

'Well, that is straightforward,' he replied, clapping me on the shoulder. 'And you shall see him. In coming to Crillon you have come to the right man. Revol,' he continued, turning to the secretary, 'this gentleman bears a message from M. de Rambouillet to the king. Take him to the closet without delay, my friend, and announce him. I will be answerable for him.'

But the secretary shrugged his shoulders up to his ears. 'It is quite impossible, M. de Crillon,' he said gravely. 'Quite impossible at present.'

'Impossible! Chut! I do not know the word,' Crillon retorted rudely. 'Come, take him at once, and blame me if ill comes of it. Do you hear?'

'But his Majesty——'

'Well?'

'Is at his devotions,' the secretary said stiffly.

'His Majesty's devotions be hanged!' Crillon rejoined—so loudly that there was a general titter, and M. de Nevers laughed grimly. 'Do you hear?' the Avennais continued, his face growing redder and his voice higher, 'or must I pull your ears, my friend? Take this gentleman to the closet, I say, and if his Majesty be angry, tell him it was by my order. I tell you he comes from Rambouillet.'

I do not know whether it was the threat, or the mention of M. de Rambouillet's name, which convinced the secretary. But at any rate, after a moment's hesitation, he acquiesced.

He nodded sullenly to me to follow him, and led the way to a curtain which masked the door of the closet. I followed him across the chamber, after muttering a hasty word of acknowledgment to Crillon; and I had as nearly as possible reached the door when the bustle of someone entering the chamber caught my ear. I had just time to turn and see that this was Bruhl, just time to intercept the dark look of chagrin and surprise which he fixed on me, and then Revol, holding up the curtain, signed to me to enter.

I expected to pass at once into the presence of the king, and had my reverence ready. Instead, I found myself to my surprise in a small chamber, or rather passage, curtained at both ends, and occupied by a couple of guardsmen—members, doubtless, of the Band of the Forty-Five—who rose at my entrance and looked at me dubiously. Their guard-room, dimly illuminated by a lamp of red glass, seemed to me, in spite of its curtains and velvet bench, and the thick tapestry which kept out every breath of wholesome air, the most sombre I could imagine. And the most ill-omened. But I had no time to make any long observation; for Revol, passing me brusquely, raised the curtain at the other end, and, with his finger on his lip, bade me by signs to enter.

I did so as silently, the heavy scent of perfumes striking me on the face as I raised a second curtain, and stopped short a pace beyond it; partly in reverence—because kings love their subjects best at a distance—and partly in surprise. For the room, or rather that portion of it in which I stood, was in darkness; only the farther end being illumined by a cold pale flood of moonlight, which, passing through a high, straight window, lay in a silvery sheet on the floor. For an instant I thought I was alone; then I saw, resting against this window, with a hand on either mullion, a tall figure, having something strange about the head. This peculiarity presently resolved itself into the turban in which I had once before seen his Majesty. The king—for he it was—was talking to himself. He had not heard me enter, and having his back to me remained unconscious of my presence.

I paused in doubt, afraid to advance, anxious to withdraw; yet uncertain whether I could move again unheard. At this moment while I stood hesitating, he raised his voice, and his words, reaching my ears, riveted my attention, so strange and eerie were both they and his tone. 'They say there is ill-luck in thirteen,' he muttered. 'Thirteenth Valois and last!' He paused to laugh a wicked, mirthless laugh. 'Ay—Thirteenth! And it is thirteen years since I entered Paris, a crowned King! There was Quélus and Maugiron and Saint Mégrin and I— and *he*, I remember. Ah, those days, those nights! I would sell my soul to live them again; had I not sold it long ago in the living them once! We were young then, and rich, and I was king; and Quélus was an Apollo! He died calling on me to save him. And Maugiron died, blaspheming God and the saints. And Saint Mégrin, he had thirty-four wounds. And *he*— he is dead too, curse him! They are all dead, all dead, and it is all over! My God! it is all over, it is all over, it is all over!'

He repeated the last four words more than a dozen times, rocking himself to and fro by his hold on the mullions. I trembled as I listened, partly through fear on my own account should I be discovered, and partly by reason of the horror of despair and remorse—no, not remorse, regret—which spoke in his monotonous voice. I guessed that some impulse had led him to draw the curtain from the window and shade the lamp; and that then, as he looked down on the moonlit country, the contrast between it and the vicious, heated atmosphere, heavy with intrigue and worse, in which he had spent his strength, had forced itself upon his mind. For he presently went on.

'France! There it lies! And what will they do with it? Will they cut it up into pieces, as it was before old Louis XI? Will Mercoeur—curse him!—be the most Christian Duke of Brittany? And Mayenne, by the grace of God, Prince of Paris and the Upper Seine? Or will the little Prince of Béearn beat them, and be Henry IV, King of France and Navarre. Protector of the Churches? Curse him too! He is thirty-six. He is my age. But he is young and strong, and has all before him. While I—I—oh, my God, have mercy on me! Have mercy on me, O God in Heaven!'

With the last word he fell on his knees on the step before the window, and burst into such an agony of unmanly tears and sobbings as I had never dreamed of or imagined, and least of all in the King of France. Hardly knowing whether to be more ashamed or terrified, I turned at all risks, and stealthily lifting the curtain, crept out with infinite care; and happily with so much good fortune as to escape detection. There was space enough between the two curtains to admit my body and no more; and here I stood a short while to collect my thoughts. Then, striking my scabbard against the wall, as though by accident, and coughing loudly at the same moment, I twitched the curtain aside with some violence and re-entered, thinking that by these means I had given him warning enough.

But I had not reckoned on the darkness in which the room lay, or the excitable state in which I had left him. He heard me, indeed, but being able to see only a tall, indistinct figure approaching him, he took fright, and falling back against the moonlit window, as though he saw a ghost, thrust out his hand, gasping at the same time two words, which sounded to me like 'Ha! Guise!'

The next instant, discerning that I fell on my knee where I stood, and came no nearer, he recovered himself. With an effort, which his breathing made very apparent, he asked in an unsteady voice who it was.

'One of your Majesty's most faithful servants,' I answered, remaining on my knee, and affecting to see nothing.

Keeping his face towards me, he sidled to the lamp and strove to withdraw the shade. But his fingers trembled so violently that it was some time before he succeeded, and set free the cheerful beams, which, suddenly filling the room with radiance, disclosed to my wondering eyes, instead of darkness and the cold gleam of the moon, a profusion of riches, of red stuffs and gemmed trifles and gilded arms crowded together in reckless disorder. A monkey chained in one corner began to gibber and mow at me. A cloak of strange cut, stretched on a wooden stand, deceived me for an instant into thinking that there was a third person present; while the table, heaped with dolls and powder-puffs, dog-collars and sweet-meats, a mask, a woman's slipper, a pair of pistols, some potions, a scourge, and an immense quantity of like litter, had as melancholy an appearance in my eyes as the king himself, whose disorder the light disclosed without mercy. His turban was awry, and betrayed the premature baldness of his scalp. The paint on his cheeks was cracked and stained, and had soiled the gloves he wore. He looked fifty years old; and in his excitement he had tugged his sword to the front, whence it refused to be thrust back.

'Who sent you here?' he asked, when he had so far recovered his senses as to recognise me, which he did with great surprise.

'I am here, sire,' I answered evasively, 'to place myself at your Majesty's service.'

'Such loyalty is rare,' he answered, with a bitter sneer. 'But stand up, sir. I suppose I must be thankful for small mercies, and, losing a Mercoeur, be glad to receive a Marsac.'

'By your leave, sire,' I rejoined hardily, 'the exchange is not so adverse. Your Majesty may make another duke when you will. But honest men are not so easily come by.'

'So! so!' he answered, looking at me with a fierce light in his eyes. 'You remind me in season. I may still make and unmake! I am still King of France? That is so, sirrah, is it not?'

'God forbid that it should be otherwise!' I answered
earnestly. 'It is to lay before your Majesty certain means by
which you may give fuller effect to your wishes that I am here.
The King of Navarre desires only, sire—'

'Tut, tut!' he exclaimed impatiently, and with some displeasure, 'I know his will better than you, man. But you see,'
he continued cunningly, forgetting my inferior position as
quickly as he had remembered it, 'Turenne promises well,
too. And Turenne—it is true he may play the Lorrainer.
But if I trust Henry of Navarre, and he prove false to me—'

He did not complete the sentence, but strode to and fro a
time or two, his mind, which had a natural inclination towards
crooked courses, bent on some scheme by which he might
play off the one party against the other. Apparently he was not
very successful in finding one, however; or else the ill-luck
with which he had supported the League against the Huguenots recurred to his mind. For he presently stopped, with a
sigh, and came back to the point.

'If I knew that Turenne were lying,' he muttered, 'then indeed— But Rosny promised evidence and he has sent me none.'

'It is at hand, sire,' I answered, my heart beginning to beat.
'Your Majesty will remember that M. de Rosny honoured
me with the task of introducing it to you.'

'To be sure,' he replied, awaking as from a dream, and
looking and speaking eagerly. 'Matters today have driven
everything out of my head. Where is your witness, man?
Convince me, and we will act promptly. We will give them
Jarnac and Moncontour over again. Is he outside?'

'It is a woman, sire,' I made answer, dashed somewhat by
his sudden and feverish alacrity.

'A woman, eh? You have her here?'

'No, sire,' I replied, wondering what he would say to my
next piece of information. 'She is in Blois, she has arrived,
but the truth is—I humbly crave your Majesty's indulgence
—she refuses to come or speak. I cannot well bring her here
by force, and I have sought you, sire, for the purpose of
taking your commands in the matter.'

He stared at me in the utmost astonishment.

'Is she young?' he asked after a long pause.

'Yes, sire,' I answered. 'She is maid of honour to the Princess of Navarre, and a ward also of the Vicomte de Turenne.'

'Gad! then she is worth hearing, the little rebel!' he replied. 'A ward of Turenne's is she? Ho! ho! And now she will not speak? My cousin of Navarre now would know how to bring her to her senses, but I have eschewed these vanities. I might send and have her brought, it is true; but a very little thing would cause a barricade tonight.'

'And besides, sire,' I ventured to add, 'she is known to Turenne's people here, who have once stolen her away. Were she brought to your Majesty with any degree of openness, they would learn it, and know that the game was lost.'

'Which would not suit me,' he answered, nodding and looking at me gloomily. 'They might anticipate our Jarnac; and until we have settled matters with one or the other our person is not too secure. You must go and fetch her. She is at your lodging. She must be brought, man.'

'I will do what you command, sire,' I answered. 'But I am greatly afraid that she will not come.'

He lost his temper at that. 'Then why, in the devil's name, have you troubled me with the matter?' he cried savagely. 'God knows—I don't—why Rosny employed such a man and such a woman. He might have seen from the cut of your cloak, sir, which is full six months behind the fashion, that you could not manage a woman! Was ever such damnable folly heard of in this world? But it is Navarre's loss, not mine. It is his loss. And I hope to Heaven it may be yours too!' he added fiercely.

There was so much in what he said that I bent before the storm, and accepted with humility blame which was as natural on his part as it was undeserved on mine. Indeed I could not wonder at his Majesty's anger; nor should I have wondered at it in a greater man. I knew that but for reasons, on which I did not wish to dwell, I should have shared it to the full, and spoken quite as strongly of the caprice which ruined hopes and lives for a whim.

The king continued for some time to say to me all the hard things he could think of. Wearied at last by my patience, he paused, and cried angrily, 'Well, have you nothing to say for yourself? Can you suggest nothing?'

'I dare not mention to your Majesty,' I said humbly, 'what seems to me to be the only alternative.'

'You mean that I should go to the wench!' he answered—for he did not lack quickness. ' "*Se no va el otero a Mahoma, vaya Mahoma al otero,*" as Mendoza says. But the saucy quean, to force me to go to her! Did my wife guess—but there, I will go. By God I will go!' he added abruptly and fiercely. 'I will live to ruin Retz yet! Where is your lodging?'

I told him, wondering much at this flash of the old spirit, which twenty years before had won him a reputation his later life did nothing to sustain.

'Do you know,' he asked, speaking with sustained energy and clearness, 'the door by which M. de Rosny entered to talk with me? Can you find it in the dark?'

'Yes, sire,' I answered, my heart beating high.

'Then be in waiting there two hours before midnight,' he replied. 'Be well armed, but alone. I shall know how to make the girl speak. I can trust you, I suppose?' he added suddenly, stepping nearer to me and looking fixedly into my eyes.

'I will answer for your Majesty's life with my own,' I replied, sinking on one knee.

'I believe you, sir,' he answered gravely, giving me his hand to kiss, and then turning away. 'So be it. Now leave me. You have been here too long already. Not a word to any one as you value your life.'

I made fitting answer and was leaving him; but when I had my hand already on the curtain, he called me back. 'In Heaven's name get a new cloak!' he said peevishly, eyeing me all over with his face puckered up. 'Get a new cloak, man, the first thing in the morning. It is worse seen from the side than the front. It would ruin the cleverest courtier of them all!'

# 24

# A Royal Peril

The elation with which I had heard the king announce his resolution quickly diminished on cooler reflection. It stood in particular at a very low ebb as I waited, an hour later, at the little north postern of the Castle, and, cowering within the shelter of the arch to escape the wind, debated whether his Majesty's energy would sustain him to the point of action, or whether he might not, in one of those fits of treacherous vacillation which had again and again marred his plans, send those to keep the appointment who would give a final account of me. The longer I considered his character the more dubious I grew. The loneliness of the situation, the darkness, the black front, unbroken by any glimmer of light, which the Castle presented on this side, and the unusual and gloomy stillness which lay upon the town, all contributed to increase my uneasiness. It was with apprehension as well as relief that I caught at last the sound of footsteps on the stone staircase, and, standing a little to one side, saw a streak of light appear at the foot of the door.

On the latter being partially opened a voice cried my name. I advanced with caution and showed myself. A brief conversation ensued between two or three persons who stood within; but in the end, a masked figure, which I had no difficulty in identifying as the king, stepped briskly out.

'You are armed?' he said, pausing a second opposite me.

I put back my cloak and showed him, by the light which streamed from the doorway, that I carried pistols as well as a sword.

'Good!' he answered briefly; 'then let us go. Do you walk on my left hand, my friend. It is a dark night, is it not?'

'Very dark, sire,' I said.

He made no answer to this, and we started, proceeding with caution until we had crossed the narrow bridge, and then with greater freedom and at a better pace. The slenderness of the attendance at Court that evening, and the cold wind, which swept even the narrowest streets and drove roisterers indoors, rendered it unlikely that we should be stopped or molested by any except professed thieves; and for these I was prepared. The king showed no inclination to talk; and keeping silence myself out of respect, I had time to calculate the chances to consider whether his Majesty would succeed where I had failed.

This calculation, which was not inconsistent with the keenest watchfulness on my part whenever we turned a corner or passed the mouth of an alley, was brought to an end by our safe arrival at the house. Briefly apologising to the king for the meanness and darkness of the staircase, I begged leave to precede him, and rapidly mounted until I met Maignan. Whispering to him that all was well, I did not wait to hear his answer, but, bidding him be on the watch, I led the king on with as much deference as was possible until we stood at the door of mademoiselle's apartments, which I have elsewhere stated to consist of an outer and inner room. The door was opened by Simon Fleix, and him I promptly sent out. Then, standing aside and uncovering, I begged the king to enter.

He did so, still wearing his hat and mask, and I followed and secured the door. A lamp hanging from the ceiling diffused an imperfect light through the room, which was smaller but more comfortable in appearance than that which I rented overhead. I observed that Fanchette, whose harsh countenance looked more forbidding than usual, occupied a stool which she had set in a strange fashion against the inner door; but I thought no more of this at the moment, my attention passing quickly to mademoiselle, who sat crouching before the fire, enveloped in a large outdoor cloak, as if she felt the cold. Her back was towards us, and she was, or pretended to be, ignorant of our presence. With a muttered word I pointed her out to the king, and went towards her with him.

'Mademoiselle,' I said in a low voice, 'Mademoiselle de la Vire! I have the honour—'

She would not turn, and I stopped. Clearly she heard, but she betrayed that she did so only by drawing her cloak more closely round her. Primed by my respect for the king, I touched her lightly on the shoulder. 'Mademoiselle!' I said impatiently, 'you are not aware of it, but—'

She shook herself free from my hand with so rude a gesture that I broke off, and stood gaping foolishly at her. The king smiled, and nodding to me to step back a pace, took the task on himself. 'Mademoiselle,' he said with dignity, 'I am not accustomed—'

His voice had a magical effect. Before he could add another word she sprang up as if she had been struck, and faced us, a cry of alarm on her lips. Simultaneously we both cried out too, for it was not mademoiselle at all. The woman who confronted us, her hand on her mask, her eyes glittering through the slits, was of a taller and fuller figure. We stared at her. Then a lock of bright golden hair which had escaped from the hood of her cloak gave us the clue. 'Madame!' the king cried.

'Madame de Bruhl!' I echoed, my astonishment greater than his.

Seeing herself known, she began with trembling fingers to undo the fastenings of her mask; but the king, who had hitherto displayed a trustfulness I had not expected in him, had taken alarm at sight of her, as at a thing unlooked for, and of which I had not warned him. 'How is this?' he said harshly, drawing back a pace from her and regarding me with anger and distrust. 'Is this some pretty arrangement of yours, sir? Am I an intruder at an assignation, or is this a trap with M. de Bruhl in the background? Answer, sirrah!' he continued, working himself rapidly into a passion. 'Which am I to understand is the case?'

'Neither, sire,' I answered with as much dignity as I could

assume, utterly surprised and mystified as I was by madame's presence. 'Your Majesty wrongs Madame de Bruhl as much by the one suspicion as you injure me by the other. I am equally in the dark with you, sire, and as little expected to see madame here.'

'I came, sire,' she said proudly, addressing herself to the king, and ignoring me, 'out of no love to M. de Marsac, but as any person bearing a message to him might come. Nor can you, sire,' she added with spirit, 'feel half as much surprise at seeing me here, as I at seeing your Majesty.'

'I can believe that,' the king answered drily. 'I would you had not seen me.'

'The King of France is seen only when he chooses,' she replied, curtseying to the ground.

'Good,' he answered. 'Let it be so, and you will oblige the King of France, madame. But enough,' he continued, turning from her to me; 'since this is not the lady I came to see, M. de Marsac, where is she?'

'In the inner room, sire, I opine,' I said, advancing to Fanchette with more misgiving at heart than my manner evinced. 'Your mistress is here, is she not?' I continued, addressing the woman sharply.

'Ay, and will not come out,' she rejoined, sturdily keeping her place.

'Nonsense!' I said. 'Tell her—'

'You may tell her what you please,' she replied, refusing to budge an inch. 'She can hear.'

'But, woman!' I cried impatiently, 'you do not understand. I *must* speak with her. I must speak with her at once! On business of the highest importance.'

'As you please,' she said rudely, still keeping her seat. 'I have told you you can speak.'

Perhaps I felt as foolish on this occasion as ever in my life; and surely never was man placed in a more ridiculous position. After overcoming numberless obstacles, and escaping as many perils, I had brought the king here, a feat beyond my highest hopes—only to be baffled and defeated by a waiting-woman!

I stood irresolute; witless and confused; while the king waited half angry and half amused, and madame kept her place by the entrance, to which she had retreated.

I was delivered from my dilemma by the curiosity which is, providentially perhaps, a part of woman's character, and which led mademoiselle to interfere herself. Keenly on the watch inside, she had heard part of what passed between us, and been rendered inquisitive by the sound of a strange man's voice, and by the deference which she could discern I paid to the visitor. At this moment, she cried out, accordingly, to know who was there; and Fanchette, seeming to take this as a command, rose and dragged her stool aside, saying peevishly and without any increase of respect, 'There, I told you she could hear.'

'Who is it?' mademoiselle asked again, in a raised voice.

I was about to answer when the king signed to me to stand back, and, advancing himself, knocked gently on the door. 'Open, I pray you, mademoiselle,' he said courteously.

'Who is there?' she cried again, her voice trembling.

'It is I, the king,' he answered softly; but in that tone of majesty which belongs not to the man, but to the descendant, and seems to be the outcome of centuries of command.

She uttered an exclamation and slowly, and with seeming reluctance, turned the key in the lock. It grated, and the door opened. I caught a glimpse for an instant of her pale face and bright eyes, and then his Majesty, removing his hat, passed in and closed the door; and I withdrew to the farther end of the room, where madame continued to stand by the entrance.

I entertained a suspicion, I remember, and not unnaturally, that she had come to my lodging as her husband's spy; but her first words when I joined her dispelled this. 'Quick!' she said with an imperious gesture. 'Hear me and let me go! I have waited long enough for you, and suffered enough through you. As for that woman in there, she is mad, and her servant too! Now, listen to me. You spoke to me honestly today, and I have come to repay you. You have an appointment with my husband tomorrow at Chaverny. Is it not so?' she added impatiently.

I replied that it was so.

'You are to go with one friend,' she went on, tearing the glove she had taken off to strips in her excitement. 'He is to meet you with one also?'

'Yes,' I assented reluctantly, 'at the bridge, madame.'

'Then do not go,' she rejoined emphatically. 'Shame on me that I should betray my husband; but it were worse to send an innocent man to his death. He will meet you with one sword only, according to his challenge, but there will be those under the bridge who will make certain work. There, I have betrayed him now!' she continued bitterly. 'It is done. Let me go!'

'Nay, but, madame,' I said, feeling more concerned for her, on whom from the first moment of meeting her I had brought nothing but misfortune, than surprised by this new treachery on his part, 'will you not run some risk in returning to him? Is there nothing I can do for you—no step I can take for your protection?'

'None!' she said repellently and almost rudely, 'except to speed my going.'

'But you will not pass through the streets alone?'

She laughed so bitterly my heart ached for her. 'The unhappy are always safe,' she said.

Remembering how short a time it was since I had surprised her in the first happiness of wedded love, I felt for her all the pity it was natural I should feel. But the responsibility under which his Majesty's presence and the charge of mademoiselle laid me forbade me to indulge in the luxury of evincing my gratitude. Gladly would I have escorted her back to her home —even if I could not make that home again what it had been, or restore her husband to the pinnacle from which I had dashed him—but I dared not do this. I was forced to content myself with less, and was about to offer to send one of my men with her, when a hurried knocking at the door arrested the words on my lips.

Signing to her to stand still, I listened. The knocking was repeated, and grew each moment more urgent. There was a little grille, strongly wired, in the upper part of the door, and this I was about to open in order to learn what was amiss, when Simon's voice reached me from the farther side imploring me to open the door quickly. Doubting the lad's prudence, yet afraid to refuse lest I should lose some warning he had to give, I paused a second, and then undid the fastenings. The moment the door gave way he fell in bodily, crying out to me to bar it behind him. I caught a glimpse through the gap of a glare as of torches, and saw by this light half a dozen flushed faces in the act of rising above the edge of the landing. The men who owned them raised a shout of triumph at sight of me, and, clearing the upper steps at a bound, made a rush for the door. But in vain. We had just time to close it and drop the two stout bars. In a moment, in a second, the fierce outcry fell to a dull roar; and safe for the time, we had leisure to look in one another's faces and learn the different aspects of alarm. Madame was white to the lips, while Simon's eyes seemed starting from his head, and he shook in every limb with terror.

At first, on my asking him what it meant, he could not speak. But that would not do, and I was in the act of seizing him by the collar to force an answer from him when the inner door opened, and the king came out, his face wearing an air of so much cheerfulness as proved both his satisfaction with mademoiselle's story and his ignorance of all we were about. In a word he had not yet taken the least alarm; but seeing Simon in my hands, and madame leaning against the wall by the door like one deprived of life, he stood and cried out in surprise to know what it was.

'I fear we are besieged, sire,' I answered desperately, feeling my anxieties increased a hundredfold by his appearance—'but by whom I cannot say. This lad knows, however,' I continued, giving Simon a vicious shake, 'and he shall speak. Now, trembler,' I said to him, 'tell your tale!'

'The Provost-Marshal!' he stammered, terrified afresh by

the king's presence: for Henry had removed his mask. 'I
was on guard below. I had come up a few steps to be out of
the cold, when I heard them enter. There are a round score
of them.'

I cried out a great oath, asking him why he had not gone
up and warned Maignan, who with his men was now cut off
from us in the rooms above. 'You fool!' I continued, almost
beside myself with rage, 'if you had not come to this door they
would have mounted to my rooms and beset them! What is
this folly about the Provost-Marshal?'

'He is there,' Simon answered, cowering away from me, his
face working.

I thought he was lying, and had merely fancied this in his
fright. But the assailants at this moment began to hail blows
on the door, calling on us to open, and using such volleys of
threats as penetrated even the thickness of the oak; driving
the blood from the women's cheeks, and arresting the king's
step in a manner which did not escape me. Among their cries
I could plainly distinguish the words, 'In the king's name!'
which bore out Simon's statement.

At the moment I drew comfort from this; for if we had
merely to deal with the law we had that on our side which
was above it. And I speedily made up my mind what to do.
'I think the lad speaks the truth, sire,' I said coolly. 'This is
only your Majesty's Provost-Marshal. The worst to be feared,
therefore, is that he may learn your presence here before you
would have it known. It should not be a matter of great
difficulty, however, to bind him to silence, and if you will
please to mask, I will open the grille and speak with him.'

The king, who had taken his stand in the middle of the
room, and seemed dazed and confused by the suddenness of
the alarm and the uproar, assented with a brief word. Accordingly I was preparing to open the grille when Madame de
Bruhl seized my arm, and forcibly pushed me back from
it.

'What would you do?' she cried, her face full of terror.
'Do you not hear? He is there.'

'Who is there?' I said, startled more by her manner than her words.

'Who?' she answered; 'who should be there? My husband! I hear his voice, I tell you! He has tracked me here! He has found me, and will kill me!'

'God forbid!' I said, doubting if she had really heard his voice. To make sure, I asked Simon if he had seen him; and my heart sank when I heard from him too that Bruhl was of the party. For the first time I became fully sensible of the danger which threatened us. For the first time, looking round the ill-lit room on the women's terrified faces, and the king's masked figure instinct with ill-repressed nervousness, I recognised how hopelessly we were enmeshed. Fortune had served Bruhl so well that, whether he knew it or not, he had us all trapped—alike the king whom he desired to compromise, and his wife whom he hated, mademoiselle who had once escaped him, and me who had twice thwarted him. It was little to be wondered at if my courage sank as I looked from one to another, and listened to the ominous creaking of the door, as the stout panels complained under the blows rained upon them. For my first duty, and that which took the *pas* of all others, was to the king —to save him harmless. How, then, was I to be answerable for mademoiselle, how protect Madame de Bruhl?—how, in a word, redeem all those pledges in which my honour was concerned?

It was the thought of the Provost-Marshal which at this moment rallied my failing spirits. I remembered that until the mystery of his presence here in alliance with Bruhl was explained there was no need to despair; and turning briskly to the king I begged him to favour me by standing with the women in a corner which was not visible from the door. He complied mechanically, and in a manner which I did not like; but lacking time to weigh trifles, I turned to the grille and opened it without more ado.

The appearance of my face at the trap was greeted with a savage cry of recognition, which subsided as quickly into silence. It was followed by a momentary pushing to and fro among the crowd outside, which in its turn ended in the Provost-Marshal coming to the front. 'In the king's name!' he said fussily.

'What is it?' I replied, eyeing rather the flushed, eager faces which scowled over his shoulders than himself. The light of two links, borne by some of the party, shone ruddily on the heads of the halberds, and, flaring up from time to time, filled all the place with wavering, smoky light. 'What do you want?' I continued, 'rousing my lodging at this time of night?'

'I hold a warrant for your arrest,' he replied bluntly. 'Resistance will be vain. If you do not surrender I shall send for a ram to break in the door.'

'Where is your order?' I said sharply. 'The one you held this morning was cancelled by the king himself.'

'Suspended only,' he answered. 'Suspended only. It was given out to me again this evening for instant execution. And I am here in pursuance of it, and call on you to surrender.'

'Who delivered it to you?' I retorted.

'M. de Villequier,' he answered readily. 'And here it is. Now, come, sir,' he continued, 'you are only making matters worse. Open to us.'

'Before I do so,' I said drily, 'I should like to know what part in the pageant my friend M. de Bruhl, whom I see on the stairs yonder, proposes to play. And there is my old friend Fresnoy,' I added. 'And I see one or two others whom I know, M. Provost. Before I surrender I must know among other things what M. de Bruhl's business is here.'

'It is the business of every loyal man to execute the king's warrant,' the Provost answered evasively. 'It is yours to surrender, and mine to lodge you in the Castle. But I am loth to have a disturbance. I will give you until that torch goes out, if you like, to make up your mind. At the end of that time, if you do not surrender, I shall batter down the door.'

'You will give the torch fair play?' I said, noting its condition.

He assented; and thanking him sternly for this indulgence, I closed the grille.

# 25

# Terms of Surrender

I still had my hand on the trap when a touch on the shoulder caused me to turn, and in a moment apprised me of the imminence of a new peril; a peril of such a kind that, summoning all my resolution, I could scarcely hope to cope with it. Henry was at my elbow. He had taken off his mask, and a single glance at his countenance warned me that that had happened of which I had already felt some fear. The glitter of intense excitement shone in his eyes. His face, darkly-flushed and wet with sweat, betrayed overmastering emotion, while his teeth, tight clenched in the effort to restrain the fit of trembling which possessed him, showed between his lips like those of a corpse. The novelty of the danger which menaced him, the absence of his gentlemen, and of all the familiar faces and surroundings without which he never moved, the hour, the mean house, and his isolation among strangers, had proved too much for nerves long weakened by his course of living, and for a courage, proved indeed in the field, but unequal to a sudden stress. Though he still strove to preserve his dignity, it was alarmingly plain to my eyes that he was on the point of losing, if he had not already lost, all self-command.

'Open!' he muttered between his teeth, pointing impatiently to the trap with the hand with which he had already touched me. 'Open, I say, sir!'

I stared at him, startled and confounded. 'But your Majesty,' I ventured to stammer, 'forgets that I have not yet—'

'Open, I say!' he repeated passionately. 'Do you hear me, sir? I desire that this door be opened.' His lean hand shook as with the palsy, so that the gems on it twinkled in the light and rattled as he spoke.

I looked helplessly from him to the women and back again, seeing in a flash all the dangers which might follow from the discovery of his presence there—dangers which I had not before formulated to myself, but which seemed in a moment to range themselves with the utmost clearness before my eyes. At the same time I saw what seemed to me to be a way of escape; and emboldened by the one and the other, I kept my hand on the trap and strove to parley with him.

'Nay, but, sire,' I said hurriedly, yet still with as much deference as I could command. 'I beg you to permit me first to repeat what I have seen. M. de Bruhl is without, and I counted six men whom I believe to be his following. They are ruffians ripe for any crime; and I implore your Majesty rather to submit to a short imprisonment—'

I paused struck dumb on that word, confounded by the passion which lightened in the king's face. My ill-chosen expression had indeed applied the spark to his wrath. Predisposed to suspicion by a hundred treacheries, he forgot the perils outside in the one idea which on the instant possessed his mind; that I would confine his person, and had brought him hither for no other purpose. He glared round him with eyes full of rage and fear, and his trembling lips breathed rather than spoke the word 'Imprison?'

Unluckily, a trifling occurrence added at this moment to his disorder, and converted it into frenzy. Someone outside fell heavily against the door; this, causing madame to utter a low shriek, seemed to shatter the last remnant of the king's self-control. Stamping his foot on the floor, he cried to me with the utmost wildness to open the door—by which I had hitherto kept my place.

But, wrongly or rightly, I was still determined to put off opening it; and I raised my hands with the intention of making a last appeal to him. He misread the gesture, and retreating a step, with the greatest suddenness whipped out his sword, and in a moment had the point at my breast, and his wrist drawn back to thrust.

It has always been my belief that he would not have dealt the blow, but that the mere touch of the hilt, awaking the courage which he undoubtedly possessed, and which did not desert him in his last moments, would have recalled him to himself. But the opportunity was not given him, for while the blade yet quivered, and I stood motionless, controlling myself by an effort, my knee half bent and my eyes on his, Mademoiselle de la Vire sprang forward at his back, and with a loud scream clutched his elbow. The king, surprised, and ignorant who held him, flung up his point wildly, and striking the lamp above his head with his blade, shattered it in an instant, bringing down the pottery with a crash and reducing the room to darkness; while the screams of the women, and the knowledge that we had a madman among us, peopled the blackness with a hundred horrors.

Fearing above all for mademoiselle, I made my way as soon as I could recover my wits to the embers of the fire, and regardless of the king's sword, which I had a vague idea was darting about in the darkness, I searched for and found a half-burnt stick, which I blew into a blaze. With this, still keeping my back to the room, I contrived to light a taper that I had noticed standing by the hearth; and then, and then only, I turned to see what I had to confront.

Mademoiselle de la Vire stood in a corner, half-fierce, half-terrified, and wholly flushed. She had her hand wrapped up in a 'kerchief already stained with blood; and from this I gathered that the king in his frenzy had wounded her slightly. Standing before her mistress, with her hair bristling, like a wild-cat's fur, and her arms akimbo, was Fanchette, her harsh face and square form instinct with fury and defiance. Madame de Bruhl and Simon cowered against the wall not far from them; and in a chair, into which he had apparently just thrown himself, sat the king, huddled up and collapsed, the point of his sword trailing on the ground beside him, and his nerveless hand scarce retaining force to grip the pommel.

In a moment I made up my mind what to do, and going to him in silence, I laid my pistols, sword, and dagger on a stool by his side. Then I knelt.

'The door, sire,' I said, 'is there. It is for your Majesty to open it when you please. Here, too, sire, are my weapons. I am your prisoner, the Provost-Marshal is outside, and you can at a word deliver me to him. Only one thing I beg, sire,' I continued earnestly, 'that your Majesty will treat as a delusion the idea that I meditated for a moment disrespect or violence to your person.'

He looked at me dully, his face pale, his eyes fish-like. 'Sanctus, man!' he muttered, 'why did you raise your hand?'

'Only to implore your Majesty to pause a moment,' I answered, watching the intelligence return slowly to his face. 'If you will deign to listen I can explain in half a dozen words, sire. M. de Bruhl's men are six or seven, the Provost has eight or nine; but the former are the wilder blades, and if M. de Bruhl find your Majesty in my lodging, and infer his own defeat, he will be capable of any desperate stroke. Your person would hardly be safe in his company through the streets. And there is another consideration,' I went on, observing with joy that the king listened, and was gradually regaining his composure. 'That is, the secrecy you desired to preserve, sire, until this matter should be well advanced. M. de Rosny laid the strictest injunctions on me in that respect, fearing an *émeute* in Blois should your Majesty's plans become known.'

'You speak fairly,' the king answered with returning energy, though he avoided looking at the women. 'Bruhl is likely enough to raise one. But how am I to get out, sir?' he continued, querulously. 'I cannot remain here. I shall be missed, man! I am not a hedge-captain, neither sought nor wanted!'

'If your Majesty would trust me?' I said slowly and with hesitation.

'Trust you!' he retorted peevishly, holding up his hands

278

and gazing intently at his nails, of the shape and whiteness of which he was prouder than any woman. 'Have I not trusted you? If I had not trusted you, should I have been here? But that you were a Huguenot—God forgive me for saying it!—I would have seen you in hell before I would have come here with you!'

I confess to having heard this testimony to the Religion with a pride which made me forget for a moment the immediate circumstances—the peril in which we stood, the gloomy room darkly lighted by a single candle, the scared faces in the background, even in the king's huddled figure, in which dejection and pride struggled for expression. For a moment only; then I hastened to reply, saying that I doubted not I could still extricate his Majesty without discovery.

'In Heaven's name do it, then!' he answered sharply. 'Do what you like, man! Only get me back into the Castle, and it shall not be a Huguenot will entice me out again. I am over old for these adventures!'

A fresh attack on the door taking place as he said this induced me to lose no time in explaining my plan, which he was good enough to approve, after again upbraiding me for bringing him into such a dilemma. Fearing lest the door should give way prematurely, notwithstanding the bars I had provided for it, and goaded on by Madame de Bruhl's face, which evinced the utmost terror, I took the candle and attended his Majesty into the inner room, where I placed my pistols beside him, but silently resumed my sword and dagger. I then returned for the women, and indicating by signs that they were to enter, held the door open for them.

Mademoiselle, whose bandaged hand I could not regard without emotion, though the king's presence and the respect I owed him forbade me to utter so much as a word, advanced readily until she reached the doorway abreast of me. There, however, looking back, and seeing Madame de Bruhl following her, she stopped short, and darting a haughty glance at me, muttered, 'And—that lady? Are we to be shut up together, sir?'

'Mademoiselle,' I answered quickly in the low tone she had used herself, 'have I ever asked anything dishonourable of you?'

She seemed by a slight movement of the head to answer in the negative.

'Nor do I now,' I replied with earnestness. 'I entrust to your care a lady who has risked great peril for *us;* and the rest I leave to you.'

She looked me very keenly in the face for a second, and then, without answering, she passed on, madame and Fanchette following her in that order. I closed the door and turned to Simon; who by my direction had blown the embers of the fire into a blaze so as to partially illumine the room, in which only he and I now remained. The lad seemed afraid to meet my eye, and owing to the scene at which he had just assisted, or to the onslaught on the door, which grew each moment more furious, betrayed greater restlessness than I had lately observed in him. I did not doubt his fidelity, however, or his devotion to mademoiselle; and the orders I had to give him were simple enough.

'This is what you have got to do,' I said, my hand already on the bars. 'The moment I am outside secure this door. After that, open to no one except Maignan. When he applies, let him in with caution, and bid him, as he loves M. de Rosny, take his men as soon as the coast is clear, and guard the King of France to the Castle. Charge him to be brave and wary, for his life will answer for the king's.'

Twice I repeated this; then fearing lest the Provost-Marshal should make good his word and apply a ram to the door, I opened the trap. A dozen angry voices hailed my appearance, and this with so much violence and impatience that it was some time before I could get a hearing; the knaves threatening me if I would not instantly open, and persisting that I should do so without more words. Their leader at length quieted them, but it was plain that his patience too was worn out. 'Do you surrender or do you not?' he said. 'I am not going to stay out of my bed all night for you!'

'I warn you,' I answered, 'that the order you have there has been cancelled by the king!'

'That is not my business,' he rejoined hardily.

'No, but it will be when the king sends for you tomorrow morning,' I retorted; at which he looked somewhat moved. 'However, I will surrender to you on two conditions,' I continued, keenly observing the coarse faces of his following. 'First, that you let me keep my arms until we reach the gate-house, I giving you my parole to come with you quietly. That is number one.'

'Well,' the Provost-Marshal said more civilly, 'I have no objection to that.'

'Secondly, that you do not allow your men to break into my lodgings. I will come out quietly, and so an end. Your order does not direct you to sack my goods.'

'Tut, tut!' he replied; 'I want you to come out. I do not want to go in.'

'Then draw your men back to the stairs,' I said. 'And if you keep terms with me, I will uphold you tomorrow. For your orders will certainly bring you into trouble. M. de Retz, who procured it this morning, is away, you know. M. de Villequier may be gone tomorrow. But depend upon it, M. de Rambouillet will be here!'

The remark was well timed and to the point. It startled the man as much as I had hoped it would. Without raising any objection he ordered his men to fall back and guard the stairs; and I on my side began to undo the fastenings of the door.

The matter was not to be so easily concluded, however; for Bruhl's rascals, in obedience, no doubt, to a sign given by their leader, who stood with Fresnoy on the upper flight of stairs, refused to withdraw; and even hustled the Provost-Marshal's men when the latter would have obeyed the order. The officer, already heated by delay, replied by laying about him with his staff, and in a twinkling there seemed to be every prospect of a very pretty *mêlée*, the end of which it was impossible to foresee.

Reflecting, however, that if Bruhl's men routed their

opponents our position might be made worse rather than better, I did not act on my first impulse, which was to see the matter out where I was. Instead, I seized the opportunity to let myself out, while Simon fastened the door behind me. The Provost-Marshal was engaged at the moment in a wordy dispute with Fresnoy; whose villainous countenance, scarred by the wound which I had given him at Chizé, and flushed with passion, looked its worst by the light of the single torch which remained. In one respect the villain had profited by his present patronage, for he was decked out in a style of tawdry magnificence. But I have always remarked this about dress, that while a shabby exterior does not entirely obscure a gentleman, the extreme of fashion is powerless to gild a knave.

Seeing me on a sudden at the Provost's elbow, he recoiled with a change of countenance so ludicrous that that officer was himself startled, and only held his ground on my saluting him civilly and declaring myself his prisoner. I added a warning that he should look to the torch which remained; seeing that if it failed we were both like to have our throats cut in the confusion.

He took the hint promptly, and calling the link-man to his side prepared to descend, bidding Fresnoy and his men, who remained clumped at the head of the stairs, make way for us without ado. They seemed much inclined, however, to dispute our passage, and replying to his invectives with rough taunts, displayed so hostile a demeanour that the Provost, between regard for his own importance and respect for Bruhl, appeared for a moment at a loss what to do; and seemed rather relieved than annoyed when I begged leave to say a word to M. de Bruhl.

'If you can bring his men to reason,' he replied testily, 'speak your fill to him!'

Stepping to the foot of the upper flight, on which Bruhl retained his position, I saluted him formally. He returned my greeting with a surly, watchful look only, and drawing his cloak more tightly round him affected to gaze down at me with disdain; which ill concealed, however, both the triumph he felt and the hopes of vengeance he entertained. I was especially anxious to learn whether he had tracked his wife hither, or was merely here in pursuance of his general schemes against me, and to this end I asked him with as much irony as I could compass to what I was to attribute his presence. 'I am afraid I cannot stay to offer you hospitality,' I continued; 'but for that you have only your friend M. Villequier to thank!'

'I am greatly obliged to you,' he answered with a devilish smile, 'but do not let that affect you. When you are gone I propose to help myself, my friend, to whatever takes my taste.'

'Do you?' I retorted coolly—not that I was unaffected by the threat and the villainous hint which underlay the words, but that, fully expecting them, I was ready with my answer. 'We will see about that.' And therewith I raised my fingers to my lips, and, whistling shrilly, cried 'Maignan! Maignan!' in a clear voice.

I had no need to cry the name a third time, for before the Provost-Marshal could do more than start at this unexpected action, the landing above us rang under a heavy tread, and the man I called, descending the stairs swiftly, appeared on a sudden within arm's length of M. de Bruhl; who, turning with an oath, saw him, and involuntarily recoiled. At all times Maignan's hardy and confident bearing was of a kind to impress the strong; but on this occasion there was an added dash of recklessness in his manner which was not without its effect on the spectators. As he stood there smiling darkly over Bruhl's head, while his hand toyed carelessly with his dagger, and the torch shone ruddily on his burly figure, he was so clearly an antagonist in a thousand that, had I sought through Blois, I might not have found his fellow for strength and *sangfroid*. He let his black eyes rove from one to the other, but took heed of me only, saluting me with effusion and a touch of the Gascon which was in place here, if ever.

I knew how M. de Rosny dealt with him, and followed the pattern as far as I could. 'Maignan!' I said curtly, 'I have taken a lodging for tonight elsewhere. When I am gone you will call out your men and watch this door. If anyone tries to force an entrance you will do your duty.'

'You may consider it done,' he replied.

'Even if the person be M. de Bruhl here,' I continued.

'Precisely.'

'You will remain on guard,' I went on, 'until tomorrow morning if M. de Bruhl remains here; but whenever he leaves you will take your orders from the persons inside, and follow them implicitly.'

'Your Excellency's mind may be easy,' he answered, handling his dagger.

Dismissing him with a nod, I turned with a smile to M. de Bruhl, and saw that between rage at this unexpected check and chagrin at the insult put upon him, his discomfiture was as complete as I could wish. As for Fresnoy, if he had seriously intended to dispute our passage, he was no longer in the mood for the attempt. Yet I did not let his master off without one more prick. 'That being settled, M. de Bruhl,' I said pleasantly, 'I may bid you good evening. You will doubtless honour me at Chaverny tomorrow. But we will first let Maignan look under the bridge!'

26

# Meditations

Either the small respect I had paid M. de Bruhl, or the words I had let fall respecting the possible disappearance of M. Villequier, had had so admirable an effect on the Provost-Marshal's mind that from the moment of leaving my lodgings he treated me with the utmost civility; permitting me even to retain my sword, and assigning me a sleeping-place for the night in his own apartments at the Gate-house.

Late as it was, I could not allow so much politeness to pass unacknowledged. I begged leave, therefore, to distribute a small gratuity among his attendants, and requested him to do me the honour of drinking a bottle of wine with me. This being speedily procured, at such an expense as is usual in these places, where prisoners pay, according as they are rich or poor, in purse or person, kept us sitting for an hour, and finally sent us to our pallets perfectly satisfied with one another.

The events of the day, however, and particularly one matter, on which I have not dwelt at length, proved as effectual to prevent me sleeping as if I had been placed in the dampest cell below the castle. So much had been crowded into a time so short that it seemed as if I had had until now no opportunity of considering whither I was being hurried, or what fortune awaited me at the end of this turmoil. From the first appearance of M. d'Agen in the morning, with the startling news that the Provost-Marshal was seeking me, to my final surrender and encounter with Bruhl on the stairs, the chain of events had run out so swiftly that I had scarcely had time at any particular period to consider how I stood, or the full import of the latest check or victory. Now that I had leisure I lived the day over again, and, recalling its dangers and disappointments, felt thankful that all had ended so fairly.

I had the most perfect confidence in Maignan, and did not doubt that Bruhl would soon weary, if he had not already wearied, of a profitless siege. In an hour at most —and it was not yet midnight—the king would be free to go home; and with that would end, as far as he was concerned, the mission with which M. de Rosny had honoured me. The task of communicating his Majesty's decisions to the King of Navarre would doubtless be entrusted to M. de Rambouillet, or some person of similar position and influence; and in the same hands would rest the honour and responsibility of the treaty which, as we all know now, gave after a brief interval and some bloodshed, and one great providence, a lasting peace to

France. But it must ever be—and I recognised this that night with a bounding heart, which told of some store of youth yet unexhausted—a matter of lasting pride to me that I, whose career but now seemed closed in failure, had proved the means of conferring so especial a benefit on my country and religion.

Remembering, however, the King of Navarre's warning that I must not look to him for reward, I felt greatly doubtful in what direction the scene would next open to me; my main dependence being upon M. de Rosny's promise that he would make my fortune his own care. Tired of the Court at Blois, and the atmosphere of intrigue and treachery which pervaded it, and with which I hoped I had now done, I was still at a loss to see how I could recross the Loire in face of the Vicomte de Turenne's enmity. I might have troubled myself much more with speculating upon this point had I not found —in close connection with it—other and more engrossing food for thought in the capricious behaviour of Mademoiselle de la Vire.

To that behaviour it seemed to me that I now held the clue. I suspected with as much surprise as pleasure that only one construction could be placed upon it—a construction which had strongly occurred to me on catching sight of her face when she intervened between me and the king.

Tracing the matter back to the moment of our meeting in the antechamber at Saint-Jean d'Angely, I remembered the jest which Mathurine had uttered at our joint expense. Doubtless it had dwelt in mademoiselle's mind, and exciting her animosity against me had prepared her to treat me with contumely when, contrary to all probability, we met again, and she found herself placed in a manner in my hands. It had inspired her harsh words and harsher looks on our journey northwards, and contributed with her native pride to the low opinion I had formed of her when I contrasted her with my honoured mother.

But I began to think it possible that the jest had worked in another way as well, by keeping me before her mind and impressing upon her the idea—after my reappearance at Chizé more particularly—that our fates were in some way linked. Assuming this, it was not hard to understand her manner at Rosny when, apprised that I was no impostor, and regretting her former treatment of me, she still recoiled from the feelings which she began to recognise in her own breast. From that time, and with this clue, I had no difficulty in tracing her motives, always supposing that this suspicion, upon which I dwelt with feelings of wonder and delight, were well founded.

Middle-aged and grizzled, with the best of my life behind me, I had never dared to think of her in this way before. Poor and comparatively obscure, I had never raised my eyes to the wide possessions said to be hers. Even now I felt myself dazzled and bewildered by the prospect so suddenly unveiled. I could scarcely, without vertigo, recall her as I had last seen her, with her hand wounded in my defence; nor, without emotions painful in their intensity, fancy myself restored to the youth of which I had taken leave, and to the rosy hopes and plannings which visit most men once only, and then in early years. Hitherto I had deemed such things the lot of others.

Daylight found me—and no wonder—still diverting myself with these charming speculations; which had for me, be it remembered, all the force of novelty. The sun chanced to rise that morning in a clear sky, and brilliantly for the time of year; and words fail me when I look back, and try to describe how delicately this simple fact enhanced my pleasure! I sunned myself in the beams, which penetrated my barred window; and tasting the early freshness with a keen and insatiable appetite, I experienced to the full that peculiar aspiration after goodness which Providence allows such moments to awaken in us in youth; but rarely when time and the camp have blunted the sensibilities.

I had not yet arrived at the stage at which difficulties have to be reckoned up, and the chief drawback to the tumult of joy I felt took the shape of regret that my mother no longer lived to feel the emotions proper to the time, and to share in the prosperity which she had so often and so fondly imagined. Nevertheless, I felt myself drawn closer to her. I recalled with the most tender feelings, and at greater leisure than had before been the case, her last days and words, and particularly the appeal she had uttered on mademoiselle's behalf. And I vowed, if it were possible, to pay a visit to her grave before leaving the neighbourhood, that I might there devote a few moments to the thought of the affection which had consecrated all women in my eyes.

I was presently interrupted in these reflections by a circumstance which proved in the end diverting enough, though far from reassuring at the first blush. It began in a dismal rattling of chains in the passage below and on the stairs outside my room; which were paved, like the rest of the building, with stone. I waited with impatience and some uneasiness to see what would come of this; and my surprise may be imagined when, the door being unlocked, gave entrance to a man in whom I recognised on the instant deaf Matthew—the villain whom I had last seen with Fresnoy in the house in the Rue de Valois. Amazed at seeing him here, I sprang to my feet in fear of some treachery, and for a moment apprehended that the Provost-Marshal had basely given me over to Bruhl's custody. But a second glance informing me that the man was in irons—hence the noise I had heard— I sat down again to see what would happen.

It then appeared that he merely brought me my breakfast, and was a prisoner in less fortunate circumstances than myself; but as he pretended not to recognise me, and placed the things before me in obdurate silence, and I had no power to make him hear, I failed to learn how he came to be in durance. The Provost-Marshal, however, came presently to visit me, and brought me in token that the good-fellowship of the evening still existed a pouch of the Queen's herb; which I accepted for politeness' sake rather than from any virtue I found in it. And from him I learned how the rascal came to be in his charge.

It appeared that Fresnoy, having no mind to be hampered with a wounded man, had deposited him on the night of our *mêlée* at the door of a hospital attached to a religious house in that part of the town. The Fathers had opened to him, but before taking him in put, according to their custom, certain questions. Matthew had been primed with the right answers to these questions, which were commonly a form; but, unhappily for him, the Superior by chance or mistake began with the wrong one.

'You are not a Huguenot, my son?' he said.

'In God's name, I am!' Matthew replied with simplicity, believing he was asked if he was a Catholic.

'What?' the scandalised Prior ejaculated, crossing himself in doubt, 'are you not a true son of the Church?'

'Never!' quoth our deaf friend—thinking all went well.

'A heretic!' cried the monk.

'Amen to that!' replied Matthew innocently; never doubting but that he was asked the third question, which was, commonly, whether he needed aid.

Naturally after this there was a pretty commotion, and Matthew, vainly protesting that he was deaf, was hurried off to the Provost-Marshal's custody. Asked how he communicated with him, the Provost answered that he could not, but that his little godchild, a girl only eight years old, had taken a strange fancy to the rogue, and was never so happy as when talking to him by means of signs, of which she had invented a great number. I thought this strange at the time, but I had proof before the morning was out that it was true enough, and that the two were seldom apart, the little child governing this grim cut-throat with unquestioned authority.

After the Provost was gone I heard the man's fetters clanking again. This time he entered to remove my cup and plate, and surprised me by speaking to me. Maintaining his former sullenness, and scarcely looking at me, he said abruptly: 'You are going out again?'

I nodded assent.

'Do you remember a bald-faced bay horse that fell with

you?' he muttered, keeping his dogged glance on the floor.

I nodded again.

'I want to sell the horse,' he said. 'There is not such another in Blois, no, nor in Paris! Touch it on the near hip with the whip and it will go down as if shot. At other times a child might ride it. It is in a stable, the third from the Three Pigeons, in the Ruelle Amancy. Fresnoy does not know where it is. He sent to ask yesterday, but I would not tell him.'

Some spark of human feeling which appeared in his lowering, brutal visage as he spoke of the horse led me to desire further information. Fortunately the little girl appeared at that moment at the door in search of her play-fellow; and through her I learned that the man's motive for seeking to sell the horse was fear lest the dealer in whose charge it stood dispose of it to repay himself for its keep, and he, Matthew, lose it without return.

Still I did not understand why he applied to me, but I was well pleased when I learned the truth. Base as the knave was, he had an affection for the bay, which had been his only property for six years. Having this in his mind, he had conceived the idea that I should treat it well, and should not, because he was in prison and powerless, cheat him of the price.

In the end I agreed to buy the horse for ten crowns, paying as well what was due at the stable. I had it in my head to do something also for the man, being moved to this partly by an idea that there was good in him, and partly by the confidence he had seen fit to place in me, which seemed to deserve some return. But a noise below stairs diverted my attention. I heard myself named, and for the moment forgot the matter.

# 27

# To Me, my Friends!

I was impatient to learn who had come, and what was their errand with me; and being still in that state of exaltation in which we seem to hear and see more than at other times, I remarked a peculiar lagging in the ascending footsteps, and a lack of buoyancy, which was quick to communicate itself to my mind. A vague dread fell upon me as I stood listening. Before the door opened I had already conceived a score of disasters. I wondered that I had not inquired earlier concerning the king's safety, and in fine I experienced in a moment that complete reaction of the spirits which is too frequently consequent upon an excessive flow of gaiety.

I was prepared, therefore, for heavy looks, but not for the persons who wore them nor the strange bearing the latter displayed on entering. My visitors proved to be M. d'Agen and Simon Fleix. And so far well. But the former, instead of coming forward to greet me with the punctilious politeness which always characterised him, and which I had thought to be proof against every kind of surprise and peril, met me with downcast eyes and a countenance so gloomy as to augment my fears a hundredfold; since it suggested all those vague and formidable pains which M. de Rambouillet had hinted might await me in a prison. I thought nothing more probable than the entrance after them of a gaoler laden with gyves and handcuffs; and saluting M. François with a face which, do what I would, fashioned itself upon his, I had scarce composure sufficient to place the poor accommodation of my room at his disposal.

He thanked me; but he did it with so much gloom and so little naturalness that I grew more impatient with each laboured syllable. Simon Fleix had slunk to the window and turned his back on us. Neither seemed to have anything to say. But a state of suspense was one which I could least endure to suffer; and impatient of the constraint which my friend's manner was fast imparting to mine, I asked him at once and abruptly if his uncle had returned.

'He rode in about midnight,' he answered, tracing a pattern on the floor with the point of his riding-switch.

I felt some surprise on hearing this, since d'Agen was still dressed and armed for the road, and was without all those prettinesses which commonly marked his attire. But as he volunteered no further information, and did not even refer to the place in which he found me, or question me as to the adventures which had lodged me there, I let it pass, and asked him if his party had overtaken the deserters.

'Yes,' he answered, 'with no result.'

'And the king?'

'M. de Rambouillet is with him now,' he rejoined, still bending over his tracing.

This answer relieved the worst of my anxieties, but the manner of the speaker was so distrait and so much at variance with the studied *insouciance* which he usually affected, that I only grew more alarmed. I glanced at Simon Fleix, but he kept his face averted, and I could gather nothing from it; though I observed that he, too, was dressed for the road, and wore his arms. I listened, but I could hear no sounds which indicated that the Provost-Marshal was approaching. Then on a sudden I thought of Mademoiselle de la Vire. Could it be that Maignan had proved unequal to his task?

I started impetuously from my stool under the influence of the emotion which this thought naturally aroused, and seized M. d'Agen by the arm. 'What has happened?' I exclaimed. 'Is it Bruhl? Did he break into my lodgings last night? What!' I continued, staggering back as I read the confirmation of my fears in his face. 'He did?'

M. d'Agen, who had risen also, pressed my hand with convulsive energy. Gazing into my face, he held me a moment thus embraced, his manner a strange mixture of fierceness and emotion. 'Alas, yes,' he answered, 'he did, and took away those whom he found there! Those whom he found there, you understand! But M. de Rambouillet is on his way here, and in a few minutes you will be free. We will follow together. If we overtake them—well. If not, it will be time to talk.'

He broke off, and I stood looking at him, stunned by the blow, yet in the midst of my own horror and surprise retaining sense enough to wonder at the gloom on his brow and the passion which trembled in his words. What had this to do with him? 'But Bruhl?' I said at last, recovering myself with an effort—'how did he gain access to the room? I left it guarded.'

'By a ruse, while Maignan and his men were away,' was the answer. 'Only this lad of yours was there. Bruhl's men overpowered him.'

'Which way has Bruhl gone?' I muttered, my throat dry, my heart beating wildly.

He shook his head. 'All we know is that he passed through the south gate with eleven horsemen, two women, and six led horses, at daybreak this morning,' he answered. 'Maignan came to my uncle with the news, and M. de Rambouillet went at once, early as it was, to the king to procure your release. He should be here now.'

I looked at the barred window, the most horrible fears at my heart; from it to Simon Fleix, who stood beside it, his attitude expressing the utmost dejection. I went towards him. 'You hound!' I said in a low voice, 'how did it happen?'

To my surprise he fell in a moment on his knees, and raised his arm as though to ward off a blow. 'They imitated Maignan's voice,' he muttered hoarsely. 'We opened.'

'And you dare to come here and tell me!' I cried, scarcely restraining my passion. 'You, to whom I entrusted her. You, whom I thought devoted to her. You have destroyed her, man!'

He rose as suddenly as he had cowered down. His thin, nervous face underwent a startling change; growing on a sudden hard and rigid, while his eyes began to glitter with excitement. 'I—I have destroyed her? Ay, mon Dieu! I *have*,' he cried, speaking to my face, and no longer flinching or avoiding my eye. 'You may kill me, if you like. You do not know all. It was I who stole the favour she gave you from your doublet, and then said M. de Rosny had taken it! It was I who told her you had given it away! It was I who brought her to the Little Sisters, that she might see you with Madame de Bruhl! It was I who did all, and destroyed her! Now you know! Do with me what you like!'

He opened his arms as though to receive a blow, while I stood before him astounded beyond measure by a disclosure so unexpected; full of righteous wrath and indignation, and yet uncertain what I ought to do. 'Did you also let Bruhl into the room on purpose?' I cried at last.

'I?' he exclaimed, with a sudden flash of rage in his eyes. 'I would have died first!'

I do not know how I might have taken this confession; but at the moment there was a trampling of horses outside, and before I could answer him I heard M. de Rambouillet speaking in haughty tones, at the door below. The Provost-Marshal was with him, but his lower notes were lost in the ring of bridles and the stamping of impatient hoofs. I looked towards the door of my room, which stood ajar, and presently the two entered, the Marquis listening with an air of contemptuous indifference to the apologies which the other, who attended at his elbow, was pouring forth. M. de Rambouillet's face reflected none of the gloom and despondency which M. d'Agen's exhibited in so marked a degree. He seemed, on the contrary, full of gaiety and good-humour, and, coming forward and seeing me, embraced me with the utmost kindness and condescension.

'Ha! my friend,' he said cheerfully, 'so I find you here after all! But never fear. I am this moment from the king with an order for your release. His Majesty has told me all, making me thereby your lasting friend and debtor. As for this gentleman,' he continued, turning with a cold smile to the Provost-Marshal, who seemed to be trembling in his boots, 'he may expect an immediate order also. M. de Villequier has wisely gone a-hunting, and will not be back for a day or two.'

Racked as I was by suspense and anxiety, I could not assail him with immediate petitions. It behoved me first to thank him for his prompt intervention, and this in terms as warm as I could invent. Nor could I in justice fail to commend the Provost to him, representing the officer's conduct to me, and lauding his ability. All this, though my heart was sick with thought and fear and disappointment, and every minute seemed an age.

'Well, well,' the Marquis said with stately good-nature, 'we will lay the blame on Villequier then. He is an old fox, however, and ten to one he will go scot-free. It is not the first time he has played this trick. But I have not yet come to the end of my commission,' he continued pleasantly. 'His Majesty sends you this, M. de Marsac, and bade me say that he had loaded it for you.'

He drew from under his cloak as he spoke the pistol which I had left with the king, and which happened to be the same M. de Rosny had given me. I took it, marvelling impatiently at the careful manner in which he handled it; but in a moment I understood, for I found it loaded to the muzzle with gold-pieces, of which two or three fell and rolled upon the floor. Much moved by this substantial mark of the king's gratitude, I was nevertheless for pocketing them in haste; but the Marquis, to satisfy a little curiosity on his part, would have me count them, and brought the tale to a little over two thousand livres, without counting a ring set with precious stones which I found among them. This handsome present diverted my thoughts from Simon Fleix, but could not relieve the anxiety I felt on mademoiselle's account. The thought of her position so tortured me that M. de Rambouillet began to perceive my state of mind, and hastened to assure me that before going to the Court he had already issued orders calculated to assist me.

'You desire to follow this lady, I understand?' he said. 'What with the king, who is enraged beyond the ordinary by this outrage, and François there, who seemed beside himself when he heard the news, I have not got any very clear idea of the position.'

'She was entrusted to me by—by one, sir, well known to you,' I answered hoarsely. 'My honour is engaged to him and to her. If I follow on my feet and alone, I must follow. If I cannot save her, I can at least punish the villains who have wronged her.'

'But the man's wife is with them,' he said in some wonder.

'That goes for nothing,' I answered.

He saw the strong emotion under which I laboured, and which scarcely suffered me to answer him with patience; and he looked at me curiously, but not unkindly. 'The sooner you are off, the better then,' he said, nodding. 'I gathered as much. The man Maignan will have his fellows at the south gate an hour before noon, I understand. François has two lackeys, and he is wild to go. With yourself and the lad there you will muster nine swords. I will lend you two. I can spare no more, for we may have an *émeute* at any moment. You will take the road, therefore, eleven in all, and should overtake them some time tonight if your horses are in condition.'

I thanked him warmly, without regarding his kindly statement that my conduct on the previous day had laid him under lasting obligations to me. We went down together, and he transferred two of his fellows to me there and then, bidding them change their horses for fresh ones and meet me at the south gate. He sent also a man to my stable—Simon Fleix having disappeared in the confusion—for the Cid, and was in the act of inquiring whether I needed anything else, when a woman slipped through the knot of horsemen who surrounded us as we stood in the doorway of the house, and, throwing herself upon me, grasped me by the arm. It was Fanchette. Her harsh features were distorted with grief, her cheeks were mottled with the violent weeping in which such persons vent their sorrow. Her hair hung in long wisps on her neck. Her dress was torn and draggled, and there was a great bruise over her eye. She had the air of one frantic with despair and misery.

She caught me by the cloak, and shook me so that I staggered. 'I have found you at last!' she cried joyfully. 'You will take me with you! You will take me to her!'

Though her words tried my composure, and my heart went out to her, I strove to answer her according to the sense of the matter. 'It is impossible,' I said sternly. 'This is a man's errand. We shall have to ride day and night, my good woman.'

'But I will ride day and night too!' she replied passionately, flinging the hair from her eyes, and looking wildly from me to M. de Rambouillet. 'What would I not do for her? I am as strong as a man, and stronger. Take me, take me, I say, and when I meet that villain I will tear him limb from limb!'

I shuddered, listening to her; but remembering that, being country bred, she was really as strong as she said, and that likely enough some advantage might accrue to us from her perfect fidelity and devotion to her mistress, I gave a reluctant consent. I sent one of M. de Rambouillet's men to the stable where the deaf man's bay was standing, bidding him pay whatever was due to the dealer, and bring the horse to the south gate; my intention being to mount one of my men on it, and furnish the woman with a less tricky steed.

The briskness of these and the like preparations, which even for one of my age and in my state of anxiety were not devoid of pleasure, prevented my thoughts dwelling on the future. Content to have M. François' assistance without following up too keenly the train of ideas which his readiness suggested, I was satisfied also to make use of Simon without calling him to instant account for his treachery. The bustle of the streets, which the confirmation of the king's speedy departure had filled with surly, murmuring crowds, tended still further to keep my fears at bay; while the contrast between my present circumstances, as I rode through them well-appointed and well-attended, with the Marquis by my side, and the poor appearance I had exhibited on my first arrival in Blois, could not fail to inspire me with hope that I might surmount this danger also, and in the event find mademoiselle safe and uninjured. I took leave of M. de Rambouillet with many expressions of esteem on both sides, and a few minutes before eleven reached the rendezvous outside the south gate.

M. d'Agen and Maignan advanced to meet me, the former still presenting an exterior so stern and grave that I wondered to see him, and could scarcely believe he was the same gay spark whose elegant affectations had more than once caused me to smile. He saluted me in silence; Maignan with a sheepish air, which ill-concealed the savage temper defeat had roused in him. Counting my men, I found we mustered ten only, but the equerry explained that he had despatched a rider ahead to make inquiries and leave word for us at convenient points; to the end that we might follow the trail with as few delays as possible. Highly commending Maignan for his forethought in this, I gave the word to start, and crossing the river by the Saint Gervais Bridge, we took the road for Selles at a smart trot.

The weather had changed much in the last twenty-four hours. The sun shone brightly, with a warm west wind, and the country already showed signs of the early spring which marked that year. If, the first hurry of departure over, I had now leisure to feel the gnawing of anxiety and the tortures inflicted by an imagination which, far outstripping us, rode with those whom we pursued and shared their perils, I found two sources of comfort still open to me. No man who has seen service can look on a little band of well-appointed horsemen without pleasure. I reviewed the stalwart forms and stern faces which moved beside me, and comparing their decent order and sound equipments with the scurvy foulness of the men who had ridden north with me, thanked God, and ceased to wonder at the indignation which Matthew and his fellows had aroused in mademoiselle's mind. My other source of satisfaction, the regular beat of hoofs and ring of bridles continually augmented. Every step took us farther from Blois—farther from the close town and reeking streets and the Court; which, if it no longer seemed to me a shambles, befouled by one great deed of blood—experience had removed that impression—retained an appearance infinitely mean and miserable in my eyes. I hated and loathed its intrigues and its jealousies, the folly which trifled in a closet while rebellion mastered France, and the pettiness which recognised no wisdom save that of balancing party and party. I thanked God that my work there was done, and could have welcomed any other occasion that forced me to turn my back on it, and sent me at large over the pure heaths, through the woods, and under the wide heaven, speckled with moving clouds.

But such springs of comfort soon ran dry. M. d'Agen's gloomy rage and the fiery gleam in Maignan's eye would have reminded me, had I been in any danger of forgetting the errand on which we were bound, and the need, exceeding all other needs, which compelled us to lose no moment that might be used. Those whom we followed had five hours' start. The thought of what might happen in those five hours to the two helpless women whom I had sworn to protect burned itself into my mind; so that to refrain from putting spurs to my horse and riding recklessly forward taxed at times all my self-control. The horses seemed to crawl. The men rising and falling listlessly in their saddles maddened me. Though I could not hope to come upon any trace of our quarry for many hours, perhaps for days, I scanned the long, flat heaths unceasingly, searched every marshy bottom before we descended into it, and panted for the moment when the next low ridge should expose to our view a fresh track of wood and waste. The rosy visions of the past night, and those fancies in particular which had made the dawn memorable, recurred to me, as his deeds in the body (so men say) to a hopeless drowning wretch. I grew to think of nothing but

Bruhl and revenge. Even the absurd care with which Simon avoided the neighbourhood of Fanchette, riding anywhere so long as he might ride at a distance from the angry woman's tongue and hand—which provoked many a laugh from the men, and came to be the joke of the company—failed to draw a smile from me.

We passed through Contres, four leagues from Blois, an hour after noon, and three hours later crossed the Cher at Selles, where we stayed awhile to bait our horses. Here we had news of the party before us, and henceforth had little doubt that Bruhl was making for the Limousin; a district in which he might rest secure under the protection of Turenne, and safely defy alike the King of France and the King of Navarre. The greater the necessity, it was plain, for speed; but the roads in that neighbourhood, and forward as far as Valençay, proved heavy and founderous, and it was all we could do to reach Levroux with jaded horses three hours after sunset. The probability that Bruhl would lie at Châteauroux, five leagues farther on—for I could not conceive that under the circumstances he would spare the women—would have led me to push forward had it been possible; but the darkness and the difficulty of finding a guide who would venture deterred me from the hopeless attempt, and we stayed the night where we were.

Here we first heard of the plague; which was said to be ravaging Châteauroux and all the country farther south. The landlord of the inn would have regaled us with many stories of it, and particularly of the swiftness with which men and even cattle succumbed to its attacks. But we had other things to think of, and between anxiety and weariness had clean forgotten the matter when we rose next morning.

We started shortly after daybreak, and for three leagues pressed on at tolerable speed. Then, for no reason stated, our guide gave us the slip as we passed through a wood, and was seen no more. We lost the road, and had to retrace our steps. We strayed into a slough, and extracted ourselves with difficulty. The man who was riding the bay I had purchased forgot the secret which I had imparted to him, and got an ugly fall. In fine, after all these mishaps it wanted little of noon, and less to exhaust our patience, when at length we came in sight of Châteauroux.

Before entering the town we had still an adventure; for we came at a turn in the road on a scene as surprising as it was at first inexplicable. A little north of the town, in a coppice of box facing the south and west, we happed suddenly on a rude encampment, consisting of a dozen huts and booths, set back from the road and formed, some of branches of evergreen trees laid clumsily together, and some of sacking stretched over poles. A number of men and women of decent appearance lay on the short grass before the booths, idly sunning themselves; or moved about, cooking and tending fires, while a score of children raced to and fro with noisy shouts and laughter. The appearance of our party on the scene caused an instant panic. The women and children fled screaming into the wood, spreading the sound of breaking branches farther and farther as they retreated; while the men, a miserable palefaced set, drew together, and seeming half-inclined to fly also, regarded us with glances of fear and suspicion.

Remarking that their appearance and dress were not those of vagrants, while the booths seemed to indicate little skill or experience in the builders, I bade my companions halt, and advanced alone.

'What is the meaning of this, my men?' I said, addressing the first group I reached. 'You seem to have come a-Maying before the time. Whence are you?'

'From Châteauroux,' the foremost answered sullenly. His dress, now I saw him nearer, seemed to be that of a respectable townsman.

'Why?' I replied. 'Have you no homes?'

'Ay, we have homes,' he answered with the same brevity.

'Then why, in God's name, are you here?' I retorted, marking the gloomy air and downcast faces of the group. 'Have you been harried?'

'Ay, harried by the plague!' he answered bitterly. 'Do you

mean to say you have not heard? In Châteauroux there is one man dead in three. Take my advice, sir—you are a brave company—turn, and go home again.'

'Is it as bad as that?' I exclaimed. I had forgotten the landlord's gossip, and the explanation struck me with the force of surprise.

'Ay, is it! Do you see the blue haze?' he continued, pointing with a sudden gesture to the lower ground before us, over which a light pall of summery vapour hung still and motionless. 'Do you see it? Well, under that there is death! You may find food in Châteauroux, and stalls for your horses, and a man to take money; for there are still men there. But cross the Indre, and you will see sights worse than a battle-field a week old! You will find no living soul in house or stable or church, but corpses plenty. The land is cursed! cursed for heresy, some say! Half are dead, and half are fled to the woods! And if you do not die of the plague, you will starve.'

'God forbid!' I muttered, thinking with a shudder of those before us. This led me to ask him if a party resembling ours in number, and including two women, had passed that way. He answered, Yes, after sunset the evening before; that their horses were stumbling with fatigue and the men swearing in pure weariness. He believed that they had not entered the town, but had made a rude encampment half a mile beyond it; and had again broken this up, and ridden southwards two or three hours before our arrival.

'Then we may overtake them today?' I said.

'By your leave, sir,' he answered, with grave meaning. 'I think you are more likely to meet them.'

Shrugging my shoulders, I thanked him shortly and left him; the full importance of preventing my men hearing what I had heard—lest the panic which possessed these townspeople should seize on them also—being already in my mind. Nevertheless the thought came too late, for on turning my horse I found one of the foremost, a long, solemn-faced man, had already found his way to Maignan's stirrup; where he was dilating so eloquently upon the enemy which awaited us southwards that the countenances of half the troopers were as long as his own, and I saw nothing for it but to interrupt his oration by a smart application of my switch to his shoulders. Having thus stopped him, and rated him back to his fellows, I gave the word to march. The men obeyed mechanically, we swung into a canter, and for a moment the danger was over.

But I knew that it would recur again and again. Stealthily marking the faces round me, and listening to the whispered talk which went on, I saw the terror spread from one to another. Voices which earlier in the day had been raised in song and jest grew silent. Great reckless fellows of Maignan's following, who had an oath and a blow for all comers, and to whom the deepest ford seemed to be child's play, rode with drooping heads and knitted brows; or scanned with ill-concealed anxiety the strange haze before us, through which the roofs of the town, and here and there a low hill or line of poplars, rose to plainer view. Maignan himself, the stoutest of the stout, looked grave, and had lost his swaggering air. Only three persons preserved their *sangfroid* entire. Of these, M. d'Agen rode as if he had heard nothing, and Simon Fleix as if he feared nothing; while Fanchette, gazing eagerly forward, saw, it was plain, only one object in the mist, and that was her mistress's face.

We found the gates of the town open, and this, which proved to be the herald of stranger sights, daunted the hearts of my men more than the most hostile reception. As we entered, our horses' hoofs, clattering loudly on the pavement, awoke a hundred echoes in the empty houses to right and left. The main street, flooded with sunshine, which made its desolation seem a hundred times more formidable, stretched away before us, bare and empty; or haunted only by a few slinking dogs, and prowling wretches, who fled, affrighted at the unaccustomed sounds, or stood and eyed us listlessly as we passed. A bell tolled; in the distance we heard the wailing of women. The silent ways, the black cross which marked every second door, the frightful faces which once or twice looked out from upper windows and blasted our sight, infected my men with terror so profound and so ungovernable that at last discipline was forgotten; and one shoving his horse before another in narrow places, there was a scuffle to be first. One, and then a second, began to trot. The trot grew into a shuffling canter. The gates of the inn lay open, nay seemed to invite us to enter; but no one turned or halted. Moved by a single impulse we pushed breathlessly on and on, until the open country was reached, and we who had entered the streets in silent awe, swept out and over the bridge as if the fiend were at our heels.

That I shared in this flight causes me no shame even now, for my men were at the time ungovernable, as the best-trained troops are when seized by such panics; and, moreover, I could have done no good by remaining in the town, where the strength of the contagion was probably greater and the inn larder like to be as bare as the hillside. Few towns are without a hostelry outside the gates for the convenience of knights of the road or those who would avoid the dues, and Châteauroux proved no exception to this rule. A short half-mile from the walls we drew rein before a second encampment raised about a wayside house. It scarcely needed the sound of music mingled with brawling voices to inform us that the wilder spirits of the town had taken refuge here, and were seeking to drown in riot and debauchery, as I have seen happen in a besieged place, the remembrance of the enemy which stalked abroad in the sunshine. Our sudden appearance, while it put a stop to the mimicry of mirth, brought out a score of men and women in every stage of drunkenness and dishevelment, of whom some, with hiccoughs and loose gestures, cried to us to join them, while others swore horridly at being recalled to the present, which, with the future, they were endeavouring to forget.

I cursed them in return for a pack of craven wretches, and threatening to ride down those who obstructed us, ordered my men forward; halting eventually a quarter of a mile farther on, where a wood of groundling oaks which still wore last year's leaves afforded fair shelter. Afraid to leave my men myself, lest some should stray to the inn and others desert altogether, I requested M. d'Agen to return thither with Maignan and Simon, and bring us what forage and food we required. This he did with perfect success, though not until after a scuffle, in which Maignan showed himself a match for a hundred. We watered the horses at a neighbouring brook, and assigning two hours to rest and refreshment—a great part of which M. d'Agen and I spent walking up and down in moody silence, each immersed in his own thoughts—we presently took the road again with renewed spirits.

But a panic is not easily shaken off, nor is any fear so difficult to combat and defeat as the fear of the invisible. The terrors which food and drink had for a time thrust out presently returned with sevenfold force. Men looked uneasily in one another's faces, and from them to the haze which veiled all distant objects. They muttered of the heat, which was sudden, strange, and abnormal at that time of the year. And by-and-by they had other things to speak of. We met a man, who ran beside us and begged of us, crying out in a dreadful voice that his wife and four children lay unburied in the house. A little farther on, beside a well, the corpse of a woman with a child at her breast lay poisoning the water; she had crawled to it to appease her thirst, and died of the draught. Last of all, in a beechwood near Lotier we came upon a lady living in her coach, with one or two panic-stricken women for her only attendants. Her husband was in Paris, she told me; half her servants were dead, the rest had fled. Still she retained in a remarkable degree both courage and courtesy, and accepting with fortitude my reasons and excuses for perforce leaving her in such a plight, gave me a clear account of Bruhl and his party, who had passed her some hours before. The picture of this lady gazing after us with perfect good-breeding, as we rode away at speed, followed by the lamentations of her women, remains with me to this day; filling my mind at once with admiration and melancholy. For, as I learned later, she fell ill of the plague where we left her in the beechwood, and died in a night with both her servants.

The intelligence we had from her inspired us to push forward, sparing neither spur nor horseflesh, in the hope that we might overtake Bruhl before night should expose his captives to fresh hardships and dangers. But the pitch to which the dismal sights and sounds I have mentioned and a hundred like them, had raised the fears of my following did much to balk my endeavours. For a while, indeed, under the influence of momentary excitement, they spurred their horses to the gallop, as if their minds were made up to face the worst; but presently they checked them despite all my efforts, and, lagging slowly and more slowly, seemed to lose all spirit and energy. The desolation which met our eyes on every side, no less than the death-like stillness which prevailed, even the birds, as it seemed to us, being silent, chilled the most reckless to the heart. Maignan's face lost its colour, his voice its ring. As for the rest, starting at a sound and wincing if a leather galled them, they glanced backwards twice for once they looked forwards, and held themselves ready to take to their heels and be gone at the least alarm.

Noting these signs, and doubting if I could trust even Maignan, I thought it prudent to change my place, and falling to the rear, rode there with a grim face and a pistol ready to my hand. It was not the least of my annoyances that M. d'Agen appeared to be ignorant of any cause for apprehension save such as lay before us, and riding on in the same gloomy fit which had possessed him from the moment of starting, neither sought my opinion nor gave his own, but seemed to have undergone so complete and mysterious a change that I could think of one thing only that could have power to effect so marvellous a transformation. I felt his presence a trial rather than a help, and reviewing the course of our short friendship, which a day or two before had been so great a delight to me—as the friendship of a young man commonly is to one growing old—I puzzled myself with much wondering whether there could be rivalry between us.

Sunset, which was welcome to my company, since it removed the haze, which they regarded with superstitious dread, found us still plodding through a country of low ridges and shallow valleys, both clothed in oakwoods. Its short brightness died away, and with it my last hope of surprising Bruhl before I slept. Darkness fell upon us as we wended our way slowly down a steep hillside where the path was so narrow and difficult as to permit only one to descend at a time. A stream of some size, if we might judge from the noise it made, poured through the ravine below us, and presently, at the point where we believed the crossing to be, we espied a solitary light shining in the blackness. To proceed farther was impossible, for the ground grew more and more precipitous; and, seeing this, I bade Maignan dismount, and leaving us where we were, go for a guide to the house from which the light issued.

He obeyed, and plunging into the night, which in that pit between the hills was of an inky darkness, presently returned with a peasant and a lanthorn. I was about to bid the man guide us to the ford, or to some level ground where we could picket the horses, when Maignan gleefully cried out that he had news. I asked what news.

'Speak up, *manant*!' he said, holding up his lanthorn so that the light fell on the man's haggard face and unkempt hair. 'Tell his Excellency what you have told me, or I will skin you alive, little man!'

'Your other party came to the ford an hour before sunset,' the peasant answered, staring dully at us. 'I saw them coming, and hid myself. They quarrelled by the ford. Some were for crossing, and some not.'

'They had ladies with them?' M. d'Agen said suddenly.

'Ay, two, your Excellency,' the clown answered, 'riding like men. In the end they did not cross for fear of the plague, but turned up the river, and rode westwards towards Saint-Gaultier.'

'Saint-Gaultier!' I said. 'Where is that? Where does the road to it go to besides?'

But the peasant's knowledge was confined to his own neighbourhood. He knew no world beyond Saint-Gaultier, and could not answer my question. I was about to bid him show us the way down, when Maignan cried out that he knew more.

'What?' I asked.

'Arnidieu! he heard them say where they were going to spend the night!'

'Ha!' I cried. 'Where?'

'In an old ruined castle two leagues from this, and between here and Saint-Gaultier,' the equerry answered, forgetting in his triumph both plague and panic. 'What do you say to that, your Excellency? It is so, sirrah, is it not?' he continued, turning to the peasant. 'Speak, Master Jacques, or I will roast you before a slow fire!'

But I did not wait to hear the answer. Leaping to the ground, I took the Cid's rein on my arm, and cried impatiently to the man to lead us down.

## 28

# The Castle on the Hill

The certainty that Bruhl and his captives were not far off, and the likelihood that we might be engaged within the hour, expelled from the minds of even the most timorous among us the vapourish fears which had before haunted them. In the hurried scramble which presently landed us on the bank of the stream, men who had ridden for hours in sulky silence found their voices, and from cursing their horses' blunders soon advanced to swearing and singing after the fashion of their kind. This change, by relieving me of a great fear, left me at leisure to consider our position, and estimate more clearly than I might have done the advantages of hastening, or postponing, an attack. We numbered eleven; the enemy, to the best of my belief, twelve. Of this slight superiority I should have recked little in the daytime; nor, perhaps, counting Maignan as two, have allowed that it existed. But the result of a night attack is more difficult to forecast; and I had also to take into account the perils to which the two ladies would be exposed, between the darkness and tumult, in the event of the issue remaining for a time in doubt.

These considerations, and particularly the last, weighed so powerfully with me, that before I reached the bottom of the gorge I had decided to postpone the attack until morning. The answers to some questions which I put to the inhabitant of the house by the ford as soon as I reached level ground only confirmed me in this resolution. The road Bruhl had taken ran for a distance by the riverside, and along the bottom of the gorge; and, difficult by day, was reported to be impracticable for horses by night. The castle he had mentioned lay full two leagues away, and on the farther edge of a tract of rough woodland. Finally, I doubted whether, in the absence of any other reason for delay, I could have marched my men, weary as they were, to the place before daybreak.

When I came to announce this decision, however, and to inquire what accommodation the peasant could afford us, I found myself in trouble. Fanchette, mademoiselle's woman, suddenly confronted me, her face scarlet with rage. Thrusting herself forward into the circle of light cast by the lanthorn, she assailed me with a virulence and fierceness which said more for her devotion to her mistress than her respect for me. Her wild gesticulations, her threats, and the appeals which she made now to me, and now to the men who stood in a circle round us, their faces in shadow, discomfited as much as they surprised me.

'What!' she cried violently, 'you call yourself a gentleman, and lie here and let my mistress be murdered, or worse, within a league of you! Two leagues? A groat for your two leagues! I would walk them barefoot if that would shame you. And you, you call yourselves men, and suffer it! It is God's truth you are a set of cravens and sluggards. Give me as many women, and I would—'

'Peace, woman!' Maignan said in his deep voice. 'You had your way and came with us, and you will obey orders as well as another! Be off, and see to the victuals before worse happen to you!'

'Ay, see to the victuals!' she retorted. 'See to the victuals, forsooth! That is all you think of—to lie warm and eat your fill! A set of dastardly, drinking, droning guzzlers you are! You are!' she retorted, her voice rising to a shriek. 'May the plague take you!'

'Silence!' Maignan growled fiercely, 'or have a care to yourself! For a copper-piece I would send you to cool your heels in the water below—for that last word! Begone, do you hear,' he continued, seizing her by the shoulder and thrusting her towards the house, 'or worse may happen to you. We are rough customers, as you will find if you do not lock up your tongue!'

I heard her go wailing into the darkness; and Heaven knows it was not without compunction I forced myself to remain inactive in the face of a devotion which seemed so much greater than mine. The men fell away one by one to look to their horses and choose sleeping-quarters for the night; and presently M. d'Agen and I were left alone standing beside the lanthorn, which the man had hung on a bush before his door. The brawling of the water as it poured between the banks, a score of paces from us, and the black darkness which hid everything beyond the little ring of light in which we stood—so that for all we could see we were in a pit—had the air of isolating us from all the world.

I looked at the young man, who had not once lisped that day; and I plainly read in his attitude his disapproval of my caution. Though he declined to meet my eye, he stood with his arms folded and his head thrown back, making no attempt to disguise the scorn and ill-temper which his face expressed.

310

Hurt by the woman's taunts, and possibly shaken in my opinion, I grew restive under his silence, and unwisely gave way to my feelings.

'You do not appear to approve of my decision, M. d'Agen?' I said.

'It is yours to command, sir,' he answered proudly.

There are truisms which have more power to annoy than the veriest reproaches. I should have borne in mind the suspense and anxiety he was suffering, and which had so changed him that I scarcely knew him for the gay young spark on whose toe I had trodden. I should have remembered that he was young and I old, and that it behoved me to be patient. But on my side also there was anxiety, and responsibility as well; and, above all, a rankling soreness, to which I refrain from giving the name of jealousy, though it came as near to that feeling as the difference in our ages and personal advantages (whereof the balance was all on his side) would permit. This, no doubt, it was which impelled me to continue the argument.

'You would go on?' I said persistently.

'It is idle to say what I would do,' he answered with a flash of anger.

'I asked for your opinion, sir,' I rejoined stiffly.

'To what purpose?' he retorted, stroking his small moustache haughtily. 'We look at the thing from opposite points. You are going about your business, which appears to be the rescuing of ladies who are—may I venture to say it?—so unfortunate as to entrust themselves to your charge. I, M. de Marsac, am more deeply interested. More deeply interested,' he repeated lamely. 'I—in a word, I am prepared, sir, to do what others only talk of—and if I cannot follow otherwise, would follow on my feet!'

'Whom?' I asked curtly, stung by this repetition of my own words.

He laughed harshly and bitterly. 'Why explain? or why quarrel?' he replied cynically. 'God knows, if I could afford to quarrel with you, I should have done so fifty hours ago.

But I need your help; and, needing it, I am prepared to do that which must seem to a person of your calm passions and perfect judgment alike futile and incredible—pay the full price for it.'

'The full price for it!' I muttered, understanding nothing, except that I did not understand.

'Ay, the full price for it!' he repeated. And as he spoke he looked at me with an expression of rage so fierce that I recoiled a step. That seemed to restore him in some degree to himself, for without giving me an opportunity of answering he turned hastily from me, and, striding away, was in a moment lost in the darkness.

He left me amazed beyond measure. I stood repeating his phrase about 'the full price' a hundred times over, but still found it and his passion inexplicable. To cut the matter short, I could come to no other conclusion than that he desired to insult me, and aware of my poverty and the equivocal position in which I stood towards mademoiselle, chose his words accordingly. This seemed a thing unworthy of one of whom I had before thought highly; but calmer reflection enabling me to see something of youthful bombast in the tirade he had delivered, I smiled a little sadly, and determined to think no more of the matter for the present, but to persist firmly in that which seemed to me to be the right course.

Having settled this, I was about to enter the house, when Maignan stopped me, telling me that the plague had killed five people in it, leaving only the man we had seen; who had, indeed, been seized, but recovered. This ghastly news had scared my company to such a degree that they had gone as far from the house as the level ground permitted, and there lighted a fire, round which they were going to pass the night. Fanchette had taken up her quarters in the stable, and the equerry announced that he had kept a shed full of sweet hay for M. d'Agen and myself. I assented to this arrangement, and after supping off soup and black bread, which was all we could procure, bade the peasant rouse us two hours before sunrise; and so, being too weary and old in service to remain awake thinking, I fell asleep, and slept soundly till a little after four.

My first business on rising was to see that the men before mounting made a meal, for it is ill work fighting empty. I went round also and saw that all had their arms, and that such as carried pistols had them loaded and primed. M. François did not put in an appearance until this work was done, and then showed a very pale and gloomy countenance. I took no heed of him, however, and with the first streak of daylight we started in single file and at a snail's pace up the valley, the peasant, whom I placed in Maignan's charge, going before to guide us, and M. d'Agen and I riding in the rear. By the time the sun rose and warmed our chilled and shivering frames we were over the worst of the ground, and were able to advance at some speed along a track cut through a dense forest of oak-trees.

Though we had now risen out of the valley, the close-set trunks and the undergrowth round them prevented our seeing in any direction. For a mile or more we rode on blindly, and presently started on finding ourselves on the brow of a hill, looking down into a valley, the nearer end of which was clothed in woods, while the farther widened into green sloping pastures. From the midst of these a hill or mount rose sharply up, until it ended in walls of grey stone scarce to be distinguished at that distance from the native rock on which they stood.

'See!' cried our guide. 'There is the castle!'

Bidding the men dismount in haste, that the chance of our being seen by the enemy—which was not great—might be farther lessened, I began to inspect the position at leisure; my first feeling while doing so being one of thankfulness that I had not attempted a night attack, which must inevitably have miscarried, possibly with loss to ourselves, and certainly with the result of informing the enemy of our presence. The castle, of which we had a tolerable view, was long and narrow in shape, consisting of two towers connected by walls. The nearer tower, through which lay the entrance, was roofless, and in every way seemed to be more ruinous than the inner one, which appeared to be perfect in both its storeys. This defect notwithstanding, the place was so strong that my heart sank lower the longer I looked; and a glance at Maignan's face assured me that his experience was also at fault. For M. d'Agen, I clearly saw, when I turned to him, that he had never until this moment realised what we had to expect, but, regarding our pursuit in the light of a hunting-party, had looked to see it end in like easy fashion. His blank, surprised face, as he stood eyeing the stout grey walls, said as much as this.

'Arnidieu!' Maignan muttered, 'give me ten men, and I would hold it against a hundred!'

'Tut, man, there is more than one way to Rome!' I answered oracularly, though I was far from feeling as confident as I seemed. 'Come, let us descend and view this nut a little nearer.'

We began to trail downwards in silence, and as the path led us for a while out of sight of the castle, we were able to proceed with less caution. We had nearly reached without adventure the farther skirts of the wood, between which and the ruin lay an interval of open ground, when we came suddenly, at the edge of a little clearing, on an old hag; who was so intent upon tying up faggots that she did not see us until Maignan's hand was on her shoulder. When she did, she screamed out, and escaping from him with an activity wonderful in a woman of her age, ran with great swiftness to the side of an old man who lay at the foot of a tree half a bowshot off; and whom we had not before seen. Snatching up an axe, she put herself in a posture of defence before him with gestures and in a manner as touching in the eyes of some among us as they were ludicrous in those of others; who cried to Maignan that he had met his match at last, with other gibes of the kind that pass current in camps.

I called to him to let her be, and went forward myself to the old man, who lay on a rude bed of leaves, and seemed unable to rise. Appealing to me with a face of agony not to hurt his wife, he bade her again and again lay down her axe; but she would not do this until I had assured her that we meant him no harm, and that my men should molest neither the one nor the other.

'We only want to know this,' I said, speaking slowly, in fear lest my language should be little more intelligible to them than their *patois* to me. 'There are a dozen horsemen in the old castle there, are there not?'

The man stilled his wife, who continued to chatter and mow at us, and answered eagerly that there were; adding, with a trembling oath, that the robbers had beaten him, robbed him of his small store of meal, and when he would have protested, thrown him out, breaking his leg.

'Then how came you here?' I said.

'She brought me on her back,' he answered feebly.

Doubtless there were men in my train who would have done all that these others had done; but hearing the simple story told, they stamped and swore great oaths of indignation; and one, the roughest of the party, took out some black bread and gave it to the woman, whom under other circumstances he would not have hesitated to rob. Maignan, who knew all arts appertaining to war, examined the man's leg and made a kind of cradle for it, while I questioned the woman.

'They are there still?' I said. 'I saw their horses tethered under the walls.'

'Yes, God requite them!' she answered, trembling violently.

'Tell me about the castle, my good woman,' I said. 'How many roads into it are there?'

'Only one.'

'Through the nearer tower?'

She said yes, and finding that she understood me, and was less dull of intellect than her wretched appearance led me to expect, I put a series of questions to her which it would be tedious to detail. Suffice it that I learned that it was impossible to enter or leave the ruin except through the nearer tower; that a rickety temporary gate barred the entrance, and that from this tower, which was a mere shell of four walls, a narrow square-headed doorway without a door led into the court, beyond which rose the habitable tower of two storeys.

'Do you know if they intend to stay there?' I asked.

'Oh, ay, they bade me bring them faggots for their fire this morning, and I should have a handful of my own meal back,' she answered bitterly; and fell thereon into a passion of impotent rage, shaking both her clenched hands in the direction of the castle, and screaming frenzied maledictions in her cracked and quavering voice.

I pondered awhile over what she had said; liking very little the thought of that narrow square-headed doorway through which we must pass before we could effect anything. And the gate, too, troubled me. It might not be a strong one, but we had neither powder, nor guns, nor any siege implements, and could not pull down stone walls with our naked hands. By seizing the horses we could indeed cut off Bruhl's retreat; but he might still escape in the night; and in any case our pains would only increase the women's hardships while adding fuel to his rage. We must have some other plan.

The sun was high by this time; the edge of the wood scarcely a hundred paces from us. By advancing a few yards through the trees I could see the horses feeding peacefully at the foot of the sunny slope, and even follow with my eyes the faint track which zigzagged up the hill to the closed gate. No one appeared—doubtless they were sleeping off the fatigue of the journey—and I drew no inspiration thence; but as I turned to consult Maignan my eye lit on the faggots, and I saw in a flash that here was a chance of putting into practice a stratagem as old as the hills, yet ever fresh, and not seldom successful.

It was no time for over-refinement. My knaves were beginning to stray forward out of curiosity, and at any moment one of our horses, scenting those of the enemy, might neigh and give the alarm. Hastily calling M. d'Agen and Maignan to me, I laid my plan before them, and satisfied myself that it had their approval; the fact that I had reserved a special part for the former serving to thaw the reserve which had succeeded to his outbreak of the night before. After some debate Maignan persuaded me that the old woman had not sufficient nerve to play the part I proposed for her, and named Fanchette; who being called into council, did not belie the opinion we had formed of her courage. In a few moments our preparations were complete: I had donned the old charcoal-burner's outer rags, Fanchette had assumed those of the woman, while M. d'Agen, who was for a time at a loss, and betrayed less taste for this part of the plan than for any other, ended by putting on the jerkin and hose of the man who had served us as guide.

When all was ready I commended the troop to Maignan's discretion, charging him in the event of anything happening to us to continue the most persistent efforts for mademoiselle's release, and on no account to abandon her. Having received his promise to this effect, and being satisfied that he would keep it, we took up each of us a great faggot, which being borne on the head and shoulders served to hide the features very effectually; and thus disguised we boldly left the shelter of the trees. Fanchette and I went first, tottering in a most natural fashion under the weight of our burdens, while M. d'Agen followed a hundred yards behind. I had given Maignan orders to make a dash for the gate the moment he saw the last named start to run.

The perfect stillness of the valley, the clearness of the air, and the absence of any sign of life in the castle before us—which might have been that of the Sleeping Princess, so fairy-like it looked against the sky—with the suspense and excitement in our own breasts, which these peculiarities seemed to increase a hundred-fold, made the time that followed one of the strangest in my experience. It was nearly ten o'clock, and the warm sunshine flooding everything about us rendered the ascent, laden as we were, laborious in the extreme. The crisp, short turf, which had scarcely got its spring growth, was slippery and treacherous. We dared not hasten, for we knew not what eyes were upon us, and we dared as little—after we had gone half-way—lay our faggots down, lest the action should disclose too much of our features.

When we had reached a point within a hundred paces of the gate, which still remained obstinately closed, we stood to breathe ourselves, and balancing my bundle on my head, I turned to make sure that all was right behind us. I found that M. d'Agen, intent on keeping his distance, had chosen the same moment for rest, and was sitting in a very natural manner on his faggot, mopping his face with the sleeve of his jerkin. I scanned the brown leafless wood, in which we had left Maignan and our men; but I could detect no glitter among the trees nor any appearance likely to betray us. Satisfied on these points, I muttered a few words of encouragement to Fanchette, whose face was streaming with perspiration; and together we turned and addressed ourselves to our task, fatigue—for we had had no practice in carrying burdens on the head—enabling us to counterfeit the decrepitude of age almost to the life.

The same silence prevailing as we drew nearer inspired me with not a few doubts and misgivings. Even the bleat of a sheep would have been welcome in the midst of a stillness which seemed ominous. But no sheep bleated, no voice hailed us. The gate, ill-hung and full of fissures, remained closed. Step by step we staggered up to it, and at length reached it. Afraid to speak lest my accent should betray me, I struck the forepart of my faggot against it and waited: doubting whether our whole stratagem had not been perceived from the beginning, and a pistol-shot might not be the retort.

Nothing of the kind happened, however. The sound of the blow, which echoed dully through the building, died away, and the old silence resumed its sway. We knocked again, but fully two minutes elapsed before a grumbling voice, as of a man aroused from sleep, was heard drawing near, and footsteps came slowly and heavily to the gate. Probably the fellow inspected us through a loophole, for he paused a moment, and my heart sank; but the next, seeing nothing suspicious, he unbarred the gate with a querulous oath, and, pushing it open, bade us enter and be quick about it.

I stumbled forward into the cool, dark shadow, and the woman followed me, while the man, stepping out with a yawn, stood in the entrance, stretching himself in the sunshine. The roofless tower, which smelled dank and unwholesome, was empty, or cumbered only with rubbish and heaps of stones; but looking through the inner door I saw in the courtyard a smouldering fire and half a dozen men in the act of rousing themselves from sleep. I stood a second balancing my faggot, as if in doubt where to lay it down; and then assuring myself by a swift glance that the man who had let us in still had his back towards us, I dropped it across the inner doorway. Fanchette, as she had been instructed, plumped hers upon it, and at the same moment I sprang to the door, and taking the man there by surprise, dealt him a violent blow between the shoulders, which sent him headlong down the slope.

A cry behind me, followed by an oath of alarm, told me that the action was observed and that now was the pinch. In a second I was back at the faggots, and drawing a pistol from under my blouse was in time to meet the rush of the nearest man, who, comprehending all, sprang up, and made for me, with his sheathed sword. I shot him in the chest as he cleared the faggots—which, standing nearly as high as a man's waist, formed a tolerable obstacle—and he pitched forward at my feet.

This balked his companions, who drew back; but unfortunately it was necessary for me to stoop to get my sword, which was hidden in the faggot I had carried. The foremost of the rascals took advantage of this. Rushing at me with a long knife, he failed to stab me—for I caught his wrist—but he succeeded in bringing me to the ground. I thought I was undone. I looked to have the others swarm over upon us; and so it would doubtless have happened had not Fanchette, with rare courage, dealt the first who followed a lusty blow on the body with a great stick she snatched up. The man collapsed on the faggots, and this hampered the rest. The check was enough. It enabled M. d'Agen to come up, who, dashing in through the gate, shot down the first he saw before him, and running at the doorway with his sword with incredible fury and the courage which I had always known him to possess, cleared it in a twinkling. The man with whom I was engaged on the ground, seeing what had happened, wrested himself free with the strength of despair, and dashing through the outer door, narrowly escaped being ridden down by my followers as they swept up to the gate at a gallop, and dismounted amid a whirlwind of cries.

In a moment they thronged in on us pell-mell, and as soon as I could lay my hand on my sword I led them through the doorway with a cheer, hoping to be able to enter the farther tower with the enemy. But the latter had taken the alarm too early and too thoroughly. The court was empty. We were barely in time to see the last man dart up a flight of outside stairs, which led to the first storey, and disappear, closing a heavy door behind him. I rushed to the foot of the steps and would have ascended also, hoping against hope to find the door unsecured; but a shot which was fired through a loophole and narrowly missed my head, and another which brought down one of my men, made me pause. Discerning all the advantage to be on Bruhl's side, since he could shoot us down from his cover, I cried a retreat; the issue of the matter leaving us masters of the entrance-tower, while they retained the inner and stronger tower, the narrow court between the two being neutral ground unsafe for either party.

Two of their men had fled outwards and were gone, and two lay dead; while the loss on our side was confined to the man who was shot, and Fanchette, who had received a blow on the head in the *mêlée*, and was found, when we retreated, lying sick and dazed against the wall.

It surprised me much, when I came to think upon it, that I had seen nothing of Bruhl, though the skirmish had lasted two or three minutes from the first outcry, and been attended by an abundance of noise. Of Fresnoy, too, I now remembered that I had caught a glimpse only. These two facts seemed so strange that I was beginning to augur the worst, though I scarcely know why, when my spirits were marvellously raised and my fears relieved by a thing which Maignan, who was the first to notice it, pointed out to me. This was the appearance at an upper window of a white kerchief, which was waved several times towards us. The window was little more than an arrow-slit, and so narrow and high besides that it was impossible to see who gave the signal; but my experience of mademoiselle's coolness and resource left me in no doubt on the point. With high hopes and a lighter heart than I had worn for some time I bestirred myself to take every precaution, and began by bidding Maignan select two men and ride round the hill, to make sure that the enemy had no way of retreat open to him.

## 29

# Pestilence and Famine

While Maignan was away about this business I despatched two men to catch our horses, which were running loose in the valley, and to remove those of Bruhl's party to a safe distance from the castle. I also blocked up the lower part of the door leading into the courtyard, and named four men to remain under arms beside it, that we might not be taken by surprise; an event of which I had the less fear, however, since the enemy were now reduced to eight swords, and could only escape, as we could only enter, through this doorway. I was still busied with these arrangements when M. d'Agen joined me, and I broke off to compliment him on his courage, acknowledging in particular the service he had done me personally. The heat of the conflict had melted the young man's reserve, and flushed his face with pride; but as he listened to me he gradually froze again, and when I ended he regarded me with the same cold hostility.

'I am obliged to you,' he said, bowing. 'But may I ask what next, M. de Marsac?'

'We have no choice,' I answered. 'We can only starve them out.'

'But the ladies?' he said, starting slightly. 'What of them?'

'They will suffer less than the men,' I replied. 'Trust me, the latter will not bear starving long.'

He seemed surprised, but I explained that with our small numbers we could not hope to storm the tower, and might think ourselves fortunate that we now had the enemy cooped up where he could not escape, and must eventually surrender.

'Ay, but in the meantime how will you ensure the women against violence?' he asked, with an air which showed he was far from satisfied.

'I will see to that when Maignan comes back,' I answered pretty confidently.

The equerry appeared in a moment with the assurance that egress from the farther side of the tower was impossible. I bade him nevertheless keep a horseman moving round the hill, that we might have intelligence of any attempt. The order was scarcely given when a man—one of those I had left on guard at the door of the courtyard—came to tell me that Fresnoy desired to speak with me on behalf of M. de Bruhl.

'Where is he?' I asked.

'At the inner door with a flag of truce,' was the answer.

'Tell him, then,' I said, without offering to move, 'that I will communicate with no one except his leader, M. de Bruhl. And add this, my friend,' I continued. 'Say it aloud: that if the ladies whom he has in charge are injured by so much as a hair, I will hang every man within these walls, from M. de Bruhl to the youngest lackey.' And I added a solemn oath to that effect.

The man nodded, and went on his errand, while I and M. d'Agen, with Maignan, remained standing outside the gate, looking idly over the valley and the brown woods through which we had ridden in the early morning. My eyes rested chiefly on the latter, Maignan's as it proved on the former. Doubtless we all had our own thoughts. Certainly I had, and for a while, in my satisfaction at the result of the attack and the manner in which we had Bruhl confined, I did not remark the gravity which was gradually overspreading the equerry's countenance. When I did I took the alarm, and asked him sharply what was the matter.

'I don't like that, your Excellency,' he answered, pointing into the valley.

I looked anxiously, and looked, and saw nothing.

'What?' I said in astonishment.

'The blue mist,' he muttered, with a shiver. 'I have been watching it this half-hour, your Excellency. It is rising fast.'

I cried out on him for a maudlin fool, and M. d'Agen swore impatiently; but for all that, and despite the contempt I strove to exhibit, I felt a sudden chill at my heart as I recognised in the valley below the same blue haze which had attended us through yesterday's ride, and left us only at nightfall. Involuntarily we both fell to watching it as it rose slowly and more slowly, first enveloping the lower woods, and then spreading itself abroad in the sunshine. It is hard to witness a bold man's terror and remain unaffected by it; and I confess I trembled. Here, in the moment of our seeming success, was something which I had not taken into account, something against which I could not guard either myself or others!

'See!' Maignan whispered hoarsely, pointing again with his finger. 'It is the Angel of Death, your Excellency! Where he kills by ones and twos, he is invisible. But when he slays by hundreds and thousands, men see the shadow of his wings!'

'Chut, fool!' I retorted with anger, which was secretly proportioned to the impression his weird saying made on me. 'You have been in battles! Did you ever see him there? or at a sack? A truce to this folly,' I continued. 'And do you go and inquire what food we have with us. It may be necessary to send for some.'

I watched him go doggedly off, and knowing the stout nature of the man and his devotion to his master, I had no fear that he would fail us; but there were others, almost as necessary to us, in whom I could not place the same confidence. And these had also taken the alarm. When I turned I found groups of pale-faced men, standing by twos and threes at my back; who, pointing and muttering and telling one another what Maignan had told us, looked where we had looked. As one spoke and another listened, I saw the old panic revive in their eyes. Men who an hour or two before had crossed the court under fire with the utmost resolution, and dared instant death without a thought, grew pale, and looking from this side of the valley to that with faltering eyes, seemed to be seeking, like hunted animals, a place of refuge. Fear, once aroused, hung in the air. Men talked in whispers of the abnormal heat, and, gazing at the cloudless sky, fled from the sunshine to the shadow; or, looking over the expanse of woods, longed to be under cover and away from this lofty eyrie, which to their morbid eyes seemed a target for all the shafts of death.

I was not slow to perceive the peril with which these fears and apprehensions, which rapidly became general, threatened my plans. I strove to keep the men employed, and to occupy their thoughts as far as possible with the enemy and his proceedings; but I soon found that even here a danger lurked; for Maignan, coming to me by-and-by with a grave face, told me that one of Bruhl's men had ventured out, and was parleying with the guard on our side of the court. I went at once and broke the matter off, threatening to shoot the fellow if he was not under cover before I counted ten. But the scared, sulky faces he left behind him told me that the mischief was done, and I could think of no better remedy for it than to give M. d'Agen a hint, and station him at the outer gate with his pistols ready.

The question of provisions, too, threatened to become a

324

serious one; I dared not leave to procure them myself, nor could I trust any of my men with the mission. In fact the besiegers were rapidly becoming the besieged. Intent on the rising haze and their own terrors, they forgot all else. Vigilance and caution were thrown to the winds. The stillness of the valley, its isolation, the distant woods that encircled us and hung quivering in the heated air, all added to the panic. Despite all my efforts and threats, the men gradually left their posts, and getting together in little parties at the gate, worked themselves up to such a pitch of dread that by two hours after noon they were fit for any folly; and at the mere cry of 'plague!' would have rushed to their horses and ridden in every direction.

It was plain that I could depend for useful service on myself and three others only—of whom, to his credit be it said, Simon Fleix was one. Seeing this, I was immensely relieved when I presently heard that Fresnoy was again seeking to speak with me. I was no longer, it will be believed, for standing on formalities; but glad to waive in silence the punctilio on which I had before insisted, and anxious to afford him no opportunity of marking the slackness which prevailed among my men, I hastened to meet him at the door of the courtyard, where Maignan had detained him.

I might have spared my pains, however. I had no more than saluted him and exchanged the merest preliminaries before I saw that he was in a state of panic far exceeding that of my following. His coarse face, which had never been prepossessing, was mottled and bedabbled with sweat; his bloodshot eyes, when they met mine, wore the fierce yet terrified expression of an animal caught in a trap. Though his first word was an oath, sworn for the purpose of raising his courage, the bully's bluster was gone. He spoke in a low voice, and his hands shook; and for a penny-piece I saw he would have bolted past me and taken his chance in open flight.

I judged from his first words, uttered, as I have said, with an oath, that he was aware of his state. 'M. de Marsac,' he said, whining like a cur, 'you know me to be a man of courage.'

I needed nothing after this to assure me that he meditated something of the basest; and I took care how I answered him. 'I have known you stiff enough upon occasions,' I replied drily. 'And then, again, I have known you not so stiff, M. Fresnoy.'

'Only when you were in question,' he muttered with another oath. 'But flesh and blood cannot stand this. You could not yourself. Between him and them I am fairly worn out. Give me good terms—good terms, you understand, M. de Marsac?' he whispered eagerly, sinking his voice still lower, 'and you shall have all you want.'

'Your lives, and liberty to go where you please,' I answered coldly. 'The two ladies to be first given up to me uninjured. Those are the terms.'

'But for me?' he said anxiously.

'For you? The same as the others,' I retorted. 'Or I will make a distinction for old acquaintance sake, M. Fresnoy; and if the ladies have aught to complain of, I will hang you first.'

He tried to bluster and hold out for a sum of money, or at least for his horse to be given up to him. But I had made up my mind to reward my followers with a present of a horse apiece; and I was besides well aware that this was only an afterthought on his part, and that he had fully decided to yield. I stood fast, therefore. The result justified my firmness, for he presently agreed to surrender on those terms.

'Ay, but M. de Bruhl?' I said, desiring to learn clearly whether he had authority to treat for all. 'What of him?'

He looked at me impatiently. 'Come and see!' he said, with an ugly sneer.

'No, no, my friend,' I answered, shaking my head warily. 'That is not according to rule. You are the surrendering party, and it is for you to trust us. Bring out the ladies, that I may have speech with them, and then I will draw off my men.'

'Nom de Dieu!' he cried hoarsely, with so much fear and

rage in his face that I recoiled from him. 'That is just what I cannot do.'

'You cannot?' I rejoined with a sudden thrill of horror. 'Why not? why not, man?' And in the excitement of the moment, conceiving the idea that the worst had happened to the women, I pushed him back with so much fury that he laid his hand on his sword.

'Confound you!' he stuttered, 'stand back! It is not that, I tell you! Mademoiselle is safe and sound, and madame, if she had her senses, would be sound too. It is not our fault if she is not. But I have not got the key of the rooms. It is in Bruhl's pocket, I tell you!'

'Oh!' I made answer drily. 'And Bruhl?'

'Hush, man,' Fresnoy replied, wiping the perspiration from his brow, and bringing his pallid, ugly face near to mine, 'he has got the plague!'

I stared at him for a moment in silence; which he was the first to break. 'Hush!' he muttered again, laying a trembling hand on my arm, 'if the men knew it—and not seeing him they are beginning to suspect it—they would rise on us. The devil himself could not keep them here. Between him and them I am on a razor's edge. Madame is with him, and the door is locked. Mademoiselle is in a room upstairs, and the door is locked. And he has the keys. What can I do? What can I do, man?' he cried, his voice hoarse with terror and dismay.

'Get the keys,' I said instinctively.

'What? From him?' he muttered, with an irresistible shudder, which shook his bloated cheeks. 'God forbid I should see him! It takes stout men infallibly. I should be dead by night! By God, I should!' he continued, whining. 'Now you are not stout, M. de Marsac. If you will come with me, I will draw off the men from that part; and you may go in and get the key from him.'

His terror, which surpassed all feigning, and satisfied me without doubt that he was in earnest, was so intense that it could not fail to infect me. I felt my face, as I looked into his, grow to the same hue. I trembled as he did and grew sick. For if there is a word which blanches the soldier's cheek and tries his heart more than another, it is the name of the disease which travels in the hot noonday, and, tainting the strongest as he rides in his pride, leaves him in a few hours a poor mass of corruption. The stoutest and the most reckless fear it; nor could I, more than another, boast myself indifferent to it, or think of its presence without shrinking. But the respect in which a man of birth holds himself saves him from the unreasoning fear which masters the vulgar; and in a moment I recovered myself, and made up my mind what it behoved me to do.

'Wait awhile,' I said sternly, 'and I will come with you.'

He waited accordingly, though with manifest impatience, while I sent for M. d'Agen, and communicated to him what I was about to do. I did not think it necessary to enter into details, or to mention Bruhl's state, for some of the men were well in hearing. I observed that the young gentleman received my directions with a gloomy and dissatisfied air. But I had become by this time so used to his moods, and found myself so much mistaken in his character, that I scarcely gave the matter a second thought. I crossed the court with Fresnoy, and in a moment had mounted the outside staircase and passed through the heavy doorway.

The moment I entered, I was forced to do Fresnoy the justice of admitting that he had not come to me before he was obliged. The three men who were on guard inside tossed down their weapons at sight of me, while a fourth, who was posted at a neighbouring window, hailed me with a cry of relief. From the moment I crossed the threshold the defence was practically at an end. I might, had I chosen or found it consistent with honour, have called in my following and secured the entrance. Without pausing, however, I passed on to the foot of a gloomy stone staircase winding up between walls of rough masonry; and here Fresnoy stood on one side and stopped. He pointed upwards with a pale face and muttered, 'The door on the left.'

Leaving him there watching me as I went upwards, I

mounted slowly to the landing, and by the light of an arrow-slit which dimly lit the ruinous place found the door he had described, and tried it with my hand. It was locked, but I heard someone moan in the room, and a step crossed the floor, as if he or another came to the door and listened. I knocked, hearing my heart beat in the silence.

At last a voice quite strange to me cried, 'Who is it?'

'A friend,' I muttered, striving to dull my voice that they might not hear me below.

'A friend!' the bitter answer came. 'Go! You have made a mistake! We have no friends.'

'It is I, M. de Marsac,' I rejoined, knocking more imperatively. 'I would see M. de Bruhl. I must see him.'

The person inside, at whose identity I could now make a guess, uttered a low exclamation, and still seemed to hesitate. But on my repeating my demand I heard a rusty bolt withdrawn, and Madame de Bruhl, opening the door a few inches, showed her face in the gap. 'What do you want?' she murmured jealously.

Prepared as I was to see her, I was shocked by the change in her appearance, a change which even that imperfect light failed to hide. Her blue eyes had grown larger and harder, and there were dark marks under them. Her face, once so brilliant, was grey and pinched; her hair had lost its golden lustre. 'What do you want?' she repeated, eyeing me fiercely.

'To see him,' I answered.

'You know?' she muttered. 'You know that he—'

I nodded.

'And you still want to come in? My God! Swear you will not hurt him?'

'Heaven forbid!' I said; and on that she held the door open that I might enter. But I was not half-way across the room before she had passed me, and was again between me and the wretched makeshift pallet. Nay, when I stood and looked down at him, as he moaned and rolled in senseless agony, with livid face and distorted features (which the cold grey light of that miserable room rendered doubly appalling), she

329

hung over him and fenced him from me; so that looking on him and her, and remembering how he had treated her, and why he came to be in this place, I felt unmanly tears rise to my eyes. The room was still a prison, a prison with broken mortar covering the floor and loopholes for windows; but the captive was held by other chains than those of force. When she might have gone free, her woman's love, surviving all that he had done to kill it, chained her to his side with fetters which old wrongs and present danger were powerless to break.

It was impossible that I could view a scene so strange without feelings of admiration as well as pity; or without forgetting for a while, in my respect for Madame de Bruhl's devotion, the risk which had seemed so great to me on the stairs. I had come simply for a purpose of my own, and with no thought of aiding him who lay here. But so great, as I have noticed on other occasions, is the power of a noble example, that, before I knew it, I found myself wondering what I could do to help this man, and how I could relieve madame in the discharge of offices which her husband had as little right to expect at her hands as at mine. At the mere sound of the word plague I knew she would be deserted in this wilderness by all, or nearly all; a reflection which suggested to me that I should first remove mademoiselle to a distance, and then consider what help I could afford here.

I was about to tell her the purpose with which I had come when a paroxysm more than ordinarily violent, and induced perhaps by the excitement of my presence—though he seemed beside himself—seized him, and threatened to tax her powers to the utmost. I could not look on and see her spend herself in vain; and almost before I knew what I was doing I had laid my hands on him and after a brief struggle thrust him back exhausted on the couch.

She looked at me so strangely after that that in the half-light which the loopholes afforded I tried in vain to read her meaning. 'Why did you come?' she cried at length, breathing quickly. 'You, of all men? Why did you come? He was no friend of yours, Heaven knows!'

'No, madame, nor I of his,' I answered bitterly, with a sudden revulsion of feeling.

'Then why are you here?' she retorted.

'I could not send one of my men,' I answered. 'And I want the key of the room above.'

At the mention of that—the room above—she flinched as if I had struck her, and looked as strangely at Bruhl as she had before looked at me. No doubt the reference to Mademoiselle de la Vire recalled to her mind her husband's wild passion for the girl, which for the moment she had forgotten. Nevertheless she did not speak, though her face turned very pale. She stooped over the couch, such as it was, and searching his clothes, presently stood up, and held out the key to me. 'Take it, and let her out,' she said with a forced smile. 'Take it up yourself, and do it. You have done so much for her it is right that you should do this.'

I took the key, thanking her with more haste than thought, and turned towards the door, intending to go straight up to the floor above and release mademoiselle. My hand was already on the door, which madame, I found, had left ajar in the excitement of my entrance, when I heard her step behind me. The next instant she touched me on the shoulder. 'You fool!' she exclaimed, her eyes flashing, 'would you kill her? Would you go from him to her, and take the plague to her? God forgive me, it was in my mind to send you. And men are such puppets you would have gone!'

I trembled with horror, as much at my stupidity as at her craft. For she was right: in another moment I should have gone, and comprehension and remorse would have come too late. As it was, in my longing at once to reproach her for her wickedness and to thank her for her timely repentance, I found no words; but I turned away in silence and went out with a full heart.

# 30

# Stricken

OUTSIDE the door, standing in the dimness of the landing, I found M. d'Agen. At any other time I should have been the first to ask him why he had left the post which I had assigned to him. But at the moment I was off my balance, and his presence suggested nothing more than that here was the very person who could best execute my wishes. I held out the key at arm's length, and bade him release Mademoiselle de la Vire, who was in the room above, and escort her out of the castle. 'Do not let her linger here,' I continued urgently. 'Take her to the place where we found the wood-cutters. You need fear no resistance.'

'But Bruhl?' he said, as he took the key mechanically from me.

'He is out of the question,' I answered in a low voice. 'We have done with him. He has the plague.'

He uttered a sharp exclamation. 'What of madame, then?' he muttered.

'She is with him,' I said.

He cried out suddenly at that, sucking in his breath, as I have known men do in pain. And but that I drew back he would have laid his hand on my sleeve. 'With him?' he stammered. 'How is that?'

'Why, man, where else should she be?' I answered, forgetting that the sight of those two together had at first surprised me also, as well as moved me. 'Or who else should be with him? He is her husband.'

He stared at me for a moment at that, and then he turned slowly away and began to go up; while I looked after him, gradually thinking out the clue to his conduct. Could it be that it was not mademoiselle attracted him, but Madame de Bruhl?

And with that hint I understood it all. I saw in a moment the conclusion to which he had come on hearing of the presence of madame in my room. In my room at night! The change had dated from that time; instead of a careless, light-spirited youth he had become in a moment a morose and restive churl, as difficult to manage as an unbroken colt. Quite clearly I saw now the meaning of the change; why he had shrunk from me, and why all intercourse between us had been so difficult and so constrained.

I laughed to think how he had deceived himself, and how nearly I had come to deceiving myself also. And what more I might have thought I do not know, for my meditations were cut short at this point by a loud outcry below, which, beginning in one or two sharp cries of alarm and warning, culminated quickly in a roar of anger and dismay.

Fancying I recognised Maignan's voice, I ran down the stairs, seeking a loophole whence I could command the scene; but finding none, and becoming more and more alarmed, I descended to the court, which I found, to my great surprise, as empty and silent as an old battle-field. Neither on the enemy's side nor on ours was a single man to be seen. With growing dismay I sprang across the court and darted through the outer tower, only to find that and the gateway equally unguarded. Nor was it until I had passed through the latter, and stood on the brow of the slope, which we had had to clamber with so much toil, that I learned what was amiss.

Far below me a string of men, bounding and running at speed, streamed down the hill towards the horses. Some were shouting, some running silently, with their elbows at their sides and their scabbards leaping against their calves. The horses stood tethered in a ring near the edge of the wood, and by some oversight had been left unguarded. The foremost runner I made out to be Fresnoy; but a number of his men were close upon him, and then after an interval came Maignan, waving his blade and emitting frantic threats with every stride. Comprehending at once that Fresnoy and his following, rendered desperate by panic and the prospective loss of their horses, had taken advantage of my absence and given Maignan the slip, I saw I could do nothing save watch the result of the struggle.

This was not long delayed. Maignan's threats, which seemed to me mere waste of breath, were not without effect on those he followed. There is nothing which demoralises men like flight. Troopers who have stood charge after charge while victory was possible will fly like sheep, and like sheep allow themselves to be butchered, when they have once turned the back. So it was here. Many of Fresnoy's men were stout fellows, but having started to run they had no stomach for fighting. Their fears caused Maignan to appear near, while the horses seemed distant; and one after another they turned aside and made like rabbits for the wood. Only Fresnoy, who had taken care to have the start of all, kept on, and, reaching the horses, cut the rope which tethered the nearest, and vaulted nimbly on its back. Safely seated there, he tried to frighten the others into breaking loose; but not succeeding at the first attempt, and seeing Maignan, breathing vengeance, coming up with him, he started his horse, a bright bay, and rode off laughing along the edge of the wood.

Fully content with the result—for our carelessness might have cost us very dearly—I was about to turn away when I saw that Maignan had mounted and was preparing to follow. I stayed accordingly to see the end, and from my elevated position enjoyed a first-rate view of the race which ensued. Both were heavy weights, and at first Maignan gained no ground. But when a couple of hundred yards had been covered Fresnoy had the ill-luck to blunder into some heavy ground, and this enabling his pursuer, who had time to avoid it, to get within two-score paces of him, the race became as exciting as I could wish. Slowly and surely Maignan, who had chosen the Cid, reduced the distance between them to a score of paces—to fifteen—to ten. Then Fresnoy, becoming alarmed, began to look over his shoulder and ride

in earnest. He had no whip, and I saw him raise his sheathed
sword, and strike his beast on the flank. It sprang forward,
and appeared for a few strides to be holding its own. Again
he repeated the blow—but this time with a different result.
While his hand was still in the air, his horse stumbled, as it
seemed to me, made a desperate effort to recover itself, fell
headlong and rolled over and over.

Something in the fashion of the fall, which reminded me
of the mishap I had suffered on the way to Chizé, led me to
look more particularly at the horse as it rose trembling to its
feet, and stood with drooping head. Sure enough, a careful
glance enabled me, even at that distance, to identify it as
Matthew's bay—the trick-horse. Shading my eyes, and gazing
on the scene with increased interest, I saw Maignan, who had
dismounted, stoop over something on the ground, and again
after an interval stand upright.

But Fresnoy did not rise. Nor was it without awe that,
guessing what had happened to him, I remembered how he
had used this very horse to befool me; how heartlessly he had
abandoned Matthew, its owner; and by what marvellous
haps—which men call chances—Providence had brought it
to this place, and put it in his heart to choose it out of a score
which stood to his hand!

I was right. The man's neck was broken. He was quite dead.
Maignan passed the word to one, and he to another, and so it
reached me on the hill. It did not fail to awaken memories
both grave and wholesome. I thought of Saint-Jean d'Angely,
of Chizé, of the house in the Ruelle d'Arcy; then in the midst
of these reflections, I heard voices and turned to find mademoiselle, with M. d'Agen behind me.

Her hand was still bandaged, and her dress, which she had
not changed since leaving Blois, was torn and stained with
mud. Her hair was in disorder; she walked with a limp.
Fatigue and apprehension had stolen the colour from her
cheeks, and in a word she looked, when I turned, so wan and
miserable that for a moment I feared the plague had seized
her.

The instant, however, that she caught sight of me a wave of colour invaded, not her cheeks only, but her brow and neck. From her hair to the collar of her gown she was all crimson. For a second she stood gazing at me, and then, as I saluted her, she sprang forward. Had I not stepped back she would have taken my hands.

My heart so overflowed with joy at this sight, that in the certainty her blush gave me I was fain to toy with my happiness. All jealousy of M. d'Agen was forgotten; only I thought it well not to alarm her by telling her what I knew of the Bruhls. 'Mademoiselle,' I said earnestly, bowing, but retreating from her, 'I thank God for your escape. One of your enemies lies helpless here, and another is dead yonder.'

'It is not of my enemies I am thinking,' she answered quickly, 'but of God, of whom you rightly remind me; and then of my friends.'

'Nevertheless,' I answered as quickly, 'I beg you will not stay to thank them now, but go down to the wood with M. d'Agen, who will do all that may be possible to make you comfortable.'

'And you, sir?' she said, with a charming air of confusion.

'I must stay here,' I answered, 'for a while.'

'Why?' she asked with a slight frown.

I did not know how to tell her, and I began lamely. 'Someone must stop with madame,' I said without thought.

'Madame?' she exclaimed. 'Does she require assistance? I will stop.'

'God forbid!' I cried.

I do not know how she understood the words, but her face, which had been full of softness, grew hard. She moved quickly towards me; but, mindful of the danger I carried about me, I drew farther back. 'No nearer, mademoiselle,' I murmured, 'if you please.'

She looked puzzled, and finally angry, turning away with a sarcastic bow. 'So be it, then, sir,' she said proudly, 'if you desire it. M. d'Agen, if you are not afraid of me, will you lead me down?'

I stood and watched them go down the hill, comforting myself with the reflection that tomorrow, or the next day, or within a few days at most, all would be well. Scanning her figure as she moved, I fancied that she went with less spirit as the space increased between us. And I pleased myself with the notion. A few days, a few hours, I thought, and all would be well. The sunset which blazed in the west was no more than a faint reflection of the glow which for a few minutes pervaded my mind, long accustomed to cold prospects and the chill of neglect.

A term was put to these pleasant imaginings by the arrival of Maignan; who, panting from the ascent of the hill, informed me with a shamefaced air that the tale of horses was complete, but that four of our men were missing, and had doubtless gone off with the fugitives. These proved to be M. d'Agen's two lackeys and the two varlets M. de Rambouillet had lent us. There remained besides Simon Fleix only Maignan's three men from Rosny; but the state in which our affairs now stood enabled us to make light of this. I informed the equerry—who visibly paled at the news—that M. de Bruhl lay ill of the plague, and like to die; and I bade him form a camp in the wood below, and, sending for food to the house where we had slept the night before, make mademoiselle as comfortable as circumstances permitted.

He listened with surprise, and when I had done asked with concern what I intended to do myself.

'Someone must remain with Madame de Bruhl,' I answered. 'I have already been to the bedside to procure the key of mademoiselle's room, and I run no farther risk. All I ask is that you will remain in the neighbourhood, and furnish us with supplies should it be necessary.'

He looked at me with emotion, which, strongly in conflict with his fears as it was, touched me not a little. 'But morbleu! M. de Marsac,' he said, 'you will take the plague and die.'

'If God wills,' I answered, very lugubriously I confess, for pale looks in one commonly so fearless could not but depress me. 'But if not, I shall escape. Anyway, my friend,' I continued, 'I owe you a quittance. Simon Fleix has an inkhorn and paper. Bid him bring them to this stone and leave them, and I will write that Maignan, the equerry of the Baron de Rosny, served me to the end as a brave soldier and an honest friend. What, *mon ami*?' I continued, for I saw that he was overcome by this, which was, indeed, a happy thought of mine. 'Why not? It is true, and will acquit you with the Baron. Do it, and go. Advise M. d'Agen, and be to him what you have been to me.'

He swore two or three great oaths, such as men of his kind use to hide an excess of feeling, and after some further remonstrance went away to carry out my orders; leaving me to stand on the brow in a strange kind of solitude, and watch horses and men withdraw to the wood, until the whole valley seemed left to me and stillness and the grey evening. For a time I stood in thought. Then reminding myself, for a fillip to my spirits, that I had been far more alone when I walked the streets of Saint-Jean friendless and threadbare than I was now, I turned, and swinging my scabbard against my boots for company, stumbled through the dark, silent courtyard, and mounted as cheerfully as I could to madame's room.

To detail all that passed during the next five days would be tedious and in indifferent taste, seeing that I am writing this memoir for the perusal of men of honour; for though I consider the offices which the whole can perform for the sick to be worthy of the attention of every man, however well born, who proposes to see service, they seem to be more honourable in the doing than the telling. One episode, however, which marked those days filled me then, as it does now, with the most lively pleasure; and that was the unexpected devotion displayed by Simon Fleix, who, coming to me, refused to leave, and showed himself at this pinch to be possessed of such sterling qualities that I freely forgave him the deceit he had formerly practised on me. The fits of moody silence into which he still fell at times and an occasional irascibility seemed to show that he had not altogether conquered his insane fancy; but the mere fact that he had come to me in a situation of hazard, and voluntarily removed himself from mademoiselle's neighbourhood, gave me good hope for the future.

M. de Bruhl died early on the morning of the second day, and Simon and I buried him at noon. He was a man of courage and address, lacking only principles. In spite of madame's grief and prostration, which were as great as though she had lost the best husband in the world, we removed before night to a separate camp in the woods, and left with the utmost relief the grey ruin on the hill, in which, it seemed to me, we had lived an age. In our new bivouac, where, game being abundant, and the weather warm, we lacked no comfort, except the society of our friends, we remained four days longer. On the fifth morning we met the others of our company by appointment on the north road, and commenced the return journey.

Thankful that we had escaped contagion, we nevertheless still proposed to observe for a time such precautions in regard to the others as seemed necessary; riding in the rear and having no communication with them, though they showed by signs the pleasure they felt at seeing us. From the frequency with which mademoiselle turned and looked behind her, I judged she had overcome her pique at my strange conduct; which the others should by this time have explained to her. Content, therefore, with the present, and full of confidence in the future, I rode along in a rare state of satisfaction; at one moment planning what I would do, and at another reviewing what I had done.

The brightness and softness of the day, and the beauty of the woods, which in some places, I remember, were bursting into leaf, contributed much to establish me in this frame of mind. The hateful mist, which had so greatly depressed us, had disappeared; leaving the face of the country visible in all the brilliance of early spring. The men who rode before us, cheered by the happy omen, laughed and talked as they rode, or tried the paces of their horses, where the trees grew sparsely; and their jests and laughter coming pleasantly to our ears as we followed, warmed even madame's sad face to a semblance of happiness.

I was riding along in this state of contentment when a feeling of fatigue, which the distance we had come did not seem to justify, led me to spur the Cid into a brisker pace. The sensation of lassitude still continued, however, and indeed grew worse; so that I wondered idly whether I had over-eaten myself at my last meal. Then the thing passed for a while from my mind, which the descent of a steep hill sufficiently occupied.

But a few minutes later, happening to turn in the saddle, I experienced a strange and sudden dizziness; so excessive as to force me to grasp the cantle, and cling to it, while trees and hills appeared to dance round me. A quick, hot pain in the side followed, almost before I recovered the power of thought; and this increased so rapidly, and was from the first so definite, that, with a dreadful apprehension already formed in my mind, I thrust my hand inside my clothes, and found that swelling which is the most sure and deadly symptom of the plague.

The horror of that moment—in which I saw all those things on the possession of which I had just been congratulating myself, pass hopelessly from me, leaving me in dreadful gloom—I will not attempt to describe in this place. Let it suffice that the world lost in a moment its joyousness, the sunshine its warmth. The greenness and beauty round me, which an instant before had filled me with pleasure, seemed on a sudden no more than a grim and cruel jest at my expense, and I an atom perishing unmarked and unnoticed. Yes, an atom, a mote; the bitterness of that feeling I well remember. Then, in no long time—being a soldier—I recovered my coolness, and, retaining the power to think, decided what it behoved me to do.

# 31

# Under the Greenwood

To escape from my companions on some pretext, which should enable me to ensure their safety without arousing their fears, was the one thought which possessed me on the subsidence of my first alarm. Probably it answered to that instinct in animals which bids them get away alone when wounded or attacked by disease; and with me it had the fuller play as the pain prevailed rather by paroxysms than in permanence, and, coming and going, allowed intervals of ease, in which I was able to think clearly and consecutively, and even to sit firmly in the saddle.

The moment one of these intervals enabled me to control myself, I used it to think where I might go without danger to others; and at once and naturally my thoughts turned to the last place we had passed; which happened to be the house in the gorge where we had received news of Bruhl's divergence from the road. The man who lived there alone had had the plague; therefore he did not fear it. The place itself was solitary, and I could reach it, riding slowly, in half an hour. On the instant and without more delay I determined on this course. I would return, and, committing myself to the fellow's good offices, bid him deny me to others, and especially to my friends—should they seek me.

Aware that I had no time to lose if I would put this plan into execution before the pains returned to sap my courage, I drew bridle at once, and muttered some excuse to madame; if I remember rightly, that I had dropped my gauntlet. Whatever the pretext—and my dread was great lest she should observe any strangeness in my manner—it passed with her; by reason, chiefly, I think, of the grief which monopolised her. She let me go, and before anyone else could mark or miss me I was a hundred yards away on the back-track, and already sheltered from observation by a turn in the road.

The excitement of my evasion supported me for a while after leaving her; and then for another while, a paroxysm of pain deprived me of the power of thought. But when this last was over, leaving me weak and shaken, yet clear in my mind, the most miserable sadness and depression that can be conceived came upon me; and, accompanying me through the wood, filled its avenues (which doubtless were fair enough to others' eyes) with the blackness of despair. I saw but the charnel-house, and that everywhere. It was not only that the horrors of the first discovery returned upon me and almost unmanned me; nor only that regrets and memories, pictures of the past and plans for the future, crowded thick upon my mind, so that I could have wept at the thought of all ending here. But in my weakness mademoiselle's face shone where the wood was darkest, and, tempting and provoking me to return—were it only to tell her that, grim and dull as I seemed, I loved her—tried me with a subtle temptation almost beyond my strength to resist. All that was mean in me rose in arms, all that was selfish clamoured to know why I must die in the ditch while others rode in the sunshine; why I must go to the pit, while others loved and lived!

And so hard was I pressed that I think I should have given way had the ride been longer or my horse less smooth and nimble. But in the midst of my misery, which bodily pain was beginning to augment to such a degree that I could scarcely see, and had to ride gripping the saddle with both hands, I reached the mill. My horse stopped of its own accord. The man we had seen before came out. I had just strength left to tell him what was the matter, and what I wanted; and then a fresh attack came on, with sickness, and overcome by vertigo I fell to the ground.

I have but an indistinct idea what happened after that; until I found myself inside the house, clinging to the man's

arm. He pointed to a box-bed in one corner of the room
(which was, or seemed to my sick eyes, gloomy and dark-
some in the extreme), and would have had me lie down in it.
But something inside me revolted against the bed, and despite
the force he used, I broke away, and threw myself on a heap
of straw which I saw in another corner.

'Is not the bed good enough for you?' he grumbled.

I strove to tell him it was not that.

'It should be good enough to die on,' he continued
brutally. 'There's five have died on that bed, I'd have you
know! My wife one, and my son another, and my daughter
another; and then my son again, and a daughter again. Five!
Ay, five in that bed!'

Brooding in the gloom of the chimney-corner, where he
was busied about a black pot, he continued to mutter and
glance at me askance; but after a while I swooned away with
pain.

When I opened my eyes again the room was darker. The
man still sat where I had last seen him, but a noise, the same,
perhaps, which had roused me, drew him as I looked to the
unglazed window. A voice outside, the tones of which I
seemed to know, inquired if he had seen me; and so carried
away was I by the excitement of the moment that I rose on
my elbow to hear the answer. But the man was staunch. I
heard him deny all knowledge of me, and presently the sound
of retreating hoofs and the echo of voices dying in the distance
assured me I was left.

Then, at that instant, a doubt of the man on whose com-
passion I had thrown myself entered my mind. Plague-
stricken, hopeless as I was, it chilled me to the very heart;
staying in a moment the feeble tears I was about to shed, and
curing even the vertigo, which forced me to clutch at the
straw on which I lay. Whether the thought arose from a sickly
sense of my own impotence, or was based on the fellow's
morose air and the stealthy glances he continued to cast at me,
I am as unable to say as I am to decide whether it was well-
founded, or the fruit of my own fancy. Possibly the gloom of

343

the room and the man's surly words inclined me to suspicion; possibly his secret thoughts portrayed themselves in his hang-dog visage. Afterwards it appeared that he had stripped me, while I lay, of everything of value; but he may have done this in the belief that I should die.

All I know is that I knew nothing certain, because the fear died almost as soon as it was born. The man had scarcely seated himself again, or I conceived the thought, when a second alarm outside caused him to spring to his feet. Scowling and muttering as he went, he hurried to the window. But before he reached it the door was dashed violently open, and Simon Fleix stood in the entrance.

There came in with him so blessed a rush of light and life as in a moment dispelled the horror of the room, and stripped me at one and the same time of fear and manhood. For whether I would or no, at sight of the familiar face, which I had fled so lately, I burst into tears; and, stretching out my hands to him, as a frightened child might have done, called on him by name. I suppose the plague was by this time so plainly written on my face that all who looked might read; for he stood at gaze, staring at me, and was still so standing when a hand put him aside and a slighter, smaller figure, pale-faced and hooded, stood for a moment between me and the sunshine. It was mademoiselle!

That, I thank God, restored me to myself, or I had been for ever shamed. I cried to them with all the voice I had left to take her away; and calling out frantically again and again that I had the plague and she would die, I bade the man close the door. Nay, regaining something of strength in my fear for her, I rose up, half-dressed as I was, and would have fled into some corner to avoid her, still calling out to them to take her away, to take her away—if a fresh paroxysm had not seized me, so that I fell blind and helpless where I was.

For a time after that I knew nothing; until someone held water to my lips, and I drank greedily, and presently awoke to the fact that the entrance was dark with faces and figures all gazing at me as I lay. But I could not see her; and I had sense enough to know and be thankful that she was no longer among them. I would fain have bidden Maignan begone too, for I read the consternation in his face. But I could not muster strength or voice for the purpose, and when I turned my head to see who held me—ah me! it comes back to me still in dreams—it was mademoiselle's hair that swept my forehead and her hand that ministered to me; while tears she did not try to hide or wipe away fell on my hot cheek. I could have pushed her away even then, for she was slight and small; but the pains came upon me, and with a sob choking my voice I lost all knowledge.

I am told that I lay for more than a month between life and death, now burning with fever and now in the cold fit; and that but for the tendance which never failed nor faltered, nor could have been outdone had my malady been the least infectious in the world, I must have died a hundred times, as hundreds round me did die week by week in that year. From the first they took me out of the house (where I think I should have perished quickly, so impregnated was it with the plague poison) and laid me under a screen of boughs in the forest, with a vast quantity of cloaks and horse-cloths cunningly disposed to windward. Here I ran some risk from cold and exposure and the fall of heavy dews; but, on the other hand, had all the airs of heaven to clear away the humours and expel the fever from my brain.

Hence it was that when the first feeble beginnings of consciousness awoke in me again, they and the light stole in on me through green leaves, and overhanging boughs, and the freshness and verdure of the spring woods. The sunshine which reached my watery eyes was softened by its passage through great trees, which grew and expanded as I gazed up into them, until each became a verdant world, with all a world's diversity of life. Grown tired of this, I had still long avenues of shade, carpeted with flowers, to peer into; or a little wooded bottom—where the ground fell away on one side—that blazed and burned with redthorn. Ay, and hence it was that the first sounds I heard, when the fever left me at

345

last, and I knew morning from evening, and man from woman, were the songs of birds calling to their mates.

Mademoiselle and Madame de Bruhl, with Fanchette and Simon Fleix, lay all this time in such shelter as could be raised for them where I lay; M. François and three stout fellows, whom Maignan left to guard us, living in a hut within hail. Maignan himself, after seeing out a week of my illness, had perforce returned to his master, and no news had since been received from him. Thanks to the timely move into the woods, no other of the party fell ill, and by the time I was able to stand and speak the ravages of the disease had so greatly decreased that fear was at an end.

I should waste words were I to try to describe how the peace and quietude of the life we led in the forest during the time of my recovery sank into my heart; which had known, save by my mother's bedside, little of such joys. To awake in the morning to sweet sounds and scents, to eat with reviving appetite and feel the slow growth of strength, to lie all day in shade or sunshine as it pleased me, and hear women's voices and tinkling laughter, to have no thought of the world and no knowledge of it, so that we might have been, for anything we saw, in another sphere—these things might have sufficed for happiness without that which added to each and every one of them a sweeter and deeper and more lasting joy. Of which next.

I had not begun to take notice long before I saw that M. François and madame had come to an understanding; such an one, at least, as permitted him to do all for her comfort and entertainment without committing her to more than was becoming at such a season. Naturally this left mademoiselle much in my company; a circumstance which would have ripened into passion the affection I before entertained for her, had not gratitude and a nearer observance of her merits already elevated my regard into the most ardent worship that even the youngest lover ever felt for his mistress.

In proportion, however, as I and my love grew stronger, and mademoiselle's presence grew more necessary to my happiness—so that were she away but an hour I fell a-moping—she began to draw off from me, and absenting herself more and more on long walks in the woods, by-and-by reduced me to such a pitch of misery as bid fair to complete what the fever had left undone.

If this had happened in the world I think it likely that I should have suffered in silence. But here, under the greenwood, in common enjoyment of God's air and earth, we seemed more nearly equal. She was scarce better dressed than a sutler's wife; while recollections of her wealth and station, though they assailed me nightly, lost much of their point in presence of her youth and of that fair and patient gentleness which forest life and the duties of a nurse had fostered.

So it happened that one day, when she had been absent longer than usual, I took my courage in my hand and went to meet her as far as the stream which ran through the bottom by the redthorn. Here, at a place where there were three stepping-stones, I waited for her; first taking away the stepping-stones, that she might have to pause, and, being at a loss, might be glad to see me.

She came presently, tripping through an alley in the low wood, with her eyes on the ground, and her whole carriage full of a sweet pensiveness which it did me good to see. I turned my back on the stream before she saw me, and made a pretence of being taken up with something in another direction. Doubtless she espied me soon, and before she came very near; but she made no sign until she reached the brink, and found the stepping-stones were gone.

Then, whether she suspected me or not, she called out to me, not once, but several times. For, partly to tantalise her, as lovers will, and partly because it charmed me to hear her use my name, I would not turn at once.

When I did, and discovered her standing with one small foot dallying with the water, I cried out with well-affected concern; and in a great hurry ran towards her, paying no attention to her chiding or the pettish haughtiness with which she spoke to me.

347

'The stepping-stones are all on your side,' she said imperiously. 'Who has moved them?'

I looked about without answering, and at last pretended to find them; while she stood watching me, tapping the ground with one foot the while. Despite her impatience, the stone which was nearest to her I took care to bring last—that she might not cross without my assistance. But after all she stepped over so lightly and quickly that the hand she placed in mine seemed scarcely to rest there a second. Yet when she was over I managed to retain it; nor did she resist, though her cheek, which had been red before, turned crimson and her eyes fell, and bound to me by the link of her little hand, she stood beside me with her whole figure drooping.

'Mademoiselle,' I said gravely, summoning all my resolution to my aid, 'do you know of what that stream with its stepping-stones reminds me?'

She shook her head but did not answer.

'Of the stream which has flowed between us from the day when I first saw you at Saint-Jean,' I said in a low voice. 'It has flowed between us, and it still does—separating us.'

'What stream?' she murmured, with her eyes cast down, and her foot playing with the moss. 'You speak in riddles, sir.'

'You understand this one only too well, mademoiselle,' I answered. 'Are you not young and gay and beautiful, while I am old, or almost old, and dull and grave? You are rich and well-thought-of at Court, and I a soldier of fortune, not too successful. What did you think of me when you first saw me at Saint-Jean? What when I came to Rosny? That, mademoiselle,' I continued with fervour, 'is the stream which flows between us and separates us; and I know of but one stepping-stone that can bridge it.'

She looked aside, toying with a piece of thorn-blossom she had picked. It was not redder than her cheeks.

'That one stepping-stone,' I said, after waiting vainly for any word or sign from her, 'is Love. Many weeks ago, mademoiselle, when I had little cause to like you, I loved

348

you; I loved you whether I would or not, and without thought or hope of return. I should have been mad had I spoken to you then. Mad, and worse than mad. But now, now that I owe you my life, now that I have drunk from your hand in fever, and, awaking early and late, have found you by my pillow—now that, seeing you come in and out in the midst of fear and hardship, I have learned to regard you as a woman kind and gentle as my mother—now that I love you, so that to be with you is joy, and away from you grief, is it presumption in me now, mademoiselle, to think that that stream may be bridged?'

I stopped, out of breath, and saw that she was trembling. But she spoke presently. 'You said one stepping-stone?' she murmured.

'Yes,' I answered hoarsely, trying in vain to look at her face, which she kept averted from me.

'There should be two,' she said, almost in a whisper. 'Your love, sir, and—and mine. You have said much of the one, and nothing of the other. In that you are wrong, for I am proud still. And I would not cross the stream you speak of for any love of yours!'

'Ah!' I cried in sharpest pain.

'But,' she continued, looking up at me on a sudden with eyes that told me all, 'because I love you I am willing to cross it—to cross it once for ever, and to live beyond it all my life —if I may live my life with you.'

I fell on my knee and kissed her hand again and again in a rapture of joy and gratitude. By-and-by she pulled it from me. 'If you will, sir,' she said, 'you may kiss my lips. If you do not, no man ever will.'

After that, as may be guessed, we walked every day in the forest, making longer and longer excursions as my strength came back to me, and the nearer parts grew familiar. From early dawn, when I brought my love a posy of flowers, to late evening, when Fanchette hurried her from me, our days were passed in a long round of delight; being filled full of all beautiful things—love, and sunshine, and rippling streams,

349

and green banks, on which we sat together under scented limes, telling one another all we had ever thought, and especially all we had ever thought of one another. Sometimes —when the light was low in the evening—we spoke of my mother; and once—but that was in the sunshine, when the bees were humming and my blood had begun to run strongly in my veins—I spoke of my great and distant kinsman, Rohan. But mademoiselle would hear nothing of him, murmuring again and again in my ear, 'I have crossed, my love, I have crossed.'

Truly the sands of that hour-glass were of gold. But in time they ran out. First M. François, spurred by the restlessness of youth, and convinced that madame would for a while yield no farther, left us, and went back to the world. Then news came of great events that could not fail to move us. The King of France and the King of Navarre had met at Tours, and embracing in the sight of an immense multitude, had repulsed the League with slaughter in the suburb of Saint-Symphorien. Fast on this followed the tidings of their march northwards with an overwhelming army of fifty-thousand men of both religions, bent, rumour had it, on the signal punishment of Paris.

I grew—shame that I should say it—to think more and more of these things; until mademoiselle, reading the signs, told me one day that we must go. 'Though never again,' she added with a sigh, 'shall we be so happy.'

'Then why go?' I asked foolishly.

'Because you are a man,' she answered with a wise smile, 'as I would have you be, and you need something besides love. Tomorrow we will go.'

'Whither?' I said in amazement.

'To the camp before Paris,' she answered. 'We will go back in the light of day—seeing that we have done nothing of which to be ashamed—and throw ourselves on the justice of the King of Navarre. You shall place me with Madame Catherine, who will not refuse to protect me; and so, sweet, you will have only yourself to think of. Come, sir,' she continued, laying her little hand in mine, and looking into my eyes, 'you are not afraid?'

'I am more afraid than ever I used to be,' I said trembling.

'So I would have it,' she whispered, hiding her face on my shoulder. 'Nevertheless we will go.'

And go we did. The audacity of such a return in the face of Turenne, who was doubtless in the King of Navarre's suite, almost took my breath away; nevertheless, I saw that it possessed one advantage which no other course promised—that, I mean, of setting us right in the eyes of the world, and enabling me to meet in a straightforward manner such as maligned us. After some consideration I gave my assent, merely conditioning that until we reached the Court we should ride masked, and shun as far as possible encounters by the road.

32

# A Tavern Brawl

On the following day, accordingly, we started. But the news of the two kings' successes, and particularly the certainty which these had bred in many minds that nothing short of a miracle could save Paris, had moved so many gentlemen to take the road that we found the inns crowded beyond example, and were frequently forced into meetings which made the task of concealing our identity more difficult and hazardous than I had expected. Sometimes shelter was not to be obtained on any terms, and then we had to lie in the fields or in any convenient shed. Moreover, the passage of the army had swept the country so bare both of food and forage, that these commanded astonishing prices; and a long day's ride more than once brought us to our destination without securing for us the ample meal we had earned, and required.

Under these circumstances, it was with joy little short of transport that I recognised the marvellous change which had come over my mistress. Bearing all without a murmur, or a frown, or so much as one complaining word, she acted on numberless occasions so as to convince me that she spoke truly—albeit I scarcely dared to believe it—when she said that she had but one trouble in the world, and that was the prospect of our coming separation.

For my part, and despite some gloomy moments, when fear of the future overcame me, I rode in Paradise riding by my mistress. It was her presence which glorified alike the first freshness of the morning, when we started with all the day before us, and the coolness of the late evening, when we rode hand-in-hand. Nor could I believe without an effort that I was the same Gaston de Marsac whom she had once spurned and disdained. God knows I was thankful for her love. A thousand times, thinking of my grey hairs, I asked her if she did not repent; and a thousand times she answered No, with so much happiness in her eyes that I was fain to thank God again and believe her.

Notwithstanding the inconvenience of the practice, we made it a rule to wear our masks whenever we appeared in public; and this rule we kept more strictly as we approached Paris. It exposed us to some comment and more curiosity but led to no serious trouble until we reached Étampes, twelve leagues from the capital; where we found the principal inn so noisy and crowded, and so much disturbed by the constant coming and going of couriers, that it required no experience to predicate the neighbourhood of the army. The great courtyard seemed to be choked with a confused mass of men and horses, through which we made our way with difficulty. The windows of the house were all open, and offered us a view of tables surrounded by men eating and drinking hastily, as the manner of travellers is. The gateway and the steps of the house were lined with troopers and servants and sturdy rogues; who scanned all who passed in or out, and not unfrequently followed them with ribald jests and nicknames. Songs and oaths, brawling and laughter, with the neighing of horses and the huzzas of the beggars, who shouted whenever a fresh party arrived, rose above all, and increased the reluctance with which I assisted madame and mademoiselle to dismount.

Simon was no match for such an occasion as this; but the stalwart aspect of the three men whom Maignan had left with me commanded respect, and attended by two of these I made a way for the ladies—not without some opposition and a few oaths—to enter the house. The landlord, whom we found crushed into a corner inside, and entirely overborne by the crowd which had invaded his dwelling assured me that he had not the smallest garret he could place at my disposal; but I presently succeeded in finding a small room at the top, which I purchased from the four men who had taken possession of it. As it was impossible to get anything to eat there, I left a man on guard, and myself descended with madame and mademoiselle to the eating-room, a large chamber set with long boards, and filled with a rough and noisy crew. Under a running fire of observations we entered, and found with difficulty three seats in an inner corner of the room.

I ran my eye over the company, and noticed among them, besides a dozen travelling parties like our own, specimens of all those classes which are to be found in the rear of an army. There were some officers and more horse-dealers; half a dozen forage-agents and a few priests; with a large sprinkling of adventurers, bravos, and led-captains, and here and there two or three whose dress and the deference paid to them by their neighbours seemed to indicate a higher rank. Conspicuous among these last were a party of four who occupied a small table by the door. An attempt had been made to secure some degree of privacy for them by interposing a settle between them and the room; and their attendants, who seemed to be numerous, did what they could to add to this by filling the gap with their persons. One of the four, a man of handsome dress and bearing, who sat in the place of honour, was masked, as we were. The gentleman at his right hand I could not see. The others, whom I could see, were strangers to me.

Some time elapsed before our people succeeded in procuring us any food, and during the interval we were exposed to an amount of comment on the part of those round us which I found very little to my liking. There were not half a dozen women present, and this and our masks rendered my companions unpleasantly conspicuous. Aware, however, of the importance of avoiding an altercation which might possibly detain us, and would be certain to add to our notoriety, I remained quiet; and presently the entrance of a tall, dark-complexioned man, who carried himself with a peculiar swagger, and seemed to be famous for something or other, diverted the attention of the company from us.

The new-comer was somewhat of Maignan's figure. He wore a back and breast over a green doublet, and had an orange feather in his cap and an orange-lined cloak on his shoulder. On entering he stood a moment in the doorway, letting his bold black eyes rove round the room, the while he talked in a loud braggart fashion to his companions. There was a lack of breeding in the man's air, and something offensive in his look; which I noticed produced wherever it rested a momentary silence and constraint. When he moved farther into the room I saw that he wore a very long sword, the point of which trailed a foot behind him.

He chose out for his first attentions the party of four whom I have mentioned; going up to them and accosting them with a ruffling air, directed especially to the gentleman in the mask. The latter lifted his head haughtily on finding himself addressed by a stranger, but did not offer to answer. Someone else did, however, for a sudden bellow like that of an enraged bull proceeded from behind the settle. The words were lost in noise, the unseen speaker's anger seeming so overpowering that he could not articulate; but the tone and voice, which were in some way familiar to me, proved enough for the bully, who, covering his retreat with a profound bow, backed out rapidly, muttering what was doubtless an apology. Cocking his hat more fiercely to make up for this repulse, he next proceeded to patrol the room, scowling from side to side as he went, with the evident intention of picking a quarrel with someone less formidable.

By ill-chance his eye lit, as he turned, on our masks. He said something to his companions; and encouraged, no doubt, by the position of our seats at the board, which led him to think us people of small consequence, he came to a stop opposite us.

'What! more dukes here?' he cried scoffingly. 'Hallo, you sir!' he continued to me, 'will you not unmask and drink a glass with me?'

I thanked him civilly, but declined.

His insolent eyes were busy, while I spoke, with madame's fair hair and handsome figure, which her mask failed to hide. 'Perhaps the ladies will have better taste, sir,' he said rudely. 'Will they not honour us with a sight of their pretty faces?'

Knowing the importance of keeping my temper I put constraint on myself, and answered, still with civility, that they were greatly fatigued and were about to retire.

'Zounds!' he cried, 'that is not to be borne. If we are to lose them so soon, the more reason we should enjoy their *beaux yeux* while we can. A short life and a merry one, sir. This is not a nunnery, nor, I dare swear, are your fair friends nuns.'

Though I longed to chastise him for this insult, I feigned deafness, and went on with my meal as if I had not heard him; and the table being between us prevented him going beyond words. After he had uttered one or two coarse jests of a similar character, which cost us less as we were masked, and our emotions could only be guessed, the crowd about us, seeing I took the thing quietly, began to applaud him; but more as it seemed to me out of fear than love. In this opinion I was presently confirmed on hearing from Simon—who whispered the information in my ear as he handed a dish— that the fellow was an Italian captain in the king's pay, famous

355

for his skill with the sword and the many duels in which he had displayed it.

Mademoiselle, though she did not know this, bore with his insolence with a patience which astonished me; while madame appeared unconscious of it. Nevertheless, I was glad when he retired and left us in peace. I seized the moment of his absence to escort the ladies through the room and upstairs to their apartment, the door of which I saw locked and secured. That done I breathed more freely; and feeling thankful that I had been able to keep my temper, took the episode to be at an end.

But in this I was mistaken, as I found when I returned to the room in which we had supped, my intention being to go through it to the stables. I had not taken two paces across the floor before I found my road blocked by the Italian, and read alike in his eyes and in the faces of the company—of whom many hastened to climb the tables to see what passed—that the meeting was premeditated. The man's face was flushed with wine; proud of his many victories, he eyed me with a boastful contempt my patience had perhaps given him the right to feel.

'Ha! well met, sir,' he said, sweeping the floor with his cap in an exaggeration of respect, 'now, perhaps, your high-mightiness will condescend to unmask? The table is no longer between us, nor are your fair friends here to protect their *cher ami*!'

'If I still refuse, sir,' I said civilly, wavering between anger and prudence, and hoping still to avoid a quarrel which might endanger us all, 'be good enough to attribute it to private motives, and to no desire to disoblige you.'

'No, I do not think you wish to disoblige me,' he answered, laughing scornfully—and a dozen voices echoed the gibe. 'But for your private motives, the devil take them! Is that plain enough, sir?'

'It is plain enough to show me that you are an ill-bred man!' I answered, choler getting the better of me. 'Let me pass, sir.'

'Unmask!' he retorted, moving so as still to detain me, 'or shall I call in the grooms to perform the office for you?'

Seeing at last that all my attempts to evade the man only fed his vanity, and encouraged him to further excesses, and that the motley crowd, who filled the room and already formed a circle round us, had made up their minds to see sport, I would no longer balk them; I could no longer do it, with honour. I looked round, therefore, for someone whom I might enlist as my second, but I saw no one with whom I had the least acquaintance. The room was lined from table to ceiling with mocking faces and scornful eyes all turned to me.

My opponent saw the look, and misread it; being much accustomed, I imagine, to a one-sided battle. He laughed contemptuously. 'No, my friend, there is no way out of it,' he said. 'Let me see your pretty face, or fight.'

'So be it,' I said quietly. 'If I have no other choice, I will fight.'

'In your mask?' he cried incredulously.

'Yes,' I said sternly, feeling every nerve tingle with long-suppressed rage. 'I will fight as I am. Off with your back and breast, if you are a man. And I will so deal with you that if you see tomorrow's sun you shall need a mask for the rest of your days!'

'Ho! ho!' he answered, scowling at me in surprise, 'you sing in a different key now. But I will put a term to it. There is space enough between these tables, if you can use your weapon; and much more than you will need tomorrow.'

'Tomorrow will show,' I retorted.

Without more ado he unfastened the buckles of his breast-piece, and relieving himself of it, stepped back a pace. Those of the bystanders who occupied the part of the room he indicated—a space bounded by four tables, and not unfit for the purpose, though somewhat confined—hastened to get out of it, and seize instead upon neighbouring posts of 'vantage. The man's reputation was such, and his fame so great, that on all sides I heard naught but wagers offered against me at odds; but this circumstance, which might have flurried a younger man and numbed his arm, served only to set me on making the most of such openings as the fellow's presumption and certainty of success would be sure to afford.

The news of the challenge running through the house had brought together by this time so many people as to fill the room from end to end, and even to obscure the light, which was beginning to wane. At the last moment, when we were on the point of engaging, a slight commotion marked the admission to the front of three or four persons, whose consequence or attendants gained them this advantage. I believed them to be the party of four I have mentioned but at the time I could not be certain.

In the few seconds of waiting while this went forward I examined our relative positions with the fullest intention of killing the man—whose glittering eyes and fierce smile filled me with a loathing which was very nearly hatred—if I could. The line of windows lay to my right and his left. The evening light fell across us, whitening the row of faces on my left, but leaving those on my right in shadow. It occurred to me on the instant that my mask was actually an advantage, seeing that it protected my sight from the side-light, and enabled me to watch his eyes and point with more concentration.

'You will be the twenty-third man I have killed!' he said boastfully, as we crossed swords and stood an instant on guard.

'Take care!' I answered. 'You have twenty-three against you!'

A swift lunge was his only answer. I parried it, and thrust, and we fell to work. We had not exchanged half a dozen blows, however, before I saw that I should need all the advantage which my mask and greater caution gave me. I had met my match, and it might be something more; but that for a time it was impossible to tell. He had the longer weapon, and I the longer reach. He preferred the point, after the new Italian fashion, and I the blade. He was somewhat flushed with wine, while my arm had scarcely recovered the strength of which illness had deprived me. On the other hand, excited at the first by the cries of his backers, he played rather wildly;

while I held myself prepared, and keeping up a strong guard, waited cautiously for any opening or mistake on his part.

The crowd round us, which had hailed our first passes with noisy cries of derision and triumph, fell silent after a while, surprised and taken aback by their champion's failure to spit me at the first onslaught. My reluctance to engage had led them to predict a short fight and an easy victory.

Convinced of the contrary, they began to watch each stroke with bated breath; or now and again, muttering the name of Jarnac, broke into brief exclamations as a blow more savage than usual drew sparks from our blades, and made the rafters ring with harsh grinding of steel on steel.

The surprise of the crowd, however, was a small thing compared with that of my adversary. Impatience, disgust, rage, and doubt chased one another in turn across his flushed features. Apprised that he had to do with a swordsman, he put forth all his power. With spite in his eyes he laboured blow on blow, he tried one form of attack after another, he found me equal, if barely equal, to all. And then at last there came a change. The perspiration gathered on his brow, the silence disconcerted him; he felt his strength failing under the strain, and suddenly, I think, the possibility of defeat and death, unthought of before, burst upon him. I heard him groan, and for a moment he fenced wildly. Then he again recovered himself. But now I read terror in his eyes, and knew that the moment of retribution was at hand. With his back to the table, and my point threatening his breast, he knew at last what those others had felt!

He would fain have stopped to breathe, but I would not let him though my blows also were growing feeble, and my guard weaker; for I knew that if I gave him time to recover himself he would have recourse to other tricks, and might out-manoeuvre me in the end. As it was, my black unchanging mask, which always confronted him, which hid all emotions and veiled even fatigue, had grown to be full of terror to him —full of blank, passionless menace. He could not tell how I fared, or what I thought, or how my strength stood. A superstitious dread was on him, and threatened to overpower him. Ignorant who I was or whence I came, he feared and doubted, grappling with monstrous suspicions, which the fading light encouraged. His face broke out in blotches, his breath came and went in gasps, his eyes began to protrude. Once or twice they quitted mine for a part of a second to steal a despairing glance at the rows of onlookers that ran to right and left of us. But he read no pity there.

At last the end came—more suddenly than I had looked for it, but I think he was unnerved. His hand lost its grip of the hilt, and a parry which I dealt a little more briskly than usual sent the weapon flying among the crowd, as much to my astonishment as to that of the spectators. A volley of oaths and exclamations hailed the event; and for a moment I stood at gaze, eyeing him watchfully. He shrank back; then he made for a moment as if he would fling himself upon me dagger in hand. But seeing my point steady, he recoiled a second time, his face distorted with rage and fear.

'Go!' I said sternly. 'Begone! Follow your sword! But spare the next man you conquer.'

He stared at me, fingering his dagger as if he did not understand, or as if in the bitterness of his shame at being so defeated even life were unwelcome. I was about to repeat my words when a heavy hand fell on my shoulder.

'Fool!' a harsh growling voice muttered in my ear. 'Do you want him to serve you as Achon served Matas? This is the way to deal with him.'

And before I knew who spoke or what to expect a man vaulted over the table beside me. Seizing the Italian by the neck and waist, he flung him bodily—without paying the least regard to his dagger—into the crowd. 'There!' the new-comer cried, stretching his arms as if the effort had relieved him, 'so much for him! And do you breathe yourself. Breathe yourself, my friend,' he continued with a vainglorious air of generosity. 'When you are rested and ready, you and I will have a bout. Mon dieu! what a thing it is to see a man! And by my faith you are a man!'

'But, sir,' I said, staring at him in the utmost bewilderment, 'we have no quarrel.'

'Quarrel?' he cried in his loud, ringing voice. 'Heaven forbid! Why should we? I love a man, however, and when I see one I say to him, "I am Crillon! Fight me!" But I see you are not yet rested. Patience! There is no hurry. Berthon de Crillon is proud to wait your convenience. In the meantime, gentlemen,' he continued, turning with a grand air to the spectators, who viewed this sudden *bouleversement* with unbounded surprise, 'let us do what we can. Take the word from me, and cry all, "*Vive le Roi, et vive l'Inconnu!*"'

Like people awaking from a dream —so great was their astonishment—the company complied and with the utmost heartiness. When the shout died away, someone cried in turn, '*Vive Crillon!*' and this was honoured with a fervour which brought the tears to the eyes of that remarkable man, in whom bombast was so strangely combined with the firmest and most reckless courage. He bowed again and again, turning himself about in the small space between the tables, while his face shone with pleasure and enthusiasm. Meanwhile I viewed him with perplexity. I comprehended that it was his voice I had heard behind the settle; but I had neither the desire to fight him nor so great a reserve of strength after my illness as to be able to enter on a fresh contest with equanimity. When he turned to me, therefore, and again asked, 'Well, sir, are you ready?' I could think of no better answer than that I had already made to him, 'But, sir, I have no quarrel with you.'

'Tut, tut!' he answered querulously, 'if that is all, let us engage.'

'That is not all, however,' I said, resolutely putting up my sword. 'I have not only no quarrel with M. de Crillon, but I received at his hands when I saw him a considerable service.'

'Then now is the time to return it,' he answered briskly, and as if that settled the matter.

I could not refrain from laughing. 'Nay, but I have still an excuse,' I said. 'I am barely recovered from an illness, and am weak. Even so, I should be loth to decline a combat with some; but a better man than I may give the wall to M. de Crillon and suffer no disgrace.'

'Oh, if you put it that way—enough said,' he answered in a tone of disappointment. 'And, to be sure, the light is almost gone. That is a comfort. But you will not refuse to drink a cup of wine with me? Your voice I remember, though I cannot say who you are or what service I did you. For the future, however, count on me. I love a man who is brave as well as modest, and know no better friend than a stout swordsman.'

I was answering him in fitting terms—while the fickle crowd, which a few minutes earlier had been ready to tear me, viewed us from a distance with respectful homage—when the masked gentleman who had before been in his company drew near and saluted me with much stateliness.

'I congratulate you, sir,' he said, in the easy tone of a great man condescending. 'You use the sword as few use it, and fight with your head as well as your hands. Should you need a friend or employment, you will honour me by remembering that you are known to the Vicomte de Turenne.'

I bowed low to hide the start which the mention of his name caused me. For had I tried, ay, and possessed to aid me all the wit of M. de Brantôme, I could have imagined nothing more fantastic than this meeting; or more entertaining than that I, masked, should talk with the Vicomte de Turenne masked, and hear in place of reproaches and threats of vengeance a civil offer of protection. Scarcely knowing whether I should laugh or tremble, or which should occupy me more, the diverting thing that had happened or the peril we had barely escaped, I made shift to answer him, craving his indulgence if I still preserved my incognito. Even while I spoke a fresh fear assailed me: lest M. de Crillon, recognising my voice or figure, should cry my name on the spot, and explode in a moment the mine on which we stood.

This rendered me extremely impatient to be gone. But M. le Vicomte had still something to say, and I could not withdraw myself without rudeness.

'You are travelling north like everyone else?' he said, gazing at me curiously. 'May I ask whether you are for Meudon, where the King of Navarre lies, or for the Court at Saint Cloud?'

I muttered, moving restlessly under his keen eyes, that I was for Meudon.

'Then, if you care to travel with a larger company,' he rejoined, bowing with negligent courtesy, 'pray command me. I am for Meudon also and shall leave here three hours before noon.'

Fortunately he took my assent to his gracious invitation for granted, and turned away before I had well begun to thank him. From Crillon I found it more difficult to escape. He appeared to have conceived a great fancy for me, and felt also, I imagine, some curiosity as to my identity. But I did even this at last, and, evading the obsequious offers which were made me on all sides, escaped to the stables, where I sought out the Cid's stall, and lying down in the straw beside him, began to review the past, and plan the future. Under cover of the darkness sleep soon came to me; my last waking thoughts being divided between thankfulness for my escape and a steady purpose to reach Meudon before the Vicomte, so that I might make good my tale in his absence. For that seemed to be my only chance of evading the dangers I had chosen to encounter.

## 33

# At Meudon

Making so early a start from Étampes that the inn, which had continued in an uproar till long after midnight, lay sunk in sleep when we rode out of the yard, we reached Meudon about noon next day. I should be tedious were I to detail what thoughts my mistress and I had during that day's journey—the last, it might be, which we should take together; or what assurances we gave one another, or how often we repented the impatience which had impelled us to put all to the touch. Madame, with kindly forethought, detached herself from us, and rode the greater part of the distance with Fanchette; but the opportunities she gave us went for little; for, to be plain, the separation we dreaded seemed to overshadow us already. We uttered few words, though those few were to the purpose, but riding hand-in-hand, with full hearts, and eyes which seldom quitted one another, looked forward to Meudon and its perils with such gloomy forebodings as our love and my precarious position suggested.

Long before we reached the town, or could see more of it than the Château, over which the Lilies of France and the broad white banner of the Bourbons floated in company, we found ourselves swept into the whirlpool which surrounds an army. Crowds stood at all the cross-roads, wagons and sumpter-mules encumbered the bridges; each moment a horseman passed us at a gallop, or a troop of disorderly rogues, soldiers only in name, reeled, shouting and singing, along the road. Here and there, for a warning to the latter sort, a man dangled on a rude gallows; under which sportsmen returning from the chase and ladies who had been for an airing rode laughing on their way.

Amid the multitude entering the town we passed unnoticed. A little way within the walls we halted to inquire where the Princess of Navarre had her lodging. Hearing that she occupied a house in the town, while her brother had his quarters in the Château, and the King of France at Saint-Cloud, I stayed my party in a by-road, a hundred paces farther on, and, springing from the Cid, went to my mistress's knee.

'Mademoiselle,' I said formally, and so loudly that all my men might hear, 'the time is come. I dare not go farther with you. I beg you, therefore, to bear me witness that as I took you so I have brought you back, and both with your good-will. I beg that you will give me this quittance, for it may serve me.'

She bowed her head and laid her ungloved hand on mine, which I had placed on the pommel of her saddle. 'Sir,' she answered in a broken voice, 'I will not give you this quittance, nor any quittance from me while I live.' With that she took off her mask before them all, and I saw the tears running down her white face. 'May God protect you, M. de Marsac,' she continued, stooping until her face almost touched mine, 'and bring you to the thing you desire. If not, sir, and you pay too dearly for what you have done for me, I will live a maiden all my days. And, if I do not, these men may shame me!'

My heart was too full for words, but I took the glove she held out to me, and kissed her hand with my knee bent. Then I waved--for I could not speak—to madame to proceed; and with Simon Fleix and Maignan's men to guard them they went on their way. Mademoiselle's white face looked back to me until a bend in the road hid them, and I saw them no more.

I turned when all were gone, and going heavily to where my Sard stood with his head drooping, I climbed to the saddle, and rode at a foot-pace towards the Château. The way was short and easy, for the next turning showed me the open gateway and a crowd about it. A vast number of people were entering and leaving, while others rested in the shade of the wall, and a dozen grooms led horses up and down. The sunshine fell hotly on the road and the courtyard, and flashed back by the cuirasses of the men on guard, seized the eye and dazzled it with gleams of infinite brightness. I was advancing alone, gazing at all this with a species of dull indifference which masked for the moment the suspense I felt at heart, when a man, coming on foot along the street, crossed quickly to me and looked me in the face.

I returned his look, and seeing he was a stranger to me, was for passing on without pausing. But he wheeled beside me and uttered my name in a low voice.

I checked the Cid and looked down at him. 'Yes,' I said mechanically, 'I am M. de Marsac. But I do not know you.'

'Nevertheless I have been watching for you for three days,' he replied. 'M. de Rosny received your message. This is for you.'

He handed me a scrap of paper. 'From whom?' I asked.

'Maignan,' he answered briefly. And with that, and a stealthy look round, he left me, and went the way he had been going before.

I tore open the note, and knowing that Maignan could not write, was not surprised to find that it lacked any signature. The brevity of its contents vied with the curtness of its bearer. 'In Heaven's name go back and wait,' it ran. 'Your enemy is here, and those who wish you well are powerless.'

A warning so explicit, and delivered under such circumstances, might have been expected to make me pause even then. But I read the message with the same dull indifference, the same dogged resolve with which the sight of the crowded gateway before me had inspired me. I had not come so far and baffled Turenne by an hour to fail in my purpose at the last; nor given such pledges to another to prove false to myself. Moreover, the distant rattle of musketry, which went to show that a skirmish was taking place on the farther side of the Castle, seemed an invitation to me to proceed; for now, if ever, my sword might earn protection and a pardon. Only in regard to M. de Rosny, from whom I had no doubt that the message came, I resolved to act with prudence; neither making any appeal to him in public nor mentioning his name to others in private.

The Cid had borne me by this time into the middle of the throng about the gateway, who, wondering to see a stranger of my appearance arrive without attendants, eyed me with a mixture of civility and forwardness. I recognised more than one man whom I had seen about the Court at Saint-Jean d'Angely six months before; but so great is the disguising power of handsome clothes and equipments that none of these knew me. I beckoned to the nearest, and asked him if the King of Navarre was in the Château.

'He has gone to see the King of France at Saint-Cloud,'

the man answered, with something of wonder that anyone should be ignorant of so important a fact. 'He is expected here in an hour.'

I thanked him, and calculating that I should still have time and to spare before the arrival of M. de Turenne, I dismounted, and taking the rein over my arm, began to walk up and down in the shade of the wall. Meanwhile the loiterers increased in numbers as the minutes passed. Men of better standing rode up, and, leaving their horses in charge of their lackeys, went into the Château. Officers in shining corselets, or with boots and scabbards dulled with dust, arrived and clattered in through the gates. A messenger galloped up with letters, and was instantly surrounded by a curious throng of questioners; who left him only to gather about the next comers, a knot of townsfolk, whose downcast visages and glances of apprehension seemed to betoken no pleasant or easy mission.

Watching many of these enter and disappear, while only the humbler sort remained to swell the crowd at the gate, I began to experience the discomfort and impatience which are the lot of the man who finds himself placed in a false position. I foresaw with clearness the injury I was about to do my cause by presenting myself to the king among the common herd; and yet I had no choice save to do this, for I dared not run the risk of entering, lest I should be required to give my name, and fail to see the King of Navarre at all.

As it was I came very near to being foiled in this way; for I presently recognised, and was recognised in turn, by a gentleman who rode up to the gates and, throwing his reins to a groom, dismounted with an air of immense gravity. This was M. Forget, the king's secretary, and the person to whom I had on a former occasion presented a petition. He looked at me with eyes of profound astonishment, and saluting me stiffly from a distance, seemed in two minds whether he should pass in or speak to me. On second thoughts, however, he came towards me, and again saluted me with a peculiarly dry and austere aspect.

367

'I believe, sir, I am speaking to M. de Marsac?' he said in a low voice, but not impolitely.

I replied in the affirmative.

'And that, I conclude, is your horse?' he continued, raising his cane, and pointing to the Cid, which I had fastened to a hook in the wall.

I replied again in the affirmative.

'Then take a word of advice,' he answered, screwing up his features, and speaking in a dry sort of way. 'Get upon its back without an instant's delay, and put as many leagues between yourself and Meudon as horse and man may.'

'I am obliged to you,' I said, though I was greatly startled by his words. 'And what if I do not take your advice?'

He shrugged his shoulders. 'In that case look to yourself!' he retorted. 'But you will look in vain!'

He turned on his heel as he spoke, and in a moment was gone. I watched him enter the Château, and in the uncertainty which possessed me whether he was not gone—after salving his conscience by giving me warning—to order my instant arrest, I felt, and I doubt not I looked, as ill at ease for the time being as the group of trembling townsfolk who stood near me. Reflecting that he should know his master's mind, I recalled with depressing clearness the repeated warnings the King of Navarre had given me that I must not look to him for reward or protection. I bethought me that I was here against his express orders: presuming on those very services which he had given me notice he should repudiate. I remembered that Rosny had always been in the same tale. And in fine I began to see that mademoiselle and I had together decided on a step which I should never have presumed to take on my own motion.

I had barely arrived at this conclusion when the trampling of hoofs and a sudden closing in of the crowd round the gate announced the King of Navarre's approach. With a sick heart I drew nearer, feeling that the crisis was at hand; and in a moment he came in sight, riding beside an elderly man, plainly dressed and mounted, with whom he was carrying on an earnest conversation. A train of nobles and gentlemen, whose martial air and equipments made up for the absence of the gewgaws and glitter, to which my eyes had become accustomed at Blois, followed close on his heels. Henry himself wore a suit of white velvet, frayed in places and soiled by his armour; but his quick eye and eager, almost fierce, countenance could not fail to win and keep the attention of the least observant. He kept glancing from side to side as he came on; and that with so cheerful an air and a carriage so full at once of dignity and good-humour that no one could look on him and fail to see that here was a leader and a prince of men, temperate in victory and unsurpassed in defeat.

The crowd raising a cry of '*Vive Navarre!*' as he drew near, he bowed, with a sparkle in his eye. But when a few by the gate cried '*Vivent les Rois!*' he held up his hand for silence, and said in a loud, clear voice, 'Not that, my friends. There is but one king in France. Let us say instead, "*Vive le Roi!*" '

The spokesman of the little group of townsfolk, who, I learned, were from Arcueil, and had come to complain of the excessive number of troops quartered upon them, took advantage of the pause to approach him. Henry received the old man with a kindly look, and bent from his saddle to hear what he had to say. While they were talking I pressed forward, the emotion I felt on my own account heightened by my recognition of the man who rode by the King of Navarre— who was no other than M. de la Noue. No Huguenot worthy of the name could look on the veteran who had done and suffered more for the cause than any living man without catching something of his stern enthusiasm; and the sight, while it shamed me, who a moment before had been inclined to prefer my safety to the assistance I owed my country, gave me courage to step to the king's rein, so that I heard his last words to the men of Arcueil.

'Patience, my friends,' he said kindly. 'The burden is heavy, but the journey is a short one. The Seine is ours; the circle is complete. In a week Paris must surrender. The king, my cousin, will enter, and you will be rid of us. For France's sake one week, my friends.'

The men fell back with low obeisances, charmed by his good-nature, and Henry, looking up, saw me before him. On the instant his jaw fell. His brow, suddenly contracting above eyes which flashed with surprise and displeasure, altered in a moment the whole aspect of his face; which grew dark and stern as night. His first impulse was to pass by me; but seeing that I held my ground, he hesitated, so completely chagrined by my appearance that he did not know how to act, or in what way to deal with me. I seized the occasion, and bending my knee with as much respect as I had ever used to the King of France, begged to bring myself to his notice, and to crave his protection and favour.

'This is no time to trouble me, sir,' he retorted, eyeing me with an angry side-glance. 'I do not know you. You are unknown to me, sir. You must go to M. de Rosny.'

'It would be useless, sire,' I answered, in desperate persistence.

'Then I can do nothing for you,' he rejoined peevishly. 'Stand on one side, sir.'

But I was desperate. I knew that I had risked all on the event, and must establish my footing before M. de Turenne's return, or run the risk of certain recognition and vengeance. I cried out, caring nothing who heard, that I was M. de Marsac, that I had come back to meet whatever my enemies could allege against me.

'*Ventre Saint Gris!*' Henry exclaimed, starting in his saddle with well-feigned surprise. 'Are you that man?'

'I am, sire,' I answered.

'Then you must be mad!' he retorted, appealing to those behind him. 'Stark, staring mad to show your face here! *Ventre Saint Gris!* Are we to have all the ravishers and plunderers in the country come to us?'

'I am neither the one nor the other!' I answered, looking with indignation from him to the gaping train behind him.

'That you will have to settle with M. de Turenne!' he

retorted, frowning down at me with his whole face turned gloomy and fierce. 'I know you well, sir, now. Complaint has been made that you abducted a lady from his Castle of Chizé some time back.'

'The lady, sire, is now in charge of the Princess of Navarre.'

'She is?' he exclaimed, quite taken aback.

'And if she has aught of complaint against me,' I continued with pride, 'I will submit to whatever punishment you order or M. de Turenne demands. But if she has no complaint to make, and vows that she accompanied me of her own free-will and accord, and has suffered neither wrong nor displeasure at my hands, then, sire, I claim that this is a private matter between myself and M. de Turenne.'

'Even so I think you will have your hands full,' he answered grimly. At the same time he stopped by a gesture those who would have cried out upon me, and looked at me himself with an altered countenance. 'Do I understand that you assert that the lady went of her own accord?' he asked.

'She went and has returned, sire,' I answered.

'Strange!' he ejaculated. 'Have you married her?'

'No, sire,' I answered. 'I desire leave to do so.'

'Mon dieu! she is M. de Turenne's ward,' he rejoined, almost dumbfounded by my audacity.

'I do not despair of obtaining his assent, sire,' I said patiently.

'*Saint Gris!* the man is mad!' he cried, wheeling his horse and facing his train with a gesture of the utmost wonder. 'It is the strangest story I ever heard.'

'But somewhat more to the gentleman's credit than the lady's!' one said with a smirk and a smile.

'A lie!' I cried, springing forward on the instant with a boldness which astonished myself. 'She is as pure as your Highness's sister! I swear it. That man lies in his teeth, and I will maintain it.'

'Sir!' the King of Navarre cried, turning on me with the utmost sternness, 'you forget yourself in my presence! Silence, and beware another time how you let your tongue run on those above you. You have enough trouble, let me tell you, on your hands already.'

'Yet the man lies!' I answered doggedly, remembering Crillon and his ways. 'And if he will do me the honour of stepping aside with me, I will convince him of it!'

'*Ventre Saint Gris!*' Henry replied, frowning, and dwelling on each syllable of his favourite oath. 'Will you be silent, sir, and let me think? Or must I order your instant arrest?'

'Surely that at least, sire,' a suave voice interjected. And with that a gentleman pressed forward from the rest, and gaining a place of 'vantage by the King's side, shot at me a look of extreme malevolence. 'My lord of Turenne will expect no less at your Highness's hands,' he continued warmly. 'I beg you will give the order on the spot, and hold this person to answer for his misdeeds. M. de Turenne returns today. He should be here now. I say again, sire, he will expect no less than this.'

The king, gazing at me with gloomy eyes, tugged at his moustaches. Someone had motioned the common herd to stand back out of hearing; at the same time the suite had moved up out of curiosity and formed a half-circle; in the midst of which I stood fronting the king, who had La Noue and the last speaker on either hand. Perplexity and annoyance struggled for the mastery in his face as he looked darkly down at me, his teeth showing through his beard. Profoundly angered by my appearance, which he had taken at first to be the prelude to disclosures which must detach Turenne at a time when union was all-important, he had now ceased to fear for himself; and perhaps saw something in the attitude I adopted which appealed to his nature and sympathies.

'If the girl is really back,' he said at last, 'M. d'Aremburg, I do not see any reason why I should interfere. At present, at any rate.'

'I think, sire, M. de Turenne will see reason,' the gentleman answered drily.

The king coloured. 'M. de Turenne,' he began,

'Has made many sacrifices at your request, sire,' the other

said with meaning. 'And buried some wrongs, or fancied wrongs, in connection with this very matter. This person has outraged him in the grossest manner, and in M. le Vicomte's name I ask, nay I press upon you, that he be instantly arrested, and held to answer for it.'

'I am ready to answer for it now!' I retorted, looking from face to face for sympathy, and finding none save in M. de la Noue's, who appeared to regard me with grave approbation. 'To the Vicomte de Turenne, or the person he may appoint to represent him.'

'Enough!' Henry said, raising his hand and speaking in the tone of authority he knew so well how to adopt. 'For you, M. d'Aremburg, I thank you. Turenne is happy in his friend. But this gentleman came to me of his own free will and I do not think it consistent with my honour to detain him without warning given. I grant him an hour to remove himself from my neighbourhood. If he be found after that time has elapsed,' he continued solemnly, 'his fate be on his own head. Gentlemen, we are late already. Let us on.'

I looked at him as he pronounced this sentence, and strove to find words in which to make a final appeal to him. But no words came; and when he bade me stand aside, I did so mechanically, remaining with my head bared to the sunshine while the troop rode by. Some looked back at me with curiosity, as at a man of whom they had heard a tale, and some with a jeer on their lips; a few with dark looks of menace. When they were all gone, and the servants who followed them had disappeared also, and I was left to the inquisitive glances of the rabble who stood gaping after the sight, I turned and went to the Cid, and loosed the horse.

With a feeling of bitter disappointment. The plan which mademoiselle had proposed and I had adopted in the forest by Saint-Gaultier—when it seemed to us that our long absence and the great events of which we heard must have changed the world and opened a path for our return—had failed utterly. Things were as they had been; the strong was still strong, and friendship under bond to fear. Plainly we should have shewn ourselves wiser had we taken the lowlier course, and, obeying the warnings given us, waited the King of Navarre's pleasure or the tardy recollection of Rosny. I had not then stood, as I now stood, in instant jeopardy, nor felt the keen pangs of a separation which bade fair to be lasting. She was safe, and that was much; but I, after long service and brief happiness, must go out again alone, with only memories to comfort me.

It was Simon Fleix's voice which awakened me from this unworthy lethargy—as selfish as it was useless—and, recalling me to myself, reminded me that precious time was passing while I stood inactive. To get at me he had forced his way through the curious crowd, and his face was flushed. He plucked me by the sleeve, regarding the varlets round him with a mixture of anger and fear.

'*Nom de Dieu!* do they take you for a rope-dancer?' he muttered in my ear. 'Mount, sir, and come. There is not a moment to be lost.'

'You left her at Madame Catherine's?' I said.

'To be sure,' he answered impatiently. 'Trouble not about her. Save yourself, M. de Marsac. That is the thing to be done now.'

I mounted mechanically, and felt my courage return as the horse moved under me. I trotted through the crowd, and without thought took the road by which we had come. When we had ridden a hundred yards, however, I pulled up. 'An hour is a short start,' I said sullenly. 'Whither?'

'To Saint-Cloud,' he answered promptly. 'The protection of the King of France may avail for a day or two. After that, there will still be the League, if Paris have not fallen.'

I saw there was nothing else for it, and assented, and we set off. The distance which separates Meudon from Saint-Cloud we might have ridden under the hour, but the direct road runs across the Scholars' Meadow, a wide plain north of Meudon. This lay exposed to the enemy's fire, and was, besides, the scene of hourly conflicts between the horse of both parties, so that to cross it without an adequate force was impossible. Driven to make a circuit, we took longer to reach our destination, yet did so without mishap; finding the little town, when we came in sight of it, given up to all the bustle and commotion which properly belong to the Court and camp.

It was, indeed, as full as it could be, for the surrender of Paris being momentarily expected, Saint-Cloud had become the rendezvous as well of the few who had long followed a principle as of the many who wait upon success. The streets, crowded in every part, shone with glancing colours, with steel and velvet, the garb of fashion and the plumes of war. Long lines of flags obscured the eaves and broke the sunshine, while, above all, the bells of half a dozen churches rang merry answer to the distant crash of guns. Everywhere on flag and arch and streamer I read the motto, '*Vive le Roi!*'— words written, God knew then, and we know now, in what a mockery of doom!

34

# ''Tis an Ill Wind'

We had made our way slowly and with much jostling as far as the principal street, finding the press increase as we advanced, when I heard, as I turned a corner, my name called, and, looking up, saw at a window the face of which I was in search. After that half a minute sufficed to bring M. d'Agen flying to my side, when nothing, as I had expected, would do but I must dismount where I was and share his lodging. He made no secret of his joy and surprise at sight of me, but pausing only to tell Simon where the stable was, haled me through the crowd and up his stairs with a fervour and heartiness which brought the tears to my eyes, and served to impress the company whom I found above with a more than sufficient sense of my importance.

375

Seeing him again in the highest feather and in the full employment of all those little arts and graces which served as a foil to his real worth, I took it as a great honour that he laid them aside for the nonce; and introduced me to the seat of honour and made me known to his companions with a boyish directness and a simple thought for my comfort which infinitely pleased me. He bade his landlord, without a moment's delay, bring wine and meat and everything which could refresh a traveller, and was himself up and down a hundred times in a minute, calling to his servants for this or that, or railing at them for their failure to bring me a score of things I did not need. I hastened to make my excuses to the company for interrupting them in the midst of their talk; and these they were kind enough to accept in good part. At the same time, reading clearly in M. d'Agen's excited face and shining eyes that he longed to be alone with me, they took the hint, and presently left us together.

'Well,' he said, coming back from the door, to which he had conducted them, 'what have you to tell me, my friend? She is not with you?'

'She is with Mademoiselle de la Vire at Meudon,' I answered, smiling. 'And for the rest, she is well and in better spirits.'

'She sent me some message?' he asked.

I shook my head. 'She did not know I should see you,' I answered.

'But she—she has spoken of me lately?' he continued, his face falling.

'I do not think she has named your name for a fortnight,' I answered, laughing. 'There's for you! Why, man,' I continued, adopting a different tone, and laying my hand on his shoulder in a manner which reassured him at least as much as my words, 'are you so young a lover as to be ignorant that a woman says least of that of which she thinks most? Pluck up courage! Unless I am mistaken, you have little to be afraid of except the past. Only have patience.'

'You think so?' he said gratefully.

I assured him that I had no doubt of it; and on that he fell into a reverie, and I to watching him. Alas for the littleness of our natures! He had received me with open arms, yet at sight of the happiness which took possession of his handsome face I gave way to the pettiest feeling which can harbour in a man's breast. I looked at him with eyes of envy, bitterly comparing my lot with that which fate had reserved for him. He had fortune, good looks, and success on his side, great relations, and high hopes; I stood in instant jeopardy, my future dark, and every path which presented itself so hazardous that I knew not which to adopt. He was young, and I past my prime; he in favour, and I a fugitive.

To such reflections he put an end in a way which made me blush for my churlishness. For, suddenly awaking out of his pleasant dream, he asked me about myself and my fortunes, inquiring eagerly how I came to be in Saint-Cloud, and listening to the story of my adventures with a generous anxiety which endeared him to me more and more. When I had done —and by that time Simon had joined us, and was waiting at the lower end of the room—he pronounced that I must see the king.

'There is nothing else for it,' he said.

'I have come to see him,' I answered.

'Mon dieu, yes!' he continued, rising from his seat and looking at me with a face of concern. 'No one else can help you.'

I nodded.

'Turenne has four thousand men here. You can do nothing against so many?'

'Nothing,' I said. 'The question is, Will the king protect me?'

'It is he or no one,' M. d'Agen answered warmly. 'You cannot see him tonight: he has a Council. Tomorrow at daybreak you may. You must lie here tonight, and I will set my fellows to watch, and I think you will be safe. I will away now and see if my uncle will help. Can you think of anyone else who would speak for you?'

377

I considered, and was about to answer in the negative, when Simon, who had listened with a scared face, suggested M. de Crillon.

'Yes, if he would,' M. d'Agen exclaimed, looking at the lad with approbation. 'He has weight with the king.'

'I think he might,' I replied slowly. 'I had a curious encounter with him last night.' And with that I told M. d'Agen of the duel I fought at the inn.

'Good!' he said, his eyes sparkling. 'I wish I had been there to see. At any rate we will try him. Crillon fears no one, not even the king.'

So it was settled. For that night I was to keep close in my friend's lodging, showing not even my nose at the window.

When he had gone on his errand, and I found myself alone in the room, I am fain to confess that I fell very low in my spirits. M. d'Agen's travelling equipment lay about the apartment, but failed to give any but an untidy air to its roomy bareness. The light was beginning to wane, the sun was gone. Outside, the ringing of bells and the distant muttering of guns, with the tumult of sounds which rose from the crowded street, seemed to tell of joyous life and freedom and all the hopes and ambitions from which I was cut off.

Having no other employment, I watched the street, and keeping myself well retired from the window, saw knots of gay riders pass this way and that through the crowd, their corselets shining and their voices high. Monks and ladies, a cardinal and an ambassador, passed under my eyes—these and an endless procession of townsmen and beggars, soldiers and courtiers, Gascons, Normans and Picards. Never had I seen such a sight or so many people gathered together. It seemed as if half Paris had come out to make submission, so that while my gorge rose against my own imprisonment, the sight gradually diverted my mind from my private distresses, by bidding me find compensation for them in the speedy and glorious triumph of the cause.

Even when the light failed the pageant did not cease, but, torches and lanthorns springing into life, turned night into day. From every side came sounds of revelry or strife. The crowd continued to perambulate the streets until a late hour, with cries of '*Vive le Roi!*' and '*Vive Navarre!*' while now and again the passage of a great noble with his suite called forth a fresh burst of enthusiasm. Nothing seemed more certain, more inevitable, more clearly predestined than that twenty-four hours must see the fall of Paris.

Yet Paris did not fall.

When M. d'Agen returned a little before midnight, he found me still sitting in the dark looking from the window. I heard him call roughly for lights, and apprised by the sound of his voice that something was wrong, I rose to meet him. He stood silent awhile, twirling his small moustaches, and then broke into a passionate tirade, from which I was not slow to gather that M. de Rambouillet declined to serve me.

'Well,' I said, feeling for the young man's distress and embarrassment, 'perhaps he is right.'

'He says that word respecting you came this evening,' my friend answered, his cheeks red with shame, 'and that to countenance you after that would only be to court certain humiliation. I did not let him off too easily, I assure you,' M. d'Agen continued, turning away to evade my gaze; 'but I got no satisfaction. He said you had his good-will, and that to help you he would risk something, but that to do so under these circumstances would be only to injure himself.'

'There is still Crillon,' I said, with as much cheerfulness as I could assume. 'Pray Heaven he be there early! Did M. de Rambouillet say anything else?'

'That your only chance was to fly as quickly and secretly as possible.'

'He thought my situation desperate, then?'

My friend nodded; and scarcely less depressed on my account than ashamed on his own, evinced so much feeling that it was all I could do to comfort him; which I succeeded in doing only when I diverted the conversation to Madame de Bruhl. We passed the short night together, sharing the same room and the same bed, and talking more than we slept—of madame and mademoiselle, the castle on the hill, and the camp in the woods, of all old days in fine, but little of the future. Soon after dawn Simon, who lay on a pallet across the threshold, roused me from a fitful sleep into which I had just fallen, and a few minutes later I stood up dressed and armed, ready to try the last chance left to me.

M. d'Agen had dressed stage for stage with me, and I had kept silence. But when he took up his cap, and showed clearly that he had it in his mind to go with me, I withstood him. 'No,' I said, 'you can do me little good, and may do yourself much harm.'

'You shall not go without one friend,' he cried fiercely.

'Tut, tut!' I said. 'I shall have Simon.'

But Simon, when I turned to speak to him, was gone. Few men are at their bravest in the early hours of the day, and it did not surprise me that the lad's courage had failed him. The defection only strengthened, however, the resolution I had formed that I would not injure M. d'Agen; though it was some time before I could persuade him that I was in earnest, and would go alone or not at all. In the end he had to content himself with lending me his back and breast, which I gladly put on, thinking it likely enough that I might be set upon before I reached the Castle. And then, the time being about seven, I parted from him with many embraces and kindly words, and went into the street with my sword under my cloak.

The town, late in rising after its orgy, lay very still and quiet. The morning was grey and warm, with a cloudy sky. The flags, which had made so gay a show yesterday, hung close to the poles, or flapped idly and fell dead again. I walked slowly along beneath them, keeping a sharp look-out on every side; but there were few persons moving in the streets, and I reached the Castle gates without misadventure. Here was something of life; a bustle of officers and soldiers passing in and out, of courtiers whose office made their presence necessary, of beggars who had flocked hither in the night for company. In the middle of these I recognised on a sudden and with great surprise Simon Fleix walking my horse up and down. On seeing me he handed it to a boy, and came up to speak to me with a red face, muttering that four legs were better than two. I did not say much to him, my heart being full and my thoughts occupied with the presence chamber and what I should say there; but I nodded kindly to him, and he fell in behind me as the sentries challenged me. I answered them that I sought M. de Crillon, and so getting by, fell into the rear of a party of three who seemed bent on the same errand as myself.

One of these was a Jacobin monk, whose black and white robes, by reminding me of Father Antoine, sent a chill to my heart. The second, whose eye I avoided, I knew to be M. la Guesle, the king's Solicitor-General. The third was a stranger to me. Enabled by M. la Guesle's presence to pass the main guards without challenge, the party proceeded through a maze of passages and corridors, conversing together in a low tone; while I, keeping in the train with my face cunningly muffled, got as far by this means as the ante-chamber, which I found almost empty. Here I inquired of the usher for M. de Crillon, and learned with the utmost consternation that he was not present.

This blow, which almost stunned me, opened my eyes to the precarious nature of my position, which only the early hour and small attendance rendered possible for a moment. At any minute I might be recognised and questioned, or my name be required; while the guarded doors of the chamber shut me off as effectually from the king's face and grace as though I were in Paris, or a hundred leagues away. Endeavouring to the best of my power to conceal the chagrin and alarm which possessed me as this conviction took hold of me, I walked to the window; and to hide my face more completely and at the same time gain a moment to collect my thoughts, affected to be engaged in looking through it.

Nothing which passed in the room, however, escaped me. I marked everything and everyone, though all my thought was how I might get to the king. The barber came out of the chamber with a silver basin, and stood a moment, and went

381

in again with an air of vast importance. The guards yawned, and an officer entered, looked round, and retired. M. la Guesle, who had gone in to the presence, came out again and stood near me talking with the Jacobin, whose pale nervous face and hasty movements reminded me somehow of Simon Fleix. The monk held a letter or petition in his hand, and appeared to be getting it by heart, for his lips moved continually. The light which fell on his face from the window showed it to be of a peculiar sweaty pallor, and distorted besides. But supposing him to be devoted, like many of his kind, to an unwholesome life, I thought nothing of this; though I liked him little, and would have shifted my place but for the convenience of his neighbourhood.

Presently, while I was cudgelling my brains, a person came out and spoke to La Guesle; who called in his turn to the monk, and started hastily towards the door. The Jacobin followed. The third person who had entered in their company had his attention directed elsewhere at the moment; and though La Guesle called to him, took no heed. On the instant I grasped the situation. Taking my courage in my hands, I crossed the floor behind the monk; who, hearing me, or feeling his robe come in contact with me, presently started and looked round suspiciously, his face wearing a scowl so black and ugly that I almost recoiled from him, dreaming for a moment that I saw before me the very spirit of Father Antoine. But as the man said nothing, and the next instant, averted his gaze, I hardened my heart and pushed on behind him, and passing the usher, found myself as by magic in the presence which had seemed a while ago as unattainable by my wits as it was necessary to my safety.

It was not this success alone, however, which caused my heart to beat more hopefully. The king was speaking as I entered, and the gay tones of his voice seemed to promise a favourable reception. His Majesty sat half-dressed on a stool at the farther end of the apartment, surrounded by five or six noblemen, while as many attendants, among whom I hastened to mingle, waited near the door.

La Guesle made as if he would advance, and then, seeing the king's attention was not on him, held back. But in a moment the king saw him and called to him. 'Ha, Guesle!' he said with good-temper, 'it is you? Is your friend with you?'

The Solicitor went forward with the monk at his elbow, and I had leisure to remark the favourable change which had taken place in the king, who spoke more strongly and seemed in better health than of old. His face looked less cadaverous under the paint, his form a trifle less emaciated. That which struck me more than anything, however, was the improvement in his spirits. His eyes sparkled from time to time, and he laughed continually, so that I could scarcely believe that he was the same man whom I had seen overwhelmed with despair and tortured by his conscience.

Letting his attention slip from La Guesle, he began to bandy words with the nobleman who stood nearest to him; looking up at him with a roguish eye, and making bets on the fall of Paris.

'Morbleu!' I heard him cry gaily, 'I would give a thousand pounds to see the Montpensier this morning! She may keep her third crown for herself. Or, *peste!* we might put her in a convent. That would be a fine vengeance!'

'The veil for the tonsure,' the nobleman said with a smirk.

'Ay. Why not? She would have made a monk of me,' the king rejoined smartly. 'She must be ready to hang herself with her garters this morning, if she is not dead of spite already. Or, stay, I had forgotten her golden scissors. Let her open a vein with them. Well, what does your friend want, La Guesle?'

I did not hear the answer, but it was apparently satisfactory, for in a minute all except the Jacobin fell back, leaving the monk standing before the king, who, stretching out his hand, took from him a letter. The Jacobin, trembling visibly, seemed scarcely able to support the honour done him, and the king, seeing this, said in a voice audible to all, 'Stand up, man. You are welcome. I love a cowl as some love a lady's hood. And now, what is this?'

He read a part of the letter and rose. As he did so the monk leaned forward as though to receive the paper back again, and then so swiftly, so suddenly, with só unexpected a movement that no one stirred until all was over, struck the king in the body with a knife! As the blade flashed and was hidden, and His Majesty with a deep sob fell back on the stool, then, and not till then, I knew that I had missed a providential chance of earning pardon and protection. For had I only marked the Jacobin as we passed the door together, and read his evil face aright, a word, one word, had done for me more than the pleading of a score of Crillons!

Too late a dozen sprang forward to the king's assistance; but before they reached him he had himself drawn the knife from the wound and struck the assassin with it on the head. While some, with cries of grief, ran to support Henry, from whose body the blood was already flowing fast, others seized and struck down the wretched monk. As they gathered round him I saw him raise himself for a moment on his knees and look upward; the blood which ran down his face, no less than the mingled triumph and horror of his features, impressed the sight on my recollection. The next instant three swords were plunged into his breast, and his writhing body, plucked up from the floor amid a transport of curses, was forced headlong through the casement and flung down to make sport for the grooms and scullions who stood below.

A scene of indescribable confusion followed, some crying that the king was dead, while others called for a doctor, and some by name for Dortoman. I expected to see the doors closed and all within secured, that if the man had confederates they might be taken. But there was no one to give the order. Instead, many who had neither the *entrée* nor any business in the chamber forced their way in, and by their cries and pressure rendered the hubbub and tumult a hundred times worse. In the midst of this, while I stood stunned and dumbfounded, my own risks and concerns forgotten, I felt my sleeve furiously plucked, and, looking round, found Simon at my elbow. The lad's face was crimson, his eyes seemed starting from his head.

'Come,' he muttered, seizing my arm. 'Come!' And without further ceremony or explanation he dragged me towards the door, while his face and manner evinced as much heat and impatience as if he had been himself the assassin. 'Come, there is not a moment to be lost,' he panted, continuing his exertions without the least intermission.

'Whither?' I said, in amazement, as I reluctantly permitted him to force me along the passage and through the gaping crowd on the stairs. 'Whither, man?'

'Mount and ride!' was the answer he hissed in my ear. 'Ride for your life to the King of Navarre—to the King of France it may be! Ride as you have never ridden before, and tell him the news, and bid him look to himself! Be the first, and, Heaven helping us, Turenne may do his worst!'

I felt every nerve in my body tingle as I awoke to his meaning. Without a word I left his arm, and flung myself into the crowd which filled the lower passage to suffocation. As I struggled fiercely with them Simon aided me by crying 'A doctor! a doctor! make way there!' and this induced many to give place to me under the idea that I was an accredited messenger. Eventually I succeeded in forcing my way through and reaching the courtyard; being, as it turned out, the first person to issue from the Château. A dozen people sprang towards me with anxious eyes and questions on their lips, but I ran past them and, catching the Cid, which was fortunately at hand, by the rein, bounded into the saddle.

As I turned the horse to the gate I heard Simon cry after me, 'The Scholars' Meadow! Go that way!' and then I heard no more. I was out of the yard and galloping bareheaded down the pitched street, while women snatched their infants up and ran aside, and men came startled to the doors, crying that the League was upon us. As the good horse flung up his head and bounded forward, hurling the gravel behind him with hoofs which slid and clattered on the pavement, as

385

the wind began to whistle by me, and I seized the reins in a shorter grip, I felt my heart bound with exultation. I experienced such a blessed relief and elation as the prisoner long fettered and confined feels when restored to the air of heaven.

Down one street and through a narrow lane we thundered, until a broken gateway stopped with fascines—through which the Cid blundered and stumbled—brought us at a bound into the Scholars' Meadow just as the tardy sun broke through the clouds and flooded the low, wide plain with brightness. Half a league in front of us the towers of Meudon rose to view on a hill. In the distance, to the left, lay the walls of Paris, and nearer, on the same side, a dozen forts and batteries; while here and there, in that quarter, a shining clump of spears or a dense mass of infantry betrayed the enemy's presence.

I heeded none of these things, however, nor anything except the towers of Meudon, setting the Cid's head straight for these and riding on at the top of his speed. Swiftly ditch and dyke came into view before us and flashed away beneath us. Men lying in pits rose up and aimed at us; or ran with cries to intercept us. A cannon-shot fired from the fort by Issy tore up the earth to one side; a knot of lancers sped from the shelter of an earthwork in the same quarter, and raced us for half a mile, with frantic shouts and threats of vengeance. But all such efforts were vanity. The Cid, fired by this sudden call upon his speed, and feeling himself loosed—rarest of events—to do his best, shook the foam from his bit, and opening his blood-red nostrils to the wind, crouched lower and lower; until his long neck, stretched out before him, seemed, as the sward swept by, like the point of an arrow speeding resistless to its aim.

God knows, as the air rushed by me and the sun shone in my face, I cried aloud like a boy, and though I sat still and stirred neither hand nor foot, lest I should break the good Sard's stride, I prayed wildly that the horse which I had groomed with my own hands and fed with my last crown might hold on unfaltering to the end. For I dreamed that the fate of a nation rode in my saddle; and mindful alike of Simon's words, 'Bid him look to himself,' and of my own notion that the League would not be so foolish as to remove one enemy to exalt another, I thought nothing more likely than that, with all my fury, I should arrive too late, and find the King of Navarre as I had left the King of France.

In this strenuous haste I covered a mile as a mile has seldom been covered before; and I was growing under the influence of the breeze which whipped my temples somewhat more cool and hopeful, when I saw on a sudden right before me, and between me and Meudon, a handful of men engaged in a *mêlée*. There were red and white jackets in it—Leaguers and Huguenots—and the red coats seemed to be having the worst of it. Still, while I watched, they came off in order, and unfortunately in such a way and at such a speed that I saw they must meet me face to face whether I tried to avoid the encounter or not. I had barely time to take in the danger and its nearness, and discern beyond both parties the main-guard of the Huguenots, enlivened by a score of pennons, when the Leaguers were upon me.

I suppose they knew that no friend would ride for Meudon at that pace, for they dashed at me six abreast with a shout of triumph; and before I could count a score we met. The Cid was still running strongly, and I had not thought to stay him, so that I had no time to use my pistols. My sword I had out, but the sun dazzled me and the men wore corselets, and I made but poor play with it; though I struck out savagely, as we crashed together, in my rage at this sudden crossing of my hopes when all seemed done and gained. The Cid faced them bravely—I heard the distant huzza of the Huguenots—and I put aside one point which threatened my throat. But the sun was in my eyes and something struck me on the head. Another second, and a blow in the breast forced me fairly from the saddle. Gripping furiously at the air I went down, stunned and dizzy, my last thoughts as I struck the ground being of mademoiselle, and the little brook with the stepping-stones.

## 35

# 'Le Roi est Mort'

It was M. d'Agen's breastpiece saved my life by warding off the point of the varlet's sword, so that the worst injury I got was the loss of my breath for five minutes, with a swimming in the head and a kind of syncope. These being past, I found myself on my back on the ground, with a man's knee on my breast and a dozen horsemen standing round me. The sky reeled dizzily before my eyes and the men's figures loomed gigantic; yet I had sense enough to know what had happened to me, and that matters might well be worse.

Resigning myself to the prospect of captivity, I prepared to ask for quarter; which I did not doubt I should receive, since they had taken me in an open skirmish, and honestly, and in the daylight. But the man whose knee already incommoded me sufficiently, seeing me about to speak, squeezed me on a sudden so fiercely, bidding me at the same time in a gruff whisper be silent, that I thought I could not do better than obey.

Accordingly I lay still, and as in a dream, for my brain was still clouded, heard someone say, 'Dead! Is he? I hoped we had come in time. Well, he deserved a better fate. Who is he, Rosny?'

'Do you know him, Maignan?' said a voice which sounded strangely familiar.

The man who knelt upon me answered, 'No, my lord. He is a stranger to me. He has the look of a Norman.'

'Like enough!' replied a high-pitched voice I had not heard before. 'For he rode a good horse. Give me a hundred like it, and a hundred men to ride as straight, and I would not envy the King of France.'

'Much less his poor cousin of Navarre,' the first speaker rejoined in a laughing tone, 'without a whole shirt to his back or a doublet that is decently new. Come, Turenne, acknowledge that you are not so badly off after all!'

At that word the cloud which had darkened my faculties swept on a sudden aside. I saw that the men into whose hands I had fallen wore white favours, their leader a white plume; and comprehended without more that the King of Navarre had come to my rescue, and beaten off the Leaguers who had dismounted me. At the same moment the remembrance of all that had gone before, and especially of the scene I had witnessed in the king's chamber, rushed upon my mind with such overwhelming force that I fell into a fury of impatience at the thought of the time I had wasted; and rising up suddenly I threw off Maignan with all my force, crying out that I was alive—that I was alive, and had news.

The equerry did his best to restrain me, cursing me under his breath for a fool, and almost squeezing the life out of me. But in vain, for the King of Navarre, riding nearer, saw me struggling. 'Hallo! hallo! 'tis a strange dead man,' he cried, interposing, 'What is the meaning of this? Let him go! Do you hear, sirrah? Let him go!'

The equerry obeyed and stood back sullenly, and I staggered to my feet, and looked round with eyes which still swam and watered. On the instant a cry of recognition greeted me, with a hundred exclamations of astonishment. While I heard my name uttered on every side in a dozen different tones, I remarked that M. de Rosny, upon whom my eyes first fell, alone stood silent, regarding me with a face of sorrowful surprise.

'By heavens, sir, I knew nothing of this!' I heard the King of Navarre declare, addressing himself to the Vicomte de Turenne. 'The man is here by no connivance of mine. Interrogate him yourself, if you will. Or I will. Speak, sir,' he continued, turning to me with his countenance hard and forbidding. 'You heard me yesterday, what I promised you? Why, in God's name, are you here today?'

I tried to answer, but Maignan had so handled me that I had not breath enough, and stood panting.

'Your Highness's clemency in this matter,' M. de Turenne said, with a sneer, 'has been so great he trusted to its continuance. And doubtless he thought to find you alone. I fear I am in the way.'

I knew him by his figure and his grand air, which in any other company would have marked him for master; and forgetting the impatience which a moment before had consumed me—doubtless I was still light-headed—I answered him. 'Yet I had once the promise of your lordship's protection,' I gasped.

'My protection sir?' he exclaimed, his eyes gleaming angrily.

'Even so,' I answered. 'At the inn at Étampes, where M. de Crillon would have fought me.'

He was visibly taken aback. 'Are you that man?' he cried.

'I am. But I am not here to prate of myself,' I replied. And with that—the remembrance of my neglected errand flashing on me again—I staggered to the King of Navarre's side, and, falling on my knees, seized his stirrup. 'Sire, I bring you news! great news! dreadful news!' I cried, clinging to it. 'His Majesty was but a quarter of an hour ago stabbed in the body in his chamber by a villain monk. And is dying, or, it may be, dead.'

'Dead? The King!' Turenne cried with an oath. 'Impossible!'

Vaguely I heard others crying, some this, some that, as surprise and consternation, or anger, or incredulity moved them. But I did not answer them, for Henry, remaining silent, held me spellbound and awed by the marvellous change which I saw fall on his face. His eyes became on a sudden suffused with blood, and seemed to retreat under his heavy brows; his cheeks turned of a brick-red colour; his half-open lips showed his teeth gleaming through his beard; while his great nose, which seemed to curve and curve until it well-nigh met his chin, gave to his mobile countenance an

390

aspect as strange as it was terrifying. Withal he uttered for a time no word, though I saw his hand grip the riding-whip he held in a convulsive grasp, as though his thoughts were "Tis mine! Mine! Wrest it away who dares!'

'Bethink you, sir,' he said at last, fixing his piercing eyes on me, and speaking in a harsh, low tone, like the growling of a great dog, 'this is no jesting-time. Nor will you save your skin by a ruse. Tell me, on your peril, is this a trick?'

'Heaven forbid, sire!' I answered with passion. 'I was in the chamber, and saw it with my own eyes. I mounted on the instant, and rode hither by the shortest route to warn your Highness to look to yourself. Monks are many, and the Holy Union is not apt to stop half-way.'

I saw he believed me, for his face relaxed. His breath seemed to come and go again, and for the tenth part of a second his eyes sought M. de Rosny's. Then he looked at me again. 'I thank you, sir,' he said, bowing gravely and court-eously, 'for your care for me—not for your tidings, which are of the sorriest. God grant my good cousin and king may be hurt only. Now tell us exactly—for these gentlemen are equally interested with myself--had a surgeon seen him?'

I replied in the negative, but added that the wound was in the groin, and bled much.

'You said a few minutes ago, "dying or already dead!"' the King of Navarre rejoined. 'Why?'

'His Majesty's face was sunken,' I stammered.

He nodded. 'You may be mistaken,' he said. 'I pray that you are. But here comes Mornay. He may know more.'

In a moment I was abandoned, even by M. de Turenne, so great was the anxiety which possessed all to learn the truth. Maignan alone, under pretence of adjusting a stirrup, re-mained beside me, and entreated me in a low voice to begone. 'Take this horse, M. de Marsac, if you will,' he urged, 'and ride back the way you came. You have done what you came to do. Go back, and be thankful.'

'Chut!' I said, 'there is no danger.'

'You will see,' he replied darkly, 'if you stay here. Come,

come, take my advice and the horse,' he persisted, 'and begone! Believe me, it will be for the best.'

I laughed outright at his earnestness and his face of perplexity. 'I see you have M. de Rosny's orders to get rid of me,' I said. 'But I am not going, my friend. He must find some other way out of his embarrassment, for here I stay.'

'Well, your blood be on your own head,' Maignan retorted, swinging himself into the saddle with a gloomy face. 'I have done my best to save you!'

'And your master!' I answered, laughing.

For flight was the last thing I had in my mind. I had ridden this ride with a clear perception that the one thing I needed was a footing at Court. By the special kindness of Providence I had now gained this; and I was not the man to resign it because it proved to be scanty and perilous. It was something that I had spoken to the great Vicomte face to face and not been consumed, that I had given him look for look and still survived, that I had put in practice Crillon's lessons and come to no harm.

Nor was this all. I had never in the worst times blamed the King of Navarre for his denial of me. I had been foolish, indeed, seeing that it was in the bargain, had I done so; nor had I ever doubted his good-will or his readiness to reward me should occasion arise. Now, I flattered myself, I had given him that which he needed, and had hitherto lacked—an excuse, I mean, for interference in my behalf.

Whether I was right or wrong in this notion I was soon to learn, for at this moment Henry's cavalcade, which had left me a hundred paces behind, came to a stop, and while some of the number waved to me to come on, one spurred back to summon me to the king. I hastened to obey the order as fast as I could, but I saw on approaching that though all was at a standstill till I came up, neither the King of Navarre nor M. de Turenne was thinking principally of me. Every face, from Henry's to that of his least important courtier, wore an air of grave preoccupation; which I had no difficulty in ascribing to the doubt present in every mind, and outweighing every interest, whether the King of France was dead, or dying, or merely wounded.

'Quick, sir!' Henry said with impatience, as soon as I came within hearing. 'Do not detain me with your affairs longer than is necessary. M. de Turenne presses me to carry into effect the order I gave yesterday. But as you have placed yourself in jeopardy on my account I feel that something is due to you. You will be good enough, therefore, to present yourself at once at M. la Varenne's lodging, and give me your parole to remain there without stirring abroad until your affair is concluded.'

Aware that I owed this respite, which at once secured my present safety and promised well for the future, to the great event that, even in M. de Turenne's mind, had overshadowed all others, I bowed in silence. Henry, however, was not content with this. 'Come, sir,' he said sharply, and with every appearance of anger, 'do you agree to that?'

I replied humbly that I thanked him for his clemency.

'There is no need of thanks,' he replied coldly. 'What I have done is without prejudice to M. de Turenne's complaint. He must have justice.'

I bowed again, and in a moment the troop were gone at a gallop towards Meudon, whence, as I afterwards learned, the King of Navarre, attended by a select body of five-and-twenty horsemen, wearing private arms, rode on at full speed to Saint-Cloud to present himself at His Majesty's bedside. A groom who had caught the Cid, which had escaped into the town with no other injury than a slight wound in the shoulder, by-and-by met me with the horse; and in this way I was enabled to render myself with some decency at Varenne's lodging, a small house at the foot of the hill, not far from the Castle-gate.

Here I found myself under no greater constraint than that which my own parole laid upon me; and my room having the conveniency of a window looking upon the public street, I was enabled from hour to hour to comprehend and enter into the various alarms and surprises which made that day remarkable.

The manifold reports which flew from mouth to mouth on the occasion, as well as the over-mastering excitement which seized all, are so well remembered, however, that I forbear to dwell upon them, though they serve to distract my mind from my own position. Suffice it that at one moment we heard that His Majesty was dead, at another that the wound was skin deep, and again that we might expect him at Meudon before sunset. The rumour that the Duchess de Montpensier had taken poison was no sooner believed than we were asked to listen to the guns of Paris firing *feux de joie* in honour of the King's death.

The streets were so closely packed with persons telling and hearing these tales that I seemed from my window to be looking on a fair. Nor was all my amusement without doors; for a number of the gentlemen of the Court, hearing that I had been at Saint-Cloud in the morning, and in the very chamber, a thing which made me for the moment the most desirable companion in the world, remembered on a sudden that they had a slight acquaintance with me, and honoured me by calling upon me and sitting a great part of the day with me. From which circumstances I confess I derived as much hope as they diversion; knowing that courtiers are the best weather-prophets in the world, who hate nothing so much as to be discovered in the company of those on whom the sun does not shine.

The return of the King of Navarre, which happened about the middle of the afternoon, while it dissipated the fears of some and dashed the hopes of others, put an end to this state of uncertainty by confirming, to the surprise of many, that His Majesty was in no danger. We learned with varying emotions that the first appearances, which had deceived, not myself only, but experienced leeches, had been themselves belied by subsequent conditions; and that, in a word, Paris had as much to fear, and loyal men as much to hope, as before this wicked and audacious attempt.

I had no more than stomached this surprising information, which was less welcome to me, I confess, than it should have been, when the arrival of M. d'Agen, who greeted me with the affection which he never failed to show me, distracted my thoughts for a time. Immediately on learning where I was and the strange adventures which had befallen me he had ridden off; stopping only once, when he had nearly reached me, for the purpose of waiting on Madame de Bruhl. I asked him how she had received him.

'Like herself,' he replied with an ingenuous blush. 'More kindly than I had a right to expect, if not as warmly as I had the courage to hope.'

'That will come with time,' I said, laughing. 'And Mademoiselle de la Vire?'

'I did not see her,' he answered, 'but I heard she was well. And a hundred fathoms deeper in love,' he added, eyeing me roguishly, 'than when I saw her last.'

It was my turn to colour now, and I did so, feeling all the pleasure and delight such a statement was calculated to afford me. Picturing mademoiselle as I had seen her last, leaning from her horse with love written so plainly on her weeping face that all who ran might read, I sank into so delicious a reverie that M. la Varenne, entering suddenly, surprised us both before another word passed on either side.

His look and tone were as abrupt as it was in his nature, which was soft and compliant, to make them. 'M. de Marsac,' he said, 'I am sorry to put any constraint upon you, but I am directed to forbid you to your friends. And I must request this gentleman to withdraw.'

'But all day my friends have come in and out,' I said with surprise. 'Is this a new order?'

'A written order, which reached me no farther back than two minutes ago,' he answered plainly. 'I am also directed to remove you to a room at the back of the house, that you may not overlook the street.'

'But my parole was taken,' I cried, with a natural feeling of indignation.

He shrugged his shoulders. 'I am sorry to say that I have

395

nothing to do with that,' he answered. 'I can only obey orders. I must ask this gentleman, therefore, to withdraw.'

Of course M. d'Agen had no option but to leave me; which he did, I could see, notwithstanding his easy and confident expressions, with a good deal of mistrust and apprehension. When he was gone, La Varenne lost no time in carrying out the remainder of his orders. As a consequence I found myself confined to a small and gloomy apartment which looked, at a distance of three paces, upon the smooth face of the rock on which the Castle stood. This change, from a window which commanded all the life of the town, and intercepted every breath of popular fancy, to a closet whither no sounds penetrated, and where the very transition from noon to evening scarcely made itself known, could not fail to depress my spirits sensibly; the more as I took it to be significant of a change in my fortunes fully as grave. Reflecting that I must now appear to the King of Navarre in the light of a bearer of false tidings, I associated the order to confine me more closely with his return from Saint-Cloud; and comprehending that M. de Turenne was once more at liberty to attend to my affairs, I began to look about me with forebodings which were none the less painful because the parole I had given debarred me from any attempt to escape.

Sleep and habit enabled me, nevertheless, to pass the night in comfort. Very early in the morning a great firing of guns, which made itself heard even in my quarters, led me to suppose that Paris had surrendered; but the servant who brought me my breakfast declined in a surly fashion to give me any information. In the end, I spent the whole day alone, my thoughts divided between my mistress and my own prospects, which seemed to grow more and more gloomy as the hours succeeded one another. No one came near me, no step broke the silence of the house; and for a while I thought my guardians had forgotten even that I needed food. This omission, it is true, was made good about sunset, but still M. la Varenne did not appear, the servant seemed to be dumb, and I heard no sounds in the house.

I had finished my meal an hour or more, and the room was growing dark, when the silence was at last broken by quick steps passing along the entrance. They paused, and seemed to hesitate at the foot of the stairs, but the next moment they came on again, and stopped at my door. I rose from my seat on hearing the key turned in the lock, and my astonishment may be conceived when I saw no other than M. de Turenne enter, and close the door behind him.

He saluted me in a haughty manner as he advanced to the table, raising his cap for an instant and then replacing it. This done he stood looking at me, and I at him, in a silence which on my side was the result of pure astonishment; on his, of contempt and a kind of wonder. The evening light, which was fast failing, lent a sombre whiteness to his face, causing it to stand out from the shadows behind him in a way which was not without its influence on me.

'Well!' he said at last, speaking slowly and with unimaginable insolence, 'I am here to look at you!'

I felt my anger rise, and gave him back look for look. 'At your will,' I said, shrugging my shoulders.

'And to solve a question,' he continued in the same tone. 'To learn whether the man who was mad enough to insult and defy *me* was the old penniless dullard some called him, or the dare-devil others painted him.'

'You are satisfied now?' I said.

He eyed me for a moment closely; then with sudden heat he cried, 'Curse me if I am! Nor whether I have to do with a man very deep or very shallow, a fool or a knave!'

'You may say what you please to a prisoner,' I retorted coldly.

'Turenne commonly does— to whom he pleases!' he answered. The next moment he made me start by saying, as he drew out a comfit-box and opened it, 'I am just from the little fool you have bewitched. If she were in my power I would have her whipped and put on bread and water till she came to her senses. As she is not, I must take another way. Have you any idea, may I ask,' he continued in his

397

cynical tone, 'what is going to become of you, M. de Marsac?'

I replied, my heart inexpressibly lightened by what he had said of mademoiselle, that I placed the fullest confidence in the justice of the King of Navarre.

He repeated the name in a tone I did not understand.

'Yes, sir, the King of Navarre,' I answered firmly.

'Well, I daresay you have good reason to do so,' he rejoined with a sneer. 'Unless I am mistaken he knew a little more of this affair than he acknowledges.'

'Indeed? The King of Navarre?' I said, staring stolidly at him.

'Yes, indeed, indeed, the King of Navarre!' he retorted, mimicking me, with a nearer approach to anger than I had yet witnessed in him. 'But let him be a moment, sirrah!' he continued, 'and do you listen to me. Or first look at that. Seeing is believing.'

He drew out as he spoke a paper, or, to speak more correctly, a parchment, which he thrust with a kind of savage scorn into my hand. Repressing for the moment the surprise I felt, I took it to the window, and reading it with difficulty, found it to be a royal patent drawn, as far as I could judge, in due form, and appointing some person unknown—for the name was left blank—to the post of Lieutenant-Governor of the Armagnac, with a salary of twelve thousand livres a year!

'Well, sir?' he said impatiently.

'Well?' I answered mechanically. For my brain reeled; the exhibition of such a paper in such a way raised extraordinary thoughts in my mind.

'Can you read it?' he asked.

'Certainly,' I answered, telling myself that he would fain play a trick on me.

'Very well,' he replied, 'then listen. I am going to condescend; to make you an offer, M. de Marsac. I will procure you your freedom, and fill up the blank, which you see there, with your name—upon one condition.'

I stared at him with all the astonishment it was natural for me to feel in the face of such a proposition. 'You will confer this office on me?' I muttered incredulously.

'The king having placed it at my disposal,' he answered, 'I will. But first let me remind you,' he went on proudly, 'that the affair has another side. On the one hand I offer you such employment, M. de Marsac, as should satisfy your highest ambition. On the other, I warn you that my power to avenge myself is no less today than it was yesterday; and that if I condescend to buy you, it is because that course commends itself to me for reasons, not because it is the only one open.'

I bowed. 'The condition, M. le Vicomte?' I said huskily, beginning to understand him.

'That you give up all claim and suit to the hand of my kinswoman,' he answered lightly. 'That is all. It is a simple and easy condition.'

I looked at him in renewed astonishment, in wonder, in stupefaction; asking myself a hundred questions. Why did he stoop to bargain, who could command? Why did he condescend to treat, who held me at his mercy? Why did he gravely discuss my aspirations, to whom they must seem the rankest presumption? Why?—but I could not follow it. I stood looking at him in silence; in perplexity as great as if he had offered me the Crown of France; in amazement and doubt and suspicion that knew no bounds.

'Well!' he said at last, misreading the emotion which appeared in my face. 'You consent, sir?'

'Never!' I answered firmly.

He started. 'I think I cannot have heard you aright,' he said, speaking slowly and almost courteously. 'I offer you a great place and my patronage, M. de Marsac. Do I understand that you prefer a prison and my enmity?'

'On those conditions,' I answered.

'Think, think!' he said harshly.

'I have thought,' I answered.

'Ay, but have you thought where you are?' he retorted. 'Have you thought how many obstacles lie between you and this little fool? How many persons you must win over, how

399

many friends you must gain? Have you thought what it will be to have me against you in this, or which of us is more likely to win in the end?'

'I have thought,' I rejoined.

But my voice shook, my lips were dry. The room had grown dark. The rock outside, intercepting the light, gave it already the air of a dungeon. Though I did not dream of yielding to him, though I even felt that in this interview he had descended to my level, and I had had the better of him, I felt my heart sink. For I remembered how men immured in prisons drag out their lives always petitioning, always forgotten; how wearily the days go, that to free men are bright with hope and ambition. And I saw in a flash what it would be to remain here, or in some such place; never to cross horse again, or breathe the free air of heaven, never to hear the clink of sword against stirrup, or the rich tones of M. d'Agen's voice calling for his friend!

I expected M. de Turenne to go when I had made my answer, or else to fall into such a rage as opposition is apt to cause in those who seldom encounter it. To my surprise, however, he restrained himself. 'Come,' he said, with patience which fairly astonished me, and so much the more as chagrin was clearly marked in his voice, 'I know where you put your trust. You think the King of Navarre will protect you. Well, I pledge you the honour of Turenne that he will not; that the King of Navarre will do nothing to save you. Now, what do you say?'

'As I said before,' I answered doggedly.

He took up the parchment from the table with a grim laugh. 'So much the worse for you then!' he said, shrugging his shoulders. 'So much the worse for you! I took you for a rogue! It seems you are a fool!'

# 36

# '*Vive le Roi!*'

He took his leave with those words. But his departure, which I should have hailed a few minutes before with joy, as a relief from embarrassment and humiliation, found me indifferent. The statement to which he had solemnly pledged himself in regard to the King of Navarre, that I could expect no further help from him, had prostrated me; dashing my hopes and spirits so completely that I remained rooted to the spot long after his step had ceased to sound on the stairs. If what he said was true, in the gloom which darkened alike my room and my prospects I could descry no glimmer of light. I knew His Majesty's weakness and vacillation too well to repose any confidence in him; if the King of Navarre also abandoned me, I was indeed without hope, as without resource.

I had stood some time with my mind painfully employed upon this problem, which my knowledge of M. de Turenne's strict honour in private matters did not allow me to dismiss lightly, when I heard another step on the stairs, and in a moment M. la Varenne opened the door. Finding me in the dark he muttered an apology for the remissness of the servants; which I accepted, seeing nothing else for it, in good part.

'We have been at sixes-and-sevens all day, and you have been forgotten,' he continued. 'But you will have no reason to complain now. I am ordered to conduct you to His Majesty without delay.'

'To Saint-Cloud!' I exclaimed, greatly astonished.

'No, the King of France is here,' he answered.

'At Meudon?'

'To be sure. Why not?'

I expressed my wonder at his Majesty's rapid recovery.

'Pooh!' he answered roughly. 'He is as well as he ever was. I will leave you my light. Be good enough to descend as soon as you are ready, for it is ill work keeping kings waiting. Oh! and I had forgotten one thing,' he continued, returning when he had already reached the door. 'My orders are to see that you do not hold converse with anyone until you have seen the king, M. de Marsac. You will kindly remember this if we are kept waiting in the antechamber.'

'Am I to be transported to—other custody?' I asked, my mind full of apprehension.

He shrugged his shoulders. 'Possibly,' he replied. 'I do not know.'

Of course there was nothing for it but to murmur that I was at the king's disposition; after which La Varenne retired, leaving me to put the best face on the matter I could. Naturally I augured anything but well of an interview weighted with such a condition; and this contributed still further to depress my spirits, already lowered by the long solitude in which I had passed the day. Fearing nothing, however, so much as suspense, I hastened to do what I could to repair my costume, and then descended to the foot of the stairs, where I found my custodian awaiting me with a couple of servants, of whom one bore a link.

We went out side by side, and having barely a hundred yards to go, seemed in a moment to be passing through the gate of the Castle. I noticed that the entrance was very strongly guarded, but an instant's reflection served to remind me that this was not surprising after what had happened at Saint-Cloud. I remarked to M. la Varenne as we crossed the courtyard that I supposed Paris had surrendered; but he replied in the negative so curtly, and with so little consideration, that I forebore to ask any other questions; and the Château being small, we found ourselves almost at once in a long, narrow corridor, which appeared to serve as the antechamber.

It was brilliantly lighted and crowded from end to end, and

almost from wall to wall, with a mob of courtiers; whose silence, no less than their keen and anxious looks, took me by surprise. Here and there two or three, who had seized upon the embrasure of a window, talked together in a low tone; or a couple, who thought themselves sufficiently important to pace the narrow passage between the waiting lines, conversed in whispers as they walked. But even these were swift to take alarm, and continually looked askance; while the general company stood at gaze, starting and looking up eagerly whenever the door swung open or a new-comer was announced. The strange silence which prevailed reminded me of nothing so much as of the Court at Blois on the night of the Duke of Mercoeur's desertion; but that stillness had brooded over empty chambers, this gave a peculiar air of strangeness to a room thronged in every part.

M. la Varenne, who was received by those about the door with silent politeness, drew me into the recess of a window; whence I was able to remark, among other things, that the Huguenots present almost outnumbered the king's immediate following. Still, among those who were walking up and down, I noticed M. de Rambouillet, to whom at another time I should have hastened to pay my respects; with Marshal d'Aumont, Sancy, and Humières. Nor had I more than noted the presence of these before the door of the chamber opened and added to their number Marshal Biron, who came out leaning on the arm of Crillon. The sight of these old enemies in combination was sufficient of itself to apprise me that some serious crisis was at hand; particularly as their progress through the crowd was watched, I observed, by a hundred curious and attentive eyes.

They disappeared at last through the outer door, and the assemblage turned as with one accord to see who came next. But nearly half an hour elapsed before the Chamber door, which all watched so studiously, again opened. This time it was to give passage to my late visitor, Turenne, who came out smiling, and leaning, to my great surprise, on the arm of M. de Rosny.

As the two walked down the room, greeting here and there an obsequious friend, and followed in their progress by all eyes, I felt my heart sink indeed; both at sight of Turenne's good-humour, and of the company in which I found him. Aware that in proportion as he was pleased I was like to meet with displeasure, I still might have had hope left had I had Rosny left. Losing him, however—and I could not doubt, seeing him as I saw him, that I had lost him—and counting the King of Navarre as gone already, I felt such a failure of courage as I had never known before. I told myself with shame that I was not made for Courts, or for such scenes as these; and recalling with new and keen mortification the poor figure I had cut in the King of Navarre's antechamber at Saint-Jean, I experienced so strange a gush of pity for my mistress that nothing could exceed the tenderness I felt for her. I had won her under false colours, I was not worthy of her. I felt that my mere presence in her company in such a place as this, and among these people, must cover her with shame and humiliation.

To my great relief, since I knew my face was on fire, neither of the two, as they walked down the passage, looked my way or seemed conscious of my neighbourhood. At the door they stood a moment talking earnestly, and it seemed as if M. de Rosny would have accompanied the Vicomte farther. The latter would not suffer it, however, but took his leave there; and this with so many polite gestures that my last hope based on M. de Rosny vanished.

Nevertheless, that gentleman was not so wholly changed that on his turning to re-traverse the room I did not see a smile flicker for an instant on his features as the two lines of bowing courtiers opened before him. The next moment his look fell on me, and though his face scarcely altered, he stopped opposite me.

'M. de Marsac is waiting to see His Majesty?' he asked aloud, speaking to M. la Varenne.

My companion remaining silent, I bowed.

'In five minutes,' M. de Rosny replied quietly, yet with

a distant air, which made me doubt whether I had not dreamed all I remembered of this man. 'Ah! M. de Paul, what can I do for you?' he continued. And he bent his head to listen to the application which a gentleman who stood next me poured into his ear. 'I will see,' I heard him answer.

'In any case you shall know tomorrow.'

'But you will be my friend?' M. Paul urged, detaining him by the sleeve.

'I will put only one before you,' he answered.

My neighbour seemed to shrink into himself with disappointment. 'Who is it?' he murmured piteously.

'The king and his service, my friend,' M. de Rosny replied drily. And with that he walked away. But half a dozen times at least before he reached the upper end of the room I saw the scene repeated.

I looked on at all this in the utmost astonishment, unable to guess or conceive what had happened to give M. de Rosny so much importance. For it did not escape me that the few words he had stopped to speak to me had invested me with interest in the eyes of all who stood near. They gave me more room and a wider breathing-space, and looking at me askance, muttered my name in whispers. In my uncertainty, however, what this portended I drew no comfort from it; and before I found time to weigh it thoroughly the door through which Turenne and Rosny had entered opened again. The pages and gentlemen who stood about it hastened to range themselves on either side. An usher carrying a white wand came rapidly down the room, here and there requesting the courtiers to stand back where the passage was narrow. Then a loud voice without cried, "The King, gentlemen! the King!' and one in every two of us stood a-tiptoe to see him enter.

But there came in only Henry of Navarre, wearing a violet cloak and cap.

I turned to La Varenne and with my head full of confusion, muttered impatiently, 'But the king, man! Where is the king?' He grinned at me, with his hand before his mouth. 'Hush!' he whispered. ''Twas a jest we played on you!

His late Majesty died at daybreak this morning. This is the king.'

'This! the King of Navarre?' I cried; so loudly that some round us called 'Silence!'

'No, the King of France, fool!' he replied. 'Your sword must be sharper than your wits, or I have been told some lies!'

I let the gibe pass and the jest, for my heart was beating so fast and painfully that I could scarcely preserve my outward composure. There was a mist before my eyes, and a darkness which set the lights at defiance. It was in vain I tried to think what this might mean—to me. I could not put two thoughts together, and while I still questioned what reception I might expect, and who in this new state of things were my friends, the king stopped before me.

'Ha, M. de Marsac!' he cried cheerfully, signing to those who stood before me to give place. 'You are the gentleman who rode so fast to warn me the other morning. I have spoken to M. de Turenne about you, and he is willing to overlook the complaint he had against you. For the rest, go to my closet, my friend. Go! Rosny knows my will respecting you.'

I had sense enough left to kneel and kiss his hand; but it was in silence, which he knew how to interpret. He had moved on and was speaking to another before I recovered the use of my tongue, or the wits which his gracious words had scattered. When I did so, and got on my feet again I found myself the centre of so much observation and the object of so many congratulations that I was glad to act upon the hint which La Varenne gave me, and hurry away to the closet.

Here, though I had now an inkling of what I had to expect, I found myself received with a kindness which bade fair to overwhelm me. Only M. de Rosny was in the room, and he took me by both hands in a manner which told me without a word that the Rosny of old days was back, and that for the embarrassment I had caused him of late I was more than forgiven. When I tried to thank him for the good offices which I knew he had done me with the king he would have none of it; reminding me with a smile that he had eaten of my cheese when the choice lay between that and Lisieux.

'And besides, my friend,' he continued, his eyes twinkling, 'You have made me richer by five hundred crowns.'

'How so?' I asked, wondering more and more.

'I wagered that sum with Turenne that he could not bribe you,' he answered, smiling. 'And see,' he continued, selecting from some papers on the table the same parchment I had seen before, 'here is the bribe. Take it; it is yours. I have given a score today, but none with the same pleasure. Let me be the first to congratulate the Lieutenant-Governor of the Armagnac.'

For a while I could not believe that he was in earnest; which pleased him mightily, I remember. When I was brought at last to see that the king had meant this for me from the first, and had merely lent the patent to Turenne that the latter might make trial of me, my pleasure and gratification were such that I could no more express them then than I can now describe them. For they knew no bounds. I stood before Rosny silent and confused, with long-forgotten tears welling up to my eyes, and one regret only in my heart—that my dear mother had not lived to see the fond illusions with which I had so often amused her turned to sober fact. Not then, but afterwards, I remarked that the salary of my office amounted to the exact sum which I had been in the habit of naming to her; and I learned that Rosny had himself fixed it on information given him by Mademoiselle de la Vire.

As my transports grew more moderate, and I found voice to thank my benefactor, he had still an answer. 'Do not deceive yourself, my friend,' he said gravely, 'or think this an idle reward. My master is King of France, but he is a king without a kingdom, and a captain without money. Today, to gain his rights, he has parted with half his powers. Before he win all back there will be blows—blows, my friend. And to that end I have bought your sword.'

I told him that if no other left its scabbard for the king, mine should be drawn.

'I believe you,' he answered kindly, laying his hand on my shoulder. 'Not by reason of your words—Heaven knows I have heard vows enough today!—but because I have proved you. And now,' he continued, speaking in an altered tone and looking at me with a queer smile, 'now I suppose you are perfectly satisfied? You have nothing more to wish for, my friend?'

I looked aside in a guilty fashion, not daring to prefer on the top of all his kindness a further petition. Moreover, His Majesty might have other views; or on this point Turenne might have proved obstinate. In a word, there was nothing in what had happened, or on M. de Rosny's communication, to inform me whether the wish of my heart was to be gratified or not.

But I should have known that great man better than to suppose that he was one to promise without performing, or to wound a friend when he could not salve the hurt. After enjoying my confusion for a time he burst into a great shout of laughter, and taking me familiarly by the shoulders, turned me towards the door. 'There, go!' he said. 'Go up the passage. You will find a door on the right, and a door on the left. You will know which to open.'

Forbidding me to utter a syllable, he put me out. In the passage, where I fain would have stood awhile to collect my thoughts, I was affrighted by sounds which warned me that the king was returning that way. Fearing to be surprised by him in such a state of perturbation, I hurried to the end of the passage, where I discovered, as I had been told, two doors.

They were both closed, and there was nothing about either of them to direct my choice. But M. de Rosny was correct in supposing that I had not forgotten the advice he had offered me on the day when he gave me so fine a surprise in his own house—'When you want a good wife, M. de Marsac, turn to the right!' I remembered the words, and without a moment's hesitation—for the king and his suite were already entering the passage—I knocked boldly, and scarcely waiting for an invitation, went in.

Fanchette was by the door, but stood aside with a grim smile, which I was at liberty to accept as a welcome or not. Mademoiselle, who had been seated on the farther side of the table, rose as I entered, and we stood looking at one another. Doubtless she waited for me to speak first; while I on my side was so greatly taken aback by the change wrought in her by the Court dress she was wearing and the air of dignity with which she wore it, that I stood gasping. I turned coward after all that had passed between us. This was not the girl I had wooed in the greenwoods by Saint-Gaultier; nor the pale-faced woman I had lifted to the saddle a score of times in the journey Paris-wards. The sense of unworthiness which I had experienced a few minutes before in the crowded antechamber returned in full force in presence of her grace and beauty, and once more I stood tongue-tied before her, as I had stood in the lodgings at Blois. All the later time, all that had passed between us was forgotten.

She, for her part, looked at me wondering at my silence. Her face, which had grown rosy red at my entrance, turned pale again. Her eyes grew large with alarm; she began to beat her foot on the floor in a manner I knew. 'Is anything the matter, sir?' she muttered at last.

'On the contrary, mademoiselle,' I answered hoarsely, looking every way, and grasping at the first thing I could think of, 'I am just from M. de Rosny.'

'And he?'

'He has made me Lieutenant-Governor of the Armagnac.'

She curtseyed to me in a wonderful fashion. 'It pleases me to congratulate you, sir,' she said, in a voice between laughing and crying. 'It is not more than equal to your deserts.'

I tried to thank her becomingly, feeling at the same time more foolish than I had ever felt in my life; for I knew that this was neither what I had come to tell nor she to hear. Yet I could not muster up courage nor find words to go farther, and stood by the table in a state of miserable discomposure.

'Is that all, sir?' she said at last, losing patience.

Certainly it was now or never, and I knew it. I made the effort. 'No, mademoiselle,' I said in a low voice. 'Far from it. But I do not see here the lady to whom I came to address myself, and whom I have seen a hundred times in far other garb than yours, wet and weary and dishevelled, in danger and in flight. Her I have served and loved; and for her I have lived. I have had no thought for months that has not been hers, nor care save for her. I and all that I have by the king's bounty are hers, and I came to lay them at her feet. But I do not see her here.'

'No, sir?' she answered in a whisper, with her face averted.

'No, mademoiselle.'

With a sudden brightness and quickness which set my heart beating she turned, and looked at me. 'Indeed!' she said. 'I am sorry for that. It is a pity your love should be given elsewhere, M. de Marsac—since it is the king's will that you should marry me.'

'Ah, mademoiselle!' I cried, kneeling before her—for she had come round the table and stood beside me—'But you?'

'It is my will too, sir,' she answered, smiling through her tears.

.    .    .    .    .    .    .    .    .    .

On the following day Mademoiselle de la Vire became my wife; the king's retreat from Paris, which was rendered necessary by the desertion of many who were ill-affected to the Huguenots, compelling the instant performance of the marriage, if we would have it read by M. d'Amours. This haste notwithstanding, I was enabled by the kindness of M. d'Agen to make such an appearance, in respect both of servants and equipment, as became rather my future prospects than my past distresses. It is true that His Majesty, out of a desire to do nothing which might offend Turenne, did not honour us with his presence; but Madame Catherine attended on his behalf, and herself gave me my bride. M. de Sully and M. Crillon, with the Marquis de Rambouillet and his nephew, and my distant connection, the Duke de Rohan, who first acknowledged me on that day, were among those who earned my gratitude by attending me upon the occasion.

The marriage of M. François d'Agen with the widow of my old rival and opponent did not take place until something more than a year later, a delay which was less displeasing to me than to the bridegroom, inasmuch as it left madame at liberty to bear my wife company during my absence on the campaign of Arques and Ivry. In the latter battle, which added vastly to the renown of M. de Rosny, who captured the enemy's standard with his own hand, I had the misfortune to be wounded in the second of the two charges led by the king; and being attacked by two foot soldiers, as I lay entangled I must inevitably have perished but for the aid afforded me by Simon Fleix, who flew to the rescue with the courage of a veteran. His action was observed by the king, who begged him from me, and attaching him to his own person in the capacity of clerk, started him so fairly on the road to fortune that he has since risen beyond hope or expectation.

The means by which Henry won for a time the support of Turenne (and incidentally procured his consent to my marriage) are now too notorious to require explanation. Nevertheless, it was not until the Vicomte's union a year later with Mademoiselle de la Marck, who brought him the Duchy of Bouillon, that I thoroughly understood the matter; or the kindness peculiar to the king, my master, which impelled that great monarch, in the arrangements of affairs so vast, to remember the interests of the least of his servants.